# VULTURES IN THE WIND

PETER RIMMER

# ABOUT PETER RIMMER

~

Peter Rimmer was born in London, England, and grew up in the south of the city where he went to school. After the Second World War, and aged eighteen, he joined the Royal Air Force, reaching the rank of Pilot Officer before he was nineteen. At the end of his National Service, he sailed for Africa to grow tobacco in what was then Rhodesia, now Zimbabwe.

The years went by and Peter found himself in Johannesburg where he established an insurance brokering company. Over 2% of the companies listed on the Johannesburg Stock Exchange were clients of Rimmer Associates. He opened branches in the United States of America, Australia and Hong Kong and travelled extensively between them.

Having lived a reclusive life on his beloved smallholding in Knysna, South Africa, for over 25 years, Peter passed away in July 2018. He has left an enormous legacy of unpublished work for his family to release over the coming years, and not only them but also his readers from around the world will sorely miss him. Peter Rimmer was 81 years old.

facebook.com/PeterRimmerAuthor
twitter.com/@htcrimmer
instagram.com/PeterRimmer_writer
bookbub.com/authors/peter-rimmer
amazon.com/author/peterrimmer

# ALSO BY PETER RIMMER

**The Brigandshaw Chronicles**

*The Rise and Fall of the Anglo Saxon Empire*

Book 1 - Echoes from the Past

Book 2 - Elephant Walk

Book 3 - Mad Dogs and Englishmen

Book 4 - To the Manor Born

Book 5 - On the Brink of Tears

Book 6 - Treason If You Lose

Book 7 - Horns of Dilemma

Book 8 - Lady Come Home

Book 9 - The Best of Times

Book 10 - Full Circle

Book 11 - Leopards Never Change Their Spots

Book 12 - Look Before You Leap

Book 13 - The Game of Life

Book 14 - Scattered to the Wind

**Standalone Novels**

All Our Yesterdays

Cry of the Fish Eagle

Just the Memory of Love

Vultures in the Wind

In the Beginning of the Night

**The Asian Sagas**

Bend with the Wind (Book 1)

Each to His Own (Book 2)

~

**The Pioneers**

Morgandale (Book 1)

Carregan's Catch (Book 2)

~

**Novella**

Second Beach

VULTURES IN THE WIND



This novel is entirely a work of fiction. Names, characters, long-standing establishments, places, events and incidents are either the products of the author's imagination or used in a fictitious manner. Any resemblance to actual persons, living or dead, is purely coincidental.

First published in Great Britain in 2014 by

KAMBA PUBLISHING, United Kingdom

10 9 8 7 6 5 4 3

# PART 1

# 1

Green pigeons burst from the wild fig tree and wheeled away upriver, frightened by the new-born cry. When the flock of birds drew level with the kraal, a second cry made them wheel again to fly back towards the sea, over the banana trees, where they cut the beach before returning to the fig tree and the feast of ripe fruit. The birdsong in the valley mingled with the chatter of monkeys and the sound of surf rolling to the shore. From the Mbeki kraal, the smoke from the cooling fire rose straight to the powder blue sky.

There was peace in paradise, food in the sea and fruit on the trees, and the news spread from the woodsman's hut to the kraal and from the kraal to the hut that men-children had been born. It was a day of great celebration and joy. They called the white boy Matthew Gray and the black boy Luke Mbeki and the families joined together to drink the thick white beer brewed from the maize corn. The harmony was tangible. Robert Gray spoke English to his wife Isalin, but Xhosa to Sipho Mbeki and Namusa his wife.

That afternoon, from the sea, Robert brought a big fat copper steenbras that he had caught from his boat and they made the fire on the beach, beside the banana trees that came to the edge of the sand, and the great fish was cooked for the families. Robert and Isalin opened slipper oysters and laid them out on trays, dropping mauve petals from the bougainvillea between the gaping, pearl-coloured shells. Sipho found a small black pearl in his oyster and luck was with them again. Bananas, mangoes, peanuts and avocado pears, filled with cooked mussel, were eaten in great quantities and, when the ball of red fire dipped behind the hills, it spread a glow of fire under the belly of heaven.

The children played in the gentle surf and the fish plopped in the river that spilled into the sea. Luke and Matthew were put next to each other under the fronds of the banana trees and their mothers fed them. Robert walked the long beach with Sipho and watched the moon rise from the sea to the right of the Gap where God had left the cliff and tipped a piece half into the sea. Behind them, the sunset was rich as blood. The men were tall and lean with the long strides of the well content. It had not always been so peaceful for Robert Gray.

In 1929, when the values of the world's shares were being adjusted downwards on an hourly basis, Robert had been a forester at Diepwalle, many kilometres to the west. Five days after that Black Monday at Wall Street in October, he had risen at dawn and found the chief forester beating a black man around the head with a heavy piece of wood. He had taken violent measures to retrieve the weapon, making Piet van der Walt turn his attention to his young forester.

"The bastard's a thief," said the Afrikaner, in the tongue they were now calling Afrikaans.

"I stole nothing, Baas," wailed the battered black man, as Robert's superior took a heavy swing at Robert's head.

Van der Walt growled, "You should mind your own business, Gray," and, as he bent to pick up the fallen log, Robert brought his knee up into the man's face. The two white men fought for less than a minute but it was enough to destroy Robert's career with the department of forestry. That afternoon he left Diepwalle for an uncertain future with van der Walt's now quiet voice still playing through his mind.

As he walked the sixteen kilometres into Knysna, the giant yellow-woods mocked his progress. "You will never work again in forestry, Gray. Mark my words." The fact that the real thief had been found at lunchtime meant nothing. If the chief forester wished to batter one of his black workers with a metre-long piece of wood, it was the chief forester's prerogative, and most likely the man would work better. That was how they thought at Diepwalle.

There was no work in Knysna, so Robert shifted off up the coast. He was a twenty-three-year-old graduate of the University of Cape Town with a degree in forestry, something else van der Walt had not liked about Robert Gray. He had moved progressively further up the coast, feeding himself from the sea and the local vegetation. After a month, he was enjoying himself and the small back pack that carried his all was as light as a feather.

He arrived in Port St Johns six months later, and then walked back from First Beach the five kilometres to Second Beach, to the mouth of the smaller river where the sea and river fishing were good, the bananas plentiful and the only two brick-built houses empty of people. Deeper in the forest he met Sipho Mbeki, whose kraal was sheltered amongst the trees and whose pigs, cattle and chickens roamed the forest. The black man had a flock of noisy geese down by the river and a dog that growled at Robert. He also had two wives and many children. In Xhosa they discussed the weather and this year's piglets and last year's piglets and the small banana crop. After three hours of sitting on his haunches, Robert came to the point.

"Who owns the brick houses with the green roofs?"

"Baas Todd in Johannesburg."

This was how the Gray family first became aware of the Todd family. It would be some time before the Todd family visited, as they only came down on holiday in December.

"You think I can build myself a hut?"

"Every man has the right to build a hut." It was the African tradition.

The work took Robert three months as he had to borrow the tools in the village of Port St Johns and buy wood and nails with the last of his forester's wages. The corner poles he cut from the forest and the roof he thatched with grass. The front of the hut was a long veranda, so even in driving rain the bedroom and lounge were dry. On cold nights he burnt driftwood in the open fireplace, the only part of the hut that was built of brick. In exchange for a fourteen kilogram Cape salmon, the local butcher gave him a hammock which he hung on the veranda for watching the beach and the sea. Very quietly, Robert drifted into the daily lives of the Mbekis. He was the only permanent white man at Second Beach. For Robert, there was nowhere more wonderful on earth.

Isalin Metcalf came to Port St Johns to paint. She had a fine arts degree from the University of Witwatersrand, and a boyfriend in the establishment who wanted her to settle down and have his babies and live in a fine house in Sandown, ride horses, give dinner parties and look decorative, while he carried on making piles of money in 'the big J', Johannesburg. Even the Depression had not dulled his wits, as when the crash came he was liquid and left selling short into a tumbling market.

The only snag with the boyfriend was that he talked about nothing but money. He even patronised her painting in public, as if he were bringing out the family dog to play tricks. It never once crossed his mind that she was serious about her painting and, when she persuaded her father to give her a year at the coast, to hold an exhibition on her return and let the public decide, he thought she would be back in the big city within a week. He fancied Isalin as much for her heavy breasts, strong, child-bearing hips and long, lean legs as he did for the whiff of rumour that her great-grandfather was a Scottish earl and the blood of kings ran in her veins. The boyfriend was also a snob.

Her work could be described as exotic paintings of the jungle with lots of tropical foliage and animals, small and large that hid among the trees. Her colours were soft pastels and the canvases big, but best of all she had the third dimension. Her art teacher had known what he was doing.

She rented a small house across the big river mouth from the First Beach and took the ferry boat to the village for provisions. She was prepared to be a recluse for her art, to prove that there was more to life than parties and selling shares short on the stock exchange. She wanted something of her own; to create something, to say something, to let the longings and passions inside her come out on the canvas and take shape that other people could see. She desperately wanted other people to feel the same way that she felt about beauty and nature and all the animals and birds on God's earth. She wanted to say it all in colour, to shout it in colour. She wanted to shout how wonderful life was through her paintings.

To be a painter, she grew her blonde hair long and hung it on one side of her face with a flower, and wore long skirts with sandals and wrap-around tops that she made herself. She tanned nude and her body was firm and ripe. She had never been penetrated and, though the longing was there, she refrained. There was a beach hidden among rocks down from her house on the cliff that let her swim naked and feel the warm salt water all over her body. She went across in the rowing boat twice a week as food went off in the heat and, with all the sea and sun and the burning energy that made her paint whenever the light was good enough, she was always hungry. She cooked big feasts for herself at night, pretended she had company and hugged herself with pleasure.

She had been on the Wild Coast for three months before she saw Robert Gray, who was now wearing hair as long as hers. He also had a beard, shoulders as broad as a woodcutter's and a tan so deep that, were it not for the penetrating blue eyes twinkling among all the hair, she would have thought him more local than he was, even more a part of the tropical Africa.

The sight of him striding down the road near the shops caught her instant attention. He was magnificent, wearing a colourful home-made shirt and shorts, no shoes, and curved pipe in his mouth which he removed to greet everyone he saw with a "Beautiful day."

She was not close enough to hear whether he was humming, but his body language sang with a song, and she fell in love from across the street. Her legs would not work and she thought her heart stopped. When the blue eyes played into her soul, she took hold of the jacaranda tree and hung there, hooked like a fish.

"You must be the painter," he called.

"Yes," she replied, without sound.

"May I come and look at them?"

"Yes," she squeaked.

They became lovers that night, and were destined never to spend a day apart for as long as they lived in Port St Johns, until the war in the desert took him away from her forever.

DAVID TODD HAD MADE MORE money in twenty years than most men dreamt about. He had founded his insurance company in 1910, shortly after the Union of South Africa was created from the belligerence of the Boer War. He had privately placed three-hundred shares of five-hundred pounds each with friends and relations, whom he talked into in the same way that he had sold insurance for Prudential.

For five years he had been their most successful salesman, working on the principle that, if he did not sell his prospect a policy and force him to save, the man would drink the money and the man's family would suffer terrible consequences. He was one of the few insurance salesmen who really believed in his product, not simply the first year's premium he earned in commission. With the new company he formed, he installed into his sales force the same belief, and the funds poured into his company. Because his mind was set on security, the company invested only in the old-established mining-houses and property, the first being Security Life's building in the fast-growing Johannesburg.

Within ten years and despite the fact that he spent two years in France and was one of the few South Africans to walk out of Deville Wood undamaged, his original thirty shareholders were all rich from their one investment and David Todd was looking to expand into England. This was a remarkable reversal of the normal trend in the insurance industry, which saw British companies taking huge profits out of South Africa, the benefit of a good colonial system. By the time he came down to Port St Johns with his large family for their annual holiday in 1930, he had avoided the pitfalls of the stock-market crash for his policyholders, and his endowment policies in Africa and Europe were showing a fine return on the policyholders' investments.

The family arrived in convoy, with the house servants and nurses for the younger children. Each of the children brought a friend, and the noise when they decanted from an assortment of shooting brakes was formidable, though they were all glad the journey was over. The road through the hills to the coast was terrible, but it gave David Todd once a year the seclusion he craved from his business. There were no telephones at Second Beach and if anyone wanted to talk to him he had to drive down and back again. He offered neither shelter nor nourishment, so generally he was left alone with his family for what he considered the most important six weeks of his year.

"Daddy, there's a new hut behind the cottage," chorused his children, soon after the main house had been opened up and he was sitting on his veranda marvelling at the sheer beauty of the scenery.

"A new hut! Where?" He put down his second cup of tea and was dragged by the hand to view Robert's hut. Isalin looked up from her painting to see six children and a man staring at her. She had heard the cars and came to the right conclusion.

"Hello; you must be Mister Todd. I'm Isalin Gray. Sipho told us all about you. Robert's fishing." The man was giving her a queer look, but did not come any nearer. "Robert, my husband. We got married last week. No, here he comes. Robert! This is the nice Mister Todd, Sipho and Namusa talked about."

"Robert Gray. Ex-forester. Now beachcomber and fisherman," said Robert, by way of introduction. "I built the house myself," he went on, following the stare of the man and the children.

"You've built it on my land," said David Todd.

"Oh how awful. Sipho thought it... I'll move it, then."

David began to smile. "You'd better come and have a drink at seven o'clock, you and your wife. I think I have a job for you if you want to stay."

Which is how the motorboat came to be and the brick houses were properly looked after and the monkeys kept off the roofs when the Todds were away at their other lives. It was also how David Todd came to be Matthew Gray's godfather and the biggest influence in his life after his parents. The Todds and Grays fitted together very nicely as the years unwound themselves and Robert was never sure which family looked forward more to the Todd's annual holiday.

SIPHO MBEKI LIVED in the same way his ancestors had lived for all their history. Nothing had changed for centuries. The cattle, goats and pigs grazed and foraged on the earth, the rain fell and made the grass grow and the young children herded the animals. The women lightly tilled a small area next to the huts and grew pumpkin and maize. The men talked a great deal and were the warriors who defended the women and children. There were no fences or permanent dwellings; the crude huts being built of poles, mud and thatch – thatch which very often leaked. There was a hole in the centre of the domed roof and a fire was made on the earth floor in the centre of the rondavel to warm the family and drive out the bugs. Everyone accepted smoke in the eye as normal. The daily workload was minimal; fetching firewood and water from the river, keeping some of the weeds out of the maize, brewing maize beer and watching the chickens and animals. Except for the last seventy years, Africa had been bountiful to its entire people, as there was so much of Africa and so few people. When the grazing was finished, the Xhosa moved onto sweeter pastures.

The land, like the rain and the sun, had no owners. To explain to Sipho that Robert had built his hut on land owned by David Todd was a lot of nonsense. There were no fences or boundaries in Sipho's life. He bred his children like his cattle, and his wealth was counted accordingly. Some lived, some died; if the calf was a heifer all the better; if the white man gave him medicine to keep more of his children alive all the better, but he had no intention of changing a way of life that had treated his family well. So long as the Zulu impis kept away, everything was fine.

There was no necessity for the Xhosa to be the mother of his inventions. He had never found the need to invent the wheel. The water came from the river on the heads of women, the firewood was close, and the animals walked on their own legs and were slaughtered next to the cooking fire. And if he wanted to go anywhere, he walked, so he could enjoy the trees, the long grass and the song of the birds. The animals were his friends and rarely did he hunt them. It was easier to kill a pig that did not run away. Sipho's horizon was limited to the valley, the river and the sea. He had twice walked the few kilometres to the village of Port St Johns and both times he had told himself never to do it again. The road started at Second Beach and he was on the road-free side of the river. The bridge David Todd had built to his house was the only encroachment on his privacy and that was used once a year.

Robert also lived like a Xhosa; except that he built his hut in a funny way, with planks and windows and a big open room in the front that made no sense whatsoever to Sipho. And Robert knew how to catch fish with a piece of string and showed him things to eat from the sea. That was the only change he had allowed in his life. He was a man content, a happy man.

Namusa was Sipho's second wife and was many years younger than her husband. The first and senior wife had stopped bearing children seven years earlier, causing Sipho to pay the high price of six good cows for Namusa, her father demanding so much for the prettiest of his daughters. She was fifteen and sixteen when Luke, her first son, was born. He proved to be her only child, and it was this lack of children that threw Luke increasingly into the company of Matthew.

This changed the course of his life. From the cradle he began to absorb the white man's culture, and learnt the English language which would be the key to all the knowledge stored in all the books in the world. Even if he could read in Xhosa, the translations would have been so strange as to mean little to him. Had anyone written in Xhosa, something which had never been done, it would have been about the tribe, which had many distinctive ways of describing a bird in flight but no word for machine or algebra. The language barrier was the limiting factor for the black man.

Luke and Matthew learned to crawl together and talk together, in a mixture of Xhosa and English, which by the time they were three had become two distinct languages and a puzzle for young Luke. Robert would understand whatever he said but Sipho only some of it. So many of the child's questions were directed at Robert, and son and father, confounded by Sipho's age, were not as close as they should have been. This brought the first glimmer of doubt into Sipho's world. The era of discontent had begun, with a harmless clash of cultures.

When the boys were five, Isalin bought a correspondence course for Matthew, and his education began as normally as it had done for his great great-grandfather. Luke was generally with Matthew during the day, and lessons were fun. It never occurred to them that they were alienating Luke from his family or leading him into conflict with the culture of his own people. What was apparent to both Isalin and Robert, who took it in turn to give instruction, was that both boys were bright and that both of them never stopped asking questions.

The only outside influence came once a year from the Todds and their friends when they were on holiday, and whatever happened in Port St Johns was light years away from their lives in Johannesburg. They might have thought it strange to see the two little boys from different races holding hands, but no one put it into words.

Robert and Isalin were largely self-sufficient. Mental stimulation for Robert had ceased with the passing years. He was deeply in love with his wife and nature and the joy of showing his son the simple ways of survival. They dangled baited string in the sea and the foolish crayfish refused to let go as the line was gently pulled out of the water. They dived together for oysters when the sea was calm and took out the Todd motorboat, launching it with skill from the beach. All manner of fish landed in the boat: seventy-fours, yellow-bellies, cape salmon, copper steenbras and black steenbras. The Indian Ocean was plentiful, and some of the fish went in to Port St Johns, the cash giving them money for the few luxuries that flavoured their lives.

Once a year the Todds took Isalin's paintings to Johannesburg and David Todd built a savings fund for Matthew's future education. Isalin's parents journeyed once to Port St Johns, were appalled by her lifestyle and never came again. Then her father died and her mother returned to England. For both of them, their only family was their own; Robert's parents both having died young.

Robert walked with Matthew along the tops of tall cliffs and they made camp down below on the beach, building their cooking fires from driftwood and sleeping above the high tide. Every day saw the father striding the cliff paths and the beaches, his tall staff rhythmically prodding the earth and sand. The boy walked two metres behind the father, idolising him, finding life so sweet, the tears of mental pain as yet unknown to him. Sometimes Luke came on their journeys but mostly it was father and son, year after year.

When Hitler walked into Poland and the second Great War broke out, they were camped out on the cliff some thirty kilometres from Coffee Bay, and it was only a week later that Robert heard the news that had taken South Africa into the war on the British side by a slim majority in parliament.

In 1940, Robert answered the call to arms and he was gone from the beach, the cliffs and the sea. The boy was left behind with his memories. The shadow of fear stalked the woodsman's hut and, for the first time in twenty years, David Todd stayed in Johannesburg, where he watched his sons march off to the war, to the train and the troopship that took the young and the best to Egypt.

In 1941 the Todd boys and Robert were infantry behind the tanks at Tobruk and all four of them died in the desert within a week of each other. They would never know the sadness of old age. They would never know the pain of being left behind. The news to Matthew Gray was more shattering than the bullet that killed his father.

A week after the terrible news reached Second Beach, Isalin packed her few things with her son and left. Separately Luke and Matthew cried the loss of their innocence.

The departure of Isalin and Matthew left Luke Mbeki washed up on an alien shore with a thirst for knowledge and nowhere to find what he wanted. Sipho was helpless. After four and a half years of formal education, Luke could read and write, do arithmetic and knew a lot about a world outside Port St Johns, outside the Union of South Africa. His years of happiness were over and he took to walking morosely up and down the hills and along the beaches alone, friendless and helplessly frustrated. The library was for white people, the school was for white people with money; in fact, the things he had learnt about were for white people with money. In her misery, Isalin had forgotten the black boy who was her son's only friend and, in his pain at the loss of his sons, David Todd never again visited his home near Port St Johns.

Luke watched the houses fall into disrepair and a pack of baboons moved into the woodsman's hut. The motorboat was washed into the river in the storm of 1942 and smashed on the rocks below the Gap. The weeds and forest quickly took over the Todds' garden and, when the gutters were ripped off in the storm, the rain soaked in through the walls. Luke could find no employment for his mind; looking after his father's cattle and pigs was not enough. When the chief wife began to abuse the second wife, Namusa, Luke's mother, in 1943, Luke ran away from home and made his way to Umtata, sixty-five kilometres inland, where he looked for work. The tide of war was shifting in favour of Britain and America but, though it was not apparent at the time, Hitler had sowed the seeds which would quickly destroy the British Empire and leave their colonised people in turmoil.

Luke was eleven when he found his first job in an English house that spoke no Xhosa. He worked in the garden, doing some of the things he had learnt from Robert Gray, and acted as an interpreter for the house staff. When he asked for books, he was given them to read and he took a path of self-education that would finally make him valuable to the African National Congress. This black political organisation had been founded in 1912 to give the black people a voice after they had been excluded from the political process when the British joined together the defeated Boer states and their own colonies of the Cape and Natal. But that was many years ahead of him. For the present, Luke dug up weeds, cut grass, watered the flowers and absorbed the content of the books he read so eagerly. By 1944, when the British and Americans went on the offensive and invaded Europe, Isalin and Matthew had fallen into poverty. They had lost touch with her aristocratic mother in England, and David Todd wanted nothing to do with anything that reminded him of Port St Johns and his sons. Her paintings sold for very little during war-time, and the one-roomed flat they rented in Hillbrow was in the poor white neighbourhood and Matthew was forced to carry a knife to defend him.

Like Luke, most of his education came from reading books as his mother had lost all interest in the world. She had grown grey and thin, her full breasts sagging to her navel. Even if Matthew had hoped for a step-father, a situation he would have found abhorrent, no man would have looked at his mother. When she died in 1945 of pneumonia for lack of the money for a dose of penicillin, Matthew found himself an orphan at the age of thirteen with a deep voice, some of his father's height and a good prospect of growing taller.

He looked fifteen, and said so when he applied for a job as office boy at the Security Life Insurance Company. Matthew was sure David Todd had forgotten all about his godson and never mentioned his name. He lied about one other matter, saying his father had died at Tobruk, and had sold life insurance for Security Life in the Transkei. He had picked up enough from the Todd children to make his story convincing. He saw the youngest of the Todd girls once in the foyer of the Security Life building but she showed no sign of recognition.

Enrolled at night school, Matthew continued his education and, when he turned sixteen and had learnt something about life insurance, he decided that selling insurance was not for him. He applied to join the sister short-term company that dealt with fire and accident business. Soon after his transfer, he took a bus to Port St Johns and walked to Second Beach to find Sipho and his bickering wives. One look at his place of happiness had him running back down the road away from the ghost of his past life. His mother had been right.

Matthew enquired extensively of Luke in the village of Port St Johns, but to no avail. No one could tell him anything about his friend. After two days, Matthew was glad to return to Hillbrow and his digs. He forced himself to concentrate on the future and began his long apprenticeship to the insurance industry with the burning desire one day to make himself rich so that the happiness he had once known would return. One day with the price of the fare he would look up his grandmother in England, but he locked Port St Johns away deep in the back of his memory.

Soon after David Todd's boys had been killed in the retreat to Tobruk and the South African army had decreed that in the future brothers would not be allowed to serve on active duty in the same regiment, David bought a ranch on the banks of the Limpopo River, close to the place where South Africa, Bechuanaland and Southern Rhodesia briefly touched. The girls were married and the Sandown house was full of memories. The Northern Transvaal was the ideal place for the recluse and the game was plentiful.

When he turned the ranch over to the wild animals, it was so achingly lonely that he and his wife were barely able to find a purpose for living as the pain of loss, past and future, drifted away with the flow of years. His business was of no further interest. His sons had been the reason for his money. Nothing existed except the monotonous pattern of eating sometimes, sleeping sometimes and walking in the bush. He did not even own a dog and he gave no more thought to his godson Matthew Gray than he did to his business. As far as he was concerned, his life had come to an end and he was simply waiting to die.

A good business, like a well-run country, takes a few years to run down when management changes for the worse. The offices of Security Life and its subsidiary company, Security Fire and Accident, began to cement themselves into their traditions. They preferred not to make decisions. They maintained the status quo and the graph of progress began to falter. By the time Matthew turned eighteen and was about to train for six months each in the Fire, Accident, Motor, Marine, Public Liability, Personal Life and Marine departments, the line on the graph was beginning to turn downwards.

No one had seen David Todd in years, which was not surprising as he had not once left his game ranch, not once even phoning the office. His solicitor held his power of attorney and, not knowing anything about insurance, only did the best he could. Then David's youngest daughter did the only thing that had any positive effect upon her father. She introduced him to his first grandson, four weeks old. All the other grandchildren had been girls.

Two years earlier, in 1948, South Africa had taken an agonising wrong turn by electing the National Party to power. Hitler had died in his bunker but a lot of new little Hitlers were being bred in South Africa, as the new punitive legislation poured out of Parliament, changing 'innocent till proved guilty' to 'guilty until innocence was approved by the government'.

The English they left alone, letting them make the money for which the Afrikaner had never been trained. First they concentrated on the poor people of mixed blood. These they legislated as 'coloured' and promptly disenfranchised. Grand apartheid, separate development, was born. All positions in government were preserved for the Afrikaner, who voted nationalist irrespective of his education and ability.

The police began to enforce a long line of regulations which would herd the black man into homelands. Every black man was made to carry a pass and any policeman had the right to demand the pass at any time of the day or night. The scum of the often gentle Afrikaner race, the poor whites, were given jobs in the police and the railways when their only qualification was to be white. More absurd legislation prevented sex across the colour bar, and the semi-literate fools sat in trees all night trying to catch offenders when an indignant neighbour suspected black and white were engaged in any kind of intercourse.

In 1950, David Todd came back to a country for which he had given his only three sons. Smuts had been tossed onto the garbage heap of history. The little grey men, hiding behind their Calvinism from which they managed to prove to themselves and no one else that God decreed the separation of the races, were in power, and all political opposition stopped. By the end of 1952, when Matthew turned twenty, David saw two alternatives: either to leave the country of his birth and run his company in England, or to stay and use his wealth to fight the Nats. He chose the latter course.

A young, good-looking man with a little money in his pocket had other things to think about in 1952, and presumed his elders knew what they were doing. The war was over, money was there to be made, and there were girls, girls, girls. Matthew took a flat in Rosebank, near the new George Hotel, and moved up in the world, a world that for him was booze, birds and business. Even in the early days, Matthew kept his social life in check during the week. He learnt to drive and bought himself a pre-war Morris Eight for ten pounds. It was to be the most exciting car he was ever to own. Happiness, fickle happiness, had returned to Matthew Gray.

David Todd had called Matthew into his office a week after returning from the bushveld, in 1950, and since then they had seen very little of each other and never on social occasions. It was as if the promise at Matthew's baptism had never been made.

"You seem to be getting along all right, Matthew," he had been told. He had stood in front of the large, well-carved desk with its green leather top. He had not been asked to sit down. "I want you to know there is no favouritism in Security Life, just results. Why did you leave my life insurance company?"

"Because life insurance contains a lot of promises that do not have to be fulfilled," Matthew responded.

"Explain yourself."

"It's a con."

"What the hell do you mean by that?" his godfather demanded.

"When they sell a policy, they tell the prospect that if the company makes twelve per cent per annum for thirty years he will receive half a million pounds. Sounds good to a man with a mortgage. What you don't tell the man is that half the compound growth rate is eaten up by inflation, that the first year's premium goes to the salesman and the second year's to the pyramid of branch and regional managers, that a quarter per cent of the capital sum is deducted quarterly and ten per cent of the interest is taken annually, all to cover so-called overheads. Which is why there is only a meagre cash value in the policy at the end of the third year. That, to be exact, forty-two per cent of every pound invested in an endowment policy goes up against the wall in overheads and brokerage."

"Who told you these ridiculous figures?" David Todd snorted indignantly.

"An actuary."

"He was talking nonsense. We provide a magnificent return for our policy holders."

"And a large cash flow for the government in prescribed investments, a phenomenal return for shareholders, to say nothing of all the largest buildings in Johannesburg."

"The buildings are an investment," David told him.

"For whom: the policyholders or the shareholders?"

"You are being rude."

"You asked me, sir, why I left the life division," Matthew replied courteously. "Short-term insurance is a calculated risk against a calculated premium. The ship floats, nothing; the ship sinks, we pay. I believe in the product. We spread the risk. Clients can do business without fear of a wipe-out."

"What about the widows and orphans?"

"Sell them insurance, pure insurance against death. Unfortunately it is only five per cent of the endowment premium." Matthew sounded firm and confident.

"I see. At eighteen years of age, you know all about the insurance industry... I was sorry to hear about your mother."

"She never recovered from Father's death."

For the first time, Matthew looked straight at his godfather, and some of his anger subsided. The pain of loss was etched into the old man's face.

"I'm sorry, sir," he said quietly.

"Maybe one day you will understand why anything to do with Port St Johns makes the pain intolerable. And you, Matthew, you above all, remind me of Port St Johns."

LUKE MBEKI WAS LUCKIER with David Todd than Matthew. In honour of his dead sons and to assuage some of the guilt he felt about making his money in a country that legislated against the majority of its citizens, David launched the Todd Scholarships. By then, Luke had fallen victim to the new pass laws, had spent many nights in prison without being charged, and was many degrees angrier with the South African political system than Matthew was with the insurance industry. Defying the pass laws which forced him to stay in the Transkei, the apartheid-engineered homeland-to-be of the Xhosa, he travelled to Johannesburg and made his way into the black township of Soweto, where he first heard about the Todd scholarships for black South Africans.

"I want to speak to Mister Todd." He found the number in the phone book, the number of Security Life's head office.

"Who is speaking?'

"Luke Mbeki."

'Who?" asked the white receptionist, who had never before been given the surname of a black man. They were either Philemon or Fred or Mary, names a white person could understand.

"Luke Mbeki. Mister Todd is a friend of my father."

"I'll put you through to his secretary." The whole discussion was repeated with the same degree of impatience at a black man wasting a white woman's time. Only when he mentioned the scholarship did he receive any attention, and then the woman asked briskly for his name and the address where she could send an application form.

"I would like to speak to Mister Todd." Ever since leaving Port St Johns, Luke had been brushed off by white people, and he knew that only a personal interview would give him any kind of chance.

"I'm sorry: Mister Todd does not speak to applicants until the forms have been completed and processed."

"Do you have a telegraphic address?"

"Of course. Seclife, Johannesburg."

"Thank you, miss." Luke put down the phone. He had had an idea.

The following day, the secretary in her ivory tower was told personally by David Todd that Mr Mbeki was going to phone and that he was to be put through immediately. Luke's call had done its work.

Two years later when Matthew was moving into his flat in Rosebank, Luke was on a boat to Durban harbour at the start of his journey to London. He found it best to keep mostly to his cabin for three weeks, the cabin staff bringing him food. He walked the decks late at night and very early in the morning. The ship was a white man's ship, and there was no place for a black man in the dining room, let alone in the bar. Luke felt more lonely than be had ever felt in his life.

Despite his bursary and a generous allowance from the Todd Memorial Trust, Luke found the London School of Economics no better for a black man than the ship, or South Africa for that matter – except for the staff many of whom leaned towards the doctrines of Marx and Lenin.

The message from Moscow was to befriend the natives from the colonies. Soviet Russia had seen the British were on a wrong premise and they were going to exploit the mistake to their own advantage. After two years at the crammer in downtown Johannesburg, Luke was at last receiving a proper education. Some of the staff went out of their way to assist him, and were willing to make a friend out of the tall black man from the richest country in sub-Saharan Africa.

Matthew had no further significant dealings with the chairman of the board until he had finished his apprenticeship, after completing six months in each of the various departments. Luke was then beginning his third year Bcom and they were both twenty-two years old. Matthew still claimed to be three years older than he actually was, and most of his friends were in their middle or late twenties. He was earning a reasonable salary, although Lucky Kuchinski and Archie Fletcher-Wood were earning considerably more.

These two were by now Matthew's most intimate friends. Lucky was in the business of selling cars, which he did with great success, and was also a womaniser second to none. Archie, the oldest of the trio by two years, was working as a salesman for an American drug company. The Americans paid well and demanded a high standard of work, income being largely derived from profit-incentive bonuses. There were no sinecures in the American drug companies in 1954. Reward was in direct proportion to results, and Matthew envied his friends' ability to increase their income by hard and accurate work. The term 'yuppie' was not then in vogue, but Archie and Lucky would undoubtedly have fallen into this category. Matthew quietly resolved that their lifestyle was one he was determined to share – and quickly.

Once again Matthew had asked for an interview with his godfather, but in his telephone conversation making the appointment he had made it clear that it was a staff member wishing to see the Chief Executive Officer. David Todd prided himself on his claim that he was available to the cleaner boy.

"This is a lot of rubbish," said David Todd, waving aside Matthew's long pondered memorandum that had preceded his visit by twenty-four hours. "Lot of damned rubbish. The insurance industry has been around much longer than you or I and every company runs on departmental lines. A marine man leaves fire insurance to the fire department."

"Why?" asked Matthew.

"Because that is what they are trained to do."

"But I have been trained in both departments," Matthew pointed out. "A client or broker can quite easily ask me about Protection and Indemnity insurance for the crew of the ship or Loss of Profits Insurance following a fire in the oil refinery. The ship and crew bring the crude oil, and the refinery turns it into petrol, diesel and a host of other by-products. They belong to one company, and in the company insurance problems are dealt with by one man."

"What the hell has that to do with throwing out all my departments? You can't get a fireman to handle the public liability risk. You can't have one man handling one client."

"Why not? I can do it."

"Sit down, Matthew," David ordered.

"If we let one man handle Caltex, he would control the account. He could move the business to another company."

"Not if we changed the account executives every three years. Like the advertising agents. The bank manager gets changed regularly for security reasons. Imagine a client being able to talk to one man about all the aspects of his insurance, instead of being transferred from one department to the next."

"The brokers work in departments," David pointed out firmly.

"They are also wrong."

"Oh, so you think you know better than the brokers as well."

"There is more paper chasing more paper between our departments, their departments and the bemused clients than in any other industry. We even use an insurance language that our clients don't understand. They give us the wrong loss of profit figures as our gross profit is not the one they see in their profit and loss accounts. There are gaps left in the covers by the departments, double indemnified by two lots of them, ours and the brokers. You can place certain consequential loss risks in the Fire, Marine or Loss of Profits department, and the client only finds out when his claim is refused for being uninsured. Fallen between three stools."

"How old are you Matthew?"

"Twenty-five, sir."

"You are twenty-two."

"My records in the company show twenty-five."

"I know that," David Todd informed him. "I also know your father did not sell life insurance."

"My father would not have sold life insurance in a fit. I needed a job. There was no one in this damn world that cared a stuff about Matthew Gray."

"Don't swear in this office."

"Sorry, sir."

"You are a maverick like your father. I like mavericks, but not in my office, not in my business. There is a system. Not everyone is bright enough to absorb all the classes of business. They have to work to a system."

"Insurance isn't such a big subject," argued Matthew. "Not nearly as large as law or accountancy. A reasonably intelligent man can be trained proficiently in five years. If we cut the mystique and cut the inefficiency, we could reduce our rates by thirty per cent and still make the same percentage profit to premium income. We would end up with half the business in this country just by being efficient, just by translating the insurance language into Anglo-Saxon English."

"It could never be done."

"Let me try," Matthew urged him.

"Not in this company. We would be reduced to chaos in a month."

"Then I must offer my resignation."

"Seeing that you want to destroy my short-term insurance company, I should think that a very good thing," replied David, leaning back in his chair. "And when you have put it in writing, come round to the house for dinner. Rule 17 in Security Life is that I never entertain staff under the rank of branch manager. I'll put in a word at Price Forbes. They may send you to London to have a look at Lloyd's. They're the best training ground for brokers in the country. You can look up Luke Mbeki."

"Luke?"

"You remember Luke?"

"Of course: I've spent years looking for Luke."

"Why didn't you ask your godfather?"

THE ONE THING Matthew had liked about Security Fire and Accident was having his own office where he could work without interruption from his fellow workers. Price Forbes thought differently and put everyone below the contact managers in rows in communal offices where a single telephone conversation could be heard by everyone, and firing paper clips from rubber bands was an antidote for boredom. If they had not promised him a boat trip to England with six months' training at Lloyd's, he would have left the insurance business and taken up Lucky Kuchinski's suggestion that he sell motor cars.

Cars were something of a mania with Matthew and as he had quickly worked out the success ratio with dating to the type of motor car used in his endless quest to satisfy his sex drive. When he was not totally concentrating, Matthew thought of women both in general and in particular. As half the staff in the Price Forbes general office were women, mostly young women, and there were no partitions, the best of his five minute concentrations were broken by the stab in his groin caused by the flash of a leg or a firm breast pushed into a deliberately too small sweater. Both Lucky and Archie were far more successful with women and Matthew put it down to their motor cars. He was taller than either of them by ten centimetres; he no longer had a spot on his face, and had so far never been the whole way with a woman. It had to be the cars.

Lucky Kuchinski was a Pole with a cleft in his chin that rivalled that of Kirk Douglas, an English accent that was better than any Frenchman's, and an idiosyncrasy of leaping into the driving seat of his convertible Chevrolet without opening the door. He also had a smile that was equally as irresistible to prospective car owners as it was to young girls.

Archie had a smart car and experience, and knew which type of woman went for Archibald Fletcher-Wood, ex-manager for Central African Airways at Mongu, Barotseland, and which ones did not. Accordingly, unlike Matthew, he wasted very little of his time on the wrong type and, though he did not boast or even mention his conquests, Matthew by the change in the young ladies' way of looking at Archie was convinced he was bedding two 'newbies' a month. He believed in spreading the happiness.

Archie rented a cottage not far from Lucky's showroom, but it was a long way from many of the girls' more permanent beds, and Archie most often entertained at home where the lighting, the music and the drinks were best suited to the willing seduction of the right young girls. Matthew envied many things about Archie, but most of all his charm. "You mustn't rush these things, young man," Archie would explain. "Give them good nosh and soft lights, and talk them into it. Make it look like a big future. Make them feel very comfortable."

Matthew had not long turned twenty-two, a fact of which both his friends were quite well aware, despite his claim of being three years older, when Archie and Lucky held a private meeting in the cottage. The subject was Matthew Gray.

"We can't let him go to England a virgin. Whatever will they think of the macho South African? Definitely not."

"We'll have to talk to Sandy," said Lucky. He was relaxing on the big, wide, specially-made-for-Archie couch with a large Bells and soda. It was his third. "He must never suspect that we provided her."

"Just telling Sandy that Matthew's a virgin will send her hormones dancing in the rafters. There are very few virgins left in Johannesburg. The more the Dutchman brings in his morality rules, the more it happens underground. Wonderful place, the big Johannesburg. Will you talk to Sandy?"

Sandy de Freitas had been through a swift learning curve with men, starting at seventeen when she thought she was in love, and fell pregnant. The young man was the son of a rich industrialist who paid for the abortion and turned Sandy sour for the rest of her life. From then on, she believed not a word any man whispered into her ear and she was determined to make as many men as possible regret her abortion and the destruction of her dreams. The abortion had been a mess and she had only been saved by a D&C in a top clinic to stop the bleeding. Sandy was sure she would never have children.

By the time Archie explained his problem, she was twenty-five and her looks had peaked. She was magnificent, with an alabaster skin and genuine firm, hard, smooth breasts that turned up. She had firm, hard, smooth, bottom cheeks that turned men crazy when they felt the tucks, and a smooth, long back that was meant to be kissed all over. She had given Archie her enigmatic smile and accepted another Bells and soda. The cocktail bar was quiet and sophisticated, and no one could overhear their conversation.

"Sandy, why don't you and I..." Archie began, wishing to settle Matthew's fate one way or the other, Sandy was also unpredictable.

"You know I never go back, Archie. Anyway, you are not rich enough. The man in my life at the moment is MD of a car manufacturer and has promised me a car."

"He's promised that car to a lot of girls. What does his wife have today? Married men are a very poor bed."

Archie leaned forward and smiled. "Actually, I know just the chap you may be interested in," he murmured. "A friend of mine; just can't make him out. Nearly my age; fine brain, terrific personality. The girls at his office all fancy him. But this chap's hard to get; you know I believe he's still a virgin! Completely unattached."

Sandy fell for the bait immediately. "You must be joking!" she exclaimed. "Tell me more."

Archie reeled in the slack. "Goes by the name of Matthew Gray. One of the tallest men in town, and a physique to fill it. He's in insurance and, believe me, this chap is going right through to the top. Talk about dynamic! It's unbelievable that no girl's got hold of him yet; I suspect he's a very hard nut to crack. Seems to take morality very seriously."

Sandy was stimulated by the challenge. "I'd like to meet this Matthew Gray," she exclaimed animatedly. "Do you think…?"

Archie was staring over her shoulder, affecting surprise. "Why, look at that!" he gestured. "Matthew himself."

"You're a devil, Archibald, a little devil... wow, he must be two metres tall."

"One hundred and ninety-eight centimetres. Matthew this is Sandy de Freitas. You probably know each other from parties."

Half an hour later, Archie withdrew and wondered when he reached the parking lot, whether either he or Sandy knew what they wanted from life. He felt slightly miffed, shrugged to himself and drove home. For the first time in months, Archie felt lonely, and put through a call to his long-standing girlfriend in Bulawayo. They had known each other from his days in Mongu, from when he came out of the bush to bustling Bulawayo in Southern Rhodesia, which everyone else would have called a dump. They spent half an hour on the phone.

That morning, Archie had been offered the job of area manager, a big career leap. There was a stipulation. Area managers had to be married. It was the American rule.

Archie spent the weekend thinking of his problem and on Sunday afternoon drew out a large piece of white paper and wrote down on the left-hand side, very neatly, the prerequisites of a wife, from sex to cooking to irritating habits. There were nineteen terms, and he gauged each item on the scale of one to ten. Then he wrote the names of five girls he was dating, including the lady from Bulawayo, across the top of the list and set to work. Archie pondered a long time, checking and rechecking before finally adding up the columns. The lady from Bulawayo came second by two points, a lady who had been waiting to marry Archie for five years.

"Will being engaged be enough to get me the job?" he asked on the Monday morning. On the Monday evening, he proposed, was accepted and on Tuesday became an area manager with a good chance of further promotion in the company.

Matthew had returned to Sandy's flat on the Friday where she had fed him a thick garlic steak and red wine. In every room of the flat, including the loo, she had burnt joss sticks. She had turned down the dinner-out invitation, wanting to play her game on home ground.

By Monday morning, she knew Matthew was totally infatuated. She was going to do to Matthew Gray what had been done to her at the age of seventeen. She was going to build him up to the highest peak, and then toss him off the mountain.

It was all too easy. As far as women were concerned, Matthew was considerably experienced in the abstract, but was a complete greenhorn in the concrete. Sandy had no trouble whatsoever in seducing Matthew and making him her slave. Then she withdrew. She became inaccessible.

One night, in desperation, Matthew went round to her flat after work and determined to stay there until she returned. But Sandy was two steps ahead of him. When the following morning dawned, she had still not returned home, and Matthew had to spend the night slumped on her doorstep.

He tried to phone her time and again, but there never was a reply. He left urgent notes in her post box. Finally, just as Sandy suspected he might be ready to give up, she phoned him at work and accepted a date with feigned eagerness. Then she simply failed to show up.

It was a game that kept her amused for a month and sent Matthew kicking doors and getting drunk for a week. He took leave, heart-sick leave.

Finally, not even the boat trip from Cape Town could turn his mind from the screaming pain of rejection. Sandy had made herself even with men far more deeply than she could ever have hoped. She had made Matthew grow up. She had hurt his feelings. She had made him violently jealous. She had also made the biggest mistake of her life by not marrying a man with the same innocence she had once possessed.

While Matthew began his rise in life, fuelled by a determination to be rich enough for the likes of Sandy de Freitas, the "but you haven't any money" ringing in his ears, Sandy began her decline. Blinded by her own hatred, she had missed her own boat.

# 2

Matthew arrived in England at the end of January 1955, when England was just beginning to shrug off the greyness of post-war shortages. There was still coal rationing, and bombed-out houses were to be seen everywhere. Heart-sick, Matthew cared little for anything and went through the motions of disembarking at Southampton and catching the train to London.

He was cold in the unfamiliar climate, but colder inside. His mind kept returning to Sandy's flat, the smell of joss sticks, her body, her voice, her smile, her swift changes of dress habits; his gut chased jealousy for hours.

No one met the boat, no one met the train – why should anyone? He knew no one in England except a grandmother he couldn't remember and a black man who would probably have nothing to do with a white South African. There was the job to which he must report on Monday, and a flat to find, or more probably a room. All his savings amounted to five hundred pounds and that was his "I can get home on my own" money and not to be touched.

At Victoria Station he bought an Evening Standard and ran his eyes down the column of rooms to let. The bedsitters were in Nottinghill Gate, Holland Park and Shepherds Bush. Price Forbes were paying him twelve pounds a week and he intended spending no more than twenty-five per cent on his accommodation. There were things to see and places to go which would all cost money. A bed was a bed, however small. He had not even looked at the women on the boat, staying mostly in the pool-bar drinking cheap, duty-free booze and chasing away his hangovers with another deluge of alcohol.

The first bedsitter he looked at was on the second floor, and when the landlady said, "No women in the rooms," he paid her the three-guineas rent and went back on the Tube to collect his suitcases from 'left luggage'. He knew he had to work out the underground train system and now was better than later.

Matthew had learnt to think of small things to keep his mind from reeling out of control. He would think back to the friendships he had made in Johannesburg, especially with Archie and Lucky. And he would at times let his mind drift back to his early life at Port St Johns, recalling the happier memories of the sun, the sea and the cliffs, while steadfastly refusing to brood on the family sorrows connected with the place.

His road in Nottinghill Gate – Sycamore Avenue as it said on his address – was off the Bayswater Road, tucked among leafy plane trees. No. 36 was at the end of the road, away from the worst of the London traffic. Matthew forced himself to enjoy and appreciate his tiny oasis of trees and comparative tranquillity so close to the heart of the world's greatest city. During his first day in London, he slept for twelve hours and, despite his conscious efforts to concentrate on the positive, his dreams were of Sandy. When he awoke, he felt mentally in tune with the heavy, grey, sullen English clouds which seemed to brood only a few metres above his little window. The day was cold and he could not find an English shilling for the gas meter. He lay back on the bed and mentally shook himself.

"Never ever let another woman get under your skin, Matthew Gray." he said aloud. And then a little while later, "Shit, I'm hungry."

Matthew's introduction to the British class system came on the Monday morning at eleven o'clock. Arriving at the office in King William Street at eight-thirty, the time he used to arrive at his Johannesburg office, he found no one but the doorman at Price Forbes House.

"Is it Sunday?"

"Work starts at nine-fifteen. What can we do for you, young man?" Matthew explained his position to the doorman, as he was to do many times during the next hour to all and sundry, it seemed. Eventually they sat him at a desk among thirty other desks where he listened to their 'weekend' conversations. At ten-thirty, he was called into the overseas director's office, and left five minutes later, none the wiser as to what he was meant to do. The fact that he was placed in the Loss of Profits department on the third floor was, it seemed, sufficient to qualify him for his two pounds a day – after deductions.

At eleven o'clock, the entire staff rose and went out for morning coffee. Insurance so far had not even been mentioned. Matthew continued to sit behind his desk, hoping that something would happen, that someone would give him some work to do. At home, by now he would have dictated enough already to keep his secretary typing all morning.

A tall, thin man, maybe seven centimetres shorter than Matthew, turned at the far door. "Coffee, old chap; we all go out to coffee. You should come with me." Matthew was not aware that the man addressing him in a plummy accent knew that David Todd owned Security Life and that David Todd was Matthew Gray's godfather. In Johannesburg, that fact had made no difference to his social life.

"Name's Gore. Oliver. Eton, 'forty-eight to 'fifty-three. Where'd you go to school, old chap?"

"What did you say?" Matthew had never been asked about his schooling at the first meeting, or at any other, for that matter. The man repeated his question, sounding slightly miffed.

"In South Africa. Not really a school. Night school."

"Oh." Oliver Gore had assumed that, with a rich man as godfather, the South African would have been sent to school in England. "You'd better have coffee with us, anyway."

'Us' were the public-schoolboys, minor and major from Eton to Brighton College. By the end of the coffee break, Matthew had taken a thorough dislike to Oliver Gore. All the man ever wanted to know was what his father or grandfather had done.

"Was he commissioned?" asked Oliver Gore, as they filed back into the office.

"No, he wasn't. My father was a private and lived in a woodsman's hut with my mother who painted pictures. My best friend was Luke Mbeki and all of us were very happy. Oh, and Luke was black, pitch black... Do you speak Xhosa?"

When Gore sat down five desks away from Matthew, the only word Matthew caught in the subsequent group conversation was 'colonial'. Apparently there was something wrong with being a 'colonial'. The head of the Loss of Profits department, four desks up the line from Matthew, still had not spoken to him by lunchtime. Matthew watched everyone else departing with their luncheon vouchers to places unknown, without sparing him so much as a glance. After sitting by himself for ten minutes, Matthew went out into the cold street to find something to eat. He did not yet own an overcoat. He trudged for some time, consciously keeping the whereabouts of Price Forbes in mind. Then he entered one of the many eating places, a self-service, took a tray as instructed, and bought a pie and a cup of coffee.

"Got y'r vouchers?"

"No. Cash. Here we are." The shop was warm, the tables full and Matthew began to feel stupid towering over everyone with a tray in his hand. To his left, lunchers pushed up further and left him room to unload his tray and sit with half his backside on the bench. His knees were a problem. "Thank you." He ate his pie in total isolation, despite the fact that there were ten other men at the table. It was the worst cup of coffee he had ever drunk in his life.

"EVERYTHING BURNS if it gets hot enough. Concrete explodes at a given temperature. If the chance of fire is small, so is the rate. Our job is to argue down the rate, not leave a client uninsured."

"What else can you teach me?" Matthew tried a smile, but the man was as frigid as an Eskimo left out in the snow.

"Do you always ask so many questions?"

"I go on asking questions until I understand. I was short on a formal education. I started work when I was thirteen. I read and ask questions. Lot of catching up. Where is the library?" The man was looking at Matthew with a queer look. "I started Plato before I left Johannesburg but I can't afford to buy books."

"Ask Oliver Gore. He has an Oxford degree in English Lit."

"What's he doing in insurance, then? What's the use of a BA in English in this job? He doesn't like colonials."

For a brief moment, the head of the Loss of Profits department, a man maybe five years older than Matthew, almost smiled. An hour later, he handed back the Rolls calculation.

"Some of the standing charges should be put in as partly variables," he was told. "We go for a beer after work on Fridays. You'd better join us. I don't imagine Oliver Gore ever imagined a colonial had heard of Socrates. Do you like music?"

"Something I know little about." He knew the man was not referring to Elvis Presley or Bill Haley and the Comets. "But I like jazz."

"There's Humphrey Littleton. Went to Eton a few years before Oliver. Chris Barber's club. All in Soho or the West End. I went to Westminster."

"I want to go there myself."

The man gave him another queer look and returned to work. Matthew was left to fend off flying paper clips from the few bored occupants of the office who appeared to have nothing better to do than flick them at anyone else whose back was turned. Only department heads worked after three o'clock on Friday. There was already a holiday atmosphere pervading the third floor of Price Forbes House.

MATTHEW'S IMPRESSION after a week in the City of London was that no one did any work, that he did more work in a day in Johannesburg than they did in a week. With a few exceptions, they were all playing a game, and it made him wonder how the British ever founded an empire. He had a strong suspicion that these people were going to waste his time.

Finding a library near his bedsitter, he withdrew the books he had listed to read and continued his self-education. Plato's analysis of right and wrong in the dialogues of Socrates and his disciples made more sense than flicking paper clips. He read through 'The Republic' and started again, struggling to maintain complete concentration and understanding. The grey skies and cold winds were unable to penetrate his small room with the double gas cooker, gas heater and sash window that looked out over the slate roofs and the chimney pots. To counter his loneliness and the loss of his friends, to stop his thoughts shifting back to Sandy, he steeped himself in literature, absorbing some of the distilled wisdom of three thousand years of Western civilisation. Once he went out with another purpose in mind, and knocked on the door of a house in Shepherds Bush. The paint had peeled from the front door. The sour smell of cooked cabbage enveloped him when the door was opened by an old woman with a face as sharp as a chisel.

"Does Luke Mbeki live here?"

"Not anymore."

"Where does he live now?"

"How would I know?"

"Didn't he leave a forwarding address?"

"You a friend of his?"

"Yes. We grew up together."

The door slammed shut less than a foot from his face. He rang the bell again and again. "Bugger off," he was told. "Never did want a bloody nigger in the first place."

He next tried the London School of Economics.

"What department?" he was asked.

"He's studying for a degree in economics."

"What's his name?"

"Mbeki."

"What?"

"Mbeki."

"There are thousands of students here."

"Aren't they listed somewhere?"

"If they are, I don't 'ave the list. Where are you from?"

"South Africa."

"Why they let you lot in, I don't know."

Finally, he wrote to his godfather and awaited news of Luke's new address. The bursary had to be paid somewhere.

On his third visit to the library, he was greeted almost like a friend, and it was the first human warmth he had been shown since leaving the boat at Southampton. The librarian had obviously noticed Matthew's keen interest in books, and had apparently decided that here was a man worth getting to know. He greeted him with something of a smile as Matthew approached his desk. But this time Matthew had something else on his mind besides books.

"I want to trace a coat of arms," he said. "A family coat of arms, I've been told. All I have is an old piece of silver."

"You need to go to the College of Heralds for that. It's only possible to look it up here if you know the name."

"My mother's name was Metcalf but the piece belonged to her mother's family. My great-great-grandfather that would be. Or so the story goes. I've lost touch with my grandmother and these people you mention may be able to help. The silver's pretty worn. Just an old snuff box. She's probably the only relative I have."

With the address of the College of Heralds in his pocket, he took the Tube the following Saturday and offered his snuff box for inspection.

"That's easy," said the man in the dark suit. "That's the crest of a Scottish earl. Do you mind if I take the box?"

"Please bring it back. It's the only connection I have with any relatives." The man raised an unbelieving eyebrow and went off, leaving Matthew at the desk. Ten minutes later, he was back.

"Did you buy this in Portobello Road?"

"My mother gave it to me. My grandmother gave it to her."

"The earls of Lothianmore."

"Is there a living earl of Lothianmore?"

"Of course. That piece of silver was made in the reign of Charles I. The one they beheaded. My armourer tells me that they also cut off the head of an earl of Lothianmore."

"Then the title must have died."

"Not at all. That title was old in the reign of Elizabeth the First."

"Where can I find the earl of Lothianmore?"

"Look him up in Debrett's. They'll give you his current address and his clubs... Are you thinking of visiting him?"

"I think I will."

"Are you from Australia?"

"South Africa."

"Why aren't you black?"

Matthew looked at the man, who was trying not to snigger, thanked him for his trouble and left the Royal College of Heralds to their patronage.

A MONTH after Matthew's unsuccessful search for his family and Luke Mbeki, Oliver Gore happened to announce that his family were heralds to the earl of Lothianmore. Matthew chanced to overhear him as they were sitting around a table in the coffee shop to which Matthew followed his colleagues every morning. Immediately he became alert.

"Do you ever visit them?" asked Matthew, showing casual interest.

"For the grouse shooting."

"Recently?"

"Last twelfth of August. Grouse season opening. Do you shoot?" The man was being sarcastic.

Matthew gave the matter some thought, and decided to drop the subject for the present. When he reached his bedsitter, there was a letter under the door from David Todd. It was the first letter he had ever received from his godfather.

Thinking again about the earl of Lothianmore, he decided to befriend Oliver Gore. He wanted an invitation to Scotland to shoot grouse. The piece of silver and the vague reference to a Scottish title had finally stirred his curiosity, and he idly wondered if kinship to an earl would make any difference to Sandy. It was going to take him years to make his fortune, but the blood-line connection was immediate and Matthew Gray still wanted Sandy de Freitas more than anything on earth. Maybe he could write to her on the earl's notepaper from the earl's castle and see if that did any good. If she was hot after money, maybe she was hot after aristocracy, however distant the relationship. He had written to her four times without receiving any reply.

Matthew was not sure if he would spend many days in the company of

Oliver Gore, but there was no pleasure without pain, as his mother had often said. He thought of his mother often and his thoughts were mostly sad. When he thought of his father, there was always a mixture of happiness and a terrible feeling of loss. His father had gone one day; his mother had declined in front of his eyes. The memories of Port St Johns returned with joy. They gave another meaning to his pursuit of happiness, his wish to be free from want and the necessity of having to rely on other people.

Luke Mbeki had found that his bursary was inadequate soon after his landlady had made his life so difficult that he looked for another room in which to stay. Apartheid was alive and well in London, though the English had not legislated for their prejudice. With so many colonies giving out British passports, the country had been flooded by people looking for an escape from poverty in their own lands. And they were prepared to work, to do the jobs the new welfare state had considered below the dignity of a large number of working-class Englishmen.

It had not taken tens of thousands of people very long to abuse the Labour government's welfare state. These were the people who took the dole and worked for cash on the side, leaving the roads to be swept by the dark-skinned immigrants. A smouldering fire had been introduced into a homogenous society, and Luke Mbeki felt the full force of the silent insidious resentment. The British were turning their backs on the empire, and they would like to exclude its people as well. The empire had been costing money and Europe seemed the better proposition. Changing gear, the new England was shedding its industrial empire and turning its shop keeping mind to trade and to the service industries, with London still at the centre of the financial world despite the free-fall in the value of the pound.

Luke moved four times before he worked out a routine for his survival, which included crane feathers, ankle and arm beads, genet tails and a magnificent leopard skin, head and all that he found among the walks in the Portobello market. If London expected a savage, then he would be their savage and dress accordingly.

Wisely, in view of the climate, Luke chose the middle of summer to cause his sensation on the Tube, at the London School of Economics and, more importantly, at the jazz club he frequented nearly every night. He had introduced the bongo drums there with mild success, which turned to near hysteria when he played them solo in full tribal costume, having his spear and cowhide shield (these had been sent to him from Soweto) against the bandstand. He followed the drum session with some magnificent leaps and bounds that Sipho had taught him in Port St Johns. Remembering the best sensations can be overdone, he had changed into jeans and a shirt before going home on the Tube, leaving his regalia at the Soho club in Greeth Street.

Matthew walked in on the act with Luke's new address in his pocket. Luke had progressed from drumming to singing in English and Xhosa, and was doing his best recollection of a war dance when an equally tall man in the audience howled back at him in Xhosa. The man, pushing his way through the crowd, mounted the small stage on the bandstand and fell into perfect step. The crowd clapped and the two giants, one black and one white, leaped and cavorted, Matthew stripping to his jeans in the smoky heat. Their excitement at seeing each other mounted in the dance as they vied for the tallest leap. With the simultaneous crash of four feet on the floor, the music stopped.

"Give a welcome to my brother," shouted Luke, and the noise was heard in the street, up the deep well from the basement. "You're an elusive bugger to track down," said Matthew. "You were out. Someone gave me the name of the club. Two sets of regalia and we'll make a sensation."

THE CASTLE at Loch Lothianmore opened to the public in May, on Wednesdays and Saturdays from 11 am to 4 pm. The earl of Lothianmore was running out of money and socialist England smiled at his indignity. The retribution of wealth was taking effect.

After three more months of listening to Oliver Gore, Matthew had foregone the opportunity of a grouse shoot (which presumably did not take place on Wednesdays or Saturdays) in favour of joining the tourist bus from Stirling. Matthew and Luke, who were now sharing a flat together, had changed trains three times before arriving at the little Scottish city and before showing their tour tickets to the bus conductor. Three Americans had asked Luke "You from America?" as they rightly assumed that a black immigrant to Britain did not ride on tour buses in Scotland.

When the bus turned through the trees and showed them the ancient pile of stones, Matthew felt a queer shiver and touched the snuff box in his pocket. He had said nothing to Luke, as many families had tales of glory in their past that were nothing more than good stories to add a little spice to wearisome lives. The bus stopped briefly at the castle gatehouse, which needed immediate repairs, before continuing down a long drive. Rhododendrons lined the route and behind them the once lush lawns had been turned into fields and were now cropped short by a flock of sheep. They continued through an avenue of tall fir trees and up to the side door of the ancient castle where the passengers began to disembark. When he stepped down and walked into the building, Matthew felt so peculiar that Luke asked him if he was feeling all right.

"I feel dizzy... Luke, I feel I've been here before." And as he walked further into the castle. "I know this place."

After ten more minutes of déjà vu, Matthew asked the tour guide if the earl and countess were in residence. "They never talk to visitors. Our family is very private."

"Your family?" asked Matthew. "Are you related to the earl?"

"I am a cousin."

"Then maybe you could take this to the earl," and Matthew pulled the snuff box from his pocket, "and say that Matthew Gray from South Africa would be grateful for a brief moment with his lordship."

"Where'd you get this, laddie?"

"From my mother, and her mother before that."

"What was your grandmother's name?"

"Her married name was Metcalf. I was never told her maiden name."

"When the others take their tea, I'll take you to Lord Lothianmore's private quarters." The man put the snuff box in his pocket and continued to lecture the tour group, repeating his twice-weekly story by rote.

Later, as the tourists lined up for their tea in an old summer house, the guide advised Matthew to wait by the door. He then returned to the castle, to return about five minutes later. He gestured to Matthew to follow him, and then led him round the back of the castle and in through a small entrance. Matthew followed him obediently along a cold, gloomy corridor.

The guide stopped outside a door, knocked, and opened it when bidden from within. He announced, "Mister Matthew Gray, my Lord," and stepped back to allow Matthew to enter. Matthew did so, finding himself in what seemed like a different world from the gloomy day outside. Although by no means ornate, the room was brightly lit and a little warmer, thanks to an electric heater, than all the cold halls of history. It was like a lounge except for a desk on the left, behind which sat a smallish, balding man not ten years older than Matthew. He was holding the snuff box.

He greeted Matthew briefly, but did not offer him a seat. "Mister Gray, can you tell me, please, how you came to be in possession of this snuff box?" he requested. Matthew told him the story in a few words.

"Do you have your mother's birth certificate?" The earl was clearly a little suspicious, although the state of his property made it evident that he was not in a position to enrich any charlatans who might claim blood relationship.

"Of course."

"She was an artist. Where is she now?"

"Dead. She did not have money for penicillin."

"Your father?"

"Died at Tobruk."

"Your grandmother died here five years ago. She was destitute. Why did your family not help?"

Matthew began to laugh and held out his hand for the snuff box. "I'll keep this as a curiosity," he said. "She walked out on my mother. A family disagreement. She was unable to accept my mother's desire for a different lifestyle, or her marriage to my father. So she practically disowned her. I am the only relative. I earn twelve pounds a week and share a flat in Shepherds Bush with a black man, my only friend, who is taking his tea with the rest of your tourists. I was curious to know if the story was true."

"Are you looking for help?"

The hackles rose on Matthew's back. "One day, Lord Lothianmore, judging by the upkeep of this place you will more likely be asking me for help." Matthew took out his wallet and a pen, wrote his name and the Johannesburg phone number of Security Life c/o David Todd on a plain card and gave it to the earl. "Phone me when you have to sell this place."

"David Todd? The insurance man?"

"He is my godfather. All three of his sons died the same week as my father outside Tobruk."

THE FOLLOWING JULY, un-tempted by the brief warmth of the English summer and repaying Price Forbes for his boat trip, Matthew caught the aeroplane back to South Africa. His search for living relatives had ended with his interview with the earl of Lothianmore.

The interviews went on for two weeks. Matthew was fully qualified with, in addition, six months' London experience. He had worked in the insurance industry for ten years and was looking for a managerial job. The representative of a Hong Kong company, head-hunting in South Africa, interviewed him twice and offered him the job of managing their chief agency with a staff of seven, six of them Chinese.

The romantic image of the East caught his imagination but, before ending up in a general office number five in a bank of desks even if he was sitting at the top, Matthew went home and wrote down carefully the way in which he would run the Hong Kong office for Swire and Maclean. He would train his staff to be account executives, each with a personal assistant (PA). These would handle all classes of insurance business for the client. They would each, including the PA secretaries, have their own offices. Claims for up to five hundred pounds would be settled by the AEs (account executives) in the client's office by cheque, and would then be recovered from the insurance company through application of the claim for system.

He estimated that he could run a highly efficient chief agency for nine per cent of premium, five per cent below Price Forbes who received a broker's twenty-two per cent average commission against a chief agency's forty per cent, as the chief agency would act as both underwriter and broker.

He received by telegram, to Archie Fletcher-Wood's cottage, where he was staying temporarily, an immediate withdrawal of the job offer. Swire and Maclean did not wish to be told how to run their business.

Archie now married and area manager for his American drugs company, read Matthew's thesis on how to run an insurance agency and, when the rejection came from Hong Kong, showed a copy of the report to his managing director. The American read it carefully and told Archie that, in his opinion, if the concept were implemented properly, Matthew would make a fortune and that, if the appointment of his insurance broker had not been dictated by Fort Worth, he would have been interested in eliminating his own insurance frustrations by handing them all over to Matthew. He told Archie to advise his friend to branch out on his own and not waste his talent on an employer.

Archie spoke to Matthew that night. "Take the best salary on offer for a year," he advised. "Save your money, build-up a prospective list of potential clients and go out on your own. If you have to, find a broker, or sell life insurance while you are building up your short-term account. Security Life will give you an agency."

At the end of August, six weeks after Matthew's return to South Africa, Gray Associates was formed, and incorporated as a private, limited-liability company at the end of the year. In his pursuit of business, Matthew forgot about castles in Scotland and Luke in London. He worked fourteen hours every weekday, keeping Saturdays and Sundays for himself. With annual life commission paid in advance, his cash-flow was positive in six weeks, and he was able to move out of Lucky's flat, to where he had gone from Archie's marital home in Rivonia. Matthew rented a flat in Sandown and settled into his new life. Once again he had found his happiness, this time in the freedom and excitement of owning his own business.

POPPY TUPPER WAS the product of an East End of London mother with a sense of humour and a father who worked in the docks but should have been given the opportunity for a better education. Poppy's mother had had her christened Poppit, and the overworked priest had not joined the first name to the second and come up with the mother's sick sense of humour. Someone had in fact popped it up her at the age of fourteen and Poppy had found it much to her liking.

Taking her brains from her father and the other lifelong-to-be habit from her mother, she had written 0-level examinations at the grammar school when she was fifteen years old, a mature girl with big breasts and the body of a go-go dancer. To the surprise of everyone outside school, Poppy passed all ten subjects, none of which were of any commercial use. She should have taken A-levels and gone to university, but her mother's side of her genes dictated otherwise. Poppy had a thirst for men and wore clothes that drew them like a magnet.

Finding no further adventure in the boys at school, Poppy looked at life's alternatives, and gave up a promising academic career to pursue a more hedonistic lifestyle. There was a lot of fun in being sixteen and a body that swivelled every male head, a face full of laughter, and brains to keep the predators from ruining her life.

She took a job in the accounts department of Security Life's head office in London and received her first tentative introduction to Africa. Being quicker on the uptake than most, she quickly mastered her trivial job and centred her attention on the good life after work. Poppy was able to do her work accurately after four hours' sleep, day after day after day. She shared a small fiat with two other girls, never ate at home and spent most nights playing away.

It was lack of private accommodation that threw her into the arms of older men who were rich enough to afford their own apartments. Poppy became quite upset when people suggested that she was digging for gold. The matter was much more simple. She liked her sex in comfort, and one climax was merely enough to leave her thoroughly frustrated and unable to sleep. Someone gave it to her in the broom cupboard in the office and she vowed never to try that one again. After two years of clubs, restaurants, theatres and music halls, Poppy was bored and looking for a new adventure when she learnt about the South African-assisted passage that was encouraging whites to emigrate.

Poppy sailed from Southampton on the Braemar Castle. She was eighteen years old, more sexy than ever and the sea voyage turned her on uncontrollably. Lifeboats, shower rooms, day cabins, anywhere was good enough, officers, crew or passengers. For Poppy, the two week voyage to Cape Town was a non-stop party. At eighteen Poppy knew exactly which men to avoid, and everyone was happy.

Matthew Gray believed in employing his own staff personally, and in the years ahead would never employ a personnel manager or an employment agency to do what he considered the vital ingredient in this business. His slogan, snatched from David Todd, was in every advertisement for staff. Two days after her train arrived in Johannesburg, one caught Poppy's attention. It read:

---

*If business isn't fun, forget it' Gray Associates are again expanding and require accounts staff in their insurance brokerage business.*

---

Gray Associates were then going into their third year of operation.

"How many 0-levels?"

"Ten."

"Subjects?" She reeled them off and showed him a leg. Very tall men turned her on.

"Can you type?"

"No"

"Go into accounts but learn to type, and then you can be my secretary. Dictaphone. No shorthand. I want a PA/secretary to think for me."

"Why me?"

"I can teach an intelligent girl insurance but I can't always teach an insurance girl intelligence. Good-looking girls in a brokerage business attract customers, insurance customers. The average age of my male staff is twenty-three. Will you join us?"

"What a pleasure."

"There is a set of Gray rules on the wall over there."

Poppy rose and read the twenty-one rules of the company. "I don't like rule seven," she said.

"Nobody does." (Rule 7 stated that members of staff were not permitted to date each other.)

"What happens if we do?"

"Both parties get fired."

"Why?"

"Internal politics are the cancer which takes the fun out of business. All my staff are unmarried. We'd never get any work done."

Poppy began to laugh: "I think I'm going to enjoy myself."

A WEEK after becoming Matthew's PA/secretary and having taken six weeks to learn how to type at a rate of one hundred words a minute, she was asked to close the door. This was only shut for private conversations, Matthew being open to his staff all day. The mini-skirt was starting out on a glorious career, and Poppy had taken to wearing the shortest she could find in the shops. There was a constant panty-flash that had been driving Matthew crazy.

"We have two alternatives," he told her, "Either you stop flashing it, or you resign now and we go out to dinner tonight."

Poppy waited for the laugh which never came. They looked at each other for a full five seconds. He was serious.

Poppy broke the silence. "There's a third alternative. You introduce me to your men friends and I'll introduce you to my girl friends. You do have some men friends, Mister Gray?"

Matthew began to smile.

"It could be good for business," she said, sweetly. She was reading his mind, but he was not thinking of clients so much as Lucky and Archie. Archie had thrown up the area manager's job along with his wife and become a trader with an import-export house.

"We'll have to do something about your name. I can't introduce you as Poppy Tupper to my friends. No one would believe it."

"Some of my friends call me Sunny."

"That'll do. You promise to stop flashing."

"You'll just have to train yourself to stop looking. Or maybe Penny will take your mind off the problem."

"Who's Penny?" Matthew wanted to know.

"My best friend. We share a flat. How about that dinner tonight? Only we'll make it for four."

"Do you prefer an Englishman who trades in commodities, or a Pole who jumps in and out of his car without opening the door? It's a convertible."

"I'll try the Pole. For starters... is he cute?"

"A dimple like Kirk Douglas' and an accent that is pure sex."

"You've talked me into it."

PRICE FORBES HAD SHOWN Matthew his first insurance summary, compiled piece by piece in each department, intelligible to men literate in insurance language but meaning no more to the client than the policy itself, a comprehensive legal document designed to stand up in court.

Over the previous eighteen months, he had sat down with the policy documents of every insurance company licensed to do business in South Africa, including Lloyd's of London, and translated the jargon into understandable English which would enable him to tell his clients what they were and what they were not insured against. The key definition of an insurable gross profit had been worded to enable a chartered accountant to differentiate between his own gross profit and that which he would wish to be paid out if his factory were to burn to the ground and his turnover be reduced to nothing.

Matthew restored communication between client and insurer, and it was not uncommon for his AEs to be told by a new client that it was the first time the client understood insurance. Matthew's reports in pursuit of new business used the same new language. New business was controlled not by the number of new clients wishing to do business with Gray Associates, but by the lack of trainable staff, people to whom Matthew could teach all classes of insurance and turn into competent account executives. Much of his after-hours work was training and motivating, teaching his people to do the job the way he knew was right.

One of his better known conditions of insurance was written in capital letters on every motor policy summary. Drunk drivers were NOT insured, a fact that worried Matthew himself! In South Africa there were no public houses just round the corner and cars were used on all social occasions. Matthew's first short-term client had been a company in the recording industry, making radio commercials and radio programmes. There was no television in South Africa in 1957. The managing director was an old friend of Archie Fletcher-Wood. The premium was modest but handled personally by Matthew as that six hundred pound commission in the first year had been vital to him.

On that Friday night when Sunny, Penny, Lucky and Matthew had enjoyed themselves so much, the MD of the sound recording studio drove a Cadillac into a tree, putting his girlfriend, a well-known model, through the windscreen. The Cadillac had come with the takeover of his company by a large record company. Fortunately, the ambulance arrived before the police, and the unconscious MD and his girlfriend were taken to hospital. By the time the police wished to take a blood test, it was too late. Matthew visited his client in hospital on the Monday soon after the accident was reported. He took a claim form and returned with a signed statement from the client saying, among other things, that the client was sober at the time of the accident. If the client had been drunk, the car, a write-off, was uninsured and the record company would be most annoyed. Worse, the model, whose face needed major plastic surgery, would be uninsured and forced to sue the driver in his personal capacity.

Matthew knew the MD was short of money. The reason for the takeover had been a personal cash flow problem. In his personal capacity, the driver, Matthew's client, would not have sufficient money to pay the doctor's bills. And the prime witness to any question of drunken driving was the model. Matthew, knowing his client's drinking habits first-hand, was sure that at five minutes to midnight on a Friday night, the chances of his client being sober were nil. It could have happened to any of them, he reasoned; young bachelors living in the fast lane.

That morning, Matthew made an urgent appointment with the general manager of the insurance company which underwrote the Cadillac. He and Matthew were personal friends, and Matthew knew his friend drank with the best of them and a little bit better than some.

"What's the urgency, Matt? Had a good weekend?"

"Superb." For a moment, the vision of Penny, naked and calling for more, took him briefly away from the point. Matthew gave a brief smile and brought his mind back to his responsibility as broker to client and underwriter.

"Have you ever been drunk behind the wheel?" he asked.

"Probably... Do you have a point?"

"We've all been drunk in terms of the law at one time or another, and most of us on a weekly basis. It goes with the job and none of us have drivers. Maybe we should. I've a claim here, signed by my client, saying he was sober when he smacked up his Caddy on Saturday night and put a top model through the windscreen. She looks awful. I just visited."

"What's your point, Matt?"

"My client was drunk, probably out of his mind." Matthew told him frankly.

"Did the police ...?"

"No. It's his word and the girl's, though I expect you could go back on his evening and prove he was motherless."

"You can't expect me to pay an uninsured claim," the general manager said firmly.

"If you can't nail down the barman, the restaurant manager and whoever, the claim from the girl will include a large sum for pain and suffering, another large sum for loss of earnings and then there's plastic surgery. If I handle that claim, I think I can keep it to the Cadillac and plastic surgery. Also you miss any messy publicity about your refusal to pay out. Even though you are quite justified, it wouldn't gain you clients."

The GM began to smile as the point became clear. "If the girl wishes to recover from your client, she will have to sue him; is that what you're saying?"

"And my client doesn't have enough money."

"Can you talk to the girl?"

"Poor kid doesn't have a chance if she sues. Can you include a nose job? I've met the girl. She said to me once she needed a nose job, though I had no idea why. Maybe she'll settle down and have kids. But not with my client. She's mad as hell at him as he wasn't even wearing his glasses. Vanity. Men and vanity.

"Can I take you out to lunch? Never eat breakfast... Have you met my new secretary?"

"You're an honest extortionist, Matthew Gray. That's what you are."

"All you have to do is withstand the temptation." He was referring to Sunny Tupper.

FOUR WEEKS LATER, the record company, itself a subsidiary of a large stock exchange-listed conglomerate, gave an instruction to all its subsidiaries to change their insurance to Price Forbes, the conglomerate's broker. At the same time the subsidiaries were told to change the group auditors, lawyers, printers, shipping agents, confirming house and bank.

The MD, recovered from his car smash and in line for the position of chief executive of the record company, a condition of the takeover, refused to change his insurance broker and, though never admitting that he was drunk behind the wheel, it seemed that he was fully aware of Matthew's successful negotiation with his now ex-girlfriend and the insurance company. The man was no fool, despite his tendency to over-drink on weekends and leave behind his glasses in the company of pretty girls. The model, in the hands of the best plastic surgeon, was well satisfied with Matthew's solution.

The confrontation came between the MD and the head of the conglomerate, one of the best-known businessmen in the country. It was said that his short-term insurance account was the fifth-largest in South Africa, worth over a million rand in annual premium. The top man bullied; the MD argued, was threatened, and told the man he could shove his takeover and that the agreement of purchase said nothing about changing insurance brokers, only bankers and auditors. Finally, the MD told the truth about the accident and of Matthew's solution, finishing with a shout that Gray Associates were the best bloody brokers in the country. The top man went quiet. Not for nothing had he built an empire, and he came up with the proposal that Gray's reported on the entire group's insurances and insisted that either the entire group changed to Gray's, or the MD changed his broker.

Matthew's summary and report system included a questionnaire which analysed a new client's insurance needs and left nothing uncovered. It went into the client's business and tailored insurance individually. There were one hundred and seventy-three companies in the conglomerate, distributed around the country, from hotels to a coal mine. Some of the subsidiaries fell under the same financial director, but it still required the completion of forty-three questionnaires and reports.

Matthew first completed Johannesburg, flew by schedule airline to Durban, Port Elizabeth and Cape Town and chartered an aircraft to visit the coal mine. By the end of his analysis, he proved the group was under-insured by twenty-four million rand on the fire and consequential loss policies, one factory building being without any insurance at all, and, with the help of the general manager who was paying the model's plastic surgeon, was able to reduce premiums by ten per cent at the higher sums insured.

The forty-three reports were given to the individual financial directors six weeks after Matthew was asked to inspect the conglomerate's policies. He had used dummy report forms to save writing out each insurance definition, now translated into English. Every one of his secretaries worked late. The excitement in the company was tangible. The head of the conglomerate, who expected to have Price Forbes pick holes in the young man's reports, was faced with a unanimous request from his financial director to change over to Gray Associates. Matthew explained his share proposal, which offered the conglomerate shares in Gray's in proportion to their annual premium. It was Matthew's idea to float his company on the Johannesburg stock exchange when he reached ten million rand in premium income.

Matthew was handed a letter of appointment to the group that was to make him open branches in Durban and Cape Town within six months. Matthew made a brief speech to his staff. The message was simple: he increased all salaries by twenty per cent. The enthusiasm rose to new heights. The company was on a roll. Gray Associates had arrived as a force in the insurance industry.

Many of the big London brokers were not happy about an upstart interfering with a system that had worked well for half a century. Some of the insurance companies, faced with redefining their policy wordings to compete, agreed that Gray Associates were disturbing the industry. Matthew, being young, failed to see the antagonism in his rush to take on new staff and open up his branches whenever he received a letter of appointment.

THE LATE NIGHTS, booze and cigarettes were catching up on Sandy de Freitas. Looking down the last year of her twenties, she was no longer sure where she was going. The married men had stayed married to their wives, the I've-got-a-lot-of-money bull shitters were easier to see through, and the real men had found their partners for life and were cutting lawns and reading bedtime stories to their children. Sandy tried to cut the same dash but her looks were beginning to fade and young girls like Sunny Tupper were infringing on her turf. Sandy tried a few of the second-time-arounders and quickly discovered why they were divorced. Her good time years were overspent and there wasn't any money in the bank. Cynically, she thought she would have done better as a hooker.

Taking stock one dreary Sunday morning on her own, something that never used to happen, she looked back on all the besotted men she had discarded in her search for the real pot of gold. All had married or drifted out of town. All but one.

Having been unable to get out as much as usual, Sandy had not seen Matthew in two years. Their eyes had met again briefly across the heads of the hedonists at the Friday night swill in the Balalaika Hotel where all the singles met to find out where the party was going to be over the weekend. Times had been when Sandy never left the Balalaika without an invitation to dinner, but now too often she went home on her own to face the Saturday and Sunday in her flat.

Matthew had never really turned her on. He had been too young and too nice. She had been able to make him do what she wanted, and, after a month, that had been boring. But now they said he was rich and the biggest aphrodisiac for Sandy was money. She looked him up in the directory on the Sunday afternoon and dialled his number, boredom having reached the stage of hurting the marrow in her bones. What she did not know was that Matthew had watched her carefully for half an hour on the Friday, at first stomach lurch turning to sadness as he watched the eye-desperation in his faded beauty. She had looked forty. The monkey on his back had climbed down and departed for ever.

"Hello, lover." He recognised the voice and felt the lurch in his stomach. He kept silent.

"Hear you're making money... You know who this is? ... Matthew?"

As the silence continued, she knew this chance had long since departed.

"Hi, Sandy. How've you been?" To Sandy, he sounded sad.

"Are you alone?" she asked.

"No. No, I'm not," he lied. Sunday afternoons were always spent quietly, taking stock of the jobs he had to do during the coming week. This time Matthew listened to the silence on the telephone line. Just before he heard the click, there was a brief, terrible sob. He looked at the dead phone and put it back on the hook.

Half an hour later he found her address in the telephone book and, with premonition pricking his nerves, drove speedily to the flat in Rosebank, the same flat. There was no answer to the ring. He called her name. A weak voice said, "Go away, you bugger. I'm going to sleep." Using a technique he had mastered when locked out of his own fiat, he slid his American Express gold card into the crack of the door and pushed back the catch. There was still a faint smell of joss sticks, incense-from the past.

"Why the hell did you do this?" he asked.

"My life's over, lover. You can't have your cake and eat it. They all went. All of them... You ever been lonely, lover?"

Matthew put the empty pill bottle in his pocket for the doctors and picked up the only woman who had taken his heart, a woman now gone and lost in the memory of his youth.

AFTER MATTHEW LEFT LONDON, Luke had kept on the flat, inviting a fellow black to share it with him. The man was from Northern Rhodesia and spent more time talking politics than anything else. Luke learnt that all the man wished for in life was the break-up of the federation of Rhodesia and Nyasaland and for the independence of the country he called Zambia. Luke's new flatmate was in his second year at the London School of Economics, which Luke concluded he would fail as the man never opened a book unless it had to do with revolutionary politics. He was going to be this Zambia's minister of finance. The quotes from Karl Marx and Mao Tse-tung came at regular, boring intervals.

"A man is frightened into working or given a personal incentive," Luke told his flat-mate. "'Each according to his need' is a licence for the bums to sit on their arses and feed off the fools who work for nothing. There are a lot of lazy buggers in this world who will work for nothing and who will hijack your utopia and have the likes of you and me working for them for nothing... and you won't get a degree in economics by reading nothing but Karl Marx."

"Then we live under the yoke of the white man for the rest of our lives, our children's lives. Communism and the party will set us free. I am being put through this university by the Russian communist party."

"What's in it for them?"

"You are cynical, Luke Mbeki."

"And you, my good friend, are naive. Nobody does anything in this world for nothing. Security Life, who pays for me, think there is a future market among the blacks for the insurance industry and the Todd Memorial Grant is a way to hedge the bet. But take advantage. Don't waste an opportunity."

Luke had completed his doctorate and booked his passage home the day the results were known, and the Edinburgh Castle had sailed in early 1960, away from the cold of Southampton. He had been away for six years and, though the reports from home were as chilling as the English weather, Dr Luke Mbeki wanted to go back to South Africa. It never once occurred to him to look for a job in England. The greatest joy he had found during his six years was in sharing the flat with Matthew, talking about Port St Johns and longing for the years of their childhood.

This time, Luke Mbeki did not make the same mistake as on his previous voyage when he had kept himself isolated, and tried to mingle with the passengers. But his efforts to break down the barriers were in vain. He kept to his lower-deck cabin, a six-berth, that, miraculously, he had to himself. He was the only black passenger on the Edinburgh Castle. They gave him a small table to himself in the dining room and gave him drinks in the bar by himself. Even the barman refused to be drawn into conversation. When he sat down on a deck chair, the space around him was cleared. No one was rude. They merely treated him as if he did not exist.

The boat sailed into Cape Town harbour at six o'clock in the morning, with Luke out on deck. The sea was calm and there was a red sunrise behind Table Mountain. He turned to look back out to sea, in the direction of the penal colony of Robben Island. There was not one cloud in the sky, the previous day's southeaster having chased away the rain. Luke's euphoria continued as the ship docked, and he disembarked with his luggage.

"Where's your pass, man?" demanded the immigration officer, ignoring Luke's passport which had been obtained by David Todd after bringing pressure to bear on the nationalist government.

"You can't come into Cape Town without a pass. Here, it says you were born in the Transkei. You either live in the Transkei or you have a pass."

"Where do I get this pass?"

"At Bantu Affairs, man. You can wait over there till I'm finished."

"May I not go and get this pass?"

"You can't come into Cape Town without a pass, man. Don't you kaffirs ever listen?"

It took Luke four hours to get through immigration and collect his luggage, a man from Bantu Affairs coming all the way to the docks to issue a temporary pass which would enable Luke to travel through South Africa to his place of birth.

"But I want to work in Johannesburg," he said to the man.

"Then you must go to the Transkei and ask them at Bantu Affairs in Umtata. I can only issue a travel pass."

"I have spent six years in England becoming a doctor of economics, and they don't employ such people in Umtata."

"It's the Law, man. If you want to work in Johannesburg, you must have a pass. Influx control, man. If the government didn't keep control of the kaffirs they'd be swarming all over Johannesburg. If you want to work in a white area, you get a pass. That travel pass is valid for one week. If the police find you after that, they lock you up. Better catch your train."

"The boat train has left."

"That's your problem. Just be in the Transkei a week from now."

"Do you know a hotel for tonight?"

"All hotels are reserved for whites. A black man can't sleep in a white area after dark. Group Areas Act."

"Then what do I do?"

"That's your problem. You missed your train."

Luke spent the night on a wooden bench in the non-white section of Cape Town station. When the ticket office opened, he was told the next train would travel the following day.

"Can't travel on that ticket, man." said the Afrikaner. Even in the non-white section of the railways, the civil servant was white. "First-class is for whites only. Where'd they give you that ticket?"

"In London."

"Better change it or they won't let you on the train."

"I'm a doctor of economics."

"I don't care if you're the king of England. If you're black, you don't travel first-class in South Africa. It's the law. Railway Act, man... You want to change that ticket for a third-class, non-white."

"Do I get a refund?"

"You'll have to fill in a form if you want a refund and then it goes to the office and then it goes to Pretoria. Takes ten days."

"Give me a third-class, non-white. May I have a sleeper?"

"You trying to be cute with me, kaffir. I don't have to change your ticket, you know. I can make you take it back to the office that issued it, see. You get benches, third-class, non-white. Why, the tickets are cheap."

"Thank you. You are most kind. Just give me what you can."

By the time Luke arrived at Johannesburg station four days after sailing into Cape Town harbour and his future, he was a wreck, hungry, unslept and dishevelled. When he phoned the Gray Associates number he expected to be blocked by the telephone operator, the same way he had been blocked trying to speak to David Todd.

"Gray Associates, good morning." The voice was light and Luke knew the girl would be pretty.

"May I speak to Mister Matthew Gray?"

"Certainly, I'll put you through,"

"Matthew Gray speaking."

"Matt, its Luke. You can't have any idea how good it is to hear your voice."

"Luke, you old bastard. Where the hell are you?"

"Johannesburg station. Third-class, non-white.

There was a pause. "Oh, shit," said Matthew down the line. "These people make me sick. I'm on my way, Luke. Hang on... Did you get your doctorate?"

"Yes, then I came home. I got to Cape Town four days ago."

"You *jawling* in Cape Town."

"No, Matt, I wasn't *jawling*."

The sight of a very tall white man hugging a very tall black man in the third-class, non-white section of Johannesburg station stopped all movement on the platform. Matthew was the only white man in the non-white section out of uniform.

"Kaffir-lover," said a white railway worker.

Matthew's right hand shot out, gripping the man's arm and dragging him round. "You want to say that to my face?"

"You're not allowed here. Non-whites only. Can't you read, kaffir-lover?"

A crowd had now gathered, all of it black. Matthew still had the man by his arm and was applying the pressure. "Take your hand off me."

"People like you make me puke." As the man pulled away from him, Matthew suddenly let him go. The sudden release shot him back into the crowd of blacks where they parted to let him fall on his rear.

"You pushed me, you bastard."

"I did not, and I have a hundred witnesses to prove it. It's people like you who are ruining this country." The sea of black faces stopped the man from repeating his threats. "One day, these people will rip you apart and the world won't lift a finger. Luke, let's get out of here." To the surprise of the on-lookers, Matthew spoke Xhosa to his friend. "Don't let people like that ruin your day."

"They already have. All the way from Cape Town."

A long, hot bath, with a T-bone steak twenty-five millimetres thick, and ten hours sleep put Luke back into the world. They had talked for hours, moving away from the cause of their anger to what they had both been doing since Matthew left London. Neither of them had been more than birthday and Christmas letter-writers, young men too embarrassed to speak of their emotions on paper. Even now, the emotions were expressed in body language rather than words. During the two-day train ride, Luke had wondered if Matthew had joined the apartheid system.

"Where they're clever, Luke, is in keeping us apart," Matthew told him over supper. "I don't even know any blacks in Johannesburg. So far as my day-to-day life is concerned, I see white faces all the time. We have a driver boy, a black girl in the printing office, and the rest of my staff are white. My clients are all white. The law stop blacks going where I socialise and if a policeman walks in here now they can arrest both of us, but in reality it will only be you. All but menial civil servants are white and Afrikaner, and schools, pensions and welfare benefits are for all intents and purposes white. Black people living in newly designated white areas get moved, forcibly removed to somewhere too far from their jobs to be economical; half the salary goes in transport. That way we live in a white world and forget about the blacks.

"The rest of the fat cats in the world don't worry about two-thirds of the world starving, so why should we, is what the advocates of our new system tell themselves. It must blow up in the end. I've heard there's widespread opposition to the pass laws, people talking about burning their pass books in mass demonstrations. But the Afrikaner is tough, Luke. Some of the little men with power over your people make Hitler look like a philanthropist. They'll use force with pleasure. Keep out of their clutches."

Next morning, Matthew was up with the dawn, and had finished three hours' work and was making breakfast when Luke awoke.

"Good morning, Luke. Feeling better?"

"Much. Do I smell bacon and eggs?"

"I've phoned my office, cancelled appointments and I'm free for ten days," Matthew told him. "After breakfast, we're driving down to Port St Johns. You want to see your father. David Todd said on the phone I should get you out of the way until he has your proper papers. He's highly annoyed you did not tell the Todd Trust you were coming back so soon after graduation. They want you to work for Security Life. There's something in your bursary to that effect.

"Just remember, Luke, however difficult it gets, not every white is a bigoted racist. There are a lot of us who know we have to share this country and its wealth. Harry Oppenheimer said the other day that the real wealth is in the people, not in the minerals. You guys have got to get educated, that's the bottom line, and you've done just that. We'll feel free in Port St Johns. You'll see. We'll walk the beach, swim, eat crayfish, oyster, catch us a mussel or two, and you can tell Sipho the wonders of London. Then I go to Australia. We're opening a branch in Sydney."

"You've done well."

"We've just over two per cent of the country's short-term premium income. We're in the top twenty brokers, but I've made a lot of enemies in the industry."

The massacre at Sharpeville took place the following day, bringing the spotlight of the world onto the cruel system of pass laws and apartheid. Matthew had been right. The blacks burnt their pass books, surging around the police station near Paarl where hundreds died in a hail of bullets. Naked racism had gone to war.

# 3

While Matthew and Luke were sitting round the cooking fire outside Sipho's hut with the sound of the Wild Coast surf pounding the soft air, Hector Fortescue-Smythe was waiting for his controller beneath a tree in Green Park, London. Between Hector and the entrance to the Cavalry Club, the Piccadilly traffic was as constant as the rain. He would have preferred being inside the club, in front of the fire with a whisky and soda, but the instruction had been emphatic and Hector knew better than to keep the Russian waiting.

Hector had been recruited at Cambridge before he went into the army to do his national service in tanks, where he had received his commission with minimal help from his father, a man Hector loved and despised in equal proportions. After his two years in the army, during which time he had heard nothing from his controller, Hector had drifted around London refusing to join his father's business. Hector wanted nothing to do with his family business because it was founded on the seat of the working man.

Hector's great-grandfather had been a chemist who had invented the first detergent, a blue that whitened clothes. He had made the discovery while in the bath in the shed at the back of the family semi-detached house in Liverpool. They lived on the corner of Sister and Bold streets, the bath and shed having been turned into his laboratory. James Smythe (the 'Fortescue' had been added by Hector's grandmother) had both an inventor's and a business brain, and refused the offer from Reckitt's to buy his patent.

He began to build his empire by selling his product in a handcart around the streets of Liverpool, leading to a factory, a large number of staff and Hector's confusion. Not having gone into the business, Hector was convinced that a rich man who inherited a business, albeit making it grow and doubling its work force, was living off everybody's work other than his own. He was not aware that retaining wealth was just as difficult as making it in the first place, it being the way of man to take away rather than to give. The pure scent of communism was the ocean air he wished to breathe. His naivety was matched only by his sincerity, a sincerity so intense that, had it been channelled to religion, it would have found Hector ensconced in a monastery.

Unbeknown to Hector, the reason for the meeting was the massacre at Sharpeville and, when his controller arrived at the appointed hour, the picture of dead black bodies strewn around the police station incensed Hector far more than his father's exploitation. There were white policemen and white soldiers with pointed rifles, and all the blacks were either dead, dying, or had their backs to the guns. They were running away as fast as their legs could take them. It did not require the Russian to point out that the dead and wounded had been shot in the back.

The controller explained in detail that Russia wished to help the black oppressed by challenging the power of the white minority government which was backed by the West. He made it clear to Hector that the capitalist West was just as guilty as the white South Africans and that the Americans and British were racist pigs, something Hector was quick to deny so far as he was concerned. The rain had run water down the photographs, and it reminded Hector of blood, the spilt blood of the poor and helpless.

"The South Africans are offering a free passage to whites to emigrate and boost their numbers, and we want you to go."

"I couldn't live in a country that did that ..."

"But you would if the blacks came to power with your help and ours, and created a one-party state, governed for the people, by the people. There is a fledgling South African communist party that was started by the white workers in 1923 during the miners' strikes.

"We wish to take control and turn it into the tool that will fan the flames of black nationalism and bring about another great victory for the working classes. We want you to apply to join the South African army. There are many ex-members of the Royal Navy at the Simonstown base where we have sent another young man. You will be a sleeper for many years, Mister Fortescue-Smythe, but, in the end, the South African communist party will control the African National Congress, having taught it how to fight a guerrilla war. Since the massacre at Sharpeville, this ANC has let us know that the time for peaceful words is over.

"They are ready to launch an armed struggle."

"Shouldn't I join that struggle?"

"You will be far less conspicuous in the white army, and far more useful to us and the communist party. You will work hard. You will agree with all their sentiments. You will learn Afrikaans and you will marry an Afrikaans girl and join their Broederbond, a secret elite, white society that controls their white nationalist government. You will be more racist than the racists. You will attain high rank, and when we tell you, and only when we tell you, will you come out of the closet."

"How long will that be?"

"Time is on the side of communism. When the time is right, mankind will be set free. We will eliminate all want. There will no longer be rich and poor but sufficient for everyone. There will be one world. One government run on the heroic principles of Karl Marx and Vladimir Lenin. It will be the greatest day on earth, and you will be part of the rejoicing."

The Russian hugged Hector twice, happy with the expression of total belief on the face of his prospect. For a moment, he thought he had gone too far.

"How am I going to find a suitable Afrikaans wife?" It was the only part that struck a discordant note.

"We will give you a list. Her father must be high in the government and the Nationalist Party of Dr Verwoerd, a man we are going to kill in his own parliament to demonstrate to our friends the strength of the communist party and our commitment to black rule. I hear you have a way with women. You may even love the girl, if you wish, but that is your business. Personally, I have never believed there is only one person for each of us. Like religion, sex is the opium of the people?'

As the Englishman walked away with his written instructions to join the South African army, instructions that bore no reference to their source, the Russian smiled to himself at how easy it was to manipulate a true believer. Such men went to their deaths with smiles on their faces. The strategy of exploiting the wrongs of racism and colonialism which he had helped to formulate in Moscow was coming together, and when they had finished they would totally control the chrome, manganese and twelve other strategic minerals that were found only in South Africa and the Soviet Union. The American Arms programme would be crippled at source. The rights and wrongs of racism and colonialism mattered as much to the Russian as the rain dripping off the brim of his hat. Power. It was all about power.

LUCKY KUCHINSKI and Archie Fletcher-Wood were bored with their lives. Chasing women, going to parties, drinking too much and having more money than they could spend had lost its edge. They needed a little excitement.

They were thirty-one and thirty-three respectively, and the idea of settling down with a wife had few attractions for either of them. Archie had tried, and had ended up with a woman who did little for herself, expecting to be entertained and pampered by Archie for what soon became a rather boring ten minutes of sex every day. The woman was always wanting something and, for Archie, one-sided arrangements had a habit of coming to a speedy end. Lucky had watched his friend, and was determined not to make the same mistake. The value of home and hearth was not worth that price to pay.

The conversation had begun on a Sunday morning after reading the Sunday papers in Archie's Rivonia cottage. The papers were screaming of the criminality of women, children and missionaries being massacred by rampaging blacks in the recently ex-Belgian Congo. The obscene rush out of Africa by the European powers had been matched only by their obscene rush into Africa during the previous century. Within months, the Belgians had decided to get their troops and administrators out of the Congo and, within fourteen days of their departure, all forms of government disintegrated and rebellious troops went on the rampage. The South African press was outraged, and the Afrikaans press, still smarting from overseas criticism over the Sharpeville massacre, said, "We told you so."

Back at the United Nations, the Russians stirred the pot and made the Americans run around like headless chickens, no one knowing whom to support or whether to condemn the slaughterous blacks or the fleeing Belgians; whether to tell the Belgians to send the para-troops back in to save women and children and evacuate the whites, or to send in a United Nations force.

The only province to retain any semblance of order was Katanga. Their leader, Moise Tshombe, wished to declare a separate state for his copper-rich country and asked the Americans to support his secession, which the Indians and Russians vociferously opposed. The Americans prevaricated and tried to get the leading lights amid the anarchy to talk to each other. It was Tshombe's carefully worded advertisement in the *Sunday Times*, calling for men of military age to help his breakaway country that caught the eyes of Lucky and Archie.

"He's recruiting a force of mercenaries," said Archie, after taking the proffered page from Lucky.

"Looks like it."

"Why don't we go?" suggested Archie. "The commies are going to take over Africa if someone doesn't do something. The Yanks are so anti-colonialist they're going to sit back and see the Russians take over exactly where the Belgians, French, British and Portuguese left off. Or, as here, the vacuum leaves a bloodbath." Archie threw the paper on the table, its screaming headline face up. "Poor sods. For every white killed and reported in the press, there'll be hundreds of blacks killed in the power struggle. Why can't people stop interfering in other people's business?"

"Self-interest," replied Lucky. "I got out of a communist state. All the shit in the Congo is an extension of the cold war. The Russians want to run the world, Buddy boy. Anyway, what are we going to do with the rest of our lives? I'm sick of jumping in and out of the car without opening the door."

"You think Matthew will want to come?"

"No... he's too busy running round the world opening branches. Never stops. Why do people go on making more and more money when they can't even spend what they've got?"

"You're jealous," teased Archie.

"Maybe. We can ask him... you want me to phone the number in the paper? There are pygmies up there. And gorillas."

"Both kinds. You think they'll give us some kind of military training? Whom shall we phone first: Matt, or the number in the paper?"

When they spoke to Matthew, he turned them down flat. He was three years younger than Archie, and his period of disillusionment had not yet arrived. The adrenaline he pumped into business was still surging through his body. Matthew was hyperactive, permanently on the go, flying twenty thousand kilometres every month in an aeroplane. He wanted to float his company on the Johannesburg stock exchange before he was thirty, and use the injection of capital to create his own conglomerate. The stock market was on a strong bull run and Matthew had targeted two of his clients as likely candidates for takeover. He knew the business of each as well as its staff and he had studied their balance sheets for years, every time he adjusted their Loss of Profits insurance. And as a broker under 'Section 20bis of the Insurance Act', he was only obliged to pay over his client's premiums to underwriters ninety days after renewal of the client's policies, and most of Matthew's clients paid him on receipt of the first statement. When Lucky asked him to drop everything and run off to fight another man's war, he had over four million rand out with the banks earning interest.

"You guys are crazy. Cool it, Lucky. What the hell am I going to do for friends if you go to the Congo? Look, I'd come over but my plane leaves from Jan Smuts for America in two hours. Talk to you when I get back. Six weeks. We're looking at Canada with the Bank of Montreal. They like our systems and want to lock them into a computer with a patent. It will mean we can prepare reports for the client, closing instructions for the underwriter, and the summary of insurance by one input. Absolute break-through if it works, which it will. The computer automatically amends everything when there is an endorsement, throwing out a new summary at the press of a button. It can print the policy document and cut out all the underwriter's overheads. Gray's will issue policies, and the insurance company will merely act as a reinsurer, saving the forty-three per cent overhead factor. I can drop the premium rates by forty per cent and make everyone the same profit."

"You lost me a while ago, Matt."

"Lucky, don't go to the Congo. Wait till I get back. Got to go."

By the time Matthew returned with everything he wanted, his friends had gone. It was the first chill wind he had felt since starting Gray Associates, but he was too busy to give it sufficient thought. The financial press had picked up the news of his joint venture with the Bank of Montreal, one of the largest banks in the world, and with Hambros Bank, the large British merchant bank. Within a week of his two best friends entering a military camp as private soldiers under Major Mike Hoare, Matthew was a celebrity. He was a perfect target. Young, tall and rich. The socialite invitations began in earnest and the background of his girlfriends moved into the rich and famous. Sunny Tupper was not sure if the change was such a good thing, but she was so busy with her own social life that she only concentrated on her business life when with Matthew Gray. Later, many years later, Matthew was to look back and tell himself that it would have been for the better if Sunny had resigned that first time around, and become his love and who knew what else. She was certainly the only woman in the business world he was ever able to trust.

Sadly, Matthew saw less and less of Luke. Luke lived in Soweto and Matthew needed a permit to visit the black township, something rarely given by the police, and none, of the watering holes were multi-racial. Occasionally they spoke on the phone, Luke working in the actuarial department of Security Life and studying for his actuarial degree. Luke rented a small house in a good Soweto suburb away from the coal stoves and the vicious poverty. He visited the Transkei and dated women and, if his Zambian friend had not given his name to the ANC recruitment officer in London, he would probably have remained non-political. He had his friends, a good job and a future. What he failed to realise was that he was one of a very few blacks in Africa with such a fortunate scenario.

WHEN HECTOR APPLIED to South Africa House in the Strand to join the South African army, he was told that he would have to become a South African citizen, and it would take five years of living there before he was eligible. Even the Russians could be wrong. The interviewing officer, a young Afrikaner by the name of Swart, all but one of the embassy staff being Afrikaans, asked him what else he would like to apply for, and pulled out a questionnaire. Hector smiled to himself when the name of the prestigious English public school that had been in existence four hundred years meant nothing to the Afrikaner. His tertiary education drew a better response. The man had heard of Cambridge.

"Did you obtain a degree?"

"Honours in industrial chemistry."

"Say that again." Young Swart interviewed some twenty people a day, all eager to emigrate to South Africa as the tax and cost of living, coupled with salary in England, made an individual's wealth in real terms about half the value it would be in South Africa, where the country was enjoying a growth rate of just under ten per cent.

"Bachelor of science, chemistry."

"And you had good marks?"

"I believe they were the best in my year." Even Hector recognised that the genes that gave him life had come from the inventor of the first detergent, leaving an indelible print stronger than the more fickle fruit of money.

Frikkie Swart took his menial job seriously, and read all the memoranda that concerned immigration in South Africa. The 'powers that be' had recognised their country's dependence on imported products of a strategic nature, and that the world would be able to use these products as weapons against South Africa in its efforts to destroy its white, non-communist government. The Afrikaners' problems were oil and arms, the lack of good artillery in the war against the British at the turn of the century having taught them a lesson. So they put into operation their plans to provide their country with alternatives to imported products. Secretly, they had formed Armscor and Sasol, the former to develop sophisticated arms and the latter to extract oil, non-existent naturally in South Africa, from coal, which was in abundant supply. Both were backed by massive government funds. Hector's qualification would make him an excellent acquisition for the country.

"It is possible we could find you a job in the chemical business, and if after five years you still wish to join our army, you could change over. Why do you wish to come to South Africa?"

"I detest socialism in all its forms, and Hugh Gaitskell in particular."

Swart kept the excitement out of his eyes. The man was too good to be true. A potentially brilliant chemist nurtured in one of the best universities in the world, and an Englishman who would probably vote NAT when he became a South African citizen.

"Do you agree with our policy of separate development of black and whites in our country, and the creation of homelands where the blacks will be able to live and vote, coming to the white areas only to work?"

"Wholeheartedly. Look what has happened in the Congo. A model colony overrun by communism and lost in anarchy. Sharpeville was unfortunate, but no one can make an omelette without breaking the eggs. You can't just go and work in America without a green card, so why should the blacks work in white cities without a permit? There has to be control in this world, something Hugh Gaitskell doesn't understand. Anyway, I think he's a communist. The unions are run by the commies, and the unions are going to put Gaitskell into power at the next election, which is why I want to get out of this country. How quickly can you get me a passage?"

"Maybe a month. Will that be suitable? You don't have a police record?"

"I thought that was only needed to get into Australia."

They both laughed like good friends enjoying an old joke "Officers in the British army do not have police records," Hector finished. "They are officers and gentlemen."

"Do you have any funds to bring to South Africa?"

"Not until my father dies, and then he'll leave the money to the cats' home. Despite being a capitalist, he is handing out millions to the labour party. He is a socialist, I know that. His public image is a contradiction. We hate each other. My mother is very aloof and has no time for me, and I have no brothers and sisters. There is nothing to keep me in England. I believe every young man should make his own way in life. I obtained a county scholarship to Cambridge, despite my father's wealth."

When he left the embassy, Hector thought he had covered all the cracks in his story. It gave him pleasure to label his father a socialist.

The Edinburgh Castle gave Hector Fortescue-Smythe none of the problems encountered by Luke Mbeki. The assisted passage (he paid ten pounds) put him in a four-berth with a blacksmith, an electrician and a sanitary engineer, people whom Hector secretly thought the salt of the earth and the people to whom he was dedicating his life. The hiccup over getting into the army was quickly turned to advantage, with Hector applying to join the secret company that Frikkie Swart confided to him was the embryo Armscor. The South African policy change in allowing the English into the armed forces was noted with interest. The Russians had only just got their Swiss national into the navy in time.

Instead of the rude demand for a pass book at immigration in Cape Town Hector was welcomed with a smile. He was told how to find his hotel that was being paid for by the South African government before flying to Johannesburg to take up his job. He had moved into the country so smoothly that there was not even a ripple left in his wake.

LUKE'S REACTION to the approach from the military wing of the ANC would have been polite and mild, probably even including a cash contribution, had he not gone to Matthew's flat on David Todd's instruction. The chairman of Security Life had judged it better not to telephone Matthew direct but to send his godson a friendly warning and some good advice: don't rock the established way of things in the insurance industry, otherwise things will start going wrong at Gray Associates.

"Hey, Luke," Matthew said on the phone when his friend asked if he might come over to the flat. "Good idea. Last time you were frightened of the cops. Come and have supper tonight, stay over and I'll drop you at your office in the morning. When you've finished work, come over here. Nice talking to you again... You okay, Luke?"

"I'm just fine, Matt. Never been better. This job keeps a man working all the time."

After supper in Matthew's apartment, Luke brought up the subject that was bothering David Todd and most of the life insurance offices. Six months earlier, Matthew had decided to analyse the different insurance policies offered by the life insurance companies to decide which one was the best. The project seemed to be simple and clinical. He wanted to know which company would give an investor placing one hundred rand every month the best return on his money.

Matthew was concerned with the fact that most maturing policies were giving the investor much less than he expected. The key words to the problem were 'estimated' and 'inflation'. The estimated capital sum thirty years down the line turned most policyholders into rich men at today's value of money. The insurance companies sold the public policies on an "if we earn twelve per cent for thirty years you will get 'x'." It was similar to asking a man the length of a piece of string.

Trying to find out each insurance company's investment policy was decidedly like trying to eat soup with a fork. All he got was a taste and nothing to eat. Generally speaking, the investor was giving the insurance company his money on trust and the insurance companies could pay him back, within reason, what they liked. And Matthew knew that an additional one per cent compound interest over thirty years was a lot of money. When Matthew approached the problem from the other direction, he hit a brick wall, except for two of the smaller companies who were trying to break into the market and saw Gray Associates as their opportunity.

Matthew asked every insurance company in South Africa to tell him how they invested the one hundred rand every month, and how much went on agents' brokerage, management commission and overheads. He then wanted to know the cost deductions for collecting interest and dividends and what insurers' commissions were for buying and selling shares in their general policyholders' portfolio. It was only after these deductions that the twelve per cent compound factor came into effect.

The questionnaire he sent them was ruthlessly simple. With the information, Gray Associates would be able to give their clients professional advice, as they did on the short-term account, where Gray's claimed they had never had a client with an uninsured loss against which he had not previously been warned in writing. To Matthew, Plato's philosophy of 'it can either be right or wrong but never in between' applied equally to operations in the free-enterprise capitalist system. Honesty was the life blood that made the system work or fail. What he failed to realise was that, at the age of twenty-eight, he was firing a large cannon at the fabric of the insurance industry that by law invested thirty per cent of their income in government bonds and erected large prestigious office blocks named after the insurance company to show their policyholders the soundness of their investments.

"It's over forty per cent, isn't it?" said Matthew, when he understood the point of Luke's visit. He was referring to the amount of the monthly investment income lost to the policyholder.

"There's the management skill in investing correctly. There are overheads in the retail industry, bringing an average mark-up of over forty per cent. You're rocking the boat, Matt, and Mister Todd says you should stop before you get hurt."

"It's a threat?"

"Friendly advice."

"Why won't they give me the figures?"

"Because the information is too damn valuable to the opposition," replied Luke. "The secrets known to certain companies which make them successful would be public knowledge. You can't patent investment skill."

"You agree that secrecy prevents the public buying the best policy every time."

"Matt, this subject's bigger than you and I. One company is pretty similar to the other, as they all run by the same rules and invest in the same stock exchange. Marketing the product is like packaging; you have to make it look good. Normally, the bigger the company, the better and the safer the investment. Get on with selling your products and stop trying to act like an actuary. It's my job to try and work out what is going to be fact in thirty years down the line. Now give me another glass of wine and let's talk about anything but business. For instance, when are you getting married?"

"And you, Luke?"

"I find it rather difficult to find young, pretty black ladies with any kind of education."

"I hadn't thought of that."

"I do, constantly. My whole social life revolves around the problem. I'm happy in the office working with challenges, but illegal shabeens in dark houses are not my idea of entertainment, and, if I walked into the Balalaika, everyone would kick me out."

"Not me. I hate the bloody system. I've got three good friends in this world. Two of them went off as mercenaries to the Congo six months ago, and the other I'm not allowed by law to entertain in my own home. The world stinks, Luke."

"It'll change."

"It'll change, all right. But whether it will change for the better is what I worry about. Look at the shit in the Congo. And no, don't lets you and I get onto specific politics. Why is everything so complicated?"

"People make it complicated. Look at the laws in this country that blatantly discriminate against my people."

"I'd rather not. They make me sick. Luke, let's get some sleep. It's two o'clock in the morning and I get up at half past six."

"Thanks for the supper."

"You're welcome."

In the dark of the night, they were woken by a pounding on Matthew's front door, bringing him out of his dreams – violent, cross-purpose dreams where he was being sucked down in a quagmire of words. He flicked on his bedside light and crawled out of bed in his underpants, looked for a dressing gown and instead pulled on his trousers.

"Okay, okay!" he shouted. "Don't wake the whole neighbourhood. Which one of my cherished clients is burning down his factory and wants me to piss on the fire?... Why can't you wait till morning?" He reached the door and pulled up the catch, "Can't you wait till morning?"

With the catch released, five uniformed, armed and very big policemen burst through the door, pushing Matthew against his own wall.

"You're under arrest."

"Who the hell are you, busting in here? Do you know who I am?"

"He's here, Sergeant."

"Bring him out. You, Mister Gray, will be charged with contravening the Group Areas Act, and your black friend is coming down to the station.

"No, Mister Gray, don't try that or we'll beat you up as well, resisting arrest." They glared at each other as Luke, half-naked, was pushed out of the flat into the night.

The last Matthew heard was a policeman daring Luke to try to run away, and the tone of his voice made Matthew sick to the pit of his stomach. As he stared back into his lounge where half of Luke's clothes had been left behind, the worst feeling he had was of impotence. There was no higher law to which he could turn for justice.

By the time Matthew woke David Todd, Luke was close to death. The police had beaten him mercilessly, trying to obtain from him the names of his accomplices in the ANC. The ANC had been made illegal some time before the arrest and trial of Nelson Mandela for perpetrating the bomb blast at the Johannesburg railway station in July 1964.

Miraculously, the only irreparable damage was to Luke's soul. His physical beating had been done by professionals who pulled him from the brink of death. David Todd and Matthew were at the hospital when Luke arrived on a stretcher, five policemen giving sworn statements that the man had tried to escape from Rivonia police station. Even the inquiry, instigated by David Todd, came to nothing but smug smiles of "We were only doing our job."

Luke spent four weeks in hospital and, when he was strong enough, Matthew drove him again to Port St Johns. Luke had changed, and Matthew was not sure whether he was now part of the hatred. They parted sadly on the beach, destined not to see each other for a further twenty-nine years. In a matter of two months, Matthew had lost his three best friends. The same pain he had felt in his fingertips so long before came back with his feeling of aching loneliness.

IT WAS SAID of Helena Kloss that mushrooms would grow on her bed sheets that she imagined the pill had been specially invented for her. Every Monday afternoon, she checked her diary and looked for evenings without a date during the coming week. She then consulted her list of current men and phoned those who had not phoned her to fill in the gaps. She had cards printed with her phone numbers, and any likely candidate was given one and told to give her a ring.

She had long yellow hair the colour of rich cream, and a skin to match. In front were heavy, firm breasts, but not too big to need a bra. Her legs were perfect beneath a mini-skirt, and the baby eyes spoke constantly to men of naughty, sexy longings, one stage further than bedroom eyes. Helena Kloss would do it anywhere, with anyone, despite her Calvinist upbringing and the fact that her father was the Deputy Minister of Defence. She was not simply a young girl who had no regard for the family name.

At a party, she handed one of her cards to Hector Fortescue-Smythe. After a year in South Africa, Hector now spoke fluent Afrikaans with an accent that was no longer an embarrassment. He had wangled his way to the party, as he was still very conscious of his need to find an Afrikaans wife of the correct background. The baby eyes had sent a message straight to his genitals, but that night the girl was occupied with someone else. He was not to know that he and the man currently in her sights were the only two men in the room who had not had the pleasure of sex with the Deputy Minister's daughter.

The most remarkable thing about her exploits was that none of it got back to mummy or daddy. Their dutiful nineteen year old daughter was always home by midnight. The fact that the father was also a senior member of the secret Broederbond may also have had something to do with it, as most of her conquests worked for the government and most of them were too scared to open their mouths. They knew about the father, but the father did not know about them and they were content to keep it that way.

Hector took out his list when he returned to his flat in Pretoria. He had moved there in order to be nearer to his job and to the girls on his list, which was updated for him by mail every six months. It was a dating service that any computer would have been proud of. And there she was, Helena Kloss, and her credentials were perfectly wonderful.

Very nervously, Hector called at the Deputy Minister's house on the appointed evening, exactly on time. He sat for a moment in his car, uncomfortably aware of his heart pounding furiously within his chest. Success now was vital. If he could win the hand of the Deputy Minister's daughter, then he would truly have hit the jackpot. The next few hours – the next few minutes, even – would probably determine the course of his entire future and, far more importantly, perhaps somehow he was already under suspicion or observation? It didn't bear thinking about!

Greatly to his relief, his reception at the Kloss mansion was very low-key. In retrospect, he might have expected that, in view of Helena's active social life, to use a euphemism. Daddy was not at home, but mummy thought Hector so nice for bringing her flowers in the continental tradition. That had been an inspired move, thought Hector. His information had shown him that the woman had grown up in Amsterdam. The girl's mother was on his side already, despite his being an Englishman.

As he drove away ten minutes later with Helena in the passenger seat, he was surprised when Helena expressed her wish to see his apartment – and immediately, before the date had even started. Something in her voice made her intentions completely obvious and Hector, despite a reservation that he may be going a little too far too soon, played along with her. Once at the apartment, Helena dispensed with preliminaries, and Hector was astounded by the sheer unrestrained energy with which she got what she wanted. For the first time, Hector began to have doubts as to his ability to survive married life with this woman. But, at least until the knot was tied, he must make every effort to live up to her expectations.

After a good supper, therefore, he suggested that he drive her back to his flat again, an invitation he had no doubt would be accepted eagerly. Wryly, he thought to himself as they drove there that it was a good thing for him that she appeared unaware of the feminine tactic of playing 'hard to get." He had privately been somewhat worried about what strategy to adopt in pursuing an Afrikaner woman. But there was no doubt what this one wanted.

Leaving her back at mummy's, well satisfied and just before midnight, Hector wiped his brow as he drove home and smiled to himself. The strenuous sporting activities of the evening had left him exhausted, although 'pleasantly weary' might have been a more positive term to use. He was sure he had found exactly what he wanted, and the Russians would be pleased with the swiftness of his progress.

No one was more surprised than Hector to be refused a second date. The panting sex-pot had turned as cold as a fish, and for a while Hector was convinced his cover was blown. He waited in fear for a week, expecting the police to pick him up for being a communist; a thought that sent shudders down his spine. For a week he was too frightened to phone and, when his courage was almost restored, the girl herself phoned him at his laboratory and asked him to take her out on a date. What Hector did not know was that the previous week had been fully booked, with an extra date for lunch on the Sunday, immediately after church.

The arrangement went on for some months, blowing alternately very hot and very cold. He did notice that once he had satisfied her sexually her interest waned, and the more climaxes he managed to draw from the young girl, the colder she became. This tendency was outside Hector's considerable experience and, had her father not been a Deputy Minister and high in the Broederbond, he would have dropped her and gone on his way. All the young girls were doing it in early 1962; the whole world was swinging. There were so many for the good-looking Hector that he never ran short. But only Helena was on his list.

Helena first met Matthew some months after Luke had slipped out of the country unnoticed through Bechuanaland to join the military wing of the ANC. Matthew was attending a cocktail party in Pretoria, thrown by one of his clients who thrived on government contracts. Matthew was new on the Pretoria scene and being so tall stood out like the beacon to paradise for the insatiable Helena Kloss. She was the only pretty girl in the room and, as most of the guests were speaking Afrikaans, a language Matthew now associated with fascist policemen, he was quite willing to talk to her in English when he found her down by his elbow, Helena being just over one hundred and fifty centimetres tall.

"The long and the short of it," she said, and gave him the full meaning with those baby blue eyes. Even Matthew smiled at the openness in such exalted company. He might have expected the same look from a whore in a Hong Kong nightclub but not from a young lady of what he presumed to be the Calvinist persuasion. When she gave him her card, he was sure that one of the rare Pretoria ladies of the night had somehow gate-crashed the party by mistake.

They chatted for half an hour, as even whores could be more interesting to Matthew than most of the Afrikaners in the room. After the terrible scene with the police and Luke, he was repulsed by the very accent, even when the person spoke English. Surprisingly for whom she was, Helena spoke English with little trace of her Afrikaans background and, as Matthew was loath to leave the party too soon and be rude to his client, the conversation continued.

As he was saying goodbye to his client at the door, he was more surprised than usual to find that his chatty friend was the daughter of one of the top men who directly perpetrated the savagery that had been inflicted on Luke, for no other reason than the colour of his skin. He dropped her card in the waste bin he passed on the way to his car and drove home to Sandown.

No one, not even the liaison office of the Fifth Commando in Johannesburg, had heard of Lucky or Archie for two months. Both had been reported lost on a patrol deep in Simba country. The only thing that was going right in Matthew's life was his business, which was booming on three continents. To counter the sickness in his stomach, he had concentrated exclusively on business during the months after he had left Luke on the beach.

When Helena phoned Matthew at his office the following Monday and suggested a date, he politely declined. When she asked why, as they had gotten along so well at the party, he was tempted to tell her the truth. Then he thought of his client, mumbled about a girl who was about to become his fiancé, and left it at that.

The fact was he had not taken out a woman since Luke's demolition in the police cell, he was still too angry to look for pleasure, although he did go for platonic drinks with Sunny Tupper, who let him talk about Luke. Again, blind to reality, he was unaware of how much his now-perfect secretary was in love with him, a fact which anyone in the office could have told him had he asked. It never crossed his mind. There was Rule 7 and staff did not mix business with pleasure.

Every time he rejected Helena's body by refusing to take her out, Matthew instructed reception to channel his calls through Sunny. This was something he disliked doing, as he believed a chief executive should be openly available to everyone at all times of the day, but his anger over the treatment of Luke was finding an outlet in the form of this Afrikaans woman, and he was afraid of losing his self-control and giving vent to an outburst that he would later regret and would do his business no good.

Sunny was only too pleased to be given the opportunity to obstruct another woman's attempts to seduce Matthew. Two more calls from Helena, which ended with Sunny putting on her worst East End London accent and the vocabulary to go with it, finally put a stop to this particular approach, but not to Helena's interest. She had even found out from party gossip that he had not dated a girl for over six months, and he was certainly not after men.

Figuring out why Matthew Gray would not take her out became an obsession with Helena, almost as much as she herself was an obsession for Hector Fortescue-Smythe, who would by now have pursued Helena anyway, whether she was on the list or not. And it was through Helena that Matthew met Hector, and found they had a lot in common. Well-read people were hard to find, and both of them liked to discuss more than the cricket score or how much money they had made. With Helena deliberately drawing Hector to places she knew Matthew frequented, they began to meet on a regular basis, with Helena making use of Hector for a reason other than sex. Little did he realise that Helena was using him as a stooge, in order to ensnare the man she really wanted.

THREE MONTHS after Lucky and Archie had disappeared somewhere in the Kivu province north of Elisabethville, Matthew made his decision. He phoned the liaison office twice a week and though he understood the problems in leaving his business, he finally made up his mind. At the regular Monday management meeting he told his shocked account executives that he was going to the Congo to look for his friends. It was the first real opposition he had encountered from any of them and, in their fear of losing their security, they told him he was being irresponsible.

"This business runs when I am in Canada or Australia," retorted Matthew. "It can run when I am in the Congo."

"What happens to the business if you're killed, Matt?"

"That's your problem."

"But you got us into the company."

"Are you complaining?" asked Matthew, rather coldly.

"Security means a lot to most of us."

"Are you saying I work for you, not the other way round?"

"You are the company, Matt."

Matthew Gray looked around his staff, seeing them for the first time with new eye – comfortable, well-paid and full of self-interest. Deliberately he kept these thoughts to himself. "Tomorrow I start. I'm going to find out what has happened to my friends."

"But, Matt ..."

"Oh, shut up." It was also the first time he had been rude to any of them.

In the ensuing silence, Sunny Tupper came in with the coffee and put the tray down. Matthew's Johannesburg branch manager told her that Matthew was going up to the Congo to look for Archie and Lucky. An expression of horror flashed over her face as she turned to look down the table at Matthew, seated at the head. Then she burst into tears and ran out of the room.

"What was all that about?" asked Matthew, quite taken aback, when she had gone.

"This guy's something else," thought the branch manager, but he held his tongue.

Matthew's mind was already back on the subject. "You'll tell our clients I am in Australia. I will phone this office whenever I can, though I'm not sure if there are phone lines coming out of Katanga."

"What do you know about warfare?" asked the youngest AE.

"Nothing at all, but I will find out. I am not going alone. There will be three of us. I have investigated the problems in depth, you can be sure of that... I have shut down my current projects or delegated where I can. I'm sure I will come back and find the company in better shape than when I left. We are on our way up and I am quite confident that you will be able to maintain the impetus during my absence. And remember, when we go public next year, you will be allocated a block of shares each, and you won't have to pay for them for five years. Share options. My guess is that you'll make more out of the shares than your salaries, and capital gain is tax-free in South Africa. Guys, if I snapped at you just now, I apologise. My friends mean a lot to me."

When he left the smiles were back on their faces. He had again offered them money.

The Viscount landed at Salisbury airport, still resplendent in its Central African Airways colours that would be gone shortly with the break-up of the federation of Rhodesia and Nyasaland. Zambia, Malawi and Southern Rhodesia were to have their own airways.

The Italian with whom he had been in contact met him at the airport, and Matthew liked the look of him when they shook hands. Aldo Calucci was thirty centimetres shorter than he, but Matthew determined never to try him out in a fight. The grip from the handshake had nearly crushed his knuckles. The smile that played up at Matthew was infectious, making him think that here was a man who might well have made his mark as a salesman.

Aldo Calucci was a broad-shouldered, thickset northern Italian with dark southern eyes and the features of an Austrian, although in fact he had no connections with this country which adjoins the north of Italy. He had come to Southern Rhodesia via Kenya, where he had worked as a white hunter who took tourists into the bush and put the big animals close enough for the Americans to shoot, but not close enough for them to kill the client.

After World War II his only clients were Americans, as no one else could afford his services. He had fought the Germans with a hunting rifle when he was twelve. His job in Southern Rhodesia had been shooting game in the Zambezi Valley to the south of Chirundu, the border between the two Rhodesias. He was now working for the British sugar giants, Tate and Lyle, who had cleared and planted sugar cane on eleven thousand hectares of land, irrigating the crop by pumping water from the mighty Zambezi River. His current job, one that took very little of his time, was to keep the elephant out of the sugar cane, as the big mammals did considerable damage with their trunks and feet as they walked through the lush-green cane, the only greenery in the dry season for a thousand kilometres around.

The problem with travelling from Chirundu to the old Belgian Congo was not so much the distance as the type of terrain that had to be crossed. Following Matthew's wish to travel to Katanga, the province in the Congo adjoining the Northern Rhodesian border, Aldo had hired a second fully-equipped Land Rover, This would be driven by his black assistant, Mashinga, to give them back-up in the event of one of the vehicles breaking down on the way, and to carry further supplies. There were no tarred roads to speak of on the route they were taking.

Optimistically, Aldo had taken two weeks' leave from the Chirundu sugar estate, but privately doubted it would be anywhere near adequate. His client did not know where to look for his friends in an area fully the size of South Africa, and did not even know if they were still alive. The wish to travel into the deep bush was a stronger urge than that of making money, but Aldo appreciated the funds to equip the expedition properly. When heading into such a situation as this, it was quite obviously essential to make sure they had everything they needed, with nothing left to chance. Preparing for the worst, barring death or captivity, Aldo had stocked up with enough supplies for several months, and there was very little room to spare in either Land Rover.

Top of the list were food and medical supplies. Obtaining food within the Congo would quite probably be difficult, if not impossible at times, with fresh water a potentially serious problem. The second Land Rover contained several large water tanks. The medical supplies were very well stocked, equipped to deal with any imaginable emergency and several that were unimaginable into the bargain. Snakebite serum was a priority. Aldo was nothing if not thorough. So far, he had never lost a client; worried as he was that this particular expedition might bring that proud record to an end he was leaving nothing to chance.

"I asked in my letter, but you never told me where you got my name," Aldo said as he loaded Matthew's gear into the back of his own Land Rover. "Not that it really matters. Here we are." He spoke with a very thick, singsong accent, and Matthew had to listen hard to understand all he was saying.

"I asked one of my friends," replied Matthew. He reminded Aldo of his past contacts with Archie, when the latter, before coming to Johannesburg, had been living in Mongu, a small town in Barotseland, in the half-forgotten, underdeveloped north western corner of the then Northern Rhodesia. Archie had spent a few months as manager of the tiny airport at Mongu, which hosted generally just one aeroplane a week.

"You and he had a scheme of flying chickens and vegetables into Mongu and aviation fuel out, so he told me," Matthew continued. "I believe some of your friends blew their car engines on your high-octane fuel. You had four hectares of land in Chirundu under vegetables, irrigation compliments of Tate and Lyle. You trucked them to Salisbury to meet the Mongu flight. Archie said you both made a lot of money."

"Fletcher-Wood, he is lost? That's it? Then we find him. What have they got in the Congo of value?"

"He was last seen on patrol in the Kivu."

Aldo gave this some thought. "Diamonds! That bastard is after diamonds. He not dead. Gone missing. Oh yes, but with a bag of yellow diamonds. We will spend tonight at the sugar estate and then drive in convoy to look for our friend. Now I know why you write me. Why you not say?"

"He mentioned you as a supplier, not a friend."

"Oh, we were friends, hunting friends, and we were not always hunting game. Me and Archie met many ladies together."

"You'd better teach me how to fire a gun."

"Oh, shit," said Aldo as he climbed into the driving seat of his Land Rover. Then he gave a shrug, put the Land Rover into gear and shot out of the parking lot.

When Hector proposed to Helena, she burst out laughing and told him she would not marry him in a fit.

"But why? We've been going out for months."

"And I've been going out with a lot of other men for months."

"But you don't sleep with them, do you?"

"Not usually, as Mother likes me home at night. Gives her a sense of security. But if you ask me whether they screw me or not, that's another story."

Instead of being put off by her infidelity, it made Hector even more determined to own the woman. Despite his original reason for wanting to marry her, he was now becoming quite infatuated with her.

"But we're so good together, Helena. Why won't you marry me?"

"First, I could think of nothing more boring than living with one man. Secondly, I don't want to be faithful to anyone, so what's the point? Third, I'd prefer to end up a fat old bag on my own than lead my parents' sort of lives. Fourth, I never screw married men." She looked at him, carefully waiting for the laugh that did not come. "And fifth, you're not rich enough. Oh, no, not for me to cook food and put clothes in washing machines when nearly every man wants my body. And while we're on that subject, what the hell's the matter with Matthew Gray? He takes more notice of you than me. Is he a faggot? Now, he's rich. If I had to forego the pleasures of my life, it would be for a rich man like Matt. And he's so big ..."

"One day I will be a lot richer than Matt."

"One day... They all dream about one day. You, working for the government! My dad lives richly but even the house is owned by the ministry of defence, to say nothing of the car and who pays the servants. You couldn't get rich if you lived to be a hundred, lover boy."

Her mini-skirt had ridden up, showing red panties, and he was sure the crotch was already wet, turning his mind to water. If this woman had been the chief witch of South Africa, he would still have wanted to marry her. He was besotted beyond distraction.

"Have you heard of Smythe-Wilberforce Industries?" Hector asked her.

"Sure, they have a factory in Germiston."

"And another in Cape Town. They are the largest private company selling into the chain stores, selling everything from detergents to rice crispies. Their turnover in this country is one and a half billion rand, representing six per cent of the company's worldwide turnover."

"Why are you telling me this?" asked Helena, sitting up straighter on the couch and involuntarily shutting off his view of her panties.

"Smythe, darling. The Fortescue part was put on the name to make it sound better than Smith or Jones. Not so common. My father owns Smythe-Wilberforce Industries through a family trust fund and, even though we hate each other, when he dies I inherit the lot, Helena Kloss, and that will put me up with the Oppenheimers, making Matthew Gray look like a pauper."

"Then what on earth are you doing out here?"

"Working my own way through life. I don't believe in reaping the benefits off another man's labour."

"You sounded like a capitalist when you talked to Daddy."

"I wanted to be my own man."

"But what's the point, with that money on the way? Don't the trust pay you now?"

"No."

"Why not."

"I told them not to."

"But you can tell them to anytime you like, can't you?"

"Yes."

"You are an enigma, Hector. A bloody enigma. Now come here and let's get down to business. Real business." The flush of revelation had made her instantly randy.

"How much is the trust worth?" she asked him drowsily, as she stroked him ten minutes later.

"Oh, I don't know. Seven hundred million pounds, I should think, after limited death duties. But please don't tell anyone, Helena. At the lab they think I'm just an ordinary bloke who managed to get a county scholarship to Cambridge. No one knows what I just told you." He was now worried that he had told her too much in his need.

"I wouldn't tell a soul," she lied.

"Are we going out to supper?"

"Not tonight, lover. I have to get home. Mother has some of those boring government officials to dinner, and one of them is the prime minister."

"You won't tell anyone, Helena," he said at her parents' door.

"Why would anyone be interested?"

When she told her father the story, before the guests arrived, it was the first time he had shown any interest in his daughter for months, and certainly in any of her boyfriends. They were speaking in Afrikaans, and he asked her to repeat the story once more. The idea of a son of one of England's richest industrialists working for Armscor was so bizarre it had to be true.

"Why would he want to come out here?" Meneer Kloss asked his daughter.

"I told you, Daddy... And he proposed to me."

"Before or after he told you about his money?"

"After I turned him down."

"If he's that rich, you'd be stupid to turn him down."

"I'm too young to get married," Helena excused herself.

"You won't say that in five years' time. I'll check out Mister Fortescue-Smythe."

"Oh, Daddy, don't look so serious. You really do think there's a communist under every bed."

"Total onslaught, Helena. It's going to be total onslaught. The communist world against South Africa standing alone... But we did it before and, though we lost the battle of the last war, within nine years our General Botha was prime minister of the Union, including their previous Cape and Natal provinces. And we can do it again."

"You really do think Hector might be a commie?"

"It's possible, yes. We have a lot of strategic minerals in this country, and the Cape sea route is vital to capitalist commerce. We are a perfect communist target, you can be certain of that."

"You'd let me marry a Brit?" She was genuinely surprised. "Oupa says the only good Brit is a dead one."

"Even oupa might change his mind for seven hundred million pounds. Why don't you ask him?... But give it a little time and don't tell your mother. She'll have you measured up for a wedding dress tomorrow morning. The boy always brings her flowers. Women! I don't understand any of them."

"Quite right – you don't," thought his daughter. For once in her young life, she had more to think about than men.

Frikkie Swart was shown into the minister's office the following

Monday morning. He had returned to South Africa six months earlier on promotion.

"Do you remember interviewing a Fortescue-Smythe?" Minister Kloss waved his hand at the seat in front of his desk for Swart to sit down. The conversation was in Afrikaans.

"The chemist?" queried Swart. Kloss nodded his head. "We don't get them that good very often on assisted passage."

"Didn't you think that odd?" the minister asked him.

"It seemed to be too good to be true."

"Maybe it was. What did he say about his father?"

"That he was a socialist and was bank-rolling the labour party's shot at power. Said socialists were communists in disguise."

"Did he now? And he told my daughter last week he had wanted nothing to do with his father as he exploited the workers. Did you know he was heir to seven hundred million pounds?"

"Oh, no, sir," exclaimed Swart, his head shooting back in surprise. "He said his father would not leave him a penny. Something about a cat's home. Brilliant chemist. Top of his class."

"Cambridge— wasn't Cambridge where they found Burgess and Maclean?"

"The two who escaped to Russia. It was Oxford or Cambridge."

"Also rich fathers. Eton, I think," murmured Kloss.

"Eton, sir?"

"Public school. Same class of school where Fortescue-Smythe did his secondary education. Did you check him out?"

"Thoroughly, sir," Swart assured him earnestly. "Don't you think your daughter may have got the workers in the wrong perspective, I mean so far as this man is concerned."

"Did he ask for Armscor?"

"I believe he did. I first offered him the oil from the coal project... How did he come across your daughter, sir? I mean, obscure government employees like myself and Fortescue-Smythe don't generally meet ministers' daughters."

When Kloss questioned his daughter that night, telling her again not to wear mini-skirts, she ignored his dress sense but confirmed emphatically that Hector had said his father was exploiting the workers.

"Keep away from him."

"What, Daddy?"

"Keep away from Hector. You may be being used."

"You don't want me to marry him?" asked Helena, in some surprise.

"No."

"But Mother said she had never even heard of that kind of money so I made a call to England. He's his father's son, all right."

"I don't want you to see him again."

"You were right about one thing, Daddy. Oupa still says the only good Englishman is a dead one. He showed me his South African war rifle with eleven notches. Rather ghoulish. Said each notch was a dead Englishman."

If Minister Kloss had wanted his daughter to marry Hector, he could not have gone about ensuring her acceptance more positively. Helena liked to do what she was told not to do... and her best friend had told her how much money it all really was, how many lovers she could have and, if the young man did not like it, she could give him a divorce in exchange for a fortune. Her friend had giggled and said that every pretty girl was sitting on a fortune. Before the Minister could start an in-depth investigation, Helena had accepted Hector's proposal of marriage and the Minister's wife had told everyone who would listen. Kloss's own father, eighty-six years old, had said there was no way that he would attend the wedding and, if he was forced to go, he would give a speech about dead Englishmen and what the hell, as he'd soon be dead anyway. He had rambled on about something that had nothing to do with either weddings or his granddaughter.

Maybe as a son-in-law I can keep an eye on him better thought Minister Kloss. He would have to make the best of a bad job.

Hector was ecstatic, but insisted that his father, the man who financed the British labour party, should not be invited.

"But you said he was exploiting the workers," said his future wife.

"Putting the workers into power is what I meant. That's what the old bastard has been doing." He had his story back on the right track.

Had she repeated that conversation to her father, Helena would have been given his full blessing for the marriage, which would probably have changed her mind. There were a lot of other men with money who fancied Helena Kloss. But she did not change her mind; the Kerk, the Dutch Reformed Church, was full of all the right people for the wedding and, when a press cutting was shown to Hector's controller, who was keeping well in the background, he could not have been more pleased.

"Sometimes you can do the right thing and enjoy it as well" said the controller.

"What's that, comrade?" inquired his companion.

"Nothing." The controller had recognised the bedroom eyes even from the photograph. "May they have lots of children," he mused. "Children are always so vulnerable, though I doubt our man will give us any trouble. We'll bury him deep, comrade, for the day when we arrange South Africa's Armageddon."

A beetle dropped in the long dry grass, and Lucky Kuchinski awoke in an instant. His body was trembling. The nightmare the beetle had broken was no worse than the reality. He listened with intense desperation, and slowly the movements faded away into the night. There was no moon, not even stars. He put his hand out for his gun, and panic took control... Then he found it, and it was the wrong way round. In the writhing of his slumber, he had turned himself round.

The heat was intense, and the large Congolese mosquitoes had punctured his flesh where the net had tangled with the contortions of his dream. Forcing himself to be calm, he brought his FN automatic rifle around inside the mosquito netting and thankfully found the trigger. Another beetle dropped outside the window and he recognised the sound. He put the gun down beside his body, and fear seeped out of him. He could identify the shape of the tree outside the broken window, sturdy enough for a Simba, one of the Katangan guerrillas, to climb and shoot down from into the room. Archie was still snoring, a sound he had not even noticed as he came awake listening for the Simba.

Finally, he fell asleep again, but the torment of his life continued. As soon as he fell asleep, his nightmare returned; only this time his gun was nowhere to be found, and the drug-crazed Simba were screaming and charging, and he was screaming... A boot hit him hard in the face. He sat up with the gun and fired out the window up at the tree.

"Lucky, young man, with all that screaming and gunfire, you'll bring every Simba in Kasai on our heads. I want to sleep."

"I was dreaming... Arch, my nerves are shot. We must get out."

"We've been trying."

"Leave the money. Run. Tomorrow, now, let's run."

"Go to sleep There is no way Archibald Fletcher-Wood is leaving behind Lobengula's gold, no chance. Those old coins, a whole sack of old coins; will help you and me live on the French Riviera, never being bored again in our lives. You will get that truck going."

"And petrol?"

"We will find more petrol on the road. If the refugees hadn't eaten every horse and mule in the Congo, we could ride into Johannesburg. The gold must have come up here on a horse. They didn't have trucks in 1896."

Archie kept himself awake for another long five minutes and eventually fell into a dreamless sleep. The hum of bees in the acacia tree finally brought him awake a few hours later. Lucky was still asleep, and a shaft of sunlight came into the room, touching a picture of sixteenth-century Holland and making Archie wish he knew more about the paintings of the old masters. The gold he knew; the diamonds he would leave behind, as he knew the penalties of illicit diamond-buying, with de Beers bottling up the world market. But pictures were out of his field.

THEY HAD STUMBLED into the farmhouse six weeks earlier, two months after losing all contact with the Fifth Commando. Archie had not been sure exactly where they were until the map of the farm, an aerial mosaic in the owner's study, had given them the first hope of escape. There were aerial photographs covering the whole of that part of the Kasai province with a set including the dead man's farm enlarged to show the coffee bushes in neat lines and water spraying overhead for kilometres. There was another enlargement of the diamond mine and the cluster of mine buildings. The man must have been richer than any man Archie had known richer than David Todd.

Gunfire and the screams of the Simba had brought them to the house. After two years of civil war, the grounds and lawns overgrown, the swimming pool stagnant and the servants gone. At first they had thought themselves under attack, but the rebels were firing the other way into the thick jungle. Not knowing who was shooting whom, they waited in thick bush all morning before advancing with caution.

The house had once been beautiful, an exquisite mansion set like a great jewel in the jungle, a copy of a chateau in France or Belgium. Everywhere in the shambolic garden, colour rioted among the creeping jungle, and multi-coloured birds, many of which Archie had never seen before, hooted and flitted in the trees. He recognised the strident 'jabo' of a peacock, and saw the bird as it fanned its tail feathers. Half a morning after death, the jungle had forgotten the rude intrusion. The lion had killed and departed, and the birds were singing.

The woman was dead, butchered by more than bullets and bayonets. She had been old, over seventy. The old man was alive. The Simba had propped him against a Louis XIV chair to watch them rape his wife and her screams were there in his eyes when Lucky found him on the floor, staring at her death and the knowledge of his own.

"Are you all right, sir?" asked Lucky in French, the second language they had taught him in school.

"Do I look all right?" groaned the old man, turning his head from his wife. "They raped her. No, why would they rape an old woman of seventy-six? No, don't try to move me. I am waiting to die, have been for years. We said we wished to die together, and now we will. Who are you, young man?"

Lucky told him and introduced Archie, and they watched him slide towards death.

"There's a walk-in safe down in the basement. These are the keys. You are welcome to anything you can carry. You remember Lobengula, king of the Matabele? The one Rhodes chased out of what he wanted to call Rhodesia? The old savage was rich in gold. All the land concessions he sold, all the ivory. Lobengula got as far as Katanga, where he died. They never looked for his gold so far to the north. It's all there. Every sovereign. I was a coin collector and found the source from which an old black was bringing me the coins. I gave him a house and all the beer he could drink for the rest of his life in exchange for the gold. What else did he wish to do but sit in the sun and drink beer with his friends? One of the happiest men I ever knew, as God had not given him the brains to think."

"You can have the gold for burying me and my wife. In my study there's a map showing you the family mausoleum. I am second generation. I would like to rest for ever with my father and mother and that lovely woman lying over there. Isn't such bliss worth all the gold of Lobengula? All the gold of the world? Enjoy your lives, young men, as they are the only ones you will have."

LUCKY WOKE when the sunbeam reached his face. His tension had fled with the darkness. A spider had spun a web from the net to the window sill. The spider, a black, furry mass of body and legs, waited in the centre for insects to fly into his web. Lucky marvelled at the intricacy of the lace work and the hours of industry. Even the spider worked for his food.

Very carefully, Lucky climbed out from his net and stepped over the sill, clutching his gun all the while. A brief deluge during this latter part of the night had washed the jungle clean. Birdsong was clear and beautiful, one of the flycatchers making a sound like liquid gurgling from a crystal water jug. The sky was cobalt blue, tinged with dust-red. Butterflies and bees moved from flower to flower and sunbirds, their collars metallic red, flitted over the cannas, dipping beaks as long as their bodies deep into the flowers for nectar.

Walking up the flagstone path, he found the old man's bench and sat, looking out over the kilometres of jungle, with his gun still at the ready.

There was only one road to the estate and the seat gave him a view of the road where it still cut through the rainforest. Monkeys chattered, competing with the tree-frogs and the crickets. The Simbas had used the road to attack the old man and his wife, and had departed with all the food they could carry. Through the trees, the great house showed none of the signs brought about by neglect. He recognised Archie's walk with the slight limp, so he took his hand from the gun and waited for his friend.

"Thought I'd find you here. Beautiful, Kuchinski. Beautiful, and oh so dangerous." Archie sat down beside him on the bench, propping his FN rifle next to his knee, a habit that had twice saved their lives.

"Not really," replied Lucky, still soaking in the beauty. "He lived here without danger for eighty years. Better to die from a bullet than to decay back to second childhood... That truck's never going to work. Rust is worse in this humidity than Durban. We'll have to walk out, Archie. Now we have the maps, we know where to go. Either we leave without the gold or stay with the gold."

"We can't stay. We'll bury the coins and come back when the country's quiet."

"Can you walk on that leg for so many kilometres?"

"I'll have to."

"You know something, Arch, I haven't been bored but I sometimes think idle, carefree boredom must be the best condition of life."

MATTHEW GRAY DROVE into Elisabethville three days after Lucky and Archie walked away from the great house. A stop at the police station gave them the headquarters of the Fifth Commando, and Matthew alone was interviewed by Major Hoare, the commanding officer.

"They're dead or deserted. More likely dead by now. Four months since the fire-fight and we haven't heard... and I don't want you rushing up to Kasai and expecting me to pull you out. Enough trouble with the nuns and priests. Why do do-gooders always think they're appreciated? Worst thing you ever do a man is a favour."

"Where was the fire-fight?" asked Matthew.

"About eighty kilometres from one of the coffee estates. They're all abandoned. No one will ever drink coffee off these bushes again. There's no food, no law and no profit in that area. Go back to Johannesburg. You are wasting my time," stated Major Hoare curtly.

"I'm sorry."

"So am I, Mister Gray. I like your safari gear. Must have cost a fortune. What do you do?"

"I'm an insurance broker."

Hoare did not even bother to shake his hand but went back to the hated paper-work on his desk.

Matthew and Aldo spoke to three men who had been in the same contact, and each of them said that Archie and Lucky were presumed dead. "And if they're not, they'll wish they were."

At the end of a week, Hoare's point was as true as it was painful. Matthew was out of his depth, and even Aldo said driving around in circles looking for dead men in Simba country was mere stupidity.

AT THE SAME time as a dejected Matthew arrived back in Johannesburg to throw himself back into his business, Archie and Lucky reached the Sankuru River, ninety kilometres northwest of the deserted house. They were dressed in the old man's clothes, and each was wearing a planter's hat that belonged to another age. They had kept their rifles but discarded the military uniforms.

Elisabethville to the south was controlled by the mercenary armies, as big a problem for Archie as the marauding Simba and Baluba. Months in the forest had shown them how to see without being seen. Since leaving the house and heading for the river, nothing had passed their way. It took them a day to make a crude raft to start the journey that would take them to the Congo River, the mightiest waterway in Africa.

Lucky had compromised with Archie, and both carried fourteen kilogram's in weight of gold coins strapped around their waists next to the skin in leather money bags they had fashioned before leaving the house to the jungle. Watching for crocodile and hippopotami, they pushed their craft out into the stream and felt the current take the logs they had lashed together with strips of bark and creepers. The water tightened the straps, breaking half of them, but the logs stayed together. The bow-saw with three spare blades was lashed to the centre log. Sixty kilometres on their journey, they heard the first rapids and with crude oars drove the sluggish raft in to the shore before the current was able to pull too fast for them to control their direction. With the bow-saw and their packs, they passed by the raging white water, threading their way along the bank, leaving the first of their three rafts behind.

"This is going to be the longest journey of our lives," shouted Archie above the roar of the water. "But at least we know where we are going."

. . .

IT TOOK them a month to reach the Congo River, where they turned west on the great expanse of the big waters. At Leopoldville they mingled with the civilians from the United Nations peace-keeping force, Archie telling anyone who asked that they were journalists for the *Daily Telegraph*. They bought clothes with a gold coin and two air tickets with five more. They were leaving the life of mercenaries for Europe, making a lifelong promise to return and retrieve the sack of gold.

In London at the end of 1962, with the coins they carried properly valued, they were richer than at any other time in their lives. While they waited for the Congo to recover from the civil war, they took a flat and prepared to enjoy themselves.

The first call they made on the telephone from their new flat was to Johannesburg. They were a little drunk, as they had been ever since getting the coins through the customs at London airport. The receptionist put them through to Sunny, who informed them that Matthew was overseas.

"Where is he?"

"He's in London, at the Dorchester."

"I love you."

INSTEAD OF FINDING his friends in the jungle of equatorial Africa, Matthew found them waiting for him in the foyer of the Dorchester Hotel. For the first time in his business life Matthew was unfit to work the following day. His journey to the Congo had not been a waste of time. The bond his search had created was now unbreakable.

MATTHEW'S CONVICTION that a badly insured client would be better advised either to put his insurance premiums in his own bank account or to insure correctly, coupled with his shares for premiums, was attractive to industrial clients. Their management had neither the time nor knowledge to ensure that their enterprises were properly covered.

To prevent his staff from making mistakes, Matthew installed a series of check-lists that were shown to him by individual account executives every Monday morning or flown to him from his branches around the world. Every day he read through flimsy copies of all letters sent out by his staff. Each night he went to bed with a note pad and pen beside his bed so that when his eyes pinged open at night and his mind gnawed at a problem he could write it down, get it out of his mind and hopefully return to sleep. There were often two pages of notes by the time he made his first cup of tea in the morning and sat at his desk in his flat to write down all the jobs he had to do for the day.

Every one of his executives was required to carry a notebook so that when something came to mind it was committed to paper. Regularly, he called for these pads and when his staff went home, he stayed in his office and went through the work on their desks, in their drawers and deep in the filing cabinets. Matthew ignored the antagonism his paranoia caused but the mistakes he corrected vindicated his rudeness. When the uninsured risk came to light with a claim, the client would blame Matthew, owner of the company that bore his name, not the account executive.

The product that finally upset the short term insurance industry was one Matthew found in America, where it was common for the oil companies to sponsor insurance brokers. The insurance target was the gas station that flew the oil company's flag but was owned independently. Being small in the way of business, the gas station owner was unable to buy competitive health care, pension and casualty insurance unless the oil company developed with a broker an umbrella programme that would couple his purchasing power with the other independents that pumped the same brand of petrol.

When Matthew introduced the programme to South Africa, he made his selected carrier, the company which would underwrite the risk but not handle the paperwork or issue individual policies, sign an exclusive agreement with Gray Associates. When Matthew's product hit the market through the sponsorship of four oil companies simultaneously, his opposition was stunned.

The group programme cut the premium of petrol stations by almost half. Before, when a competing broker attacked an account, the holding broker was able to offer his client the new rate of premium from the new company, it being understood that insurance companies offered the same rates to all incorporated brokers. Matthew had not been prepared to do the other brokers' work for them and the exclusive carrier, common practice in America, was the result.

This time Matthew had overstepped the mark and antagonised every broker and insurance company but one in the country. His friend who had paid for the model's plastic surgery gave him a friendly warning: "Not my company, Matthew. Good luck to you. You offered me the scheme and I turned it down. But I'll tell you this in all earnest. The others won't tolerate any attack on close to six per cent of the nation's short-term insurance premiums. They're after you. You're breaking their rice bowls. Drop your garage programme before you get hurt. There are times when tactical retreats pay large dividends. This one's too big all at once. Come in somewhere else at a small market."

Matthew, overworked to the point of breaking, ignored his friend's advice. He was to regret it.

DURING THE EASTER RECESS, while Matthew was in America, disaster struck Gray Associates. Person or persons unknown broke into the head office accounts department and removed three locked filing cabinets, containing eighty per cent of the accounts records. If the burglars had waited another month until the company moved from mechanised accounting to mainframe computer, the effect of the loss would have been minimal. As it was, the company was unable to send out client statements, reconcile insurance company statements or produce a balance sheet without going back to the files in each account executive office throughout South Africa to recreate the company's general ledger.

Matthew flew back to face the biggest crisis of his life. The police found not a fingerprint, not a clue. In years to come, not a trace of the documents, the perpetrators or the filing cabinets was ever found. Matthew heard not even a rumour. What he found was a terrible silence.

Finally, a team from the auditors put the accounts back to normal. It took three months and drained the bank account of Grays, paying what the insurance companies said they were owed with little money coming in from clients. They came through and began to build again, but not before Matthew relinquished his exclusive underwriting authority for his garage programme.

Selecting the life insurance company that provided full investment disclosure guaranteeing not to increase deduction percentages during the life of the pension, Matthew went back to his oil companies with a proposal to offer the petrol station owners and their staff a pension fund with benefits equal to those offered by the oil companies to their salaried staff, benefits considerably better than those available in the insurance market to individuals purchasing retirement annuities. The fact that not all the short-term business was going through Gray Associates mattered little to the oil companies. With bulk buying, they had reduced the petrol station premiums.

The pension plan was given full sponsorship, letters going out from Gray's offices on special notepaper showing the Gray and oil company logos. Very deliberately, Matthew obtained exclusive rights to the brokerage on any pension fund placed on the plan. The other brokers were welcome to use the pension plan, only they would not receive commission. Every branch manager, account executive and trainee account executive was trained to present the programme. Three days after the letters arrived, the petrol stations received phone calls requesting appointments. Gray's hit the market with every available member of the staff. The appointment success rate was ninety-four per cent and the close rate fifty per cent. Before Matthew's competitors had time to realise the implications, Gray's were the top new business broker in the country.

As Matthew had planned it, it was the life insurance offices that reacted. Luke Mbeki was not available and this time the call came from Matthew's godfather directly.

"Matthew, I want to see you in my office."

"I'm very busy with my oil company programme."

"Tomorrow at ten o'clock."

Matthew surmised his godfather was very annoyed, and smiled with satisfaction when he put down the phone. The call had come from Security Life sixty days after the launch.

The introductions in the office were no different.

"Matthew, what the hell are you doing?"

"Making a pisspot full of money."

"Last time they burgled your general ledger."

"You know about that? So it was the insurance companies."

"I have no idea who it was, only that it happened. This time you are trying to force full disclosure from all the Life companies. Luke told you why that is impossible." The memory of Luke hung with them for a moment.

"Progress, Mister Todd. Status quos in business or politics do not last."

"I will not have my godson creating such a hiatus in the insurance industry," snapped Mr Todd. "Once is enough."

"Are you sure you knew nothing about that break-in over Easter? Are you saying my methods benefit my clients and not you? Are you telling me you are price-rigging and, because you generate so much money to lend the government, they keep quiet? Are you saying you're right and I'm wrong?" There was silence as they glared at each other.

Matthew continued. "Now, what I think is that your current arm-twisting is the unjust face of capitalism, that what you are threatening me with is not the real free-market system, but the capitalist system according to the fat-cat bankers and insurance companies. You know something, I don't like insurance anymore."

"Then get out of the industry."

"Buy me out."

"How much do you want?"

"For my sixty-seven point one per cent of Gray Associates, calculated at two and a half years' annual brokerage income, six point three million rand in cash. Now, if you will excuse me. The two oil companies not on our programme wish to see me, and I have an appointment with the railway workers union about a fully disclosed pension fund. I am also thinking of forming my own insurance company, and have an option to purchase the President Insurance Company and a life office that prefer to remain anonymous. If you buy me out by twelve noon tomorrow, I will sign a five-year agreement to keep out of the insurance industry."

SUNNY TUPPER HAD NOT GONE into the office the day after the take-over. She was sick to the pit of her stomach. She was sure that life had passed her by; worse, she had seen the hurt in Matthew's eyes, not the triumph he was trying to portray for the benefit of his staff.

The industry had wanted him out and now they had succeeded, but in the process they had also succeeded in ruining her life and those of most of the staff. A young, independent company was fun. Working for Security Life, one might as well join the civil service. She no longer even had a job to enjoy, let alone hopes for the future – the hope that one day he would fall in love with her and return the burning passion that was eating her life.

When she came back after wallowing in self-pity, she found Matthew cleaning out his desk.

"Leaving so soon?" she asked.

"I never did like working for other people. What are you going to do, Sunny? You going to stay on?"

"I'm going back to England."

"Why?"

"Oh, Matt, are you really that stupid? I've been in love with you for seven years."

Matthew stared in surprise for a moment. "Well, at least rule seven doesn't apply anymore." In his embarrassment he tried to make a joke of it. "You've done well with your shares. Give you a good start."

"Didn't you hear?"

"Sunny, I'm hollow inside. Empty. Nothing. I've got nothing to return. I don't even know what I'm going to do this afternoon."

"Take me to lunch, to dinner."

"That's a pleasure, Sunny. You know that."

"As a date."

"I'm not too good at dating people these days," Matthew excused himself. "Maybe I'll visit London. There's Lucky and Arch. Rumour has it Luke's in London working for the ANC... I think I want to be alone, Sunny. For a while. I'll take a rain check. I'll find you in London if I come over. I want to walk the beach and find out where I am. I'm only thirty-three ... seems such a waste of effort."

He was looking round his office. He shook his head and went back to emptying the last of the drawers. "Leave your London number with Life Security, Sunny. And thanks for the years. Best damn secretary a man ever had, and when you came you couldn't even type... Do you know what's happened to that model car that was on top of my desk? Sunny?" He closed the last drawer and looked up. She was gone.

"Now I really am on my own." said Matthew Gray. He hunched his shoulders and left his office for the last time, rubbing the side of his hand along the big sign by the lift: "Gray Associates (Pty) Ltd. Incorporated Insurance Brokers."

# PART 2

# 1

Matthew Gray bent forward against his seat belt to look out of the small window of the Boeing 707 at the approaching runway at Heathrow airport, London. He watched, fascinated, as the big wings levelled, taking the air pressure from the ground and the aircraft touched the tarmac twice before running smoothly. As the South African Airways pilot put all four engines into reverse, Matthew sat back into his seat letting the nervousness of arrival take pleasant control as expectation and apprehension mingled with the reality of arriving in a foreign country.

It was New Year's Day, one year exactly since he had sold his business. The aircraft turned at the end of the runway and taxied back to the terminal. There was a slight flurry of snow outside, but he could see nothing on the tarmac. The aircraft taxied up to the tunnel and turned. Everyone in the aircraft stood up when the plane stopped moving; all except Matthew. First out of the aircraft would not be the first with the luggage. Matthew's orange card was still valid and the frequent-traveller privilege would give him his luggage personally instead of waiting at the conveyor belt. He was quickly through the foreign nationals arrivals and stood for five minutes until the luggage reached the terminal building. A hostess brought him his suitcase, the same one that had travelled with him for so many years.

"Enjoy your stay."

He smiled back. She was pretty. "We're at the Cumberland Hotel."

"I'll see how it goes." He had flown with her many times before but had never taken up the invitations. Air hostesses were even more transient than Matthew Gray.

Customs made him open his suitcase. Rhodesia's recent declaration of independence had even had an effect at Heathrow airport. The English, Matt smiled to himself, were as mad as hell at the Rhodesians. Harold Wilson was moving swiftly towards mandatory sanctions, something that would only be effective with the co-operation of South Africa.

But such help Prime Minister Verwoerd was unlikely to give the British Government. South Africa and Rhodesia were the last bastions of white rule in an Africa which only ten years earlier had been almost entirely controlled by European colonists. The South African government considered Ian Smith and his rebels as blood brothers, allies in the fight against communism and the anarchy which they maintained always accompanied black rule. On a more practical level, there was no way that Verwoerd's government wanted a hostile black state on their northern border.

The curt attitude of the customs officer contrasted with the pleasant reception Matthew had always received in the past. This was the first cool wind that would turn to an icy freeze. He was tempted to say that the Scots were never welcome in England but shrugged instead and made his way out through to the exit to a shoulder-wrenching handshake from Archie Fletcher-Wood. Archie was the main reason for his journey, the second being the message from Sunny Tupper saying that if he came over to England she would tell him the whereabouts of Luke Mbeki.

Matthew had waited until the previous March before buying a Land Rover and driving deep into the Okavango Swamps in Botswana to rejuvenate his soul and give his mind and body a rest from business He stayed in the swamps for three months hiring a canoe and guide drifting through the waterways among the tall reeds and between the islands day after day swimming when the sun grew hot, pulling into the shade of the big acacia trees during the fiercer heat of the day, watching the birds, the big game and the fish jumping in the waters that were so well filtered that Matt could put a mug in the water and drink. He had driven for two days using the four wheel drive with skill before taking the dug-out canoe. It was as far from the realities of the twentieth century as Matt could go to think.

His wealth had been carefully invested in the shares at Anglo American, South African Breweries and de Beers Consolidated, shares in gold, coal, industry, tourism, the growth shares and blue chips of South Africa. The growth was part of his plan and he had worked in silence, not one member of the insurance industry bothering to phone him and wish him well. His old clients phoned until he changed the number in his Sandown flat.

The clinically efficient service he had regimented in Gray Associates had changed to the more casual, old-boy routine the broking industry preferred. "Don't worry, old chap, we'll make sure they pay your claim. You can always rely on us." Matthew had preferred to rely on the legally binding written word of an insurance contract. It was an aspect of selling his shares that had never crossed his mind, that Security Life would be unable, with their vast financial resources, to provide his clients with the same efficient service.

When he returned from the Okavango delta, he sat in the study of his flat and made his plans, swimming in the pool and visiting his old haunt in the Cock and Hen bar at the Balalaika Hotel. He was tanned the colour of mahogany.

"What are you up to these days Matt?"

"Not much. No point in working if you don't have to. Buy you a drink?"

"Thanks. You look well. Now come on – what are you up to?"

"Nothing." But the far-away look spoke louder than any words.

The prospects in Matthew's plan included Archie Fletcher-Wood and Hector Fortescue-Smythe, the latter becoming more of an enigma as Matthew researched his background. What the man was doing in South Africa made no sense at all.

"What do you want to do first?" asked Archie in the car as they drove away from the airport, back towards the city of London.

"Find the nearest pub that serves draft Guinness and have a pint. Good to see you, you old sod. I missed you."

"Next you'll be wanting a kiss... we'll get nearer my flat before we start drinking. You said you had something important to ask?"

"Over a pint, Arch. Where's Lucky?"

"He's given up the quest. Found himself a woman and moved in."

"Is he going to marry her? Be a pity. I have a detailed and workable scheme for getting your gold, diamonds and paintings out of Zaire."

Archie turned quickly to look at Matthew. "What makes you suddenly interested in my problem?"

"I have a need for the money."

"You must have three million quid in the bank, and you want money?"

"Sixty million pounds, to be exact."

"What for, Matt?"

"Not even you, good friend, will be told that until I'm ready... You think it's going to snow properly?"

"Never does much in London."

"Do we have a double date tonight?" Matthew was smiling to himself.

"She can't wait to get at you and all your money. You sound like the old Matt again. There was a time when you were only talking business."

"Sorry, Arch. That's all over. Never again. I learnt a lot building Gray's."

THE WELL-BANKED COAL fire glowed red in the Crown and Anchor, two blocks from the flat that Archie would not be able to afford for very much longer. The coins of Oom Paul Kruger were almost spent, and Archie's prospects were as low as his bank account. He was thirty-nine years old and had nothing to show for it, save a multitude of memories. He had listened to Matthew for an hour and a half, not even going to the bar to refill their pints.

"It may work, Matt, but the cost is way beyond Lucky or me. I'm pretty skint, just now. Have to find a job."

"Quarter of a million pounds! I have checked each link in the chain. Nothing that can be prearranged has been left to chance. We even go on a fitness course."

"All right. So we go. We come back. How much do you want?"

"Half of everything, and an undertaking in writing that you and Lucky will place your proceeds in a discretionary trust of which I am the sole trustee. I will probably double your money within three years and neither of you will be able to fritter it away... the main rains in the Congo will be over by the end of April."

"I can't last till then, Matt."

"I will pay your rent and expenses."

"We could get ourselves killed."

Matthew ignored the statement. "Do you remember Hector Fortescue-Smythe? Chap who married the Minister's daughter. Don't like his father-in-law, for what that's worth. Nasty piece of work, Meneer Kloss. The new bureau of state security comes under his portfolio, and that's a licence to kill anyone who doesn't agree with the NAT government. The story goes that Hector is the son of James Fortescue-Smythe, the CEO of Smythe-Wilberforce Industries. Now I didn't believe it, quite frankly, as there have been many con men and ne'er-do-wells in Africa, from Kenya down to the Cape. Hector makes less sense, since I paid for a quiet investigation, than he did before. Not only does he inherit the controlling shareholding but, when he turns thirty at the end of the year he is made joint chief executive in terms of his great-grandfather's will; the old man left his company to all of his descendants, not one in particular. And Smythe-Wilberforce control massive investment funds outside their core business.

"What I want to find out is why Hector is living in South Africa, speaking Afrikaans like a Dutchman and, rumour has it in Pretoria, will be, if he isn't already, the first Brit ever to be made a member of the Broederbond, the inner sanctum of Afrikaner establishment and the think-tank that invented apartheid. Why they let him in is a big question. Daddy-in-law's influence must be prodigious. But what's in it for Hector? What's he going to do at the end of the year when he inherits joint control of a multi-billion empire?"

"Bring all the money into South Africa?"

"Joint control stops bad investment. Some may come in, yes, I hope so. I have made it my business lately to cultivate Hector despite his wife, who has not changed her habits, of which everyone is aware except Hector. The curious thing about the man is his deep intelligence, despite the blind spot when it comes to his wife. He would make a superb captain of industry instead of fiddling around in the development section of Armscor. I'll take a bet his family company invests vastly more funds in research than Armscor, however vital it is to South Africa to circumvent the arms embargo. The man does not make sense and I want to know why."

"Cambridge are looking at a business course for non-graduates who have done well as entrepreneurs. Harvard has a programme. I am going up to see if I am eligible. The course lasts two weeks and the prototype starts next week. If the first one doesn't make sense, they'll sling it. Imagine, fifty smoking guns with little formal education but proven track records arguing with Cambridge dons! The mind boggles. Theory and practice head-on … Hector was at Cambridge for three years, and I have a theory. The boy was totally conventional until he came down from Cambridge... You want another pint?"

Matthew went up to the bar and returned to their corner table with white froth sliding deliciously down the sides of both glasses. "Now let's talk about women," he laughed. "Enough business. When can we get hold of Kuchinski?"

"He's joining us tonight with his bird."

"To your wealth, to hell with your health," said Matthew, raising his glass and drinking deeply, all the time looking at Archie. Deep inside, his eyes were still smiling, the flecks of green among the softer brown sparkling in the glow of the firelight.

"To our wealth and our health," responded Archie and they both laughed, making the barman look across at his only two customers before returning to polishing beer glasses.

THE WEEK before going to Cambridge, Matthew spent time familiarising himself with the numismatic world, the collecting of coins. As he suspected, there were some Kruger sovereigns worth more than others. The problem was rarity. Between his coin-calls, he visited art galleries and auctions specialising in Old Dutch masters. He finished with a list of people dealing in the rare and precious. There was something about tradition, genuine reputation and knowledge that made Matthew realise why London and its people successfully survived the centuries. Before his journey he had visited de Beers in Main Street, Johannesburg.

The last night before travelling by train to Cambridge, Matthew put a call through to Sunny Tupper and asked her out to dinner.

"Is this a date?"

"It isn't business." There was a slight pause before she agreed to the arrangements.

They met in the foyer of the Savoy Grill, Matthew arriving first in a new suit he had had made for him in Saville Row, something he knew was necessary to create the right tone in the coin and art circles. His accent had proved a problem but the image of South Africa, mixed in with diamonds and Hollard Street, gold and deep-shaft mining, had gone some way towards mitigating the circumstances. Gentle inference had been his way to confidentiality; that and the prospect of business.

In a lonely cellophane pack, Matthew carried a single yellow orchid, flecked at the throat with drops of blood, the flower exquisite in its perfection. She was wearing green as he had known she would, and his stomach did a small turn of excitement when she walked into the small room off the restaurant. It seemed that she had spent some of the money paid out by Security Life for her Gray share options on clothes, and the result left nothing of the eighteen-year-old who had first walked into his life with a terrifying name and accent straight from the London docks. Before, his ex-secretary had been sexy to the point of distraction with mini-skirts, see-through blouses and hot pants that earned their name every moment she wore them. Now she was cool, elegant and sophisticated, twenty-five years old and beautiful.

"I like the suit, Matt."

"I like the dress... Maybe we've come a long way since first we met. Do you remember those first few days?" With his arm at her back, he led her through into the best restaurant in London, and gently put her into the ornate chair with its plush seat cushion and ivory-clad arms that suggested the drawing rooms of the rich.

Sunny was thinking back to their first meeting. "I wish I'd resigned and gone on a date... How are you? Got over selling Gray's? What are you up to? How's Archie?" They both laughed and lapsed into looking at each other. For Matthew, it was like dining with a very familiar stranger, new and yet old, exciting yet proven. It was not the feeling of brief encounter like the one he had felt the night he arrived in England, the double date with Archie. On that particular night, the social cogs had turned smoothly, as he and Archie had both known they would when they smiled at each other in mutual recognition. The bedroom with the woman Archie had provided had been as inevitable as the first dry Martini expertly served with a lighted flash of lemon peel to tang the surface of the gin.

"I'll tell you what, Sunny, you talk the first half-hour, and I'll keep the drinks coming. Then we'll talk of Luke Mbeki, but first we order the full menu and get that out of the way."

"Is this a date, Matt?"

"Oh yes. You can bet your bottom dollar. I haven't seen anything looking so good in all my life."

"You mean that, don't you?"

"Sure." She was shaking her head with a smile almost of exasperation. After five minutes he took her hand across the table, the first physical contact they had ever felt.

Compared with the Okavango delta, the River Cam was a stream, but Matthew only noticed the antiquity, feeling the awe of centuries of learning and the same déjà vu he had felt in Scotland. He walked around staring up at the old buildings, knowing nothing of their history but understanding that here was the fountainhead of the English speaking world, the origin of its knowledge distilled by the centuries of man's learning. He had never felt so small and insignificant. For hours he wandered, wondering, wishing to know, frustrated by his own lack of learning. Africa had so little in comparison with so much civilisation, each spurt of knowledge gained from the labour of the nation's very best, generation after generation.

The business management seminar was at Trinity College, the same college that had educated the scientific mind of Hector Fortescue-Smythe, and Matthew set about looking for tutors who had known the man during his days at Cambridge. It was less difficult than he had imagined, as Hector had been a brilliant undergraduate, something that added more fuel to the enigma. The man was steeped in this history, and had gone out to Africa to spend an insignificant life dreaming up technology that had already been invented but kept from South Africa by political pressure.

Ever since leaving London, Matthew had found Sunny intruding into his thoughts, something that in the past had only happened when he needed a job of work done and thought of the best person to do it. Their evening together had left him light headed, a little scatter-brained and unable to give his total concentration to the projects ahead. Instead of resenting the mental intrusion, he was glad of the intermittent flashes that came to him of a girl he had used before as an office machine, a cog in the vital process of making his money. Over one dinner, he had learned more about the girl than he had found out during seven years of daily contact.

They had agreed to visit Luke on Matthew's return from Cambridge, but she would still not tell him anything about his 'twin'. All she had said was that he might not like what he saw, but they had let the shadow drift away from their table and concentrated instead on themselves. Not once had he mentioned business, and that was definitely a first for Matthew Gray. He was glad the main rains in Zaire would not be over for another three months.

The man who had lectured Hector in chemistry was very forthcoming, pleased to meet someone who knew his pupil.

"He doesn't make sense," Matthew finished.

"You'll enjoy the MBA seminar. You entrepreneurs are a different breed. I think it's the one category of men we could never train at Cambridge." He was smiling a little condescendingly, thought Matthew, but so be it if the man would give him his time. "Now tell me why you want to know about Hector? The real reason, Mister Gray?"

At the end of half an hour, Matthew had spilled out his frustrations and explained his plan of action, omitting only the store of wealth in Zaire.

"You should win. You say you had no formal education. Amazing. One of my colleagues is deep in the study of genetics. I suspect he would find you a case worth studying. What are your politics?"

"You mean, socialist or capitalist? Racist or reformist?"

"Socialism, communism against capitalism will do. Your African politics are part of this cold war, though Korea, Malaya, Suez and the Congo are hot enough. Not my subject."

"I had never thought of that."

"Come, come, Mister Gray. You are a man who has thought of most things, and the way we govern ourselves must have been high on your list. Politics is the other, equally important side of the economic coin."

"I don't think either of them works, and history has proved it," stated Matthew. "No one would say capitalism was the solution in 1930, any more than British socialism seems to be working now. They both work to a degree. Does that help you?"

"You don't subscribe to your government's view that a communist with horns rests under every bed in South Africa, just waiting to jump out?"

Matthew laughed. "The NATS are paranoid. Now take Hector's father-in- law. This man thinks he is holding back the tide of history. Maybe he is."

"When we are young, we subscribe to ideals without reservation. We think in the birth of our first understanding that we have the solutions to man's problems... Are you a friend of Hector's?"

"Not really. I like him. I enjoy his ability to think and argue logically. Time with Hector is time well spent."

"Then get him out of South Africa and as far away as possible from his father-in-law. Even go and see his father. I know what Hector's doing. I thought he had matured but he hasn't, obviously."

"What are you trying to tell me?"

"Hector joined the communist party when he was here at Cambridge. I may have been the influence, for which I am deeply sorry. The movement, like so many others, was hijacked, Mister Gray. People use ideology as a weapon. They don't really believe in justice or an equitable distribution of wealth. They believe in power. Our mutual acquaintance is being used, and if it does not kill him it will certainly ruin a very promising life."

MATTHEW WAS ACCEPTED for the seminar and joined the other fifty students to listen to economic professors theorising the way to wealth. Matthew had to smile, as did the rest of the adult students, when the floor was opened to questions and the reality of business moved swiftly from man to man, leaving academics with problems they never knew existed.

To be accepted, Cambridge had used the same rules as Harvard. A man's wealth had to be self-made, not inherited, and he had to have created business with a turnover in excess of three million dollars before he was thirty, and to attend the course before he was thirty-five. In the days that followed, Matthew talked and argued with like-minded men from right around the English speaking world. The seminar was a success, and Matthew walked away with new knowledge and a list of business contacts that would otherwise have taken years to make.

Returning to London and spending every evening with Sunny, Matthew called James Fortescue-Smythe at his London office, and was unable even to reach the great man's private secretary. Sunny was having a problem, which she would not explain, in taking him to Luke Mbeki. Hiring a car and making Sunny take the day off from work, Matthew drove down into the countryside, having first established from three judicious phone calls that Hector's mother stayed at home most of the day and that her husband only returned to his country estate at the weekends. Putting speculation about such a life style out of his mind, he drove deep into the Surrey countryside, stark in its winter coat, the only green being the yew trees and the holly.

Matt studied the cold landscape silently for a long while. "No wonder my ancestors emigrated," he said eventually. "How can anyone enjoy this climate?"

The small roads wound through villages, and at one they stopped for lunch and the comfort of a log fire.

"You want to come back to Africa, Sunny?"

"What are you saying, Matt?"

"Come and live with me."

"We're not even lovers... Is something wrong?"

Matthew laughed happily. "No. Nothing wrong. Marriage frightens the hell out of me. I thought maybe you could break me in gently."

"Why don't you live in England?"

"That is quite impossible. I would prefer to live in a mud hut and eat mealie meal porridge. I can't even see the stars in England. No space. I would not be able to see far enough into the heavens to yearn for my destiny, locked up in a brick house with brick walls and the sky just over my head. I have to go into the bush regularly to purify my soul. Okavango. I learnt there how insignificant the loss of Gray's insurance brokers figured in my life. It did not matter, camped out on an island listening to the hippo and stoking the fire to keep off the lion. I was just another animal, alive and related to all God's miracles.

"Africa is real. Today's Europe was made by man. No, I will live and rest my bones in Africa. We will buy ourselves a smallholding at Halfway

House, between Johannesburg and Pretoria. Keep horses. A cow to milk. An African man must have cows to pay for his bride. There'll be sun and dry earth, a pool to swim in and stars to count each night. We'll be happy."

"Six months," countered Sunny.

"What about six months?"

"I'll live with you for six months on two conditions."

"Spit it out." Matt suggested, leaning back and eyeing her curiously.

"You make love to me tonight and, if you don't marry me after six months, I come back to England. I want kids as well as you."

"We'll dine again at the Savoy. Let's get to see the lady and drive back fast. Never before in my life have I been so nervous... I wonder if she knows her son is a communist?" he said after a while.

THE DAY MATT went looking for Luke Mbeki in London, his 'twin' was nearly ten thousand kilometres away in the rebellious colony of Rhodesia. He was sitting dripping wet under the warm rain in a forest of Mopani trees on the banks of a small river that was raging with flood water.

He had met up with his Matabele counterparts, all communist-trained guerrillas like himself, on the north bank of the Zambezi River in the newly independent Zambia. The rains were good, and they had come across Lake Kariba in pouring rain that cut visibility to ten metres but stopped any rebel police from seeing the three makoris of the insurgents. They were linked, at Luke's suggestion, by rope to prevent them drifting off across the great expanse of man-made lake, the second-largest in Africa. Luke led the first boat and took them across to a lonely landing, where they buried the canoes under grass-some fifty metres from the edge of the rising water, Luke fixing the position as accurately as possible.

Luke had brought the expedition forward a month when he realised that the girl making the enquiries was an emissary of Matthew Gray. Luke had no wish to defend his new principles, however sure he was of their correctness, with Matt. A slogan coined by Luke in a training camp eighty-five kilometres north of Moscow, 'One settler, one bullet', was on the lips of the cadres of the newly-forming guerrilla armies of Africa, who were to fight the colonial or settler governments that refused to hand over power to the people.

The wars of liberation in Southern Africa had begun. The Russian and Chinese inspired wars which would return the blacks of Africa to their lands of milk and honey, free of exploitation and government by foreigners. The Nguni people were going to liberate their lands. One settler, one bullet. What Luke refused to acknowledge, even in the back of his mind, was that Matt also ranked as a settler. The rancher and his wife ran cattle over six hundred square kilometres, a herd of just under a thousand beasts that were regularly dipped against tick borne disease. The rancher and his black herd-boys chased the animals into the dip-tanks from horseback, riding all day, for day after day in the burning heat. The man's children had left for the bright lights of Bulawayo, but work continued on the ranch, and life, much quieter but still rewarding, went on the same in the old house on the banks of the small river.

Luke was camped on the opposite bank among the thick Mopani trees, a couple of kilometres upriver, away from barking dogs and the white man's labour force. They sat without fire or comfort throughout the night and, shortly after three o'clock by Luke's watch, the rain stopped, but the trees dripped water till the dawn came spreading through the trees, a clear and crystal dawn with a sky clean blue and a fierce sun searching for drops of rain on the leaves of the trees, sparkling like a million diamonds. Luke, the only African National Congress fighter among the Matabele of the Zimbabwe African Peoples' Union, waited throughout the day, which grew steadily hotter. They dried their clothes, bringing the curse of the Mopani flies to cluster round their eyes and noses, tiny irritating flies that no amount of brushing stopped from crawling into nostrils and eyes. The dusk approached, the men stood to under Luke's command and the attack got under way.

The rancher and his wife, both in their sixties, were drinking sundowners on their long stoep, watching the great ball of fire that was the sun sink below the horizon, giving way to the approaching night. They were talking softly, the talk of long custom, when Luke fired the first rocket at the stoep and blew the old couple straight to eternity. By the time Luke led his men back to the canoes, the cry of 'one settler, one bullet' still rang in his head. Luke's revenge had begun.

MATT AND SUNNY had been lovers for a week not leaving her flat except to buy food. Sunny had resigned from her job by telephoning and their bags were packed for Africa. There was peace in their souls, after a strange week which had started with their drive into the countryside. The front door of The Cedars had been opened by an elderly lady.

"My name is Matthew Gray ..."

"Wait there until I find my glasses. I like to see new people when I talk to them... Here they are. Now, what can I do for you, young man?"

"I have come down from Trinity College, Cambridge, where the former tutor of Hector Fortescue-Smythe told me to see his father or mother. Mister Fortescue-Smythe would not take my call and neither would his secretary, so I would be very obliged if I could speak to the lady of the house?" Listening to his formal words echoing in the hallway of the house, Matthew smiled.

"I am Hector's mother... Oh, don't look so surprised. He was born when I was forty-two. I had two other sons and a husband who were all killed in the wars."

"I am so sorry."

"So was I at the time. They killed my first husband in 1918 and my boys in 1940. I was a suffragette. Capitalist wars. Ordinary people were slaughtered by the millions. You have word of my son? Have you met his wife? What is she like – Dutch, I believe? Is he in trouble?"

"The tutor thinks he is a communist."

"Everyone has the right to his own opinion." the lady replied, a little tartly.

"The communists are banned in South Africa. He can be sent to jail."

"Why are you concerned? What do you want? People always want something."

'I am looking for a business partner with great deal of money, and one of the people on my list is your son. I do not recruit partners without knowing who they are, and I find your son an enigma."

"You want the money, but not the man if he is a communist? How much do you want from my son? How much?"

"Risk and loan capital of thirty million pounds."

"And how much do you plan to put into the venture?" The tone of voice was sarcastic.

"Thirty million pounds and the expertise to provide an above average return on capital. I do have a track record," Matt stated.

"And you wish to warn us so that Hector will return to the capitalist fold before his thirtieth birthday?"

"His father-in-law is the head of BOSS, an organisation I believe similar to the German Gestapo, and I have first-hand knowledge of their methods. Hector, I believe, has joined the secret society which is the cement of the Afrikaner establishment, and he is working in the most secret government-funded company to give South Africa a military capability to enforce the ideology of apartheid, none of which marry well with a man who was a communist sympathiser at Cambridge, if not a card-carrying member. The tutor thinks he is a sleeper under deep cover and instruction from

Moscow. I believe marrying Helena was part of a preconceived plan. I can think of no other reason for marrying her. The parents accepted Hector, despite being English, as he was an answer to a very serious problem."

"And what problem was that?"

"The lady is a slut, Missus Fortescue-Smythe."

"You had better come in and sit down, and start from the beginning."

"There is a lady in my car outside who would also like to hear the story. It would save me repeating myself."

"Does she know Helena?" asked Missus Fortescue-Smythe.

"Yes."

"Would she also call my daughter-in-law a slut?"

"Why don't you ask her yourself?"

"Will you take a cup of tea?" the lady offered.

"That would be most kind."

"And some crumpets, I think." Matt was at the door, returning to fetch Sunny, when the old lady spoke. "And remember, Mister Gray, when you are telling your story, that I am also a communist – not card-carrying as you say, but a true believer in the way of life that might just stop war and starvation and the degradation of three-quarters of the people on this planet. One central government. There is enough for everyone. How can we have mountains of surplus food in Europe and starvation in Africa? Why?"

Matt turned back from the door and thought for a moment. "Ideologies," he then answered her. "The slogans of ideologies are simple. The nature of man is not. The reality of what you want will mean that a small percentage of society, those who willingly work for the satisfaction of achievement, will be forced to create the food and goods for the lazy masses. Most people do not work unless they are made to work.

"You were right when you asked me what I wanted. We all want something. We don't give it away. I have created wealth in my life, and jobs and a good living for many. I wish to create more. Neither you nor anyone else will ever create your utopia merely by finding a way to distribute the food. Someone has to pay. No farmer will produce a surplus to give it away, or break his back for a gaggle of lazy fellow humans who prefer to live off the charity of others! Work, education, dedication. Not a permanent attack of gimmes; give me this, give me that. Feed a man for a year, and you have to feed him for the rest of his life. That is not a slogan, but a fact. I too have read Karl Marx. A wonderful theory. He would have starved in the real world of wealth creation. There is no substitute for hard, justly-rewarded work... I will go and call Sunny. Her feet will be freezing cold, and the fault will be mine."

MATT LAY in the warm bed, his hands behind his head and Sunny fast asleep at his side. The old woman had listened very carefully for a long time, asking questions but saying little else. He had let Sunny describe Helena's way of life, and Sunny had found it difficult not to sound like a bitch. They were both convinced that Hector knew all about his wife's affairs but ignored them for the more important political advantage his marriage brought him.

When they left, the old woman thanked them for coming, and Matt thought she meant what she said. She was still there by the open door, ignoring the cold, when Matt looked back from the bottom of the long, cedar-lined driveway. He was not sure whether he had made a friend or an enemy.

Turning to the present, Matt began to tickle Sunny's back very gently until she stirred, snuffling, half-awake and wanting to go back to sleep.

"I have a surprise."

"You're going to make love to me."

"That, too." He nibbled the lobe of her ear. "I have a job scheduled in two months' time, and a berth on the Lloyd Triestino's, 'Europa', out of Venice, in three weeks' time. Tonight we are taking the boat train from Victoria Station and beginning a slow, lazy journey home to Africa. We will explore Europe quickly, Egypt more slowly, and call at all the ports of East Africa from Mombasa to the clove island of Zanzibar.

"While I am away, executing a job that will bring great wealth to myself, Arch and Lucky Kuchinski, you will search for the perfect smallholding and we will live happily ever after in the African sun. We will be happy for ever. Nothing will interfere. And when you are very good for a very long time, I will take you down to Port St Johns and Second Beach and show you where the 'twins' were born."

They lay awake, holding each other, not wishing to emerge from the warmth of the bed.

"You don't think he's avoiding me, do you?" asked Matt, thinking of Luke. "Why do you shiver?"

"Someone ran over my grave... Matt, make love to me."

• • •

A WEEK after the Fokker Friendship of TAP landed at Jan Smuts airport, Johannesburg, from Beira in Mozambique, bringing Matt home with Sunny from the last port of call on their voyage, three aircraft took off from Rand airport. In the lead Beechcraft Baron, Matthew sat beside the pilot, with Archie Fletcher-Wood, and Lucky Kuchinski in the passenger seats behind.

The second aircraft, also a twin-engine Beechcraft Baron, was loaded with aircraft parts, paid for by Matthew as a present to Rhodesian United Air Carriers (RUAC), whose supply of spares had been rudely cut off by United Nations mandatory sanctions which forbade member nations any trade with rebel Rhodesia. Matt had happily signed a certificate for Beechcraft, USA, stating that the parts would not be supplied to any destination prohibited in terms of UNO resolutions or American law.

The third aircraft was a much larger Beechcraft King Air, from which all seats other than that of the pilot had been removed and the fuselage crammed with an assortment of tubes and four long aerodynamic floats that had been made for Matthew from plans he had obtained in England. The Johannesburg engineering company that had done the job had been a client of Gray Associates.

The flight of three aircraft was met at Salisbury airport by Aldo Calucci who had taken extended leave from the sugar estate. With the co-operation of customs and the Royal Rhodesian Air Force, the parts were delivered into the hands of RUAC. The tripod of a Vickers light machine gun was welded into place in the doorway of the second Baron, and an agreement in detail reached with the Rhodesian department of customs and excise to provide Matthew with airway bills and certificates of origin 'to be listed' for works of art, antique gold coins and uncut diamonds after Matthew had agreed to purchase in Rhodesia with hard currency large quantities of Sandawana emeralds that he would resell as Bolivian on the world markets.

The rains in Zaire would not be over for another month, and the quartet went into immediate training under the supervision of the Rhodesian SAS. During the sea voyage through the Suez Canal and down the east coast of Africa, Matt had watched his diet and worked out his nearly two-metre frame in the ship's gymnasium for five hours a day. The expedition demanded that he be in superb health and physical fitness. Archie's old leg wound had healed completely.

In mid-May the aircraft took off again from Salisbury airport having been repainted in camouflage green and fitted with long-range fuel tanks that would take the aircraft round hostile Zambia to Luanda in the

Portuguese colony of Angola, flight plans having been filed by RUAC. At Luanda, the King Air and armed Baron were left behind, and Matt and Archie flew with the senior pilot northeast across the neck of Angola into the still strife-torn ex-Belgian Congo that was under the military rule of General Mobutu. Following the mighty Congo River, they turned east at Kwamouth and followed the Sankuru River, flying fifteen metres above the tallest trees that clustered close to the water. The rains had been strong and the river was running fast, but they found what they were looking for without incident and flew back to Luanda on a direct flight plan over the Central African jungle.

The following day, with the help of the Portuguese air force who were fighting a three-pronged guerrilla war against the FNLA in the north of Angola, the Marxist MPLA in the centre and UNITA in the south, the two Barons were taken by road transport to the dam that supplied the city with fresh water. Within two days, the aircraft were converted to seaplanes, riding high on long floats that reached the nose and tail of the aircraft. After successful test flights, Matt was satisfied.

"We'll go in at first light."

Dawn on the dam was violently shattered by four powerful engines, sending a flock of flamingos away from the rising sun that was reflected in the mirror calm water. Crocodiles slid into the water as the two Beechcraft Barons taxied down the lake, high on their new floats, and turned into the gentle wind for take-off. Matt, Archie, Lucky and Aldo were dressed in camouflage flak-jackets with lightweight South African army boots on their feet.

The aircraft climbed to two thousand metres and flew over the four-hundred-year-old Portuguese colony, passing well laid out coffee plantations at regular intervals. Angola was a major world exporter of coffee beans, the estates being owned and run by the Portuguese, who had lived in Angola for four generations. There was no sign of the FNLA guerrillas, but they crossed two heavily guarded transport columns, the pilots tipping their wings in salute. Nearing the Zairean border, the aircraft dropped to treetop height again, following the Congo and Sankuru rivers to the point in the latter selected by Matt for landing. The river had been divided by a long island and the pilots touched the water in the calm of an oxbow lake. They waited for five minutes with the engines idling, but nothing happened.

With the engines silent, they remained near the aircraft for the rest of the day, landing their equipment through the swamp that came down to the water's edge. They camped under mosquito nets on a ridge from which they could see the river. Their arc of fire was thirty degrees and, when the dusk faded to the dark of night, Matt was unable to see the end of his outstretched arm.

The jungle was alive with the sound of insects and birds, and Aldo twice heard the cough of the leopard and once, quite a distance away, the roar of a male lion. He would have been happier with a fire, but the ex-Belgian Congo was still controlled by heavily armed bandits, warlords who were left alone by the central government in Kinshasa. Anarchy ruled. They were ninety kilometres from the coffee plantation and the abandoned house, Matt having circled the now derelict building on his reconnaissance. The two ex-mercenaries from Hoare's Fifth Commando slept through the night; Aldo and Matt did not. On the aircraft moored close to the river island, the pilots slept badly, cradling FN rifles on their laps.

Archie, with Matt, Aldo and Lucky following him, led the way as they rose with the dawn, cutting their way through the jungle. They were each carrying twenty-seven kilograms of equipment and FN automatic rifles. They covered thirteen kilometres on the first day and camped deep in the jungle, exhausted.

"How did you walk with a wounded leg?" Matt asked Archie.

"Fear, Matt."

Again they made no fire, eating cold food and chewing biltong, the dried meat of the Boers. Matt, exhausted from taking the last front position with the panga, slept through the night.

Each day the pace increased. At the end of the week, they were unable to find the house, having passed the compass fix that Matt had verified from the air. Breaking radio silence, Matt called the aircraft, still anchored in the Sankuru River.

"Can't find the bloody house," he told the pilot. "You guys okay?"

"Bored. We're camped on the island."

"The trees and creepers are too thick. You'll have to come over and guide us in. Drop a flare. Talk to you overhead."

With the help of the aircraft, they found the house that afternoon. The buildings had deteriorated badly, with thick creepers pushing down the walls, but most of the roof was still in place, although covered by the encroaching jungle.

"No one's been anywhere near the place," said Lucky, leading them into the room where he and Archie had found the dying Belgian. The paintings were exactly where they had left them. Within ten minutes, Archie had recovered the coins and the key to the safe, all of which he had buried next to the mausoleum. There were sixteen paintings, eight per pair, and before the light had gone the large frames had been hung on the slings made especially for the job in Johannesburg.

That night, they lay down in the old house next to their treasure, but nobody slept. They were all too close to their dream. The flare had attracted no attention.

Matt rose in the middle of the night. "Let's get out of here. No one's sleeping. Sling the paintings between the poles and use your torch."

At two in the morning, they walked back into the jungle, waking a troop of vervet monkeys that came screeching down from the branch of a tree. The adrenaline in all four men was screaming.

Three days later, the aircraft returned to Rand airport and underwent conversion to civilian use, the floats having been detached from the Barons in Luanda, along with the machine gun. Matthew began his discussion with carefully selected legal practices in Johannesburg, meeting the senior partner of each firm at the lawyer's home, away from the eyes of the public.

They had returned with everything they went for: the coins and pictures had been taken into a customs bonded warehouse awaiting transport to Europe, and the yellow diamonds escorted from the airport by de Beers security guards. The following day, de Beers deposited an amount of 3.4 million Rand in Matthew's bank account at Rissik Street, equal to twenty per cent of the wholesale value of the gems. It was exactly half of what de Beers would have paid the Belgian for his diamonds, the second half being kept in a trust account by de Beers at Matthew's request. The same day, lawyers in Belgium, Holland and France were instructed to send registered letters to the thirty-seven living relatives of the Belgian planter.

The party at the newly-acquired smallholding at Halfway House had caused the only wound of the operation, Lucky cutting his head while trying to leap from a closed car without using the door. Sunny had treated the head wound in a fit of giggles, also aggravated by the Maharajah Chotapegs, a drink concocted with a cube of sugar drenched in pink angostura bitters, washed down with best Cape brandy and the glass filled to the top with a sparkling wine.

Archie Fletcher-Wood had taken to singing Irish songs at the end of the bar in the sun room that opened onto the long stoep and the swimming pool. At the end, Aldo Calucci could, it seemed, now speak only Italian, though the girl he was talking to with such emphasis did not appear to mind, as she was also drunk and sentimental. The party was a great success. Matthew and Sunny had never been happier in their lives.

On the fourth day after the men's return from the jungle, buy orders were given to eleven stockbrokers by different firms of lawyers to purchase ordinary shares in Security Holdings, the pyramid company created by David Todd to protect his controlling interest in Security Life and Security Fire and Accident, which in turn owned Gray Associates. The shareholding chart locked in Matthew's safe gave a total breakdown of David Todd's shareholdings, property investments and cash reserves. All the shares bought by Matthew's lawyers were registered in nominee names, and not even a whiff of the operation reached David Todd.

Seven days after returning to South Africa, Matthew again left Sunny alone in their new home and flew to Amsterdam to address the relatives of the man buried by Lucky and Archie deep in the African jungle. Simultaneous translation into Dutch, French and Flemish had been arranged by the Dutch legal firm when Matthew stood to thank everyone for coming to the meeting. By the time he had finished explaining the reason for his visit, the lawyer's large room was reduced to chaos, all thirty-seven relatives refusing to accept Matthew's offer of ten per cent of the realised value of all assets, subject to legal ownership of the coins and paintings being granted to Matthew Gray, a prerequisite for selling the items at an auction. Without authentication, Matthew's spoils were worth less than ten per cent of their true value.

When the shouting subsided and Matthew had registered the mood of ungrateful people who a week earlier knew nothing about coins, diamonds or paintings, he stood up again to talk to the wall of righteous indignation. "No problem," he smiled, packing the photographs they had taken of the Belgian's house and paintings back into his briefcase and snapping it shut, "I will return everything from whence it came, and you kind people can go and get it back yourselves. Good morning, ladies and gentlemen. Have a nice day."

By two-thirty that afternoon, thirty-seven affidavits had been signed and notarised, transferring ownership to Matthew Gray, and were delivered to his hotel, from which Matt had been watching the barges and people on the neighbouring canal for two unhurried hours. Neither then nor in the future did a single one of the relatives thank him for risking his life for their new-found wealth.

The following day, the paintings and coins arrived at Heathrow airport,

London, and were met by Matthew and an art dealer who specialised in Dutch masters. The dealer would supervise the sale of the paintings at Sotheby's, the proceeds of which were to follow the gold Kruger coins into a discretionary trust account of an international firm of accountants on the Channel Island of Jersey. By the time Matthew had finished realising the assets, neither customs duty, inheritance tax nor income tax were paid to any government and the funds were free from exchange control. In one sense he made the money disappear, as at no time was the money or the shares in Security Holdings registered in his, Archie's or Lucky's name. Even the trust company in Jersey was instructed to hold the security shares in the names of nominees.

Soon after the art dealer, selected by Matthew on his previous visit to London, had sold the first painting for its true market price, buy orders were placed by the trust company to purchase Security Holdings shares on the London stock exchange. David Todd had listed his company on the London exchange some years earlier to provide him with sterling funds to expand into the United Kingdom market. Even more quietly, the Kruger coins were offered to the world's coin collectors in small parcels. Matthew, unable to re-enter the insurance market in South Africa for another three and a half years, was in no hurry. There was also the need to purchase the Security Holdings shares gradually over a period of time, for fear of pushing up the price.

BEFORE FLYING BACK to South Africa, Matthew again followed up the leads given to him by Sunny, but failed to locate Luke Mbeki or anyone who even knew his name. At one point he was told to bugger off and mind his own business, which told him something. Luke, his twin, was no longer available to Matthew Gray.

Sitting in his room at the Savoy Hotel, pondering his final rejection, Matthew received a phone call from reception, saying that a man wished to see him downstairs. Matt hurried to the lift, excited at the prospect of seeing Luke again. They would go out and visit all their old jazz clubs, and talk till the sun came up. Matt's heart was full of happiness; now he knew friendship transcended politics and race.

When he reached reception, there was no tall black man smiling a big welcome, and Matt looked at Hector Fortescue-Smythe in shock and dismay. Then he recovered and put out his hand.

"Matthew. Sorry about not giving a name. Mother gave me a ring... Is there anything wrong? When you first ..."

"Hello, Hector. No, nothing wrong. Disappointment which has nothing to do with you, I am afraid. I thought it was Luke."

"Luke?" Hector kept any surprise from his expression, though his stomach gave a sharp jolt. He had seen Luke Mbeki in the strictest of confidence the previous day.

"Luke Mbeki. We were born in Port St Johns on the same day. I must have talked about him... How long are you in London? Of course, you must be here to take over joint control of the family firm."

"Not really... May we go up to your room?"

"I'm sorry I pried into your business, Hector, but when I spoke to your mother..."

"Mother liked you Matt. I want to explain."

"Come on up. Damn! I was so looking forward to seeing Luke."

Hector gave his warmest smile, confident again. "I am sorry to be so disappointing."

Matt went up in the lift in silence, sure that the conversation was going to be embarrassing. He should have ignored the Cambridge don's request to do a good deed. People never thank anyone for doing them a favour.

"You want a drink, Hector?" he invited, in the room. There was a private, well-stocked bar in every suite at the Savoy.

"Whisky, no water."

"There was some Dimple Haig here last night."

"You here on business."

"Oh, yes... how does that look? Hector, I'm very sorry. I should not have gone to see your mother. You and Helena ..."

"Cheers, Matt."

"Your good health." Matt was squirming.

"You didn't have an affair with Helena, though, did you?" asked Hector.

"No. No, you have my word."

"Relax. I know. I'm not so bloody stupid not to know my wife is screwing around... You ever had a woman who really, but really, turned you on?"

"Yes." Matt immediately had a picture of Sandy de Freitas, and smelt the pungent scent of joss sticks.

"The fact is, it turns me on even more. I think we're all a bit kinky, but some more than others. I always know when she's had it during the day. Some of the swelling is still there ...Does this shock you?"

"No," said Matt, swallowing his own whisky, to which he had added ice and water. "I mean, what you do in private... if the sex is good ..."

"Oh, it's very good. Which is why everyone, including you thinks I don't know what's going on. We'll probably grow out of our lusts."

"Does her family know? Look, I'm sorry. It has nothing to do with me."

"They knew about Helena's insatiable sex life well before I did. You see, at least I give her some respectability. They are very grateful. We're not having children just yet. I mean, who on earth would know who was the father?" He gave a hollow chuckle. "I wouldn't like to bring up someone else's kid. And then there's the family millions. Oh, and by the way; whatever my old tutor pushed into your ears, I am not a communist. We all flirted with great ideals at Cambridge, and then we grew up to the realities of the world. I went to South Africa to get away from my inheritance. You as a self-made man should see my problem. Life must be a challenge for me. And for you too, I suspect.

"Inheriting millions is boring. You are merely a custodian of someone else's property. It doesn't belong to you because you did not make it yourself. There's far more fun getting somewhere in this world than arriving. My work with Armscor challenges my mind to its limits. Yes, and I know what you said to Mother, that what we work on has already been produced in Russia or America. But are you sure? I don't know American secrets, so what we develop is new, mint, the first in man's history so far as I am concerned. The excitement and sense of achievement is just the same. Now being joint CEO of Smythe-Wilberforce would keep me well out of the R and D and leave the fun to the real scientists.

"I am over here to look for a man who will receive my power of attorney to act on my behalf as joint CEO. My lawyers say such a move is incontestable in terms of great-grandfather's will. And if Helena does decide to settle down and have my children, they can make their own decisions about money and running the old firm. Maybe you would like the job, Matt?"

"No, not me, I've enough on my plate."

"You see what I mean. Even you are unwilling to take over someone else's company." Matt remained silent. "Mother wouldn't say what you wanted the money for, but it can probably be arranged. You made a big impression on Mother."

"I don't think I need the money after all. But thank you, Hector. And for not wanting to punch me on the nose."

"Don't be silly. I could never even reach." They both laughed, and ten minutes later Hector left the Savoy and took a taxi to another part of London. He was smiling in the back of the taxi, and wondering idly how many men his wife had screwed while he was away.

• • •

AT EALING BROADWAY, Hector dismissed the taxi and took the Tube to the next station, where he hailed a second taxi, arriving at his destination an hour after leaving Matthew's room at the Savoy Hotel.

The meeting was in the basement of an old Victorian house that had seen better days. The room smelt damp under the fog of cigarette smoke and the ripe smell of bodies that had not seen sufficient soap and water. Hector refrained from wrinkling his nose and took his place at the table. The meeting had been called by the South African communist party, with Hector in the chair.

The slightly 'what-ho' look he put on as Helena's cuckolded husband and Armscor boffin had gone. His eyes examined his co-workers one by one, and reduced the conversations around the table to silence. Hector waited – keeping them under control before involuntarily touching the lobe of his ear. There were five members of the SA communist party in the room, all white, and twelve members of the African National Congress, all black. There were no women. Luke Mbeki was not present, having received his instructions the previous day before returning to Lusaka in the newly independent Zambia, the capital of the liberation movement being funded and armed by Russia.

"I asked you here to meet Father Porterstone who is being sent to Soweto to run a small Church of England mission and to train black members of the church. Over the next few years, the Father will select a black clergyman for high office in the church, a man dedicated to liberation theology, the black nationalist cause, but above all the African National Congress. Our man will be your man, but we will pay the bills. Moscow has provided a one hundred thousand pound fund which will be paid to the church through Soweto, through a donation from the British Trade Union Council, an organisation dedicated to the anti-apartheid cause. I want you to give the Father and his protégé every assistance in the years to come. However, none of you are to contact the Father openly while you are inside South Africa. It is essential that myself and my colleagues shall not be shown to have links to your organisation, as we wish to have the political support of the Americans as well as the Russians.

"The civil rights movement in America will ensure that WASP politicians in Washington use the whites in colonial and racist Africa as convenient whipping boys to assuage their own consciences and attract their own black vote. My party must not stand in the way of this American support, which has forced the British government to do everything in its power to bring down the Smith regime in Rhodesia. Our propaganda experts will be assisting you in an orchestrated plan to link the American civil rights movement with the anti-apartheid movement, isolating the Vorster government of South Africa, turning them into the pariahs of the world. World opinion and sanctions will put you into power and your people will be liberated... AMANDLA!" shouted Hector, stretching his clenched fist high above his head as he stood erect to give the black power salute. If he had kept his arm out in front with the hand flat and pointing at his audience, he would have given the perfect Nazi salute. The return cry of "Amandla! Power!" was generated by the same hysteria of nationalism, and was equally deadly to anyone who disagreed with the party.

The Reverend Andrew Porterstone did not believe in God, but what he did believe in was the communist philosophy of Marx and Lenin. He believed sincerely in reward according to a man's need and the equal distribution of earth's bounty among all men and women. Andrew, like Hector, was the product of the English public school system from a middle-class, wealthy family that provided him with all the material comforts of life, including a tertiary education. World order by one-World government had suggested to Andrew the obvious solution to man's poverty, greed, waste, ignorance and constant wish to wage war.

Born at the end of 1926, he had turned eighteen after the Normandy landings in Europe and, though he put on uniform for the last few months of the Second World War, all he saw was the destruction, the aftermath, and none of the fighting. When he entered the rubble of Cologne, he was not sure whether the RAF was any better than the Luftwaffe in bombing women and children, despite Andrew having spent 1940 through to 1944 under a hail of German bombs, delivered and self-propelled, eleven kilometres from the heart of London. Only when a V1 had taken out his school during the summer holidays of 1944 was he sent north to avoid the bombs, Englishmen of his class believing they could take anything the Germans could fly across the English Channel.

When he reached Oxford to read physics, philosophy and economics, he was an easy target for the Russian agents preparing the way for the Cold War and world domination. Andrew swallowed the utopia of world hegemony in one piece and never wavered from his convictions. The party, with a view to liberation theology being applied alongside liberation movements in Third World countries, concluded that there was a need to infiltrate the soft targets of the Christian churches that always sided with the oppressed in the name of Jesus Christ. The few communist party members in the know joked about the church and the revolutionary parties being made for each other in heaven. Andrew Porterstone was sent to theological school by the British communist party with funds channelled to it by the trade union movement of Great Britain, which was successfully and very quickly taking the 'great' out of Great Britain.

Now at the age of forty Andrew was being placed in position to put communists into strategic positions in the Church of the Province of Southern Africa. Trade Unions were banned in the prosperous South Africa of 1966, but the church was ripe and ready for infiltration. Andrew, settling into his seat aboard the 707 of South African Airways bound for Johannesburg, was going to enjoy himself. Finally his real work was about to begin and he was as ready and dedicated as any man had ever been in pursuit of his life's goal.

MATTHEW GRAY WAS LOOKING FORWARD to seeing Sunny and spending long days at his new smallholding at Halfway House. The small farm was twenty-five kilometres outside Johannesburg, with a strong borehole that watered the nine hectares of pasture in the dry season growing enough grass for two good horses and eventually, when Matthew considered his horse riding good enough, a string of polo ponies. Not only did the sport itself appeal to Matt, he was attracted to the people who played polo. They liked animals, were rich and good for business. And polo clubs were that much more exclusive than golf clubs.

Matt settled into his window seat, well satisfied with the funds in his Jersey trust account and the progress made in buying Security Holdings shares. He deserved a holiday, and there was no better way of spending it than on his own property, on his own horse with his own girl. The antique ruby ring his art dealer had searched out for him was in his pocket, and he did not even care if customs charged him the right amount of duty. The central stone was a 4.8-carat, square cut Burmese ruby, richer in red than any sunset Matt had ever seen. Clustering the jewel were small diamonds, but it was the ruby that would reflect the lighter yellow in the green eyes of his lady.

The plane was due at Jan Smuts airport at nine o'clock South African time that evening and, just in case his bar was empty of champagne, he had two bottles of Charles Heidsieck 1947 in his suitcase to complete the surprise. This time, after so many cancellations, he had not warned Sunny he was on his way home. The ring, the champagne and Matt were going to make up for his business preoccupations. Sunny was going to have all his attention for the first time in weeks. The fat man next to Matt leaned forward to look out of the window while the plane climbed away from the thick haze that covered London below him. Matt closed his eyes and was soon fast asleep. When he awoke, he found his head resting on the comfortable shoulder of the fat man next to him. As he jerked awake, he noticed the white dog-collar round the man's thick neck.

"Sorry, reverend. Nodded off."

"Best way to travel," replied Andrew Porterstone.

By the time the two men had shared lunch and supper in close proximity, they had enthusiastically agreed to meet again in Johannesburg.

"Do you belong to a church?" the reverend asked Matthew.

"No, that I've never done. I've never even been baptised. I was born in a rather wild place. Dad was killed in the war and my mother died when I was thirteen."

"You should join the Church of England. Or the Church of Scotland." They had learnt a lot about each other on the fifteen hour flight, and both men laughed companionably.

By the time the plane came in to land, Matt was overexcited. "Normally I would give you a lift but no one knows I'm arriving," he apologised.

In the rush of arrival at customs and immigration, they forgot to exchange telephone numbers. In the taxi halfway to his home, Matthew shrugged. He had met many people on aeroplanes around the world with whom he had vowed to remain friends for life. They never met again, but it made the boring process of air travel more agreeable. He mentally wished the Reverend Porterstone the best of luck and dismissed him from his mind. His watch read ten past twelve, the plane having been delayed by a minor technical problem at Nairobi airport. Sunny would be asleep, but he would soon change that. His excitement had created a tension throughout his body.

"Drop me at the gate. I want this to be a real surprise." The taxi driver took his double fare and turned to drive back to the airport. There was a KLM flight due in at ten past one.

Matthew was left at his gate with his suitcase. After opening and closing the metal catch, he walked the three hundred metres up the driveway towards his darkened house. The night was dark with no moon, and limited cloud cover obscured most of the stars. He stumbled once over a pile of horse-droppings. The horses kept the grass short in the long driveway.

Reaching the front of the house, Matt was surprised to find a 45O SLC Mercedes parked under the pagoda. Putting down the suitcase with the two bottles of champagne, Matt walked round his darkened house. At the back there was a light, and the sound grew stronger and very familiar.

When he reached the window of his bedroom, the pain of betrayal was absolute. On his bed, on his lady, was a strange man pumping rhythmically, with the familiar voice frantically calling him to climax.

Softly, agonisingly, Matt retraced his steps, opened the door to his garage and put his suitcase in the boot of his car. This time he was not going to smell joss sticks for the rest of his life. As quietly as possible he reversed out of his garage, turned his Chevrolet Malibu in the wide courtyard and drove down the driveway, out of her life.

# 2

Chelsea de la Cruz was created from a bloodline of Nguni, Portuguese, English, Irish and French, and had taken from each member of her ancestral parentage the perfect genes. She was tall, long-legged and high-breasted with perfect, tight buttocks. Her features were aquiline, her eyes dark brown and her hair pitch-black and smooth. The most startling of her European features was the dark soft-brown skin.

From the age of twelve, she had noticed that not a man looked at her without his eyes saying he wanted to take her to bed, there, now and quickly. The flame she created in men was an instant fire and, by the age of fifteen, she had begun to use that fire to her own advantage.

She had grown up in Mozambique, her mother with an English background and her father a small time store owner in Villancoulos, who had progressed to owning a holiday resort island. Ostensibly they were Portuguese but, in reality, both of them had mixed Nguni and European blood. In early 1966, with the Portuguese army fighting a guerrilla war against Frelimo, a war that would eventually push the Portuguese out of Africa after four hundred years, Chelsea met a South African tourist who was visiting her father's coral island to fish for marlin, and took him up on his invitation to visit Europe. She was seventeen.

The man, realising that apartheid laws in South Africa prevented him from achieving his ambition in that country, flaunted the excitement of Europe and, with permission from her parents who only wished the best for their daughter, flew her by light aircraft to Lourenco Marques and by

TAP to Lisbon. When the man flew to London on business, Chelsea, now clothed exquisitely, went along, despite the arrival of the man's wife in England the following day, leaving Chelsea without a chaperon. But she spoke English, had a six month visitors' visa, a thousand pounds from her lover and an excitement that rivalled her lover's lust for her body. Chelsea lived for music, and rhythm was in every sinew of her body. She moved to music as she moved to men, in perfect harmony. With the young Londoners she jived all night and eked out her money by taking a bed-sitter in Nottinghill Gate, where her dark skin felt more comfortable among the immigrants from the British West Indies. She was so happy that she was ready to fly, and Africa was as far from her mind as the moon.

MATTHEW GRAY HAD DRIVEN BACK to Jan Smuts airport and caught the first Air France flight to Nice and Paris, getting off at Nice to catch his breath. At the start of the flight he had felt utterly sick at heart; thoughts of suicide even fluttered briefly through his mind. The bitterness of having been deceived and betrayed, first by Sandy and now by Sunny, almost crushed him. But it was not long before his natural resilience took over, although the deep wounds on his soul were still there. He would get over this, he told himself grimly. But in the meantime, he just wanted to forget. And the best short-term cure he knew was alcohol. Then he would set his mind to enjoy life again.

He had drunk steadily all the way back to Europe and needed a night's sleep before he could really start to party. There was only one way in his mind to dispel the smell of joss-sticks and the voice of his about-to-be wife striving for her climax, and that was in the beds of women, many women, all types of women. One-man-one-girl relationships were out. Lucky and Archie were right. If you had money, spread the happiness; and Matt, when he woke from a sound sleep in a good French Riviera hotel, was ready and willing. If he broke ladies' hearts and they believed his stories of instant love that was their problem. He had had enough problems of his own.

Paris followed Nice and London followed Paris, where he moved into Archibald Fletcher-Wood's new flat in Baker Street, an upmarket version of Archie's previous luxury flat. Though the capital stayed in the Jersey Trust, income was paid to Archie and Lucky every month. Only Aldo had returned to Africa with his lump sum payment, to buy a game ranch lower down the Zambezi from Chirundu, where he would build his hunting lodge for rich tourists from America.

The party was on, and the three friends went on a sexual rampage, competing with each other for more and more women in their hedonistic frenzy. After the first week in London, the pain of Sunny's betrayal had gone, along with the smallholding which he had sold from under her feet. No one was ever going to do that again to Matthew Gray.

LUCKY HAD PURCHASED a convertible and was back to his old tricks, weather permitting. One gash in the top of his head ensured that he checked the roof and pushed the button to wind back the canopy. Then he leapt out. After a week he was not sure whether a saloon car was not more appropriate for his age and the English climate.

The dark girl with the sexy continental accent giggled when he leapt over the side. "Aren't you a little bit old for that kind of thing?'

"You get known for doing something stupid."

"I don't know you,"

"You will." Lucky was still confident. "You want to come back to the flat?"

"No, thank you."

"We're having a party on Saturday night."

Without further argument, Lucky drove her to Nottinghill Gate from the jazz club. He was prepared to wait for really good ones.

"You want to come up for coffee?" she asked at the door to the house.

"No. thanks. Saturday, nine o'clock. What's your name?"

"Chelsea de la Cruz"

For the first time, with the hood down, Lucky opened the driver's door and climbed into his Aston Martin DB4. She was still standing on the step under the street light. He could smell the lime trees. Their eyes met for a moment, but neither of them waved as he drove away.

THE FOLLOWING DAY, Matthew took a taxi into the city of London, having listened to Lucky describing the attributes of the girl he had danced with at the jazz club. Lucky was not usually so effusive but, by the time the taxi reached the Monument, Matt was thinking of business rather than girls. Now, after Sunny, to wait another three and a half years before returning to the insurance business was impossible. Could he find some way around the agreement he had signed with David Todd without violating his integrity?

The Queen's Counsel was as dry as the dark woodwork in his office.

Matt took a leather-bound seat with the stuffing coming out. He was not offered coffee or anything else. He would have to get used to the English way of doing business, Matt told himself.

"Mister Gray, I have read the documents of sale and my opinion is that you are perfectly entitled to conduct insurance business in the United Kingdom, provided you do not take business from Security Holdings. Under British case law, an agreement may not prevent a man from earning his living."

"You mean if I start an insurance company but refrain from attacking David Todd's clients, there is nothing he can do?"

"That is exactly what I mean."

"Are you sure?"

"Mister Gray ..."

"You said it was your opinion."

"My opinion, Mister Gray, is always right."

"Thank you. How much do I owe?"

"You will receive an account through your solicitor. Good day."

"Good day, Sir George." Outside on the pavement, Matt wanted to jump in the air and stamp his feet. The barrister had not even discussed his problem. The old fool was so sure.

THE THREADNEEDLE INSURANCE Company had tried a madcap scheme about which the Scotsman should have known better. He had given underwriting authority to an Australian who had promptly insured large numbers of Sydney taxi cabs, a well-known bad insurance risk. At considerable loss, the Threadneedle had withdrawn from Australia shortly before the Scotsman died.

The company was run exclusively by a general manager. Matthew retained a balance sheet from the English authority that monitored the solvency of insurance companies. The Threadneedle underwrote small lines on the fringe of Lloyd's and a portfolio of personal insurances relating to the three partners' clients, where the industrial business had been placed with Lloyd's underwriters. The short-term account was of little interest to Matt, as he preferred broking 'fire and accident' business rather than underwriting the risks.

What had caught his eye in his search through the few privately owned insurance companies was the Threadneedle's licence to transact long-term insurance, the life insurance that had made David Todd rich. The company was right for a takeover, but old ladies were traditionally conservative and Matt's lawyer's approaches by telephone had been flatly refused. They would not even discuss the matter. Their sentimental ownership of the company was worth more to them than a larger income.

The morning of the party Lucky had arranged left Matt searching for the key to unlocking the sister and the widows. Matt walked from Baker Street to Hyde Park on a beautiful day in August, preoccupied and not even looking at the pretty girls. Some wealthy Londoners were horse riding but the smell of fresh horse manure did not make him think of Sunny Tupper. He had been told his fortune by one of the old ladies who owned Threadneedle, and even the lure of visiting his ancestral home would not make him go up to Scotland to visit the other, unless there was no alternative. It had to be the lady with the young boy.

Progressing along this line of reasoning, he determined to leave the booze alone at the party and drive down to Surrey in the morning. This time he would make an appointment and, with his mind made up, he strode back to the flat and put through a call to the number given by his solicitor. He had been relieved to find the lady did not have a double-barrelled name.

"Missus Holland?"

"No. Do you want to speak to her?... Ma, there's a man on the phone." Matt only had to wait a moment.

"Missus Holland. This is Matthew Gray. I made a mistake in asking my solicitor to talk to you about the Threadneedle Insurance Company, and I hoped I could call tomorrow and discuss my proposition further."

"Where are you from, Mister ...?"

"Gray. G-R-A-Y. From Africa, Missus Holland.'

"Wow!" He heard the voice that had answered the phone. "Have you seen a lion in the wild?"

"I'm sorry, Mister Gray. That is my son. I picked up the extension."

"I last saw a lion in about May," Matt answered the boy.

"I was in the Congo. That's in central Africa. We were right in the jungle." He had sensed the boy's interest in lions could be turned to advantage.

"Come down early," said the boy, almost overcome with excitement. "Wow! Lions! I never met a man who had met a lion in the wild! Wow, wait till I tell my friend."

"Shall we say eleven o'clock?" suggested Mrs Holland. Matt could feel that she was smiling. "Maybe you would like to stay for lunch and give my boy a geography lesson? Ask at the shops in the village. Godalming is not very large. My husband's family have lived here since the seventeenth century."

"Thank you. And my name is Matthew. Matt. I'll look forward to meeting you and the boy."

ARCHIE HAD FOUND a caterer who had trained at the Dorchester Hotel, and the food laid out in the dining room was as good as anything in London. The fork supper had recently reached England from America, along with manhattans and daiquiris. There were no Maharajah Chotapegs. Matthew stayed in his room working, keeping close track of the progress of his shares and money. The purchase of Security Holdings shares had slowed, as institutions sensed there was a predator in the market. The ordinary shares had risen by six per cent, and Matt decided to withdraw his buy order on the Monday and sell half his shares to confuse the market. He would buy the shares back at a lower price. The idea of selling a parcel short intrigued him for a long moment of speculation. He would wait until Tuesday. Matt wondered if David Todd had started an investigation into the new buyers of his shares.

Matt was sure his godfather would find only a smokescreen. That week, there had been a small item in the social column of the *Daily Telegraph,* announcing the arrival of David's grandson at Oxford University, on a Rhodes Scholarship from Bishops School in the Cape. The boy had to be good, and the idea of stiff competition increased Matt's enjoyment. There had to be more than money in business. There had to be fun. David Todd had been right, and Matt smiled to himself as the noise level rose from the large reception room with its small wooden dance floor at the one end. The fun was to be found back in business for Matthew Gray.

Adjusting his evening dress, something that rested well on his broad shoulders, accentuating his height, he opened the door to his bedroom and walked down the plush carpet to survey the talent. He was impressed with what he saw. There was not one woman in the room whom he would rate below eight points out of ten on his scale of talent or looking at them over the age of twenty-five. Every one of them was well groomed and expensively dressed causing him to make a mental note to ask his co-hosts what the ladies did for a living. Professional ladies were off the visiting list of Archie and his friends, and listening to the different accents of the girls, Matt was still unable to place the speaker in the right social class, but he was sure of only one thing: the girls were not all from the middle and upper classes. That accent he had worked out through the art dealer, the solicitor, the QC and his distant relative in Scotland. Not all their daddies were rich.

As the next idea game to him, he laughed out loud, covered the gesture with a wave to Archie's current girlfriend who was not a day over nineteen and joined the party. Keeping to the promise he had made to himself, he filled his empty brandy glass with Canada Dry ginger ale at the makeshift bar. There he saw the black girl talking intimately with Lucky Kuchinski and agreed with Archie that she would rate a nine, if not a ten.

She was perfect, the big lips of the wide mouth making the sexiest 'come on' he could see at the party. The girl had put on a rich orange lipstick over-painted with white. The result even kept the men's eyes away from the deep cleavage made by her large breasts. She was wearing crimson coloured velvet hot pants, and her legs went on forever. Matt had a flashback of the beach at Port St Johns and it was the nostalgia and sudden homesickness, homesickness for his real home that made him go across to talk to the girl. Instinctively, he knew she came from Africa, direct from Africa and not via America or the West Indies. Lucky introduced him as his best friend.

The three friends had a golden-rule. They never poached each other's girlfriends. Pity. But a rule was a rule, and Lucky's friendship was worth more than any woman. Matt left them alone and went off to see what else he could find. By midnight, sober and knowing a lot more about many of the girls' source of income – sponsors, usually married – he took himself off to bed and locked the door. He lay awake in the dark for ten minutes, the party noise muted by the thick walls, playing his idea through his mind. He was smiling when he fell asleep, and dreamed of Port St Johns and a tall black girl with a large inviting mouth. He slept for eight hours, woke as fresh as a morning in the mountains, dressed for the country after a long soak in the bath, and walked through the lounge, not looking too carefully. There was at least one body behind the sofa snoring gently. The flat was a mess. Matthew felt it wonderful to walk out on a Sunday morning without a trace of a hangover.

THE HOUSE WAS HIDDEN among firs and elms and, even before he drove up to the front door, it was obvious that the Hollands had seen better days. The lawns were unkempt and dandelions grew profusely in what once had been a tennis court, the back netting sagging in disrepair from rusted poles. The net posts still stood, but the net had long since gone.

Geoffrey Holland had died six years earlier, leaving the Threadneedle Insurance Company as his main asset. The consequences of the ill-advised foray into Australia were apparent in the long grass and peeling paint. The unearned income tax at nine and six in the pound had also taken its toll, along with death duty and the prohibitive property taxes of the Wilson Labour government. The front door to the house opened before Matt was out of his Jaguar XJ6.

"Are you the man who saw a live wild lion?"

"That's me. And who are you?"

"Jonathan Holland. I'm going to boarding school next year. My father went to Charterhouse and so did grandpa. Where did you go to school?"

"I didn't, Jonathan. There wasn't any money."

"Mummy said there isn't any money but I'm still going to Charterhouse. How big was the lion?"

"I brought a photograph."

"Why are you so tall?"

Matt laughed, and followed the young Holland into the house that had belonged to his family since the early eighteenth century. Matt had done his research. Waiting in the drawing room for Jonathan's mother, Matt speculated how long the house would stay in the family, with the boy twenty years away from making real money, even if the opportunity for making it still existed. The boy himself, sharp as a nail, kept up the questions while studying the photograph of the lion Matt had taken in the Congo with the last two exposures in his film.

They had reached the flying boats to find the pilots over on the island. While they were loading the paintings, a pride of lions, the cubs almost fully grown, had chased them off, shattering the myth that cats did not swim. From the cabin of the Beechcraft Baron, with the window open, Matt had photographed the male before they lifted off from the river. The mane was almost black and the eyes a cold, calculating yellow. Looking back, Matt had seen the lion watching the seaplanes without even bothering to get up.

Man came and went in the Congo, but the lion was still the king of the jungle.

Mrs Holland had come into the room without Matt noticing and, when he looked up from the photograph, he knew what she was thinking. She had the sad look of a single parent seeing her son excited in the company of a man.

"I didn't see my father after the age of seven," Matt said, standing up. "He went to war and never came back." And for Matt, the pain was as great at that moment as it had been when his own mother had explained that his father was never coming home, never again walking down the long sand of Second Beach. Never fishing. Never being there to answer any of his questions... No one said anything for a moment, not even the twelve year old boy.

"Maybe one should start by talking about Jonathan, and then see how my ideas for the Threadneedle fit into the picture." In his moment of pain, Matt knew exactly how to gain control of the long-term licence and keep the short-term company alive and well for Jonathan to take over when he had gone through school and an insurance apprenticeship under Matt's guidance. He would enjoy doing for the boy what had not been done for him.

"Jonathan, go out into the garden. Mister Gray wishes to talk business."

"Can you take me to see a wild lion?"

"If your mother agrees to my suggestions," Matt smiled.

Matt stayed for the most comfortable Sunday lunch he could ever remember and, by the time he left to drive back to London, Mrs Holland had agreed to go up to Scotland at Matt's expense. Matthew himself would see the Lloyd's broker who would then be asked to convince his mother to sell fifty-one per cent of her shares. Matt would need a Lloyd's broker when he took over Security Holdings, buying back his own company in the process. Putting Jonathan Holland through school was a small extra price to pay for the licence. Matthew Gray was back in business.

Six weeks later, on a Wednesday morning at half past eleven, Matt was sitting in the lounge of their flat with his long legs stretched out in front of him. Archie was playing patience, and cheating. Outside, the October rain was coming down in a steady drizzle. Lucky was pacing the shaggy white carpet having been cooped up in the flat for three days. Matt had been waiting a week to bring up the subject he wanted to discuss with them. He was smiling.

"Never thought I could be rich and bored," said Lucky.

"Sit down, Kuchinski," ordered Archie.

"The red queen," said Lucky, stopping to look over his shoulder at the game.

"Thank you."

"You're welcome," Lucky continued to pace.

"Last week I bought us an insurance company," Matt began casually.

"Us?"

"With some of your trust money."

"We can't party forever. Boring."

"So what has that got to do with an insurance company?"

"We're going to run it together. The three of us. Life and pensions. And it's going to be fun."

"How can insurance ever be fun?" asked Archie, stacking his cards.

"First, I am going to put you two through an intensive training course. Life insurance is far simpler than fire and accident. The success of a life company is in the selling and the investment premiums. I want you two to help me with the selling by training a sales force that will outperform our conservative competitors."

"Matt, you can't be serious," protested Archie.

"Between us, we have a list of two hundred and twelve single, very attractive and mostly intelligent young girls between the ages of seventeen and twenty-five. I've checked out the backgrounds of forty-three of them. Only six have regular jobs with monthly salaries. The rest live off the party set, mostly older, rich men who find our friends better company than their wives. Only when they come into our set do they meet single men, which is why we never have problems with good looking girls when we want to throw a party. In another age, the girls would be mistresses in the classic sense with a town house down the end of a pretty mews and a visitor twice a week. All the girls I checked want a good time while they are young, but none of them wish to sell their bodies for cash. What I propose to do, with your help, will give them a far greater freedom of choice. We will give them financial independence. The 'I don't need you in a fit' money that will enable them to look after themselves."

Lucky had stopped pacing and Archie had put the cards back on the table. Both of them were looking steadily at Matt.

"Oh, you clever shit," said Archie, slapping his knee. "You think it will work?"

"What?" said Lucky for whom the proverbial penny had yet to drop.

"He is going to use all those lovely ladies to sell his policies, and you and I, Kuchinski, are going to be their bosses."

Matt watched them think it through before he continued. "The lapse ratio will be remarkably low as a married man never wants his wife to know about other women. The girls will be trading their charms for more than a temporary flat in the West End and a charge account at Harrods.

The good ones will even become rich in their own right, and you two will be doing what you do best. Chatting up the ladies."

"And I was thinking of going back to Africa," said Lucky in awe.

At the end of December 1966, just before Christmas, Matthew bought fifty-one per cent of the Threadneedle Insurance Company, which in turn sold the licence to operate life insurance to a new company in which it would hold a minority twenty per cent share, Matthew's Jersey trust owning all but five per cent of the balance. The company was called Lion Life, Matt dealing the owner of the well-known Lion Building Society a five per cent shareholding for not contesting the name and allowing the new company to use a similarly rounded logo to that which had been seen for years at every tube station in the London Underground. Matt had learnt the value of sponsorship and familiarity in Gray Associates.

The Threadneedle general manager had had little interference for twenty years and his only interest was in keeping his job. The debacle in Australia had not been of his making and he had made it clear after the event that AC Entwistle would never have insured a taxi, let alone an Australian taxi. The company, for lack of the shareholders' knowledge and time in running it, had fallen by default into the manager's hands, a manager without a shareholding.

He was fifty-seven years old, bald, fat and pompous and, when Matt phoned for an appointment, his intention being to explain the new situation in person, he ran straight into trouble. The man had a secretary who had shrivelled up on the job protecting her boss. When she refused to give Matthew an appointment without being told his business, he hoped he had not forgotten his short term insurance in the eighteen months that had elapsed since selling his company to Security Life.

For half an hour, he pondered the idea of leaving Entwistle where he was, under strict financial control, doing neither harm nor good, while Matt himself concentrated on Lion Life in different premises. Then the devil in him took over and on went his coat.

An hour later, he was standing at what barely qualified as a reception desk. Matt wanted to laugh. It only needed high stools and quills for the place to have been straight out of Dickens. It was no wonder that the company had not increased its dividends in thirty years. There were three rows of desks occupied by old men in dark suits, bald-headed or grey, with an elderly woman at each end sitting in front of typewriters that had been bought before the Second World War. The smell of old dust and antiquated central heating mingled with the cluster of wet raincoats hanging on umbrella stands inside the door.

An old lady with dyed hair turned genteel orange in patches with bright red lipstick and caked powder on an old face, asked him his business. Appalled at the reality of what he had bought and the magnitude of the task ahead, he was unable to speak. His eyes swept over the ancient tomb, resting on the glass cage that housed the general manager. When his horrified gaze returned to the old lady, she gave him a wink. Her old eyes were sparkling with merriment. Matt, taller than anyone in the room by a foot and younger by twenty years, must have looked as incongruous to them as they did to him. He began to smile and then chuckle.

"Do you have an appointment?" They were sharing a good joke and Matt felt better. The staff may be old, he thought, but this one had a sense of humour.

"That's the problem. Mister Entwistle's secretary wouldn't give me one."

"He's not busy." She said it in a way that told him Mister Entwistle was not often very busy. "I'll see what I can do."

"Tell him Missis Holland sent me."

"How is Missis Holland? And Jonathan?" She was on her way to the glass cage. It was obviously a family business and, unless he wished to replace the staff and pay a large sum in severance pay, he had better tread softly. The company had at least managed to stay in business, which seemed a miracle in itself.

"Whom shall I say is calling?" she called loudly from the door to the GM's enclosed, half-glass office.

"Matthew Gray." As if jerked by a puppet-master, the entire staff looked up.

"Where are you from?"

"Africa." Everyone sat up and put down their pens. If he wished to address his new staff, he certainly had their attention.

Either the old lady or the GM was deaf, it would appear, though Matthew doubted this. The old girl was putting on a show. "Mister Gray from Africa," she almost shouted as she threw open the half-glass door and beckoned Matthew into the only office in the company that enjoyed a carpet – a very old carpet, Matt noted, as he put out his hand to the startled man behind the desk. A lady in the corner of the room, obviously the protective secretary, was about to protest the intrusion when it was announced in an equally loud voice that everyone could hear, "Missus

Holland sent 'im." The 'H' in Holland being pronounced with great emphasis.

"And what can I do for you, Mister Gray? You wish to insure your house? Your car? We have very good personal line policies, and we always pay our claims promptly. Very promptly, Mister Gray. Would you care for a chair? Thank you, Missus Barton... Missus Barton is a little deaf. Her husband runs our mail room. The little area behind the filing cabinets." Entwistle laughed at what he thought was a joke. "We don't waste money on overheads at Threadneedle. Now what can I do for you, Mister ...?" Mrs Barton closed the door to his office, shaking the cage.

'Gray. G-R-A-Y. Matthew Gray. I would like to see your books."

"Ah, you must be from the government." Unlikely with a South African accent, Matthew thought.

"No. Mister Entwistle." He had not taken the offered seat and now turned to look at the open plan office through the glass. Everyone was still looking up from their work. "Maybe it would be better if I spoke to the entire staff. Will you be kind enough to call them all together?"

"Whatever for?"

"Because I own the company and I intend to run it hands-on. And one of the first things we are going to do is to get to know each other and go through every file and every account book."

When Matthew turned back to him, all colour had drained from the general manager's face. "We only have an audit once a year," he protested.

"Not anymore. Where are the accounts records?"

"In the safe."

"Then you'll be kind enough to give me the keys."

"I wish to resign."

"As you wish... I have no reason to be vindictive but I do wish to increase the company's profits and salaries. Maybe it would be better if you told me what you have done, and that way we can keep it to ourselves. I have been aware of your twenty-five year old mistress for some months. In fact, I have had the pleasure of entertaining the young lady. I suspect her flat is rented in the name of the company, among other things. I would be obliged if you would give me your resignation in writing. Now. And while your secretary is typing it, she can make out one for herself."

"I wish to leave immediately."

"I have no problem with that."

When the letters were typed and signed, Entwistle began to clean out his drawers.

"You can leave that. Anything of a personal nature will be returned to your home."

"There's no fool like an old fool," muttered AC Entwistle, as he prepared to leave the company he had joined in 1931.

"Mister Entwistle?" said Matthew as the two old people were leaving.

"Yes, Mister Gray."

"You will go on early retirement, and an amount equal to ten per cent of your pension will be deducted to pay back what you have taken over the last many years."

"You won't tell my wife?"

"Oh, and Mandy has moved out of the flat."

"What will happen to Mandy?"

"Fact is, I gave her a job. The ten per cent was her idea. She's a very nice girl. I won't say all the things she said about you, but none were nasty. She did say you were kind. Hence the ten per cent." Matt even felt sorry for the old man who had lost his job and his mistress, his meaning for life, all in the space of ten minutes.

"Give her my love." AC Entwistle closed his door for the last time and, with his head up and followed by his secretary of twenty-seven years, walked to the umbrella stand. He took his bowler hat and put it on his head, then he put on his raincoat and retrieved his umbrella. With the perfectly rolled umbrella on his left arm he offered his secretary his right, opened the outside door to the office and left with dignity, leaving Matthew feeling like a thief. Dismissal was not the kind of Christmas present he liked giving people. Maybe Mandy had been worth the price for AC Entwistle. He hoped so. Deflated, he sat down behind the GM's desk and contemplated his next move. He counted the staff outside in the general office. There were eighteen, in addition to the man he could not see behind the filing cabinets. Right then he could have done with Sunny Tupper as secretary, but then the other, more vivid picture of her clouded his thoughts, and he put that idea out of his mind. Tomorrow was Christmas Eve, and he was not going to start anything before the new year. They were all looking at him and they were all his, for better or for worse. He looked at his watch. It was half past three. They all had to be told and the sooner the better. He stepped out of the small office.

"I expected Mister Entwistle to tell you what was going on, but he has left the company at his own request, on learning I had purchased control of your company. Any others of you who do not wish to work for me may do the same, but I hope you will stay. My name is Matthew Gray and I come from South Africa, though my ancestors come from Scotland. On the second of January, I will take over running the day-to-day business with two of my associates, Mister Archibald Fletcher-Wood, an Englishman, and ..." Matt stopped in his tracks. For the life of him he had no idea of Lucky's Christian name. "And Lucky Kuchinski, a Pole." He would leave the rest of that for them to work out.

"The other two men will be running a new life company which will feed you short-term business" He wondered for a brief moment if he should mention the girls. "We will be moving to larger premises, though as yet I don't know where. Now, as I go round, please introduce yourselves. I know Missus Barton and I believe Mister Barton is in our vast mail room behind the filing cabinets." It was the best he could do for a stale joke, but the laughter came. His new staff were as nervous as he was, and he sat on the side of a front desk.

"Your company has been bought by Jersey Island Trust, not a South African company, though I do have experience in that market, along with the Canadian, American, Australian and Hong Kong markets where Gray Associates operated for me in the past. That company is now owned by Security Holdings, a company with which many of you will be familiar, especially its English subsidiary. Please carry on as you were, and all of you have a merry Christmas... Missus Barton, where is the nearest pub you could recommend?"

"The Green Man."

"Everyone is welcome to join me there when you are finished. Now let me shake all your hands, and then Missus Barton and her husband can show us where to find the Green Man, though I have a suspicion you all know exactly where it is." This time the laughter was genuine.

At the end of January the staff were moved to the second floor of Jupiter House and the ground floor was gutted by office renovators. Within two weeks, the walls were painted, offices created, carpets laid, and each underwriter, fire, marine and accident, installed in a front office easily accessible to the brokers needing additional lines to complete their Lloyd's slips. Next to the underwriters was a plush reception area for Lion Life and Threadneedle Insurance, and behind the single desk, opposite the warm, colourful sofas that matched the rich maroon carpet, sat Chelsea de la Cruz. Her UK work permit had been granted the week before, pending the granting of permanent residence. Mrs Barton was heard to comment that not even she had looked that good in her youth.

By the end of January, all the Gray Associates systems, methods and procedures had been introduced to the Threadneedle with surprising alacrity which had everything to do with Matthew increasing salaries by ten per cent across the board with, in addition, his old bonus system, linked to premium written and profit achieved in the three departments. Two of the old staff resigned under the new pressure of work and were not replaced.

At the end of February, Matt invited small groups of brokers to cocktail parties in the reception area, where the Lion Life girls mingled with the brokers who would feed the Threadneedle with new business. Matt was not allowing the girls into the Life field until they were properly trained, with Archie and Lucky satisfied there would be no misinformation given to clients. Initially there were only four Life products to be sold, lifted with slight variation from Security Life in Johannesburg, Matt rationalising that they had his systems, so why should he not have theirs. The Life Company would be launched with extensive local advertising and a paid-up capital of five million pounds.

On the first of February, Threadneedle's capital had been increased by two million pounds by a rights issue, the rights only taken up by the Jersey Trust as the other shareholders had insufficient money. The underwriting capacity of the Threadneedle was increased by three hundred per cent, making it worthwhile for the young brokers to call when they were unable to complete their slips in the room at Lloyd's.

Matt estimated that Chelsea attracted half the visitors. The old underwriters started to dress smartly, and the Fire underwriter appeared with a nicely fitting toupee which sent Mrs Barton into a fit of giggles. By judicious prodding and a succession of half-pints of beer in the Green Man before the cocktail parties started, Matt had convinced her to visit a hairdresser of his choice at his expense, and her hair was turned a very smart silver. Her clashing make-up was also changed. When she returned, she had undergone such a metamorphosis that it was Mister Barton's turn to chuckle.

At the end of April 1967, the Lion Life girls were given carefully selected lists of potential clients, men working in the Baltic Exchange, the stock exchange and the merchant banks. In the month of May, from twenty-five well-trained girls, all of whom registered between seven and ten on the Richter scale, premium income from single-premium payments exceeded three hundred thousand, and annualised monthly premiums with an average life of twenty-five years was one hundred and eighty-nine thousand pounds. What some of the girls did in return, under the heading of customer relations, was their business and not discussed by directors. The girls had been warned that any publicised indiscretion would cost them their jobs.

By the end of that year, both companies were causing Matthew to work fourteen hours a day six days a week. Matt's alcohol intake was limited to four drinks an evening and, though his lunch guests thought he was drinking gin and tonic in his favourite restaurant, the owner poured from a special Beefeater bottle of gin that was full of pure tap water. He had never been so busy, even in Johannesburg, and enjoyed every minute of his days.

Despite Lucky's attempts, his charm had not worked on Chelsea and, even before the carpets had been laid in the renovated ground floor, Matt had found his own flat and moved in with Chelsea de la Cruz. Matt had written a careful letter to the girl's parents in Villancoulos, and all thoughts of Sunny Tupper or Sandy de Freitas left his mind for ever. The girl made no demands going off to the jazz clubs on her own if Matt was too busy with work. They had the ideal relationship until the end of 1967, when Chelsea met Luke Mbeki at a Soho jazz club off Greek Street and fell in love for the first time in her life.

Luke Mbeki had been back from Lusaka for a month when he saw the black girl on her own in Chris Barber's jazz club, where the music was traditional and the smooth notes of Chris Barber's trombone much to Luke's liking. Being the only two blacks in the room, they had drifted towards each other and Luke had asked her to dance, doing his own version of jive. They said little while they were dancing, the noise level being too high for extended conversation.

"You want a drink?" Luke eventually asked her.

"Sure. There's a pub in Greek Street."

"I know. Used to come here a lot."

"Where've you been?"

"Zambia. You ever heard of Zambia?"

"Sure, I come from Mozambique."

"What are you doing here on your own?" queried Luke.

"My boyfriend works day and night. Owns an insurance company."

"Sounds old."

"He's thirty-five and as tall as you," smiled Chelsea.

"Black?"

"Not by skin colour but he's African by birth and a lot else."

"Do you love him?"

"I'm only eighteen. Lots of time to fall in love."

"Where do you live?"

"You ask a lot of questions," laughed Chelsea, "Where do you live? What were you doing in Lusaka? Where do you come from?"

"Port St Johns. That's in the Transkei. My name's Luke Mbeki."

Chelsea had gone cold. Even before he gave his name, she knew who he was and that the best thing she could do for herself was to get out of the club alone and never see Luke again. Her mind wanted to go one way, but her body took her up the narrow stairs beside Luke, and the calm waters that surrounded her life were whipped up into a storm, a storm that would rage around her, taking her eventually back to Africa and the horrors of war.

When she resigned from Lion Life and moved out of the flat, Matt asked her if the new guy was nice and whether he would look after her properly.

"He's nice." There was no point in denying that she had another man.

"Do I know him?"

"He's not one of the crowd."

"Then be happy, Chelsea. Have a good life." Matt shrugged, and went and got himself drunk for the first time that year. Once again he had been working too hard.

There was always a price to pay for everything. The next day he phoned Archie and left him in charge of the business, catching a plane to Johannesburg and, after a short delay, the Air Rhodesia Viscount to Salisbury. Aldo Calucci met him at the airport and, by the time he reached the game farm on the banks of the Zambezi River, looking across the river to Zambia, Matt was feeling better. This time he had not given the girl even a small piece of his heart.

THE HUNTING CAMP had been built of pole and dagga, reed-thatched with a large *boma* in the centre where the small game was roasted over an open fire. At night, Aldo, with a .375 cradled on his knee, sat with his paying guests around the big fire that burnt whole trees, the trunks being pushed into the centre of the fire as they gradually burnt away. From the camp the hunter would have been able to lob a stone into the Zambezi River, but the slope up from the water was too steep for the hippo to charge. Acacia trees, flat canopies to the heavens, shrouded the camp at night and gave it shade during the day. Mosquitoes and tsetse were bad at dusk, but the wood-smoke offered some protection.

Aldo had collected an American journalist from the same flight. Ben Munroe was writing a series of articles for *Newsweek* on newly independent African states, and he wanted an inside look at rebel Rhodesia. He had given hunting his excuse to get into the country, which was, of course, isolated from the rest of the world by mandatory United Nations trade sanctions.

There were three other Americans in camp when the Land Rover returned. The camp had been well looked after by Mashinga, who had followed Aldo into his new enterprise. When they sat round the *boma* on Matt's first night, London and Chelsea felt as far away as the moon. Above them the stars were bright in three distinct layers, a lacework of sparkling jewels.

Matt had walked away from the fire to look at the night, having the urge to pray in his excitement at being home in the bush. The plop of the bream rising to feed on the river flies was exactly the same sound as was made by the mullet in the river at Second Beach. For a moment, with the slap of wet fish on still water, Matt was a small boy in Port St Johns with his father again, and none of the pain in his life had even begun. He walked away downriver carrying his rifle, to see the heavens without the dancing firelight dimming the wonder his eyes beheld.

"You want eat food," Aldo called in his thick, northern Italian accent and bad English. A hippo grunted from the water, while the tree frogs screamed from the acacia trees to his right, answered by frogs from the river, the symphony of a thousand castanets. Far away on the Zambian side of the river, a pack of wild dogs barked with the excitement of the chase, and a hyena laughed hysterically. Further downriver, in the pale, beautiful light of the stars, a sable antelope drank at the water's edge, the tall, scimitar horns just visible in the starlight. A dove called in the night, and was silent.

Hungry from the evening's game viewing in the Land Rover with Mashinga, Matt re-joined the other men around the fire. With a hunting knife and a plate, he cut slices of the well-cooked bush pig and sat down on a log to eat. Aldo passed him a tin mug full of red wine from the Cape, and he gave his salute to the company and drank. The wine was better than any French vintage he had drunk in the City of London.

Aldo smiled, showing white teeth. "The wine is good, Matt? Good to see you. Matt is my best friend. How is Archie? We old friends. All of us old friends. How you like my camp?"

"The second best place on earth"

"Where's the best, London?" asked Ben.

"Port St Johns in the Transkei. I was born there."

"Met a guerrilla leader in Lusaka who was born in Port St Johns."

"Luke Mbeki." replied Matt, pushing pork into his mouth with his fingers. "He's my twin. How is Luke? He avoids me."

"Twin? You want to tell us?" Ben looked sceptical.

"You want to tell me you're here to hunt and not to write?" Matt laughed.

"Writers write. They can't help it."

"Tell Luke when you see him he's still my friend."

"I'll remember. What's going to happen in Rhodesia, Aldo?"

"There going to be a war," replied Aldo, with an air of inevitability.

"You going to win?"

"No. Neither are they. All we do is kill lots of people. You want more pig, anyone? Go and cut."

"The blacks want independence," said Ben.

Aldo looked at the reporter, choosing his words carefully. "They want many things they not got. A war will not make them rich. Not make them like you and me. A war make them poor, very poor. Politicians not worry about people. Only power. Their power. Always same. Out here, in bush it obvious. I always see clearly from a long way away. Tomorrow we shoot a lion and you all go home like men. There one lion on the licence and Ben write about it. Matt, you watch."

"Prefer not to, Aldo. I like live lions, not dead ones."

"He old and one bad foot. Good head. Good trophy."

"You go and shoot. I'll stay in camp and fish for tiger fish."

"What is difference?"

"The tiger fish don't look at me before I pull them out of the water."

"You can't eat a tiger fish any more than a lion."

"Then I'll fish for bream ..." His friend, Luke, now a guerrilla leader. Matt shuddered at the thought, and went cold.

IF THE WHITE Afrikaner had not invented apartheid, the Americans would have had to look for another whipping boy to assuage the aspirations of their civil rights movement. Ben Munroe was conscious of the hypocrisy, but castigating the whites in Africa made good copy and, whether *Newsweek* bought his articles or someone else's, it was a living. Drawing attention to a United Nations that applied sanctions when fifteen years earlier they had been happy to have the whites of Southern Rhodesia fight alongside them in Korea was not what the Americans wanted to hear. In 1950, the same National Party had been in power in South Africa, and the white settlers had ruled Rhodesia. But that was before Little Rock.

In the article, he wanted to write that Matthew Gray, exploiter of the black man, was the bad guy and the good guy was Luke Mbeki, the gallant guerrilla fighter who was going to liberate his people. Ben knew the white Americans had a bad attack of guilt as the Negro in his country had been treated a lot worse than the Afrikaner was now treating the tribes of Africa. Ben sensed a sensational, on-going story paralleling the lives of Matt and Luke. He would be able to give faces to the appalling wealth disparity created by apartheid. The human interest would make him famous. Luke Mbeki had told him that not all settlers needed the bullet, that he had grown up with a white boy. And now he had met the twin. With great patience, Ben stalked his prey while the other members of the shooting party stalked the old lion with the good head.

The first article was a sensation, read by Luke in Lusaka and Matt in his new office on the second floor of Jupiter House. None of the facts were wrong. Luke had been taken from Matt's flat and beaten up by the South African police, but his friend had not sold him to the police, as inferred in the article. Luke even picked up the phone in his Lusaka apartment to speak to Matt.

"He's not like that," she shouted.

Chelsea was crying.

"I know ..." then he put down the phone. Matt was the one weakness in his struggle for the freedom of his people. He could not afford to be sentimental. They were both victims.

FOR A WEEK, Matt was a dubious celebrity and only stopped the sniping of the American and British newspapers by calling a televised press conference to challenge any reporter to interview him with Luke Mbeki on camera. He appealed to Luke to get in touch with him and describe their childhood together.

"Luke Mbeki is my friend and I am his. That is a fact. We were born on the same day in Port St Johns and educated by my mother. We are twins, one black, one white, but inseparable twins and, whatever the politicians do to us, that fact will never change."

For weeks Matt waited expectantly for Luke to contact him. He worked harder in his effort to forget the accusations. By the middle of summer, Chelsea and Ben Munroe were out of his mind. By the time his restraint clause expired, Lion Life would be ready to go public.

On the 30 September 1968, Threadneedle Insurance doubled its dividend while Jonathan Holland spent his first term at Charterhouse. In

October, Edward Todd Botha played rugby for Oxford University. He had turned twenty in May.

In Johannesburg, his grandfather David Todd was now certain that someone was buying his shares. He was also sure that Lion Life was using a slight variation of his products but was told he could do nothing to stop their plagiarism. He was now eighty-two years old and chief executive of Security Holdings, waiting for his grandson to join the company. Then he would appoint a committee to run the business until Edward had the accumulated experience to take over. It had crossed his mind that Matthew might be that predator, but he had done so much for the boy; it would not be Matthew Gray. Anyway, he was tired and wanted to rest. He had done more than most people in a lifetime.

THE LIFE OFFICE ASSOCIATION OF LONDON met at the request of two of its senior members at the end of November, with thick fog swirling up to the city from the Pool of London. The meeting was well attended, and took place in the boardroom of a firm of accountants who lent their large room to major clients for such occasions.

The chairman, a man in his late fifties, was suffering the consequences of eating for many years in the best clubs and restaurants in the capital. He was a man who had been honoured by his queen with a sword tap on the shoulder, though he had not been able to receive the occasion on his knees, as to kneel and rise again was a physical impossibility. He was a jolly man with a broad minded disposition. Inside the fat that comprised his cheeks sat merry little eyes that twinkled when all was going well. That day at the end of November was an exception, and the twinkling eyes were dimmed while his large belly rested uncomfortably on the polished board table. How the pin-stripe trousers stayed attached to his body was a secret known only by the chairman and his tailor, some people saying that not even his wife knew the method of fixing or suspension. Sir Cedric was a successful man... he called for order.

"Geoffrey gave me his opinion in private, and I don't want any minutes taken of this meeting." The cream of London's life insurance industry subsided into silence as the chairman let his un-twinkling eyes search the room. Every member had been suited in Saville Row, and every one of them looked as well polished as the table. To add to the richness of the gathering, all but two of the twenty-seven members present were smoking the best of cigars even before they had partaken of luncheon. The chairman, aware of the needs of his own well-covered frame, had wisely called the meeting in the morning. He would take them all to his club when the matter of Lion Life had been dealt with, as dealt with he was determined it would be. Colonials, let alone unconventional colonials, were not welcome in the city of London.

"Geoffrey, you had better tell everyone what you told me." Geoffrey stood up with some difficulty. He too was overweight and under-haired.

"They are using young girls to sell their policies, and it is my opinion that these girls are kicking back more than money to their customers. As you know, sharing of agents' commission with the customer is illegal."

"As is prostitution," interrupted the chairman, his own indignation getting the better of him.

"The Lion Life girls are fornicating with their clients."

"Disgusting," a man said from the side of the table, while three of the members were forced to turn their heads away from the proceedings as they were unable to control their smiles.

"Do all of the salesgirls do this?" asked one of them, barely containing his laughter.

"I believe so."

"Do they do it before or after they receive the signed proposal form?"

"What on earth does that matter?"

"One is payment. The other is thanks. I do not believe the latter is illegal. Neither fornication nor adultery is illegal in the United Kingdom. I suspect that most of the clients are married?"

"We believe so."

"Then it is the wives who should be calling this meeting."

"Do you know the close rate of Lion Life is three times greater than any office represented at this table?"

"I'm not surprised," said another of the members, who had turned his head from the chairman to avoid the penetrating eyes.

"I believe all the girls are hand-picked, well-trained, highly motivated and, above all, extremely pretty. What else would you expect?"

"Lion Life is trading at an unfair and illegal advantage."

"Unfair, maybe; illegal only if the policy is taken out on the promise of sex. You must prove these girls are selling sex and not insurance."

"Then I will prove my point," said Geoffrey. "I will take out a policy with Lion Life.

"And stand up in court afterwards and say you had sex with a prostitute! Whatever would Doris have to say about that!"

"I won't actually have sex; don't be silly. I'll record her sales pitch." The younger member said nothing, though he would have given a large sum of money to be a fly on the wall when the pitch was made. The chairman closed the meeting, saying that they would return when Sir Geoffrey had completed his research.

THE CALL CAME through to the new receptionist. She was very, very tall and Nordic, whereas Chelsea had been black. Her body shape was amazing, especially in that everything was half as large again as normal.

"You wish to have one of our sales ladies call at your flat this evening?" the receptionist asked on the phone. "Please give me your name, and your home and office phone numbers, and I will put you through." The Nordic beauty barely heard the name and was refused both phone numbers.

The receptionist switched the PABX and Lucky came on the line. "Another of those calls, Lucky."

"Put him through... yes, good morning. My name is Lucky Kuchinski; I am a sales manager, Mister ..." There was silence for a moment and the line went dead. A minute later, the switchboard rang again, and Geoffrey gave a false name and false phone numbers. "We'll ring you back, Mister Halifax."

A minute and a half afterwards, the same voice, badly disguised, said his name was Geoffrey Gould and gave the number of his club, a club that was always discreet. "We'll call you back, Mister Gould" By the time she had phoned the number and asked for Mr Gould, to be told Sir Geoffrey was not in the club just then, the Lion Life receptionist was enjoying herself. She talked again to Lucky, who walked across from his office to have a chat with Matt.

"Geoffrey Gould," he said to Matt. "Got a knighthood by giving Wilson a quarter of a million for the party. Deputy chairman of life offices association. What do we do, Matt?"

"Sell him a policy. It's what he says he wants."

"He's CEO of the largest life office in Britain."

"Then he'll understand the better value of our policies with its full investment disclosure. He'll know that money put in Lion Life will grow faster than money put into his own company. Full disclosure by all life offices is what the public needs. He may see the benefit of honest selling. Gould... probably Gold, originally, Jewish. Put Janet on the job."

Janet Landau put a call through to the club and was called back by Sir Geoffrey an hour later. A meeting was arranged in Janet's flat for the following evening.

When the LOA of London reconvened its meeting on the Thursday, Sir

Geoffrey played back the tape he had recorded. Janet Landau had made her sales pitch in a slow, husky voice, describing the Lion Life Policy and the full financial position of investment charges, brokerage and overheads. The machine was turned off by Sir Geoffrey. Then he folded his arms in indignation.

"She was dressed so you missed nothing. Lights dim. In her own flat. Big couch. Soft music. Poured me a stiff whisky."

"What happened?" asked the chairman.

"I bought the policy. Had to. I mean..."

"And then?"

"Nothing. She said I would have to undergo a medical and she'd arrange that the following day."

"And then what happened?"

"I went at eleven o'clock and was accepted that afternoon. Three hundred pounds a month for the next fifteen years. When I'm sixty-five ..."

"By the sound of your tape recording, you made a good investment."

"Did she provide you with sex?"

"No. Not even a second whisky, I'm afraid. She said her husband was due home in ten minutes and I got out of that flat as fast as I could... And do you know something else. She was Jewish." This time, three of the members burst out laughing and the twinkle returned to the chairman's eyes.

"Expensive but educational." said the chairman, and closed the meeting.

MATTHEW GRAY INTRODUCED mass marketing to Threadneedle Insurance and Lion Life at the same time. The sponsor was British Petroleum. Matthew, always attacking the top, had written a short, succinct letter stating that he could reduce the short-term insurance premiums of BP service stations by forty-two per cent if BP sponsored a programme for their marketers. The pension programme would give the staff of the garages the same benefits as a BP salaried employee. They would not require a medical and was transferable within the BP dealers' network. Matt said he would call the BP chairman on the telephone and make an appointment.

Six months later, after the policies had been scrutinised by the BP financial director and his staff, Matt was able to launch his program to the BP dealers, using a special letterhead which included the BP logo. The result was in line with his earlier experiences, only this time he was able to cut out the broker and the broker's commission. A mainframe IBM computer had been installed and programmed to process new business brought in by the team of men Matt had trained to call on each of the dealers individually to sign up the policies. A policy and a summary of the policy's conditions in intelligible English were then sent to the dealer, while his petrol account with BP was debited monthly with the insurance premium. One cheque was received by Matt from BP, who programmed the payment at minimal cost. The accounting cost saving to Matt, passed onto the BP dealer, was eighteen per cent of the gross premium.

By the end of 1969, the whole of Jupiter House was occupied by Matt's companies and Mrs Holland found that she could afford to renovate the family manor house that was ready to fall down. Matt went down to the house during the school holidays and gave Jonathan a father's encouragement and, in the spring of 1970, flew the boy to Rhodesia where Aldo Calucci introduced him to a live lion.

The bush war in Rhodesia had yet to start, though Luke Mbeki, not far from Aldo's camp on the Zambezi River, was training guerrilla fighters to infiltrate across the river in dugout canoes. These were used to cache arms throughout the rebel colony in preparation for a full-scale attack from Zambia by the forces of Joshua Nkomo, and later from Mozambique by the forces of Robert Mugabe. Though Luke and the Rhodesian police knew what was happening, the public did not, and Jonathan Holland spent the most exciting two weeks of his life three kilometres from a major ZIPRA cache of RPG rockets, launchers and mines, AK47 rifles and boxes of well-sealed ammunition.

When the boy returned to Charterhouse for the summer term he told everyone he was going out to Rhodesia to grow tobacco when he left school. At the camp had been three tobacco farmers with wide-brimmed hats, short shorts and veldskoens, talking of vast hectares of green tobacco, despite the British inspired sanctions. The presence of real men and live lions had been too much for the fifteen year old boy.

In the summer of 1970, six months after his restraint clause expired, Matt made his hostile bid for Security Holdings, announcing that he owned twenty-three per cent of the company. At the same time, Lion Life was sold into Threadneedle Insurance company in a reverse takeover, giving Lion Life shareholders control of Threadneedle Insurance, which was then floated on the London stock exchange. Shares in a company established in 1928 were easier to market. Security Holdings shareholders were offered either cash for their shares or shares in Threadneedle

Insurance. One of the major buyers of the shares was Smythe-Wilberforce Industries.

A week after the offer was made public, David Todd had a heart attack. The man who had fought for South Africa at Delville Wood in World War I was dead. Back from Oxford, Edward Botha, the sole beneficiary of David Todd's Security Holdings shares that had been left to him in a death duty-free offshore trust, took over the company and announced to the press that he would fight the hostile takeover. He was twenty-two years of age.

The only person in the financial markets who did not underestimate the boy was Matthew Gray. He had started young himself and with a quarter of Edward Todd Botha's education. Matt was also aware that Botha had the Afrikaner establishment behind his determination to retain control of what had been his grandfather's company. If Matt was not careful, he was about to fight the Boer War all over again.

Realising the strength of the opposition, Matt put Archie Fletcher-Wood in charge of his pyramid company, Lion Holdings, and returned to South Africa. When he stepped down from the plane at Jan Smuts airport, he stamped twice on the tarmac. He was glad to be home. He was thirty-eight, and fitter than most men of thirty. Not a hair had been lost of his strong head of hair, though a trace of grey was showing through the rich brown. His back straight and making the best use of his nearly two-metre height, he strode across to the terminal building. Fifteen years after founding Gray Associates, he was home again to buy back his company.

He went through customs quickly and found himself a taxi. Three-quarters of an hour later, the taxi dropped him at the Balalaika Hotel where he booked in, sending his luggage to his rondavel by bell-boy. Then he walked across the few metres from reception into the Cock and Hen bar.

It was six-thirty in the afternoon and some of the team had already arrived. Felix, the barman, was polishing a glass.

"Hi, Matt! What you drinking?"

"Oudemeester."

"You never change. Felix, an *odie* for Matt. Where've you been, Matt? Haven't seen you for a while. You see those two birds down the bar," his old bar acquaintance said, dropping his voice to a whisper. "That's real talent, and it's Friday night." Outside in the tall trees, pigeons were calling to each other as the cars arrived and the young single set of Johannesburg came to their watering hole.

It was as though he had never been away.

# 3

Teddie Botha found Security Holdings to be a lot less secure than his grandfather had led him to believe. Very simply, the old man had lost control of management and the capital growth figures, published with the authentication of the auditors, were dubious, if not an outright lie. Large sums of policyholders' money had been badly invested and there were assets shown in the balance sheet that Teddie knew should have been written off years earlier. American banks lending to Third World governments were aware of the same cold shadow of bad debt.

The main problem was that the buildings put up in the boom of the sixties were less than fully occupied and the loans made by Security Life were no longer covered by the resale value of the properties. A pessimist would even have said that the solvency rate of the company was in jeopardy and that actuarially Security Life was unable to fulfil its future commitments when guaranteed policies and death sums insured were taken into account. The best thing for Security Life policyholders was a Lion Life takeover, but the company was not a mutual office and policyholders had no say in accepting the offer.

Teddie's first task as chief executive was to fire some of the senior staff, cut overheads and strengthen his balance sheet. But to do any of these things while under attack would have been suicidal. Security Holdings shares would have tumbled, making the offer irresistible. Teddie Botha needed a white knight, someone who would buy a parcel of his own trust shares so that he could use the money to follow a rights issue and increase the company's capital. The alternative was to sell the short-term company, which included Gray Associates, an asset that had been in decline ever since his grandfather had bought the company. Brokers had been disinclined to support Security Fire and Accident when it owned a firm of insurance brokers who competed for their business.

HECTOR FORTESCUE-SMYTHE SPENT HALF an hour on the phone to his mother in England. His father had contracted Parkinson's disease and his mother now ran the company with the lawyer Hector had appointed as trustee. Only when the South African interests were concerned did Hector have anything to do with the family company. He was very concerned with the impending world revolution and the role that this would have him play in South Africa. He and the Reverend Andrew Porterstone had placed seven black priests in strategic positions within the Church of England in Southern Africa, and all seven were successfully preaching liberation theology to the black congregations, placing the horrors of apartheid in the perspective they deserved and drawing from the world community funds that would further the revolution. Carefully the men were drawing Caesar and God into the same camp. In public and in private, the black clergy sided with the black nationalist cause, which was firmly controlled by the communists. When the time came, the black nationalist movement would hand over South Africa into the Soviet camp.

The idea of controlling a major life insurance company with its vast investment assets appealed to Hector's real desire in life. Revolutions needed money. With care, through a controlling shareholding, he would be able to direct funds from policyholders' pension funds into the cause of world revolution. By the time the policyholders asked for their pensions, capitalism would have been abolished in South Africa and the assets of all life insurance companies, banks and mining houses nationalised. His mother's suggestion on the telephone had been made to benefit Smythe-Wilberforce. Hector saw a better use for the funds.

Security Life's problems had been brought to his attention by his father-in-law, who had no wish to see a South African asset fall into British hands. The subject had been mentioned to a colleague over dinner, neither of them considering Hector to be of any consequence in the discussion. 'Inconsequential Hector' was how Hector liked to be seen. Teddie Botha's father, the man who had married David Todd's youngest daughter and was a member of the Broederbond that Hector was still waiting to be asked to join, had approached the Afrikaner establishment on behalf of his son. Hector said nothing, not even smiling in the knowledge that his family owned sixteen per cent of Lion Life, purchased on his mother's recommendation following her earlier good impressions of Matthew Gray.

The day after his phone call with his mother, Hector took a day's leave from Armscor and went to see Edward Botha, having told him over the phone that his mother controlled sixteen per cent of Lion Life, something of which Matthew Gray was blissfully unaware, the shares being held by nominees. Hector had asked that the meeting take place in the strictest confidence. He would introduce himself as Mr Smythe at reception. Teddie would understand when he heard what Hector had in mind. Seven weeks after Hector concluded his business with Teddie Botha, by which time his mother had bought another four per cent of Lion Life on the London stock exchange, Hector called on Matthew in his new flat next to the Balalaika Hotel. Matthew thought the visit was purely a social one, and was happy to see his friend. Matt's visit to conduct an investigation at Cambridge still gave him the cold shivers for having made a fool of himself.

"How's Helena?" he asked, handing Hector a glass of beer.

"Oh, she hasn't changed. The latest is the tennis pro at the Inanda Club."

"Didn't know Inanda had a tennis pro."

"Neither did I. One of these days she'll get her name in the newspapers and then her daddy will not be pleased."

"And how is your esteemed father-in-law?"

"As bigoted as ever. I can talk to you, Matt. These bloody Dutchmen think they can herd the black man like so many cattle. Their policy of forced removal to tidy up the tribes is going to backfire. I believe firmly in white-man rule, but they keep shooting themselves in the foot."

"You tell that to your father-in-law?"

"You must be joking."

"You lead a strange life, Hector."

"Most people have unfaithful wives, and most people have jobs they'd rather not have. At least I have a job I enjoy."

"You still turned on by Helena's habits?"

"Funnily enough Matt, not anymore. I'd get a divorce if the honourable minister would refrain from putting me through the mincer and kicking me out of the country."

"You could always run Smythe-Wilberforce!"

"That's why I came to see you, Matt. We own twenty-one per cent of Security Holdings direct and another seven per cent through nominees, bought on the open market."

"I thought someone was bidding up the shares... Are you here to buy my Security shares or to offer yours?"

"Neither. Smythe-Wilberforce wants joint ownership of the company, with you as chief executive. You control the running of the business and we handle investment. Their expertise and experience exceeds your own, Matt. We own a unit trust in England through our merchant bank. They'll give you an even greater edge over your competitors. Your market techniques and their investment skills will make Security and Lion a world player."

"What has this to do with Lion?"

"Mother says we own twenty per cent of Lion. She was impressed with you, Matt. I told you so at the time. She thinks Security and Lion should merge to strengthen the Security balance sheet. You are aware of some potentially bad debts in their property portfolio?"

"Hector, how did you buy twenty-one per cent of Security away from the market?"

"Told Teddie I was a white knight. What I did not tell him was whose white knight. The lad wants to make a rights issue. Very commendable. Bright but young."

"And you tell me you're a socialist!" Matt was chuckling. The man was now a total enigma.

"Not me, Matt – mother. She's the brains. I just do what my mother tells me to do... Do you have any more beer?"

TEDDIE BOTHA CONTROLLED his breathing and tried to see straight. His adrenaline was pumping harder than it had at the Oxford versus Cambridge game at Twickenham. With a conscious effort he brought his temper under control. It was not the first time he had been swindled, he told himself and, most likely, it would not be the last. He processed different thought lines for half an hour and then put a call through to Matthew Gray at his office.

"Mister Gray, you and I have never met each other but my mother speaks fondly of you when she knew you as a small boy. I believe you owe the Todd family a favour."

"That was before your grandfather orchestrated my eviction from the insurance industry."

"But he bought your company."

"After he threatened to ruin me. I was upsetting the market, according to your grandfather."

"May I come and see you?"

"Of course."

"I'll be right across. They tell me you're back in your old office in Rissik Street."

"I try not to be over-confident, Teddie. If my takeover fails, I will launch Lion into the South African market."

"But you don't have a trading licence and government refuses to issue any more."

It was obvious to Matt that the boy had played rugby on the wing. Short, stocky and very fast. He stood up to shake hands, towering over Teddie Botha, who showed no reaction to Matt's size.

"You set him up, of course." Teddie's temper was beginning to rise, despite his breathing exercises outside the door.

"No, I did not."

"You're a liar, Gray."

"Either Matt or Mister Gray. That English habit of surnames I find rude. They must have anglicised you at Oxford."

"They did not."

Matt sat back behind his desk. "You want to sit down. The one mistake a lot of people. make in this world is underestimating the Brits." Matt deliberately chose the word used by the Afrikaner when referring to the English.

"You're a Brit."

"Now there you are very wrong. I'm South African, born and bred. Your mother also had a British surname. Teddie, Edward, Mister Botha—whatever you prefer. Please sit down. I don't yet have a secretary but I do make a good cup of coffee... There is always a way out of a problem that is satisfactory to all, and the compromise is often better than you think.

"First, we should both know never to trust Hector Fortescue-Smythe. Not only did he buy your shares under false pretences, but his mother bought twenty per cent of Lion Life on the open market, registered in nominees so I was unable to see who really owned a fifth of my company. Smythe-Wilberforce want a Security-Lion merger, which has its attractions for your policyholders and saves me from opening offices throughout this country. They will have joint control with me, unless you and I enter into a private consortium agreement very much unbeknown to our friend Hector... You have a great future. The education I never had. I have the experience. Together we can become a major force in the world insurance industry.

"What I have in mind is a conservative agreement which ensures that you and I are obliged to offer our shares to each other first if we wish to sell. There will be equal voting rights in the consortium, with the committee chairman having a casting vote. For the first five years I will be chairman, then we will rotate control of the consortium annually. I am a lot older than you are so, if you are patient, your time will come. I do not have children, nor a woman I would like to be their mother. If we fight each other, the public will be made aware of the weaknesses in your balance sheet before the problem can be corrected. A merger is the right thing for your policyholders, and in my business they always come first. Now will you sit down and let me make us a cup of coffee."

When the placated young man left his office with an earnest handshake, Matt sat back in his swivel chair, picking at a loose button in the arm. He had tracked down his old chair and desk and bought them back, giving in their place to the astonished owners a brand new chair and a brand new desk. They were the first furniture he had bought for Gray Associates, and Matt was sentimental.

He was nearly thirty-nine and, in the calm of not running a company, only speaking to Archie on the phone every day, he had had time to appraise his private life, his lack of wife and children. What he was, rather than who he was, got him dates. Girls went for his money and power, and they were more often the wrong type, young ladies on the way up or looking for the wine and roses for the rest of their lives. They were pretty, accommodating ladies after his money.

Sunny had said she loved him and bedded another man when his back was turned. Sandy de Freitas had never been one to wait for potential to mature. Chelsea had been a question of convenience for both of them. She had the body and he had the job. Idly, he started analysing some of the others, coming to the same conclusion. Good looking, easy women after his money, or what rubbing shoulders with his money would bring to them materially.

He looked at his watch. It was too early to go to the Balalaika and there was no one he wanted to take out to dinner. He missed Archie and Lucky.

On the banks of the Zambezi River, while Matt was contemplating the emptiness of his social life, Aldo Calucci had found tracks that were not made by animals. The client had been left at the Land Rover while Aldo ranged out looking for the spoor of the kudu that was all that was left on the American's licence.

Mashinga had been right. The reputed army of Joshua Nkomo, said to be training in Zambia under Russian command, had crossed the river. The spoor he was looking at, six distinct prints of army boots had been moulded in Soviet Russia.

Glancing across the two hundred metres to his Land Rover where the American was sitting comfortably, waiting to be taken to his kill, Aldo followed the spoor towards the river. Within ten metres the tracks petered out suddenly, replaced by skilful brushwork from a broom made of acacia thorn. Someone had been careless, though the brushwork told Aldo without doubt that he had crossed the tracks of a terrorist incursion.

It had been a little over five years since Ian Smith had declared the colony independent of British rule. With his .375 hunting rifle wrapped over his shoulder, hanging comfortably, Aldo skilfully followed the brushwork to its source. Very carefully he dug with his hands in the soft river sand. It was not necessary for Aldo to open the long box wrapped professionally in oilskin to know that inside were Russian-made automatic rifles. The long arm of the communists had finally reached into his valley and the peace of his life was shattered.

"You found something?" called the American, making Aldo flinch. He was one of those more unpleasant clients: rude, loud-mouthed and a lousy shot. All his trophies had been fired at simultaneously by Aldo.

"Nothing."

"Then what are you digging?" The man had damn good eyes.

"Thought I find crocodile eggs."

"Let's get a move on. Just sitting here's costing me three hundred dollars an hour. I want that kudu by lunch."

From a hill a kilometre away on the Zambian side of the big river, Luke Mbeki watched the hunter uncover the seventeenth cache he had placed in the Zambezi Valley.

"He's found the bloody guns," he said, in a mixture of Xhosa and English. "Now we'll have to take him out with his tracker. When the client leaves, we'll attack with knives and leave the bodies to the jackals. By the time someone makes a noise, the bodies will be bones and our tracks washed clean by the rains."

"And when he takes the client back to Salisbury, he will tell the police." The ZIPRA commissar was smug. He resented a Xhosa being in command of a company of Matabele. The Matabele were Zulu and hated the Xhosa, Mzilikazi, the founder of their nation, having deserted Shaka with his regiment and fought his way north, over the Limpopo River, to the land they now called Rhodesia.

Luke watched Aldo return to the Land Rover and continue the hunt. They heard the almost simultaneous crack of two rifles three hours later.

Leaving his client by the kill to admire his handiwork, Aldo went back to his vehicle and called up Mashinga on the field radio. It was the first time he had been able to get away from the American. They spoke briefly and, when the Land Rover returned to camp, Mashinga was ready to leave.

"We leaving for Salisbury now," Aldo told his client. "There's a big rain coming. You have plane to catch tomorrow night; we going out now before the road floods. You finished licence. Good hunt, hey. You very good shot. Not many clients shoot so good."

"Where do I stay tonight?"

"At Meikles Hotel. My expense. Now we go."

"What's the hurry?"

"The rains, my friend; they come quick, we go quick." As he drove down the track away from the river, a small patch in his back was burning, even with Mashinga sitting over the tailboard scanning the bush. Aldo wished the American would stop talking. Only when they reached the tarred road to Makuti did he relax. At Sinoia, he reported his find to the BSAP.

Well before dark, Luke heard the chopper and moved his men further back into Zambian territory. It took a stick of the Rhodesian Light Infantry half an hour to find the cache. Aldo's directions had been specific.

The following Monday, with his client safely back in the States and blissfully unaware that he himself had become the hunted, and at the same time that Matthew was moving into David Todd's old office as a result of his successful takeover bid, Aldo Calucci and Mashinga joined the Rhodesian army and returned to their valley. The bush war had begun on the Sunday night with sporadic attacks on isolated farmhouses throughout the rebel colony. Now he would hunt men, the most exciting of all-the game.

1971 WAS a boom year for South Africa and the economy grew at a faster rate than that of either Japan or America. The prices of gold and strategic minerals were high and the rains were good. New businesses were starting every day in Johannesburg, and skills poured into the country from an England trying to recover from a socialist government. This was a golden age of full employment with the economy dragging the blacks into the main-stream as the white population was not large enough to service the boom.

In London, the anti-apartheid movement met in crisis, having confined their work to stopping sporting ties with apartheid South Africa. Their conclusion was now to smash the South African economy with international trade sanctions. An impoverished black community would be more easily controlled by the ANC and its communist party ally.

Hector did not attend the meeting, preferring to orchestrate the hate campaign from an adjacent house, away from the eyes of the public. Revolutions were never started on full stomachs. The South African blacks would have to starve to gain their freedom... what was life without freedom? What was life under colonialism? What was life under apartheid?

The slogans were fed to the hungrily receptive media, and in America the shouts turned to screams as the politicians skilfully turned the wrath of the Negro away from his own slum to castigate the five million whites in South Africa who had created the only African economy after Rhodesia that worked. One-man dictatorships to the north of Rhodesia joined the battle of words, feeding the hatred and turning their own people away from their own decline into self-inflicted poverty. From the Arabs to New York, from Cairo to Lusaka, from Vietnam to Cuba, the politicians screamed at the last vestige of colonialism and Hector hugged himself with excitement.

MATT MET Margaret Weeks at the launch of the first Lion Life product in South Africa. She was twenty-nine years old, with red hair, grey eyes touched with yellow streaks the colour of a male lion, and the walk of a dancer. The grey-yellow eyes had the look of a predator, coupled with the innocent smile of an angel. Her sexual attributes were not outstanding, but two other factors made her appear different to men. The first of these was her cunningly disguised desire to have whatever she wanted in life, which she generally accomplished with keen intelligence and the innocent smile which made her look as though butter wouldn't melt in her mouth. The second was the wealth of her father. The two were possibly not unconnected.

CB Weeks was one of three rand billionaires in South Africa, and he controlled a large mining and industrial empire founded by his father in the nineteenth century. Margaret's grandfather Jack had been a personal friend of Cecil John Rhodes, the founder of Rhodesia and the Rhodes scholarship. At the time of Rhodes' premature death, grandpa Jack picked up the loose ends of the De Beers empire and made them his own, leaving his wealth and responsibilities to his only son in 1923. CB Weeks had avoided the pitfalls of the stock-market crash in 1929 and by the time Matt met his daughter and only child, had increased the family wealth considerably. CB Weeks and his mining conglomerate had only two problems in September 1971: the age of CB who had married late in life and his lack of a son to carry on the empire.

Margaret Weeks ran her own public relations company, using her family and social contacts to further the aims of clients lucky enough to secure her services. A company could not just approach Margaret to act as their PR, but had to be approached. Ever since Matthew Gray had come from nowhere, as it seemed to most people in South Africa, to take over the third largest insurance company in the country, CB Weeks had been following his fortunes. When Margaret made her approach to Security Lion Holdings, she did so, on her father's instructions.

When she finally shook hands with Matt, she had already decided to be his wife and knew as much about him as he knew about himself. She gave him the angel smile, and began a carefully prepared conversation in subtle praise of Matt himself, his person and his achievements. She knew that men rarely fail to respond to charm and admiration and she tried hard to persuade Matt to talk about his career himself. But Matt, in such circumstances, portrayed the strong, silent type. He appeared relatively uninterested and taciturn, and she could elicit little response from him.

Margaret lay in bed that night wide awake and quite perplexed. She was either losing her touch, which she doubted, or there was something wrong with Matthew Gray. If it had only been her father's wishes she might have sought ways to cut him off publicly, but in any case to find a man who did not respond to her charms was a challenge. A little boredom had crept into Margaret's life, which Matthew was going to remove.

Later in the week, she phoned him and asked him to lunch. She arrived dressed exquisitely, in a long patterned dress; she knew well enough that revealing clothes did not suit her. Far better, she thought, for a girl who was not angelically formed to keep the man guessing rather than make it obvious that she was no Miss South Africa. Discreet covering was her policy.

"I really appreciate our relationship together, Matt," she began, over lunch. "You're the sort of man whose company I'd enjoy on social occasions."

Matt smiled and shook his head. "Let me put your mind at rest," he suggested. "I have a list of rules in my business, and Rule 7 says: no staff or business associates. We didn't have the rule in London, and it worked out badly."

"Then perhaps I had better resign your account."

"Margaret, what's this all about?" he asked, eyebrows slightly raised in surprise.

"I wouldn't want business to stand in the way of our developing a better relationship," she replied, letting a tinge of sadness come into her eyes.

"Running a business is rather a lonely life most of the time – don't you find it that way? There are times when I'd just love to be able to relax and know my associates as more than just business people. I've met too many men at parties who are just out for a good time, and I really feel the need to bridge the gap sometimes. I like to find a middle-of-the-road course between strict business and high living. Don't you ever get fed up with girls who are just after you for your money or your body, and then, when they've had enough, dump you and find somebody else?"

This touched a raw nerve in Matt, as it was meant to do. He had no idea that Margaret had uncovered some of his past history. He nodded.

"I suppose you're right," he responded after a moment's reflection.

"I prefer parties to be a little different," Margaret continued. "Good fun but a little more, well perhaps intellectual is the wrong word. I'm holding one this Saturday night, actually. Many young girls about my age will be there – secretaries business people, models and so on. The Inanda set which Lucky Kuchinski has been trying to break into for months. Bring him along with Archie – that is, if I can persuade you to join us. You'll all have a lot of fun, I'll guarantee. How do they like being back in Africa?"

"We work well as a team," replied Matt abstractedly, as he led himself to the conclusion that a party held by a business associate was a different matter from a private relationship.

"In more ways than one." Margaret was folding her napkin and pushing back her chair. "Now I must be off. Lovely lunch Matt. We'll be seeing you." She gave him one last smile and walked away through the tables without turning back.

Matt wasn't quite sure just how interested in him she really was, which was just as Margaret had intended. He gradually came to the conclusion that she really did fancy him but, as she had not imposed herself on him at all, it would be safe for him to proceed with caution. The attraction of meeting the Inanda set at Miss Weeks' party was an incentive he could not bring himself to refuse.

"Can't be after my money, though," he said to himself as he signed the bill. "Not in her family. That's for sure."

It was a finely-tuned public relations exercise and, by the end of 1971, Margaret and Matt had been photographed at the polo in Inanda, the Nico Malan theatre in Cape Town and Beverly Hills Hotel at Umhlanga Rocks in Durban, along with the monotonous series of charity functions designed to prove the rich were caring. CB Weeks waited hopefully for a wedding announcement but was careful not even to suggest that Matt would be ideal to succeed him at Wits Mining, as he was aware of the touchiness of a self- made man, having suffered his father for years while he was learning the business.

Matt was comfortable with Margaret, in and out of bed, although she did not allow him to bed her until they were engaged, and only occasionally after that. This was not because of any higher moral standards than any other girls who had had their dubious effect on Matt's life, but simply because she dared not run the risk of satiating Matt before the marriage and having it possibly fall through.

Matt's interest in her was, however, tinged with another reality. The fact that he was nearing the dreaded forties gave him the shudders. There was only one thing he did not wish to do, and that was to grow old. He was not in love with her in the way that he thought he had been in love with Sandy de Freitas; he did not love her as he had certainly loved Sunny Tupper; he was not even physically compatible with her as he had been with Chelsea de la Cruz; but he was comfortable, and it was comfort he prescribed for a man of thirty-nine on the brink, as he thought, of old age.

Christmas came and went, and business had never been better, the 1969 dip in the stock exchange having given way to a raging bull market. He needed a wife and children to complete his life and if, by the age of thirty-nine going on forty, he had not found his soul mate, what made him think he would find her in the future? The great love was not to be his, and he could not afford to wait any longer. In the whole affair he was the last to think of marriage but, when it was put to him by Margaret that she was turning thirty soon and wanted children, she struck the right chord of sympathy, and Matt agreed to a winter wedding when the midday weather on the highveld was invariably sunny and hopefully warm. In that way they would be able to go to Europe in the summer for their honeymoon, Matt fancying the Scottish Highlands when the whin was in full bloom.

Lucky and Archie were horrified, but agreed to toss a coin to see which one of them would be the best man. Finally, despite Matt thinking that Johannesburg would be the venue for the wedding, St George's Cathedral in Cape Town was booked, and the dean of Cape Town, the Reverend Andrew Porterstone, was asked and agreed to marry the couple. Many of Margaret's charities included the assistance of Andrew Porterstone, a man tipped shortly to return to England to be made a bishop in the Church of England.

Surprisingly, Andrew Porterstone was unable to recollect his journey by air with Matt as, when he had mentioned to Hector that he had met a Matthew Gray on the plane, Hector had told him to keep away from the man, refusing to give any kind of reason. Matt had started apologising for not following up on their conversation, saying he had still to be christened.

"Maybe you can join your first-born in the font," Andrew said jovially, still feigning not to remember their long conversation in the aircraft.

The President Hotel was booked for the reception, CB Weeks not wanting five hundred guests ruining his lawn, and the invitations were sent all round the world. Very deliberately, Margaret warned her press contacts not to speculate on her future husband joining the mining industry. She would only have a real hold over Matt when she had borne him his children.

Ben Munroe was now back in the United States, following popular trends as usual by producing virulent articles in violent opposition to the Vietnam war. The news of South Africa's proposed 'wedding of the year' reached his office in New York.

Altogether, Ben had sold four articles on South Africa, but none of them had been about Matt after that first and most successful. Friends close to the civil rights movement asked him to drop the Gray-Mbeki connection, saying that Luke's life could be in jeopardy from the bureau of state security still run by Minister Kloss with Germanic efficiency. But the big establishment society wedding was too much for Ben to resist, and he booked himself and his camera on a flight to Johannesburg, determined this time really to show up the wealth of the whites in contrast to the poverty of the blacks who, he considered, were slaves in everything but name, paid a pittance to work all day, travelled four hours to and from work to live in shacks that leaked and to eat pap and beans.

With all the right credentials from his friends in the American civil rights movement, after assuring them that Luke Mbeki would not come into his article, Ben and his camera were whisked round Soweto, Johannesburg's 'South-Western Township', the worst parts; Guguletu, the worst parts; and the wastelands of the Transkei interior to where tens of thousands of blacks had been forcibly removed so they would lose their South African citizenship in the great apartheid plan of separate, independent homelands for the tribes of South Africa. He was, of course, not shown the better areas of the townships where the rich black people lived in palatial homes. Those were quite irrelevant. The emphasis was entirely on the squalor, the poverty and the inadequacy of the sewage, electricity and water supplies. Ben, rightly, was horrified, indignant and utterly disgusted, so that when he filmed Matt's new palatial home-to-be in Sandhurst, the best suburb in Johannesburg, along with the bride's father's homes in Johannesburg, Cape Town, Durban and Zululand, all of which he was forced to photograph from the air, he was ready to write the most scathing article of his career. *Newsweek,* always happy to bash the whites in Africa, paid him a large sum for his trouble and featured on their front cover the jailed leader of the African National Congress, Nelson Mandela, imprisoned on Robben Island, just across the water from the President Hotel where he was staying in Cape Town. When the magazine article was published a month before the wedding, it caused an indignant stir right across the world. Matthew Gray and CB Weeks were thought of by the world as examples of the twentieth-century's worst kind of exploiters, worse than the cotton barons of nineteenth-century America, who were thought to have had at least some kind of charm.

WHEN MATT FINISHED READING the article, he felt sick to his stomach. Then, a week before the wedding, a newspaper owned by a mining house that constantly competed with CB Weeks broke what they claimed was the real story behind the wedding. Margaret, like all women, had had to confide in someone, gloating to her best friend about the prospect of fulfilling her father's most ardent wish to find him a successor whom she could control, keeping Wits Mining in the Weeks family for a third and, hopefully, fourth generation. Her best friend was a very good friend of Helena Kloss, and the two always confided in each other, both being equally unfaithful to their husbands. Helena asked her friend to repeat the story all over again, this time making a recording her friend knew nothing about... Helena had a long memory, and men who spurned Helena Fortescue-Smythe, nee Kloss, invariably paid a bitter price.

Twice in a month, Matt felt utterly nauseated. The truth always rings clearly in the ears when it is stripped of the music. The following day, not to be left out and lose circulation, the rest of the press corps revealed that they had been asked not to publish the fact that CB Weeks had found himself a successor that his daughter would be able to control. With the prospect of a take-over of Security Lion and top management for Wits Mining, both sets of shares rocketed on the Johannesburg stock exchange... CB Weeks refused to comment, Margaret also refused to comment, but Matthew Gray was nowhere to be found by the press, by Archie or by Margaret. No one knew where he was.

The terrible possibility of being stood up four days before her wedding caused Margaret great anguish. The hours went by and no one, not even the police, could tell her what had happened to her fiancé. For three long days, there was silence. Margaret and CB Weeks did not know whether to cancel the wedding or wait for Matt to come out of hiding. They did not even know what the man was thinking, or whether he was hiding from them or the press.

When Matt finally called his press conference, he had the full, undivided attention of the world's media. Four networks beamed the event live around the world. Amid the full splendour of the house that was no longer destined to be his family home, Matt sat stern-faced and uttered not a word.

His lawyer stood up and spoke into forty-three microphones, reading the statement that Matt had spent three days composing.

"My client, Matthew Gray, has today resigned from the boards of all his companies in South Africa, England, Canada, Australia and Hong Kong. My client has today broken his engagement with Margaret Weeks, and guests and friends are notified that the wedding will not take place tomorrow at St George's Cathedral. He requests that the food be taken to Guguletu and given to the poor. Following is my client's statement:

'It is the right of labour to withhold their labour. It is the right of capital to go where it finds the best return. It is the right of the press to tell the truth. It is the right of man to choose his religion. It is the right of man to be free. It is also the right of management to withhold their management, and today I have exercised that right.

'It appears that the world considers my creation of wealth to have been a sin against humanity; that I and my companies are parasites, feeding off the poverty of the people rather than giving them jobs and creating wealth to lift this country from the degradation of poverty. It was that which was my intention, but I am told that not only have I failed to give the others what I never had myself but that also, by inference from the press, I have achieved the opposite, adding to the misery of the mass of our people, I must consider my peers. Not everyone can be wrong and I the only one in the right.

'I have therefore signed documents, irrevocable documents, that return my wealth to the people I am supposed to have injured. This includes all shares registered in my name, trusts controlled by me for my portions of those trusts, all property and material goods. As I sit before you now, my net worth stands at five thousand rand, which I intend to use to get me as far away as is physically possible from this life that is apparently so wrong. The proceeds of my wealth will be distributed equally and evenly to every man, woman and child in this country who does not have the legal vote. It will be paid out through a leading bank against presentation of the hated pass book. It will feed every family in South Africa and the homelands for one day, after distribution costs have been deducted by the bank. Bon appétit.'

"My client is not prepared to answer questions, now or in the future. He thanks you for your time."

A month later, when the press had finally given up looking for Matthew Gray, Archie received a hand-written letter through his lawyer, dated a month earlier.

---

*Dear Archie*

*The only regret I have is in severing my friendship with you and Lucky, friendships I consider the best thing that happened to me since my father died at Tobruk. There is in place a consortium agreement with Teddie Botha which gives him first refusal on my Security Lion shares, some of which he will be able to afford, but not enough to retain control. I suggest you talk to him, you and Lucky, to join forces to control the company for the benefit of policyholders. He will make a superb CEO in a few years' time.*

*As you read this letter, I am not dead, suicide not being my style. I have decided to go away and live a different life, but I will always remember our friendship. Give my regards to Lucky.*

*Your old friend, Matt.*

---

A week after Archie gave up the hope that Matt would return to his office, he approached Teddie Botha and together they purchased enough of Matt's shares to keep control of the company. The shares having dropped a third of their value following Matt's precipitous conference. For Archie, the fun had gone out of business and much of his life. Matthew had been the pivot around which all of them had revolved.

But there would be life after Matthew Gray, for himself and Security Lion. Ordinary people and life itself, he told himself, always went on. Lucky had gone off on a monumental binge and he, Archibald Fletcher-Wood, ex-Congo mercenary and sometime playboy, had been left to run a multi-million empire. Gratefully, he handed over the responsibility to Teddie Botha. In the same week, Margaret announced her engagement to one of the Inanda set, and Wits Mining shares picked up a little of their losses. The fiancé was an accountant with a legal degree who had been one of the world's permanent students, finally coming out of varsity at the age of twenty-eight. CB Weeks would groom him well.

IN LUSAKA, Luke pondered the hurt of his friend, before throwing the pain on the pile alongside all the other problems of the struggle. He had enough problems of his own trying to kick the white farmers out of Rhodesia.

IN SCOTLAND, where the whin was in full bloom, a rich buttercup-yellow, the earl of Lothianmore cursed his luck and the stupidity of his relations. "He's thrown away all that money that would have saved the family. If he wanted to give it away, why in hell did he not give it to me instead of a bunch of niggers. I'm his flesh and blood, for God's sake."

He and his family were now living in five rooms, damp, cold, wet rooms built five hundred years earlier for sturdier men of Lothianmore, and the National Trust was doing its best with the rest of the pile of stones. The grounds had shrunk to twenty-one hectares, which they had turned into a fun park for day trippers.

SUNNY TUPPER, back in England after a bad marriage to the owner of the 450SLC Mercedes, cried for what should have been and cursed her own stupidity. She was thirty-three, her looks were fading, and she was bored with flitting from man to man. Above all else, she knew how Matt was feeling and for a brief moment of hope thought he would contact her that he was running away to her. The days passed and nothing happened. Nothing ever happened any more.

BACK IN AMERICA, Ben Munroe finally achieved what he had been aiming for: a staff job at *Newsweek*, the security he craved along with the chance to travel the world at someone else's expense. He had arrived, and he rejoiced each day at his success.

AT JAN SMUTS AIRPORT, Johannesburg, another celebration was taking place. Hector was seeing off his friend and fellow-revolutionary, the Very Reverend Andrew Porterstone, bishop-designate, the two dedicated communists enjoying fully the irony of the situation. Andrew was to become a major force in the anti-apartheid movement from his new base in the slums of north London. The black priests who would take over the Church of the Province of Southern Africa were firmly in place and the people in Moscow considered Andrew more valuable in London, helping to orchestrate the destruction of the South African economy through trade and financial sanctions. The two friends shook hands warmly, looking deeply into each other's eyes.

"We're going to win," said Hector.

"I know," said Andrew, smiling the jovial smile that was becoming so well known around the world. "And may God bless you all," he said, turning to the press and the television cameras. He had given his well-prepared speech about the horrors of apartheid, so now he could walk out and step aboard his plane. The warm feeling of success coursed through the blood in his veins, and it was better than any artificial stimulant known to man.

When the revolution came, the world would hold hands in the name of communism, not in the name of God. There would be government by the people, for the people, and he would be among the illustrious few to control the mechanism of the totalitarian, all-embracing world government. At last there would be peace on earth and goodwill to all men, as anyone wanting it any other way would be eliminated.

IN PRETORIA, the capital of apartheid South Africa, while Luke was breathing real meaning into his slogan 'one settler, one bullet' in the northwest corner of Rhodesia, Minister Kloss was coining another phase that would galvanise the whites of South Africa: "Total onslaught."

His bureau of state security understood the minds of those who fermented the black revolution. They knew that without the total onslaught of communism there would be no military threat from Angola to Mozambique, from South West Africa to Rhodesia, and he determined no quarter should be given in order to maintain civilised government. If the West did not know what was being done to it in the name of anti-colonialism and anti-apartheid, then he did, and the surrogate armies of Moscow were not going to be allowed to destroy the calm and order of white-ruled Africa.

He knew that, without the white man in Africa, without colonisation, there would not be even a vestige of wealth in the subcontinent. That Africa, left to its warring tribes, would reduce itself once again to poverty, famine and anarchy. He also knew that, without apartheid, the separate development of the races, there would not be a white left in Africa. It had never been the whites' intention, as they trekked through Africa, to adopt the lifestyle of the blacks, to reduce themselves to the lifestyle of savages who had not even invented the wheel. The genes of white and black were as different as a mud hut and an air-conditioned brick house, and the Afrikaner *volk* had no wish to live in mud huts. The *volk* would fight for the civilisation they had created. The youth of the country would be called up into the armies. Armscor would be instructed to develop weapons suitable for bush warfare.

The rest of the world, blinded by their hedonistic lifestyles built on borrowed money, could go to the hell they deserved for bending their knee to the manipulations of communism. The *volk* had fought the British Empire at the height of its power for three long years, and they would fight whoever now sought to take away their land. Every able-bodied man between the ages of eighteen and twenty-five who had not done his national service would be called up into the defence force. The mailed fist of law and order would prevail. If the world and communism wanted it otherwise, Minister Kloss told his colleagues in the cabinet, they would have to buy every Afrikaner. Once before the British had failed, despite their concentration camps and a million troops fighting twenty thousand Boers. With their Bibles and their rifles, they would defeat the powers of evil.

. . .

THE LAST THING Teddie Botha expected when he opened his private mail at the end of the winter, and the last thing he needed, was a request from the state president to attend a training camp at Voortrekker Hoogte. He was twenty-four years old and had previously avoided the draft by being at university. Without thinking much of the problem – he and Archie had as many as they could handle – he dictated a letter to the authorities explaining who he was and thought nothing more of it. He had been surprised that the government letter required him to report in three weeks' time. He instructed his secretary to register the letter.

Five weeks later, two men in uniform, wearing red caps and funereal expressions, pushed past his secretary into his office. Teddie looked up into the cold eyes of a sergeant of the military police.

"Are you Edward Todd Botha?"

"Yes," replied Teddie, the moisture drying in his mouth as quickly as if he had looked up a tree into the eyes of a leopard.

"You will come with us."

"But ..."

"Man, you want me to pick you out of that fancy chair." The sergeant moved to go round his desk, and Teddie sprang to his feet in alarm.

"What the hell's going on here?" demanded Archie, coming into the room at the secretary's request. "Who the hell are you two?"

"This man is a deserter."

"Don't be bloody silly. Do you know who he is?"

"Edward Todd Botha. And he's under arrest." He put a hand under Teddie's elbow, and Archie watched his new CEO being marched out of his office. Appalled, he sat down in Teddie's chair. The nightmare had returned.

"Are you now the managing director?" asked Teddie's secretary with a smile, as she returned to the office. "Can I get you some coffee? Mister Botha has a meeting at two-thirty and another at four. If we start now, I can brief you on the meetings. The sergeant said Mister Botha will be away for two years and three months. Something about Mister Botha being in the stockade for the first three months." The girl looked ready to burst with suppressed laughter.

Archie began to laugh, and the secretary joined him. There was nothing else for him to do. Then he sat and waited for his coffee, his mind a blank.

Finally, he thought carefully about his predicament. He had got Archie and Lucky out of the Congo, even with a gunshot wound in Archie's leg. He would get them through this one until some sanity returned to life.

Where the hell was Matthew, and why did that bitch have to come into Matt's life?

He chuckled again for a moment. Teddie in the glass house.

Then he put a call through to the bureau of state security and spoke to Minister Kloss. They had met each other through Hector and Helena. The man was brief and rather curt. Had his own problems, probably. The minister would see what he could do about the three months detention. Nothing else. Two years would be a long time for both of them. Where the hell was Matt?

THEY HAD MADE Aldo Calucci a lieutenant and put him in charge of seven men skilled in the ways of the bush. One of them was Mashinga, Sergeant Mashinga of the Rhodesian African Rifles. Aldo they had commissioned into the Rhodesian Light Infantry, a white regiment. The rest of his men were from the RAR, all of them Shangaans and none of them friends of the Matabele.

The rains had broken a week earlier, coming late, at the beginning of November, and the tsetse and mosquito in the Zambezi Valley concentrated on the one white man, despite the dye that made him look as dark as his troopers.

They all stank, as the smell of soap travelled far in the bush and the men were at war. They had succeeded in finding seven of the ZIPRA arms caches and in each case moved further down the valley before giving the helicopters the co-ordinates. Silently, the arms had been removed and taken back to base camp at Karoi, one hundred and fifty kilometres away in the heart of the white tobacco-growing area. All the rifles, grenade launchers and land mines were of Russian origin, given to the liberation movements to promote the just and glorious struggle. The older arms dumps were more difficult to find as the bush had grown over to cover the small traces of man's disturbances, but the arms would last a hundred years, lethal and giving power to their owners.

Aldo's men camped without fire and moved with the greatest caution, having many times cut the spoor of the guerrillas sent into the valley to track the trackers who were destroying their work. Every gun had to be carried into the valley through many kilometres of hot, dangerous and fly-infested country. Luke and Aldo with their men, circled each other, laying ambushes and moving on, living off the bush, eating rats and snakes, roots and berries, one day hunter, one day hunted, man hunting beast, lion hunting man, buffalo watching from the thorn thickets, leopard from the tall acacia trees, honey badgers, small and vicious, from the disused holes of ant bears, vultures circling for week-old carrion, eagles high on the wind seeing and telling no one, the valley deadly, beautiful and cruel. For three months they circled each other, never making contact. Chelsea, back in Lusaka, was certain her man was dead. The silent war of the bush.

CHARTERHOUSE SCHOOL HAD BEEN like a prison for Jonathan Holland, and he was determined that no son of his would ever be subjected to an English boarding school. The food had been lousy, the heating inadequate, the toilet facilities feudal, and the discipline and traditions something he could well have done without. Whoever it was who said that school days were the best years of a man's life needed his head read. Leaving England was a way of getting as far as possible from his school days, none of which had been enjoyable, not even the holidays, as these gave way to another term at school and another round of the popularity stakes. If you didn't curry up to the right people, you were as good as dead.

Jonathan was an average kind of boy, though Charterhouse led him to believe that he was some kind of a freak for not playing soccer, preferring rugby football, and not thinking that athletics and running round and round a track was the height of a boy's achievement, instead of a pain in the butt. Jonathan preferred tennis. This was a form of exertion which didn't include pain. Tennis was a pleasure; house runs and the mile round the track were agony, and Jonathan Holland unwisely said so, thereby receiving the cold shoulder from the boys and masters alike.

Worse still, he liked the theatre and the annual school play, the Shakespeare the boys were studying for 0-level that year. Jonathan was a romantic, and romantics were thoroughly disliked at public school. His housemaster had even told his mother that he did not think her son was going to amount to much in life, and everyone, including Jonathan with his imposed inferiority complex, had been surprised at his obtaining seven 0-levels and two A- levels. These were good enough to get him into Oxford in those days had he wished to go, but the thought of more of the same way of life gave him the silent screams. If they did not like him, then he did not like them, and he would go away and find another country that did not require a man to be popular to get on. There was one thing Jonathan disliked even more than Charterhouse: arse-creepers. The place had been full of them.

So, in 1972, Jonathan Holland, eighteen years old and with the dew of youth still wet on his face, arrived at Salisbury airport with the determination to become a tobacco farmer and wear a wide-brimmed hat. Everything about Africa fascinated him, including the whiff of war and fighting a losing cause. Anything, but anything, was better than going up to the city of London every day for the rest of his life and sitting behind a desk.

His mother had been happy for him that his father's company was still there to train him for a top position, despite the family's small percentage of shares. Matthew Gray had kept his word and, if the man had not disappeared into thin air, Jonathan knew he would have been frog-marched into the dull, dreary and depressing world of the insurance industry. But a man took his chances when he saw them and, leaving his mother a note that would break her heart, he bought a return ticket to Rhodesia to prevent them from sending him back at Salisbury airport. With the six hundred dollars left from his savings, he entered the country of his dreams, ostensibly as a visitor.

Knowing that his money was going to have to last a long time, he took the bus into Salisbury and bought himself a copy of the *Rhodesia Herald*. There were three rooms to let, and he walked into the foyer of the new Meikles Hotel where he was relieved to see a strong contingent of well-tanned men in shorts and bush shirts who had obviously left their wide brimmed hats in their trucks outside. Explaining to a very nice lady at reception that he had just arrived in the country and did not have enough money to stay in the hotel, he asked to use the phone. Instead of treating him like a lunatic, having seen plenty of Jonathans in her time, the girl took his newspaper with the rooms marked with a cross and left him standing alone with his one suitcase. In between her job she made three calls and came back to him with a big smile on her face.

"You're in luck. Missus Rankin has a room in her flat, and the block's nice and just up the road. You won't need a car to come into town and she sounded very nice. Her son is in the army, which is why she's let the room. The last lodger also got his call-up papers. You English?"

"Yes, from Surrey. Do you know Surrey?"

"Born in the Vumba. That's near Umtali. You can leave your case with me and walk up to Second Street to Missus Rankin. I've written down the address. Your first visit to Rhodesia?"

"My second."

"If you like the room, then you can come back for your suitcase. Safe as houses with me. My name's Jennifer, but they all call me Jen."

"Jonathan Holland. Thanks, Jen; you're a gem." They both laughed at his weak pun, and Jonathan handed over his suitcase to a complete stranger, keeping his passport and money in his jacket pocket. The tweed jacket felt much too hot for February in Rhodesia. He had forgotten the seasons were about-face in the southern hemisphere. With the jacket over his shoulder, he walked out into the sun. The great adventure of life had begun, and he had never felt happier.

Mrs Rankin was as nice as Jennifer and equally friendly, taking only a week's rent in advance and demanding no deposit. "If we like each other, you pay me every week, but I am sure you and I won't have problems. You remind me of my son. He's in the valley. You'd better go back and fetch your suitcase. Here's the key. Have a beer in the Captain's Cabin. Beers are good in Rhodesia... Welcome to the best country in the world. If you want anything, you ask me. You'll be all right. There's a bar lunch in the Captain's Cabin that's cheap. You can use my kitchen but don't make a mess. Don't do meals, as the ladies like their independence. We're a very independent lot in Rhodesia."

James Bell, known as Ding-dong to some of his friends, sat at the bar in the Captain's Cabin, mentally scratching his head. He had tried farming three times, selling cars once, insurance for a week, and had gone out into the Urungwe prospecting for gold and anything else he could find to make him rich.

He was twenty years old and been out from Scotland for two years and three months. It had taken him four months to realise that the last farmer was not going to pay him a bonus when the tobacco crop was in. He had been paid fifty dollars a month as a learner assistant, but the farmer charged him Salisbury prices for eggs, milk and vegetables that were produced on the farm. They had parted enemies in the middle of the reaping season, leaving James to walk halfway to Salisbury before he could cadge a lift. With men like that, he was not going to build up capital to buy his own farm in his lifetime, and James hated working for other people.

When Jonathan walked into the Captain's Cabin to have a beer and his first lunch in Rhodesia, James was fresh out of ideas. If he could not make a fortune in Rhodesia, there was nothing left but to jump into the Makabusi River, float into the Zambezi and end up drowned in Beira. But fortune and six hundred dollars sat beside him at the next bar stool, though he was too busy looking into the bottom of his beer glass to notice.

Jonathan ate his lunch ravenously, large hunks of bread and cheese and pickled onions. Jonathan was particularly partial to pickled onions, something they had never heard of at Charterhouse. He was feeling on top of the world and wanted to share the joy and excitement. There was no one to his left and only a man of his own age next to him, the next two bar stools being empty. They were on a kind of an island of their own at the bar, and Jonathan felt a kinship with his neighbour in his new country. They were young men adrift in the heart of Africa, tough and resolute, and should be talking to each other.

"You mind if I buy you a beer?" asked Jonathan, brightly.

"You can drown me in the Makabusi for all I care."

"Oh dear. One of those days. Used to get them at school. Maybe a whisky?"

He heard his companion's Scottish accent, a well-educated accent but with a pleasant burr of the country to the north of England. James had not been able to afford a whisky for months, and came out of his depression to look at the bright-eyed and bushy-tailed young man next to him. It almost made him sick. How could anyone be so cheerful on a Monday? He had his mouth half open to say no when a flood of words broke over him and he was forced to shut it again.

"You must be Scottish. I'm Jonathan Holland. Mother says there's Scots blood somewhere in the family. Just arrived. Found a room already. What's the Makabusi? You been on a tobacco farm? You know an Italian called Aldo Calucci? What kind of whisky? Malt? Ice? Plain? Bet you drink it neat. Have a double. Never seen a sad Scotsman with a double Malt in his belly. What's your name?"

James began to laugh, a pleasant, warm laugh that made the men sitting at the table behind them look up from their drinks and smile. "Make it a double malt. No ice, no water. My name's James Bell, Ding-dong Bell, but I usually hit the people who call me that when I'm drunk. And I'm broke."

"Then I'll buy the drinks and you tell me all you know about Rhodesia, and when you're drunk I promise not to call you Ding-dong Bell. Maybe your knowledge and my six hundred can get us both on the right track."

James looked at Jonathan, then at the whisky, and shook his head. It would be far too easy. Innocence of such quality was far too rare.

An hour later, they were in Bretts, having left the stale atmosphere of the Captain's Cabin. Two hours later, they walked to Le Coq D'or and, when Mrs Rankin opened the door after midnight, the key-fumbling having roused her, she found two young men as drunk as fiddlers. Her lodger was singing his school song. She put them both to bed without a word of reprimand. She missed her son more than she had realised.

. . .

JONATHAN WOKE on his first morning in Rhodesia with a little man in the front of his head who was wielding a hammer and cold chisel. At first he had no idea where he was, or who was snoring in the next bed. For a horrible moment he thought he was back at boarding school, but the little man in his head was telling him otherwise.

"Morning, old boy."

"Where the hell was I last night?"

"You'd better tell me!"

A week later, when the capital was down to five hundred and sixty dollars and Jonathan had been finally dissuaded from going tobacco farming, having found out that none of the farmers had wide brimmed hats in their trucks, he thought the time had come to use his return ticket and that his life would be reduced to insurance and the 7.32 up to Waterloo.

His new friend was still sharing his room and he was still paying for everything himself, though the genes of his long-dead reinsurance-broker father were telling him that what he had learnt in a week from James was cheap at the price and a lot cheaper than going down the same road to nowhere. He would have a long holiday, building up memories, and then go back and dig himself a rut for the rest of his life. The excitement of Matthew Gray and Aldo Calucci had vanished with the men, as the phone just rang at the game farm on the banks of the Zambezi and no one knew the whereabouts of the owner.

"It'll have to be joining the police or going back to England," he told James the following Monday, a sober, more realistic Monday. "And going into the police would be like going back to school. All that discipline."

"I have one idea," said James. "We can collect beer bottles and take them back to the breweries. They give two cents a bottle to whoever brings them back and most people just sling them in the dustbin. We need lots of blacks on bicycles going round the suburbs and bringing bottles back to us. We give them five cents a dozen, load up our truck and off to the breweries. How many bottles can we get on a truck?"

"I have no idea, Ding-dong, but it's probably the only chance I have of not ending up behind a desk."

"We'll have to buy the bicycles and hope they don't run off with them."

"That bit's wrong. They must supply their own bikes. They're in business for themselves like we are. Half for them, half for us. I buy the truck. They bring the bicycles. Cut out the chancers. I presume the breweries only take back bottles like that in truckloads."

"You sure you haven't been in business?" asked James.

"I used to sell stamps at school. During my first two years, Mother was rather short of money. The roof leaked in the house. The death duties cleaned us out. If it hadn't been for Matt, we'd still be broke. He just disappeared. No one's heard a word from him in nine months. Just dumped his millions and vanished. I really worry about him. You'd like Matthew Gray. Nearly two metres tall and had made his millions on his own."

"What made him go all funny?"

"I don't think he went funny. Just had enough of them. Rather like me at Charterhouse. He wanted to get as far away from them as possible. Probably in Hong Kong or deep in the Burmese jungle. First we go and see the breweries and get it in writing they'll buy back our bottles for ten cents a dozen. Then we look for a good truck. Just as well you can speak kitchen kaffir."

"Fanagalo sounds better. I like the blacks." On the way out, Jonathan paid Mrs Rankin another week's rent, adding fifty per cent extra for his friend.

Five months later, in July, Madge Holland received a letter from her son, informing her that he was not returning to England. He was carting bottles back to the local breweries and had gone into scrap metal, sending the rusty iron down by railcar loads to the Rhodesian iron and steel company at Redcliff where it was needed for the smelting process. With sanctions biting the Rhodesian economy badly, no one could afford to throw away anything that could be used again. They were going to buy a three-tonne truck and had employed a driver; Ding-dong was the best friend he had ever had, and they were going to make a fortune.

Madge smiled wryly, as she had not imagined the heir to the manor going into the scrap business. She cried a little and felt very sorry for herself. Then she looked at her options. She was forty-nine, had not even been out with a man since her husband had died, and the only thing left in her life was her son. The PS on the letter had been very simple: "Mum, why don't you come out? There's nothing left for you in England."

Even if he did not mean it, she would go and find out. She booked a flight on South African Airways, as British Airways were not allowed to fly to the rebel colony, and let the manor house on a year's lease. Life had not begun for her at forty. Maybe it would begin at fifty. Terrified at what she was doing, she told herself all the way to the airport that she had nothing to lose. As the plane prepared to take off for Africa, she thought of the tall man who had walked into their lives and started this odyssey. She was sure he was dead, poor man. How could the newspapers be allowed to tell such lies? To Madge Holland, Matthew Gray was one of the few good men she had ever met. Even AC Entwistle would agree with that. How could the man have been stealing from them for all those years? Her husband had trusted him. If it were not for Matthew Gray, they would all be destitute. She did not even feel the plane lift off the soil of England.

Six months after Madge Holland arrived in Rhodesia, Caetano of Portugal was overthrown and the Portuguese, no longer backed by the home government, were forced to run out of Mozambique and Angola, leaving behind Marxist states. The communists had reached the north eastern border of Rhodesia and, apart from the small border with South Africa, they had the country surrounded. Then the Americans were kicked out of Vietnam by the communists, and a flood of second-hand weaponry flooded into Africa from communist China, along with battle trained instructors.

South Africa, seeing the total onslaught reaching their borders, sent paramilitary police to Rhodesia to fight the communists. The bush war intensified, and at last the Smith government admitted that it was a war and not merely a series of sabotage attacks. The Rhodesians, drawing on their knowledge from the war in Malaya, the only war in which the communists were defeated by counter-insurgency forces, fought in the bush, hunting the terrorists like deadly game, fighting man against man. The kill rate rose to thirty to one, and the average life span of a guerrilla fighter, once inside Rhodesia, was ten days. Luke Mbeki wept for his men, and the Chinese and Russian instructors called for more recruits.

Promised the white man's farms, the white man's cars and the white man's jobs, a large number of the black youth of southern Africa responded to the drums of war. In Mozambique the great victory turned to civil war as Frelimo, the newly appointed government, took on Renamo, another political faction, who were backed by the Rhodesian government. In Angola, the civil war flared on three fronts after the MPLA, backed by Russia and their surrogate army of Cubans, seized power before there could be any such foolishness as a free and fair election by the people.

The war against the Portuguese had been about power, not about people. And the losing guerrilla movements of the FNLA and Unita, who had also fought the Portuguese, wanted their share of the spoils and appealed to South Africa for help. Within days, when the South African invasion reached the outskirts of Luanda, the Angolan capital, the Americans realised that it was madness to continue backing apartheid South Africa, even against their mortal enemy. The civil rights movement and the United Nations would have hounded them to hell.

South Africa withdrew under American pressure, and the vultures came lower. The whole of Africa, with all its strategic minerals and gold, was within the grasp of the Russians. In a frenzy of activity, they flooded arms into Ethiopia, Cuban troops into Angola, gave arms to Swapo in South African-controlled South West Africa, and forced Luke and the ZIPRA-ZANIA high command to commit thousands of young, inadequately trained troops to the Rhodesian slaughter, using the United Nations to howl in disgust when the Rhodesian army crossed international borders in hot pursuit.

Politically, the Russians stood very much higher than the Americans on the moral mountain of anti-colonialism and anti-white. While Teddie Botha was fighting his way back to South Africa in command of his tank, the Russian empire reached the zenith of its power, with its resources stretched to breaking point. The problem for the Russians with Africa and Far East Asia was that nothing came back in return. There was no financial reward, only political. The new nations of Africa and Asia, the new Marxist states, were run, by and large, by megalomaniacs disguised as statesmen, terrorists who would kill their mothers for power, disguised as presidents.

The peoples of Africa began to starve, and the vultures flew lower. The Western world said not a word, saving their rhetoric for the white pigs in Rhodesia and the neo-Nazis in South Africa. The white countries of Southern Africa became ruled by the police and the army. Laws were passed, giving them dictatorial powers. Southern Africa was in a state of military and economic war.

The only thing that had not turned against them was the weather. The rains were good. The crops grew. The people, buffeted on both sides, were able to feed themselves. It was said in Africa that you follow or lead, or get the hell out of the way. Most people chose to get out of the way.

# PART 3

# 1

At the artists' colony in Port St Johns, no one owned a television set or bought a newspaper. They were seven kilometres down the Wild Coast from the village of Port St Johns and they were generally self-sufficient in food and stimulants. Vegetables were grown, pigs ran in the limited coastal forest, and fish were taken from the sea.

The other essentials were paid for by selling their art, mostly rather bad art – it was the way of life that was more important – to the summer tourists who thought the long-haired, head-banded, kaftan-clad artists a real attraction. They bought the carved objects, the hand-beaten jewellery, hand-tooled leather and the canvases without frames for a small sum and either treasured them as holiday souvenirs or threw them in the trash can when they reached home. What they paid for was the atmosphere of peace and tranquillity in one of the last hippie colonies on earth.

The girls were mostly young, deeply tanned and without make-up, their bodies as they swam in the big, rolling breakers a picture of health. The home-made bikinis of soft leather added to the sensual attraction. The men were bearded, long-haired and well-muscled from manual labour. All had the look of serenity that had long since vanished from the civilised world. They were freaks who did not wish to hear of war. They smoked dagga which they grew themselves, freaking out in the warm sun and treading the soft white sand while listening to the waves. They were happy.

Among them was a tall man who looked to be in his early thirties. He was their leader, and it was said by some that he had found the colony by walking up the coast from Cape Town, the journey taking him nearly a year. His voice was soft, and the sun and sea had bleached the few traces of grey in his brown hair. His beard was long and wispy, and wound up under his chin. His eyes were a soft blue, and he was the only one in the colony who did not smoke dope.

If the tourists bought him a beer at the Vuya restaurant, the one commercial establishment with its store near the colony, he drank it with pleasure. If they bought him wine, he drank it with greater pleasure, and he always smiled with the crow's-feet of sun and pleasure etched into the deeply tanned part of his face, framed by the centrally parted hair and the full growth of beard. He wore colourful, home-made clothes and never wore shoes. The soles of his feet were rock hard, insulated alike against the hot sand of the day and the cold nights of winter. The only thing no one uncovered was his past. In the colony, no one cared.

Mark, as he called himself, built his own shack and introduced a water system for the colony, using the force of gravity to conduct water from the river higher up in the forest. He built a small distillery and made a white liquid that danced them high among the stars. He listened to their pains, if they had any, and encouraged their art. He was the father of the colony.

The Transkei was a product of apartheid, a self-governing homeland ruled by the Xhosa blacks. Mark had been with them for almost two years when he gave the artists' colony its first surprise. "I'm going to build a house," he said.

He had gone to the local chief and exercised his right to a hut site, choosing a place tucked into the cliff overlooking a beach of his own, where the tumbled oysters collected after a storm.

"You have to be born in the Transkei to be given a site," said one of them.

"I told the chief I was born in the Transkei."

"And he believed you?" Mark smiled, and the colony watched as the man cut into the cliff with pick and shovel to clear a level site for his permanent home. He had looked for a long time on his way up the coast for a place to live, and here he was going to stay.

It took him six months to cut into the earth and rock, making shelves of the rock formations and digging a reservoir for the rainwater he would collect from his roof. Then be built his one-roomed home from driftwood he had collected over the years. The house was in the shape of a rondavel, thatched with reeds, and had a view forever overlooking the oceans.

Nine metres below, the sea lapped or pounded depending on its mood.

Some days the sea was smooth and the sun sparkled on a million ripples. Some days it was rough, and rolled in thunderously to below his house in white-topped waves from a kilometre or more off-shore. Some days the gannets and skuas dived on the sardine shoals and the colony launched their boats and rowed out to the fish, Mark taking the big oars at the front of his boat. Some days it rained and squalled, and the Wild Coast earned its name. Apart from the tourists who bought him drinks no one came to Mark and whatever was in his mind he kept to himself. Away from the eyes of his friends he wrote, but the pages were never seen. He wrote carefully in a good, educated hand and locked the papers in a chest which was wedged between his shelves. The chest was his only secret and no one ever saw what was stored inside.

"What's in the chest, Mark?"

"My business." It was the only time anyone heard him come close to being rude.

LORNA ROSENZWEIG HAD a real talent which her mother and father refused to realise. She was nineteen, with an oval face and a rich olive skin that turned to dark brown in the sun, sometimes giving her problems in the summer when she boarded a bus in Cape Town where coloureds sat at the back. If they told her to, she sat in the back with the coloureds and often went there on her own if a seat was empty.

She painted in pastels, rich in colour. Her teacher at secondary school had taught her how to draw, and the pictures in her mind were easily transferred onto canvas. She was a happy child, happiest in the garden of her parents with her paint box and a sheet of white paper for canvas. When she left school, she wanted to go to the Michaelas Art School. Her father and mother disagreed, the rift in the family becoming close to violent.

Lorna was adamant that she was going to be a fauna artist. Her father was adamant that she was going to Cape Town University to study medicine like a good Jewish girl. One Thursday when her parents returned from work, she had gone, taking a small suitcase and leaving behind everything else she owned in the world. The note said she had gone to Israel to join a kibbutz. The note was untrue. She had gone to Port St Johns to the colony of artists. Her father searched a large part of Israel for his daughter without success, which was not surprising. His daughter had decided she was going to be a famous artist.

She had arrived at the colony in summer, so her skin was a rich brown all over, her hair bleached from rich brown to light brown, and only her blue eyes told of her Caucasian heritage. When he first saw her on the beach, walking step by gorgeous step, Mark saw the most beautiful girl in his life. She came across the soft white sand to him and dropped a towel down next to him. When her towel was straight, she sat down, stretching her long brown legs centimetres away from Mark's.

"Hi, I'm Lorna and I want to join your colony."

"I'm Mark."

"I know. Isn't this place just beautiful?" They sat together for some time looking out to sea. "You want to come for a swim?"

"Just watch the gully near those rocks. Current rips out to sea."

When they both dived into the waves at the point where the sea stopped them running any further, they were laughing.

From the edge of the beach, among the wild banana trees, Martin with the black beard remarked quietly to the lady with whom he shared his life, "Never heard him laugh before."

"About time he took a lady into his bed. At first I thought he was queer."

"Mark's not queer."

Mark's stride was twice that of Lorna's, and she had to hurry to keep up with his leisurely pace. They walked along the cliff-top in the early morning sun on their way to Third Beach. He had found her a room in a hut with a girl who made jewellery, and the first thing the girl had done was to plait Lorna's hair. To Mark she was his daughter, the one he had never had but always wanted.

A look at her paintings had stopped him putting her in with another painter. His mother had been a painter, and he recognised the real talent that Lorna's parents had failed to understand. Artistic jealousy was a vice Mark disliked and he avoided the problem whenever possible. The purpose of his life was to live in harmony and he carefully nurtured the peace and calm of his colony.

They reached Third Beach two hours after leaving the colony. The tide was out, leaving the rocks exposed for about three hundred metres, the same black colour, wet from the sea, as the mussels. There were myriads of black mussels and below them, just under the surface of the water, were the big slipper oysters that provided Mark with much of his nourishment.

They made a camp on the deserted beach, then Mark headed for the dry rocks and dropped into a gully. A bag was strapped to his side and, before submerging, he pulled down the goggles and took a long, deep breath. The crayfish scuttled out from under the big rock that he moved with ease, the sea water giving it buoyancy. Swiftly catching two, he came up for air. Lorna was bending over the rocks above his head, and was not wearing the top to her bikini.

Mark went down again with a new lungful of air and looked for the smiles of the oysters as they sucked in the sea, filtering the plankton with the gentle flow of the waves. He came up again with six big oysters, causing the girl standing watching him a metre away on the rocks to smile. Eight dives filled his bag, and he came ashore.

"Please, Lorna, put on a vest or something. I'm old enough to be your father."

"You can't be."

"Believe me."

"How old are you?"

"We've agreed to talk of the present," Mark insisted with a smile.

"Then why did you bring me here?"

"To enjoy the beach. To enjoy the crayfish cooked on a fire. To eat the freshest, bestest oysters in the world. To feel the sun on our bodies, to listen to the oyster catchers, the ones over there with red beaks. To watch the plovers and the gulls on the wind... Now, help me find some dry wood, and we'll make the fire and eat. I'm starving."

"Who are you really?"

"What you see, Lorna. As I am. There's nothing else."

She gave him a crooked look, one plait hanging. She had put on a T-shirt that had fallen in the sea.

"It's not going to work," she said.

"What?... You got the matches?"

"My being your daughter... What do you do all day?"

"There you go. Leave it alone and take what we have," insisted Mark, gently.

"That's what I want to do, you mug."

Mark, reduced to silence, gave his full attention to opening the oysters with his penknife. They were big and luscious, the big flesh of the oyster cradled in mother-of-pearl. From the back pack he had carried up the coast he took a lemon he had picked from the tree by the Vuya, cut it in half and squeezed two drops onto each open oyster where he had set them out on a rock.

"Bon appétit."

"Bon appétit." The brown nipples stood out through the white cloth of her T-shirt. He controlled the surge of passion. That side of his life was over; the years had seen to that. She was young enough to be his daughter, he told himself for the third time since getting out of the water.

It was a beautiful day.

Wherever he went she was there, watching him, smiling at him with a smile that told him he was being a fool. All day long and for most of the night, he thought of her. Everything he did related to Lorna, and in desperation he began to avoid the girl, finally taking his back pack and going down the coast on his own, sleeping in the open or in the sea caves that dotted the coast, trying each day to leave her behind.

The calm and peace of his life was shattered. It was ridiculous. He knew she was twenty-four years his junior and, if he did not look his age, it was due to the way of life, the diet, the sun, the exercise. Physically he was stronger than he had ever been, but he was forty-four years old and until now he knew he had never been in love.

He had often wondered what it was really like. Now he knew. All consuming, a total preoccupation, a permanent longing to be in her company. There was no fool like an old fool, and he lengthened his stride and walked on down the coast, his every heartbeat screaming with the pain. He wanted all of her. Mind, body and soul.

MARTIN with the black beard stood knee-deep in the lagoon, watching the mullet below the mirrored surface with deep concentration. The fig tree on the bank and white fluffy clouds was reflected far below the fish. Slowly he moved closer to his prey, his toes searching the bed of the lagoon, his throwing net ready for the lunge.

The weather had been bad for a week, and he was hungry. So were his cats, his woman and their dog. The dog was so quick that, when he walked with him into the village, the villagers said he was in the dirt bag before the local dogs had smelt the garbage. There were forty or more mullet in the shoal, lazily swimming around, unaware of the hungry eyes above the surface of the lagoon.

Martin stalked the fish for half an hour, and then he threw his net, sending it out in a perfect ring, the weights poised evenly to plunge into the water, dragging the net down over the fish. Gently, Martin pulled on the cord, drawing the net and pushing his catch to the back, making a long bag of the net with the mullet deep inside. The drawstring pulled the neck shut as he drew his catch out of the water, a writhing, silvery mass in the afternoon sun. From the shore, a pair of hands began to clap. Lorna had been watching from the time Martin had walked into the lagoon with his net.

"How many?" she called across the still water. She was sitting with her knees up under the fig-tree. As she spoke, a flock of green pigeons burst from above her and flew off swiftly up the river, away from the colony, towards the Xhosa village further up.

"Come and help me get them to the bank"

She came towards him, wading through the shallow water of the lagoon, disturbing the perfect reflection of the trees and the sky. She slipped in her excitement and, when she rose, reaching towards the net full of fish to help, Martin's loins surged with his own excitement, making him turn his body away. If Mark did not want the girl, every man in the colony, black, white and brown, lusted after her. She had no idea what effect she had on the men and, unless Mark did what she so obviously wanted him to do, there would be trouble. The men were hungry and the women jealous, and the girl had only been with them a month.

"Hold the net closed while I shorten the bag in the net... There we go. Keep it shut as I drag. Must be thirty big ones. We'll all eat tonight."

"I'm hungry."

"So am I," replied Martin, and not only for the fish. She would be less provocative if she wore no clothes at all.

By the time they had lugged the fish to the bank of the lagoon, the pigeons were back in the fig tree and Martin's body was under control. Together they carried the fish to his hut and the daggered eyes of his woman. Only Lorna had no idea of the problem she was causing. Lorna was in love, and nothing else came into focus. She saw nothing but Mark.

"May I take one up to Mark?"

"You do that," said the woman unkindly. 'And you can take it now."

"Thanks, Melissa. Isn't it a lovely day? Martin, you're so clever." The girl stretched and rose. Martin tried not to watch her walking away, but his eyes would not move from the cheeks of her buttocks pushing out of the kidskin leather of her bikini.

"You touch that girl and I'll chop it off" said his woman. The thought was better than a cold shower.

Sven was a tall, blond man who carved driftwood and had not been sure whether he preferred men or women until he saw Lorna. For the moment, as he covetously watched her walking across the beach to the Gap and Mark's rondavel, he was strongly heterosexual. If it were not for Mark's height and strength, he would have gone for the girl, whether she liked him or not. He had raped a boy once and nothing had come of it, the boy turning gay and doing what Sven wanted once he had broken him in. He watched her till she climbed between the rocks and started up the winding path through the wild banana trees to the big hut on its perch overlooking the cove.

"And I'll bet she's a virgin," he said to himself. "That kind of innocence has to be virgin."

Mark had seen her coming and gone out of the back of the house, running away from his problem. From the bushes above, he saw her put the fish in the box next to his door and leave. Then he came out of hiding and walked down to the cove for a swim. There were two closed oysters washed up on the small patch of sand. He picked them up, trying not to think of the girl, and walked back to his house. It had been the longest month of his life.

Sven watched her again, his desire mounting, only his fear of the giant in the hut above the cove stopping him from going out and bringing her back to his hut. It was dusk and no one would see.

Barbara, Baba the jewellery lady, was plump and rather pretty, and welcomed Lorna back to their hut with a proprietary smile, putting her arm round the girl, her hand hanging over the shoulder, her small plump fingers softly touching the brown skin in the V made by the girl's shirt.

"Baba, we've got a fish. Martin's so clever," she had called, and Baba had taken the fish and used the excuse to give the girl a hug, feeling the firm, big breasts against her own. It had been a long month for Baba the jewellery lady.

"Have a joint."

"You know I don't smoke, Baba."

"You can have a puff of mine."

"If it makes you happy. What do I do?"

"Just suck in, baby. Suck it in."

Lorna, all thumbs with the wet joint, did what she was told. "Hey. It's gone to my head."

"That's what it's meant to do."

"My brain feels so clear... shall we grill or fry the fish over the fire? There's still some rice and I took some herbs from Mark's herb garden. He really has green fingers."

"Can we talk about anything but Mark?" asked Barbara. "He's told you he's too old. I think he's gay. Never goes for the women."

"He can't be gay the way he looks at me," said Lorna confidently. "We'll do the fish on the braai and boil the rice and herbs... Baba, why do you look at me like that? Is something wrong?"

"Nothing, baby. Have another drag. Why don't you and I get high?" Lorna took a deep puff right down into her lungs, held it there as Baba had shown her, and let it out slowly.

"That's my baby. Come and sit next to me."

An hour and a half later, Lorna was as high as a kite, and the fish tasted better and the rice tasted better than any food she had ever eaten. Baba was just about to make her final ploy when Sven came to visit.

"I've got some moonshine. Want to share?"

"Sure," said Baba, thinking quickly. Maybe a threesome was what was wanted as the girl still kept moving away. "Have some grass. Let's have a party. I like your new shirt, Sven. Come and sit between us."

MARK HEARD the girl scream He had not been able to sleep and was sitting in a wooden chair he had made himself, enjoying the moon's gentle light, so colourless on the still Indian Ocean.

It had been three and a half years since he had been unable to sleep at night. The girl now invaded his dreams making him wake with a fierce hunger. He heard the scream again and turned his head into the soft wind of the hot summer night. He was naked, his long body stretched out in the moonlight. Twice he had been down to bathe in the sea, careful not to splash and attract the sharks. Sharks were more dangerous in the dark of the night. The wind puffed drying the last of the water on his body.

"Get your hands off me! Please! Please, Baba... Sven, I said no!" Then came another scream, this time of pain, and Mark ran down the path and onto the beach, fighting the sand in his frenzy of speed.

Baba the jewellery girl fled when she saw what was coming, but Sven was on top of Lorna, trying to penetrate her vagina, the membrane holding back on his lurching thrusts. She had twisted her hips and had bitten through his cheek, the blood sending Mark insane. He picked Sven off the girl with one hand and hit him with the other, breaking his jaw. The crack of bone was distinct in the night. Sven fell back across the hot ashes of the fire, spinning onto his face and pushing his stiff erection into the coals. He screamed and ran off over the beach for the sea, while Mark picked up the bloodied girl and carried her back across the sands. Lorna clung to him. Over to their right, Sven plunged his scorched genitals into the sea, still screaming.

"Are you hurt? Did he ...? The blood! You're covered in blood... You'll have to stay with me." He walked up the path and down to his cove, taking her with him in his arms into the water, deeper and deeper, washing her clean, gently dunking her in the ocean. Then he walked back to his rondavel and lowered her onto the big wooden bed he had built of driftwood, lighting a candle to look at her wounds. She was smiling at him, her face clean and innocent again.

"Make love to me, Mark. Please, it's the only way I'll be clean inside, if you love me." Very gently, using all the years of his experience, Mark consented.

Lying back with his girl in his arms, he could still see the moon washing the ocean, stars higher in the sky, the Southern Cross clean in the pattern of heaven. Then they slept, until the dawn woke the birds and they went back to the sea, naked happy and fulfilled. The great peace of arrival had finally come to the man.

CHELSEA DE LA CRUZ was lonely, frightened and pregnant. She loathed Lusaka. She had grown to hate the grasping people, both men and women, in the liberation movement, who warred with each other as often as they warred with the soldiers of Ian Smith.

She had never been accepted in all those years except in Luke's company. When he was away they left her alone fighting their own political battles that Chelsea found petty and personal. On the ground in Rhodesia, ZIPRA guerrillas of Joshua Nkomo, the father of the nation were fighting guerrillas of Robert Mugabe's ZANLA, killing more of each other than whites. The Patriotic Front was in disarray as the two liberation movements fought for the right to run Rhodesia without the other. Patronage was to be in the hands of one party.

Chelsea had gone off the pill six months earlier, desperate to cement her relationship with Luke. Her parents had been forced to flee Mozambique, not even taking the furniture. They wrote sad pathetic letters from Portugal, refugees too old to start again. Chelsea was sure that most of her parents' letters were being deliberately lost and all of them read before they reached the small, two-roomed flat that was home to her and Luke – when Luke was not fighting in the war that propaganda failed to convince her was going so well. There were too many new faces too few of the old.

She was twenty-five and relied on Luke for every cent she grudgingly spent. The movement paid her rent and gave her a monthly allowance that would stop the moment they killed her Luke. When she went for the money, her deep fear was to be told there was nothing for her. Men went missing, and then the money stopped. Even had she wished to leave Luke, she had no money to pay for her flight. She was trapped, and now she was pregnant. She longed for her days in Villancoulos, for her days in London.

After four months she was sure that Luke was dead, and at the end of the month she ran out of money. She would have to ask and then be told. Some times before now she had thought of writing to Matthew Gray, but now he was gone and probably dead. And, four months pregnant, no one else would look at her any longer.

She waited another two days with her misery, and then walked the dusty blocks to the offices of the ANC.

"Am I still on the list?"

"No one said take it off."

"Thank God for that. I'm pregnant."

"Are you now? I am sure comrade Mbeki is overjoyed."

"He doesn't know. Where is he? Will they talk to me in the office?"

The girl looked at her with sympathy, but there was nothing she could do.

"There's a war on. When we win the glorious victory."

Struggling to control her hatred, Chelsea forced herself not to tell the girl to stop talking propaganda. Judging by the situation in Mozambique, she and the rest of the people would be a lot worse off when the victory came and Russia stopped funding the ANC. A few would prosper, but not her Luke. He fought because he believed in the struggle, not to get a position of power and wealth. He believed in the cause and justice for the people, and he was a damned fool.

She kept back her tears until she was outside in the street. She had food for a month. She wiped her face dry. In Mozambique very few people had food for a month. And a month was a long time.

LUKE WAS NOT in the bush fighting the war, but back in Soweto, where cheap labour for the whites was supplied. Here the workers rose at five in the morning to fight their way onto the crowded trains that took them into the white man's city and the menial jobs that kept them alive. Luke was back at the heart of his own revolution, spending weeks fermenting unrest among his people and keeping out of the hands of the police, never sleeping in the same house for longer than three days. The police wanted Luke Mbeki, he knew that, and their powers did not require a warrant or even a trial. If they found him, they would put him in jail and kill him slowly. He knew all about the South African police.

The white people in South Africa were too powerful to be overthrown by a guerrilla army. The liberation movements were having enough trouble in Rhodesia with the white farmers and a white army that never exceeded three thousand in the field at any one time. And ZIPRA alone had committed ten thousand troops, deployed below Lake Kariba and around the Victoria Falls.

There was a new strategy and it would work in South Africa among the sprawling black townships, among the filth and poverty created by apartheid. They would make the townships ungovernable. The new comrades would compel the people to force the government to commit such atrocities that the world would crush apartheid. The children were to boycott the schools, refusing to be taught in Afrikaans. In June, the children and students would barricade the streets of Soweto, burning tyres and throwing petrol bombs at the police. They would set Soweto on fire, burning any building owned by the government. They would rise victorious from the rubble if it took them fifty years. They would tear down apartheid brick by brick.

One settler, one bullet. The great revolution was about to begin. Luke had not thought of Chelsea for over a month. There were other things on his mind.

THE SOWETO RIOTS WERE SHORT, violent and deadly, the police acting exactly as Luke had intended. They shot children in the streets, putting a ring of steel around the township while they crushed the unrest. The ANC had enough martyrs to last them for years and at last the world community took notice and the noose of trade sanctions tightened, helping significantly to impoverish the country.

The rage of hatred swept through the blacks of South Africa, and the ones that wanted to fight were channelled out of the country through Botswana to military training camps in Zambia, Tanzania, Russia, China and Cuba. Among the stench of burning tyres and burning flesh, Luke slipped out of the country. Black schooling had collapsed and two generations of children would find themselves without a proper education. Their elders in their wisdom and search for justice had impoverished them for ever.

AT THE TIME of the Soweto riots, Hector Fortescue-Smythe, the sleeper, warned Moscow that Armscor was about to explode an atomic device in the Namib Desert in South West Africa. The Russians let it be known in the

United States Senate, a US spy satellite picked up a flash, and every newspaper in the world reported the explosion. The screws of sanctions, flamed by Soweto, turned quick revolutions. The white apartheid government was put on the run and Swapo guerrillas were infiltrated from southern Angola into northern South West Africa, into Ovamboland. A second front had been opened against the white racists of Southern Africa.

WHEN CHELSEA OPENED the door to the flat, Luke was standing there well pleased with himself. He had been away for eight months.

Luke put a hand to her belly. "It will be a boy. We need lots of men for the struggle."

Chelsea felt sick. All he ever thought about was the struggle. She was breeding fodder for the white man's cannons and there was nothing she could do to stop it. This was the real world, a constant, bloody nightmare.

"How long are you home for, Luke?"

"Enough time to look after you and the baby."

"Are we going to be married?"

"Why not? Every boy has to be certain of his father ... we will have a big wedding to celebrate the start of the revolution. Invite all our friends. Comrade Nkomo will be our guest of honour. We will invite Comrade Tambo to come from London. You are so beautiful Chelsea. Let us go to our bed and make love."

"It won't hurt the baby?"

"I would never hurt my son."

FRIKKIE SWART WAS USHERED into the office of the minister in charge of state security. To Frikkie, Minister Kloss appeared remarkably calm considering the political circumstances. The man looked as if he had just played a relaxed game of golf and that Soweto riots and atomic bombs never entered his head. He looked the perfect example of confidence, a man in control, a man enjoying his power.

Since rising to the number three position in the South African embassy in London, Frikkie had served the ministry of foreign affairs in four countries before finding himself posted to the bureau of state security. He preferred diplomacy to spying, but a government employee did what he was told to do. He handed the file to the minister and stood to attention while it was read, needing the comfort of the door behind his back.

"The sod's been using me," Frikkie said in Afrikaans. The minister looked away from the file and out of his window in the Union Building at the beautifully kept lawns and gardens three storeys down below. The sun was shining, the sky cloudless; it was a typical day on the highveld. "Have him arrested fast. I don't care about his British passport." The minister nodded his head and Frikkie made for the door.

"Are you married?" the minister asked just before he disappeared from view.

"No, sir."

"That's a good thing."

When Frikkie shut the minister's door carefully, he had no idea why his lack of a wife was a good thing. The fact was that he knew it was a disadvantage in his career, but women intimidated Frikkie Swart. He preferred a book of rules and the regulations to go by.

HECTOR WAS a whole day ahead of his father-in-law, and when the police arrived at his nice house in Sandown (he had preferred living in Johannesburg rather than Pretoria) he was long gone, having crossed the Botswana border on his way to Gaborone and a plane to London, quite satisfied with a job well done. The missile and nuclear programme had been far too dangerous to allow it to come to fruition. He was looking forward to joining Andrew Porterstone in the anti-apartheid movement and had even thought of standing for parliament. He had some good friends in the British labour party, all of them reporting ultimately to Moscow.

HELENA'S BABY-BLUE eyes were full of the tears of frustration. For fourteen years she was sure that she had been deceiving Hector, and all that time he had been using her. She required no prompting from her father, and instituted divorce proceedings immediately. She was going to screw him for every Smythe-Wilberforce penny he possessed and live the rest of her life in luxury without the interference of a husband. She hated him. She had always hated him. He had just made her affairs so much more convenient.

Back in England and visiting the Cedars, a house his father had not visited for two years – which suited Hector as he disliked scenes with his father – Hector was totally relaxed for the first time since receiving his instructions from his controller in Green Park so many years earlier.

"She won't sue you for any money?" asked his mother.

"It'll cost her father his job."

"Never underestimate a scorned woman," she warned him.

"She was only using me."

"That is my point. Once the divorce is through, you had better find yourself a proper wife. I want some grandchildren."

"I'm nearly forty," Hector replied with an air of resignation.

"Then find yourself a young wife."

"Yes, Mother."

"That's my boy. Have a biscuit with your sherry."

The day after Helena instituted divorce proceedings, her father received a brown envelope containing photographs and a list that ran to eleven pages. Four of the men on the list were his friends and contemporaries. The list read like a who's who in Pretoria.

The girl's appetite had been prodigious. Hector had clearly been only too well aware of his wife's adultery. Looking at the photographs, Minister Kloss found his own daughter disgusting. She was an embarrassment to him and the country. He thought carefully for a moment.

"Are you free for dinner, Mister Swart? Tonight at my house... I want you to meet my daughter. Her husband, as you know, has run away. A traitor to this country. You have not met Helena?"

"I have not had the pleasure."

The unintentional double meaning that could have been inferred from Swart's innocent response went unnoticed by the minister. "Then you shall tonight," he replied. "She is deeply shocked by her husband's desertion, you understand."

Half an hour later, the minister visited his daughter and showed her the photographs. Even she was surprised.

"How the hell did he ...?"

"Your husband works for the Russians. You were had, Helena, in more ways than one. Now I want your word that a quiet divorce and a new marriage, this time arranged by me and not the communists, will lead to your complete discretion." The minister spoke with grim determination, making it clear that his decision was not to be opposed.

"Who is he?"

"Come to dinner with your mother and me tonight. The man will do exactly as he is told. You are thirty-three years old. Have some children. Grow up, Helena, before you ruin your life."

"I hate Hector."

"So do I. So do I."

. . .

ARCHIE FLETCHER-WOOD WAS SO tired that he could scream. That morning there were twelve notes on the pad next to his bed, and each one represented a period of broken sleep. He had tried alcohol and sleeping pills, but both had made him feel worse the following day, and every day there were more and still more decisions to be made.

He had begun to curse the day he had ever met Matthew Gray. He wished the damned Kruger Rands of Lobengula had stayed in the jungle, lost for another seventy years. He was one year off fifty, and if he did not get off the spinning wheel he would die. Lucky had done the clever thing by refusing to go on the board, leaving him to train the sales force and come and go as he wished.

Archie was finally at the end of his tether. This time Teddie Botha was not going to put him off with a holiday and assurances of how much he was needed. This time he was going to resign and find himself a place in the country. Get a housekeeper to look after him. And sleep. When he reached Teddie Botha's office, there was no doubt in his mind.

"Arch. You can't; I've just been called up for three months. There's shit in South West. The Cubans are pouring troops into Angola. You'll be on your own again, I'm afraid. You look terrible. Why don't you take the day off and go and have some sleep?"

"Because I can't sleep, goddammit! This bloody job and this bloody company have got me so I can't goddam sleep. No one makes any decisions on their bloody own. They bloody well wait for me or you."

"That's my point. Go down to the cottage at Umhlanga Rocks till the end of the week. I have to report to my unit on Monday."

"Why the hell did Matt...?"

"I don't know. He was your friend, not mine. And don't even think of doing a Matthew Gray. The staff and policyholders can't have two directors leaving them in the lurch. If we want to own something, Archie, we have to be responsible. Ownership and position carry great responsibilities in this life. There is always a price to pay. For myself, I prefer to run things. And so do you... why, you're so good at it. And you are, Archie. You did a bloody good job for two years on your own, and together we run a first-class company. Our figures are second only to the Old Mutual. Look on the bright side."

"But I can't sleep."

"Sea air and Umhlanga. That'll do the trick. Now, are we or are we not going to expand the life company into Australia, despite not being allowed to own controlling interest?"

"Keep out of Australia," advised Archie, somewhat tartly. "Place is run by socialists. Socialists are only good at borrowing money. They leave someone else to pay it back."

"Are you serious? No to Australia?"

"Totally bloody serious. Now can I go to sleep?"

"I'm sorry about the army, Arch."

"Then stop laughing." Teddie kept looking at him with a grin until Archie laughed.

"I'll look at what's on your desk," Teddie agreed.

"Thanks, Teddie."

"And remember; there's no pleasure without pain."

"My mother told me that ever since I was six."

"And she was right."

NO ONE in the colony took Carel van Tonder seriously, which was exactly as he wanted. He was the buffoon, the butt of jokes, the poet who wrote crazy words in both official languages, whether they were read in English or Afrikaans it made no difference. The whole lot of them were gibberish. He was one of the first to move into the old huts that were meant to have been for tourists but in which even the hardened visitors who came down to fish the big Cape salmon refused to stay, as the roofs leaked when it rained, the water when it did actually flow through the rusty old taps was brown, and there was no electricity. The only advantage was the setting, up on the hills overlooking Second Beach, with a clear view down the sands to the Gap over the top of two deserted houses with roofs that had once been green.

A black man had been sold the property with fourteen huts when Transkei received its independence, when people who were white in the Transkei were forced to sell their properties. What happened was that the apartheid government in Pretoria gave the white owner the market price for his property and gave it to the Transkei government for redistribution to black Transkeians at a fraction of the original price.

It was grand apartheid at its best, as in exchange all blacks who were Xhosa, wherever they lived, were made citizens of the Transkei, could vote in the Transkei and own property there. It was the political way of getting them out of South Africa, while physically keeping their labour. It was one of man's more twisted inventions, and it did not work from whichever angle it was viewed. Even the blacks who received the white houses did not have enough income to maintain their political gifts, and the holiday houses of an earlier era fell into disrepair, which suited the purpose of Carel van Tonder.

Carel encouraged the idea of an artists' colony and urged the black man to rent his huts to down-and-out whites for very low monthly rentals that were still greater than the man was earning at a tourist camp for fishermen. The artists put some effort into restoring the huts and making them habitable, and when Mark arrived a water system was restored. It had been a puzzle to Carel how Mark knew from where to draw water when he and others had searched for a fresh water supply without success. Mark even found pipes that had been used before, and all within a week of moving into one of the huts. Carel was sure there was more to Mark than Mark was prepared to say. They were most likely both of them fugitives from the law.

Carel owned the only motorised transport in the colony, an old bakkie with which he spent hours tinkering and which became the butt of a string of jokes. But what Mark and the rest of them did not know was that the engine was new, along with all the other working parts. Just the exhaust had been holed to sound terrible and there were stones in the hub caps. When he went off to write his great incomprehensible poems, everyone laughed again. He said he covered his costs by bringing back vegetables that he sold in the village to the stores, bringing back a few cabbages for the colony to eat.

But it was not the cabbages that made Carel his money but the dagga hidden beneath. Carel was the centre of a sophisticated ring that slipped dagga out of the Transkei to the markets of the world. Seventeen kilometres past Third Beach, at the end of a goat track, stood a thatched hut, inhabited by an old, sleepy black man whose job it was, on the appointed night, to shine his torch out to sea. The Transkei coast was a darling for smugglers as the Transkei government did not own a navy. It had not crossed the mind of a single person in the colony of Port St Johns that Carel van Tonder was anything but a mildly eccentric fool.

But they were wrong. Mark had followed his tracks and found the hut and the old man, and identified the contents of the black bags stored in the huts. Mark had shrugged. Everyone had something to hide. Who was he to care? But he did watch Carel van Tonder with new respect. Then Lorna had come into his life, and everything else had flown out of the window.

The two of them would have remained ignorant of each other if the Transkei, an independent country so far as Pretoria was concerned, had not allowed gambling under their laws, which were different from those of the Republic of South Africa, where anti-gambling laws were strictly enforced. People in the colony came and went, drifters most of them, attracted to a lazy life and cheap 'pot'. Mark and Carel were different. They intended to stay, Carel at least until his cut of the export crop, laundered for him into property in Florida – specifically Fort Lauderdale where there was a number of South Africans in the yachting industry – was sufficient for him to attain a new identity and live the life of a rich man for the rest of his life. Wealth and happiness were synonymous to Carel.

Watching Mark look so happy in a loincloth, a tall staff in hand and a catch bag for oysters and crayfish, Carel decided it was a facade. The man was running away. It was not possible for such an individual to be happy living like a hippie. A man needed a smart house, swimming pool, a big car, air conditioning and, above all, the great sophistication of civilisation. Mark and the rest of the colony were only one step up from the blacks, better organised but still living a hand-to-mouth existence that often left them cold and hungry. And if any of them became sick, they did not have a cent to pay the doctor. When they were too old for manual work, they had better get themselves washed out to sea for the sharks. No, a man only had one life, and the good life was in Fort Lauderdale among the rich, not in Port St Johns among a bunch of drifters who smoked grass. The irony of his dislike was totally lost on Carel van Tonder.

At the end of August, two men arrived in a car that put Carel's bakkie to shame and, when they stepped out and walked down to the beach, they were very excited, pointing to the features of natural beauty: the Gap with its great chunk of cliff half-fallen into the sea, the long white beach, palm-fringed, with sand so soft that it squeaked when walked upon by bare feet, the blue-green, turquoise-white roller perfection of the sea, and the rolling hills that gave everyone a view of heaven on earth in a climate that was only cold at night during the winter. It was the perfect spot for a luxury gambling resort, with the port of St Johns reopened so that the river estuary could be made into a vast yacht basin for the rich. The tarred road from Umtata had to be completed and the sand bar removed from the estuary of the river, but the ultimate paradise was there to be taken.

Mark, happier than at any time in his life, was on the beach with Lorna when the dark-suited men came down, intent on changing everything.

"Hi! You guys live there? Isn't this place something? Can you imagine what it would be like with a luxury hotel, cabanas, a casino, yacht marina, golf course and an airport? This place would come alive. And if those people in Umtata take what we offer, it'll all happen."

Mark and Lorna looked up at the men in horror, Mark thinking faster than he had done for years. One of the men was concentrating his attention on Lorna, who was sunbathing topless. It was a perfect day in August without a wind and the Wild Coast sea was as gentle as a lamb, making a lapping sound as it licked the shore among the sea-snails looking for their food and the sand-pipers scuttling backwards and forwards with the ebb and flow of the Indian Ocean.

"Wouldn't work, I'm afraid," said Mark to the other man, who was only slightly less interested in Lorna. "No fresh water."

"We'll build a dam."

"No catchment area for a hundred and sixty kilometres. The big holiday resort idea has been tried here more than once, and fails every time for lack of water."

"Where do you get yours?" The man did not like being put off by a long- haired hippie with a red headband who had no idea of business or how to make real money. "There'll be good jobs for all of you."

"We don't want jobs," said Lorna.

Mark answered the question. "There's a river pool that fills up slowly in the hills that gives us what we need, but water can never be wasted. Enough for twenty families."

"What do you know about developments?" asked the second man rudely. Lorna had turned on her stomach. "If you throw enough money at anything, the problem goes away."

Mark shrugged his shoulders. "Who's the developer?"

"We put a project together and sell it to the institutions. Create an investment opportunity. The insurance companies have millions to invest every day, and they can't invest outside South Africa Exchange control. The yields on the stock exchange are less than two per cent."

"Water, my friend. Don't forget to tell the investors about water. Because if you don't, someone else will. The huts behind you are an example of a development that went wrong. Those two houses at the end of the beach with the green roofs have fallen down. You had better look somewhere else."

"How long have you been here?"

Mark opened his mouth, shut it and smiled. "Long enough to know about the water problem."

Carel had come up, seen Mark's hesitation and wondered for the first time what the man looked like without the beard. Mark had not been overawed by the city men with a big car, and had tried to chase them off. A small crowd from the colony had gathered, and now they watched the men walk back to their car.

"You think they will?" asked someone. No one answered, and slowly everyone but Carel drifted back to his or her business.

"You and I may need to talk." said Mark.

"What about?" asked Carel.

"Black bags under cabbages for one thing. You had better have your people keep watch on those men. Get the registration of the car."

"I don't know what you are talking about."

"Have it your own way." shrugged Mark casually.

THERE WAS no moon that night and, when the old black man went out of the hut twenty-seven kilometres down the coast from Third Beach to have a pee, he looked up from his ablution to see a ship anchored out to sea, the silhouettes visible to his trained eyes. He took his time and went back into the hut for his torch. The Baas had only brought twenty black bags, but the ship had come a month early, sitting where it was on the sea in exactly the right position.

He walked slowly down the goat path where the boats and the dassies kept the short, wind-lashed grass even shorter, to the cliff-top where a gentle slope enabled the men from the small boat that would come ashore to load the black bags and take them out to the ship. On the beach, in the lee of the tall cliff, the small beach was pitch black, and if the sea had been anything else but dead calm he would not have heard the voices down below.

Quickly, he walked back without shining his torch. The police were waiting, but the boat would not come ashore unless he shone his light. Taking the few possessions that he treasured on his old back, he moved off down the cliff path in the direction leading away from his hut, which he was sure the police were going to burn to the ground.

After five minutes and a few hundred metres, he was forced to stop and put down his load. He was a very old man; his wife had died and his children gone to work on the gold mines, forgetting their elderly father. All he had in the world were the few things that he put on the ground, the old thatched hut and the little food the Baas brought him to shine his torch out to sea and make sure the black bags were kept dry. Now they were going to burn his hut, and the tears ran down the old, craggy face and splashed unseen on the ground, the ground where his ancestors had ruled so long ago, when the cattle were fat and the people had not gone away to the city of gold, Johannesburg.

He sat down next to his cooking pot, his fighting stick and the two old blankets. Where was he going? For an old black man without a tribe and without his children, there was nowhere to go. He was very lonely. Why had life given him so little? He pulled the blankets over his old, skinny legs and his old, skinny shoulders, and turned his eyes back towards the small beach and the men who would come up and burn his hut and let him die all alone on the cliff. Maybe the wind would blow his bones into the howling sea.

First, the light out to sea caught his eye. It was flashing. Then he saw the flashing light from the beach below his old hut and he knew it was not the police. All night with the blankets keeping him warm, he heard the men unloading the boats that came in from the sea to the beach. In the darkest part of the night, the ship's engines got under way and the boats stopped coming in to the shore. Half an hour later, the voices stopped, but the old man stayed in the comfort of his blankets and waited for the dawn.

Then he walked back to his hut and, when he looked down on the beach, the tide was in, washing the sand clean of the footprints. He lit his cooking fire and let the new sun warm the chill from his bones. The gods had been good to him. The evil had gone away, and an old man could sit in the sun for another day and remember the days of his youth when the body was strong, his wife was alive and beautiful, and the sound of his children came up from the shore.

Three days before the wedding in Lusaka, Luke was called back into the bush to arbitrate between the ZIPRA and ZANLA commanders in the field, to stop them from fighting each other. Chelsea was left alone to have the baby.

She had persuaded Luke to buy her a gold chain as a wedding gift. She returned it to the jeweller and said that comrade Mbeki wanted his money back and would choose another present when he returned from the bush. With the money, she took a bus to Lubumbashi in Zaire. The papers she showed the border guard were covered in official ANC and ZIPRA stamps. It was enough, as the border guards were unable to read. Then she walked into the Portuguese consulate and told them her story.

When Luke came back from his successful meetings in the bush, his woman had gone. There was no note. No one knew. Nothing. Luke sat in the one big chair in the flat and for the first time questioned the worth of it all. He was sick of people squabbling for petty power. He was sick of the Russians dictating his every move. He began to question in his mind the sincerity of some of the leaders in the liberation movements. And now Chelsea had run away with his child.

He sat for a long time with his memories and his fears and, when the child in him found its way back to the peace and gentleness of Port St Johns, there was a great yearning in his soul to run away, to leave them all to fight the battles that were growing progressively further from the ideals of liberating the people and progressively nearer to the grandiosity of individuals who wanted to be kings. Luke Mbeki had the terrible feeling that once again he was being exploited.

"I want to go and look for my woman," he said to the commissar that afternoon.

"Women who run away are never worth finding. You work for the struggle, comrade Mbeki. Don't forget. Without the struggle you have nothing. Anyway, she was not one of us."

They stared at each other for a few moments, and then Luke looked down and left the office. He took a car from the pool and drove out into the bush. He had to think. He had to renew his faith.

THE BLACK CAR returned to Second Beach the following week. Mark was walking back to his hut with a small orange tree he had been given by a tourist.

"You want a beer?" the man in the suit called from the stoep of the thatched Vuya restaurant that overlooked the beach.

"Thanks why not? You back again... I'll have a Castle. My name's Mark."

"We know. We believe you are the unofficial head of the colony. We want you to give us some help."

"Not me. I'll drink your beer but that's as far as it goes."

"People seem to think you were born here."

"That's very nice."

"Otherwise you wouldn't have been given a hut site."

"Very observant."

"And you know the local paramount chief, which is why you are left to your own devices. My name is Jake, and these are some of the people who wish to invest their money."

"What do you want for the price of a beer?"

"To know why you have warned the paramount chief against our development."

"I've told you. No water."

"One way or the other, water can be supplied if the casino can make enough money. We think it can. Why don't you join us as a consultant to make sure the local environment is looked after? That's what you want. We'll pay you well."

Mark began to laugh, a good, strong belly laugh. "Money. We don't need money. Cheers. The beer's nice and cold."

Another man leant across the wrought-iron white table. "Hi, I'm Bernard Strover from Security Lion. We're putting up the money. You must have heard of Security Lion. We're second only to the Old Mutual."

"Never heard of you, I'm afraid."

"You lived in the bush a long time?"

"All my life. Which is why I like it here as it is."

"A bit primitive."

"We're very happy, Mister Strover. That's what counts. The new world has a habit of taking away happiness. We find a life without television and newspapers more to our taste."

"You not heard of the Soweto riots?"

"No. No, we haven't."

"You really are bush-happy. Have another beer. The company pays."

"I'd like that… Lorna," he called. "Come and join these nice men. They're buying free drinks and they don't even have to pay for them. You see, I want our kid to grow up in harmony, not strife. You keep your riots and your casino."

"But not our beers," said Bernard Strover,

"Especially not when you can put it on your expense account. How long have you been with the company?"

"Three years. We're about the fastest-growing major company in South Africa."

"How nice for you. Just be sure to tell them there's no water, or they might find growth a little slower."

"Why not join us for lunch and a bottle of wine?"

"My pleasure. Lorna told me only this morning she is going to have a baby." Under the table he squeezed her hand. He was so happy that at this moment anybody could be his friend.

Luke had taken food and water for a week. He had driven far, to the banks of the Kafue River where he camped under a tall acacia tree, hanging his mosquito net from a branch of the tree. His genes as a black man may have helped him from contracting malaria, but he was allergic to the bites. The clouds were building up daily, the prelude to the start of the rains, and it was hot and humid. The rains would come within weeks.

For a while he had cried silently, remembering the girl who had made the harsh reality of his life a little softer. The hugs and smiles. The gentle talk. Sanity away from all the killing and hate. He was getting old and tired, and the permanent fighting, bickering, arguing and making of points had worn him down. And it all had to end. Smith was still in power and South Africa was still the ruler of grand apartheid.

He was not even sure about Zambia. The government had naively flooded the world market with copper, having nationalised the great copper mines that had been the financial strength of the old federation of the Rhodesias and Nyasaland. Instead of bringing the great wealth Kenneth Kaunda had expected for his people, the price of copper had crashed; the Japanese were miniaturising everything and the need for copper continued to drop sharply. Kaunda had driven the whites off their farms and given the land back to the people, but there were so many more people, and the men who went back to the land had forgotten how to farm and they grew enough only for themselves. Food for the first time had had to be imported into Zambia where the rains were good and the soil so fertile.

The white civil service had been told to go back to England and patronage, favours for political support, had replaced the competent whites with incompetent blacks who treated their jobs as a sinecure, doing little work and earning their salaries by supporting the one-party Marxist state. The funds left in the national bank by the British had gone, and UNIP, the people's party was borrowing money to feed the people. The Russians were giving them guns and money to fight Smith, and the army of Nkomo was the big source of revenue for Zambia, but the crops were small and the copper mines bankrupt. There was no single place in Africa to which he could point that was doing better.

The standard of living in post-colonial Africa was dropping and the Boers were laughing at them; even the killings in Soweto had made not one of them change his ways. And Smith under mandatory world sanctions was doing better economically than any country to his north. The commissars told the bush soldiers a very different story, but Luke knew these stories were lies. He read the papers in England. He saw the flourishing white farms in Rhodesia. He even understood how the money was made in South Africa. And it all came down to the need for good management.

Luke swam in the river, keeping a lookout for crocodiles and watching the weaver birds building furiously in the reeds, hanging their nests above the floodwater line. Kudu came down to drink in the evening, and lions roared. The tension subsided but the sadness stayed, the pain of loss, the hopelessness of knowing that he had lost his own child and wondering who was going to look after his boy.

He thought of his alternatives one by one, discarding them all. He was part of the struggle, for better or for worse, and the struggle was dangerous for those who tried to swim against the current. He had made his choice many years ago when the police had almost beaten him to death for visiting his friend. Thinking back, making himself think back, the hatred boiled; hatred generated by frustration and the need for revenge. At least, when the struggle was won, those pigs would pay the price. That he would see to; that he would see to with pleasure.

On the second day, he packed the mosquito net in the car and drove back to Lusaka. There was work to be done. First they would win the struggle, then they would kill the pigs, and then they would find a way of running the country. 'One settler, one bullet.' It was the only way.

And if Chelsea wanted to run away from the struggle, that was her business. Later he would find his son and bring him back to a South Africa free of apartheid, free of the white man's rule. They would return to the old ways and live like men. Amandla! Power to the people! Rule by the people for the people.

When Luke drove back from the river, he was singing.

ON THE DAY that Luke was posted to southern Angola to be the ANC liaison officer to Swapo in their fight to free the mandated territory of South West Africa they called Namibia, his son was born in a clinic in Lisbon, Portugal. Chelsea called the lusty, perfect child John. John de la Cruz. Her son was Portuguese. The motherland had not forgotten the children of its colonies. The whole of Europe was open to both of them, with Portugal applying to become a member of the common market. Chelsea took a job as a receptionist for an insurance company. Even in Lisbon they had heard of Security Lion.

THE WEDDING of Mark and Lorna took place when the sun came up from the sea and spread its light on the hut above the cove. Garlands of flowers hung from the beams of the hut, the front door, the open windows, the trees, and the wooden, home-made furniture out in the sun around the big fire that had burned and cooked all night.

Bride and groom were in white robes, feet bare, the only colour being their red headbands and the garlands of flowers around their necks. Mark's beard had been washed, combed and cut neatly for the first time. Lorna's hair was long and smooth, and hung around her face and down the back and front of her robe. They spoke into the silence of the morning.

"Before you people and the memory of my mother and father, do I, Mark, take Lorna to be my wife, a wife I will cherish all the years of my life."

"Before you people and the love I have for this man and the child within me, I, Lorna, take Mark to be my husband for all the years of my life."

The groom bent low to kiss the bride, and the drifters and artists, painters and potters, musicians and craftsmen, women and men, white and black in harmony for the day of celebration, the children running riot, the dogs barking, and monkeys chattering from the trees united to join the noise of joy and wish them happiness for all the years of their lives. The ox, spitted and roasted over the pit in front of the hut, was shown to the guests for the first time as if it had not been turned over the fire for a day and a half; the ox was a gift from the groom to his bride and to all the people of the colony and surrounds. Only Carel van Tonder wondered where the money had come from for the ox.

Beer, brewed by Mark with the help of the featherman and the driftwood carver, was served with the white fire liquid distilled to perfection from peaches and pears by the painter who only painted naked, pregnant women on outsize bulls. The balladeer sang a song he had written, for once remembering his words. The lady painter who painted big, wonderful jungle pictures, full of hiding monkeys and deer, sang along with the balladeer in a sweet, gentle voice that was heard far away in the hills. The sculptor, who had acquired a vast piece of local marble that had taken a month to shift to the colony from the quarry upriver of Port St Johns, drank a quart of beer in ten seconds and presented the bride and groom with a large chip off the block carved into the shape of a dove.

It was a day of joy that none of them would ever forget and, when the paramount chief came to give his official approval, the party grew and spread to the beach. When the sun went down, the celebrations were building to their climax: fires burned on the beach, great driftwood fires, and fish were cooked in the coals; great pots of mussels and oysters, rich in crayfish stock, and vegetables bubbled over the fires, hung from tripods well above the flames.

The people smoked, and the smell of pot drifted in the still night air. They danced in rings, round and round, singing, the cultures of black and white mingling in the summer air of an African night. Some of the guests, exhausted, slept under the trees, only to wake and start again. The night sky was free of cloud and clear to the third layer of the stars, and the heaven sparkled with a billion jewels, twinkling with the joy of eternal life. There was peace and goodwill to all men on earth and in the heavens. It was the reason for all life.

# 2

While Mark and Lorna were enjoying the exquisite optimism of new life with all its beauty and potential, Africa was seething in the aftermath of the post-natal depression. Generally speaking, the new nations were monsters of personal greed, broken promises and repression. The rulers cared nothing for the people, using whichever rhetoric, communism or capitalism, brought them the most in aid and military hardware. Instead of feeding the people, they crowned themselves emperors, presidents for life, fathers of the nation, destroyers of colonialism.

Two of the more imaginative dictators, one who crowned himself in the likeness and pomp of Napoleon Bonaparte and the other the product of a military coup in the aftermath of the British rush from Africa, dined on their opponents, keeping the choicer parts of thigh and buttock in the fridge to be enjoyed more slowly. They literally ate their opposition.

The misery in new Africa, primed by Russian and American rivalry, made Shaka Zulu look like a philanthropist. Wars spawned wars and the tribes of Africa were set against each other's throats. The flames of anarchy burned bright. In Angola, Castro, at the request of his Russian masters, sent troops to support the Marxist-oriented MPLA against the American-backed Unita. In Mozambique the Rhodesians created the Renamo monster to be at the throat of the Marxist Frelimo. In Rhodesia, a few whites, modern-day Canutes, stood in the way of Russian-backed ZAPU and Chinese-backed ZANU. In South West Africa, a country ruled by

South Africa following a mandate received in the aftermath of World War I, Cuba and Russia backed Swapo against the Pretoria regime.

In South Africa, itself, Russia supported the ANC against the Pretoria regime and forced the Americans, prompted by their own civil rights movement, to back a programme of sanctions to impoverish the only wealth still left in Africa. The Russians and Americans shared the frenzied desire to control the world, destroying the last outposts of colonialism, and Attila the Hun would have been proud of them.

Luke Mbeki, stoking his part of the fire, began seriously to consider whether he and his friends were not being used. And for Luke the comprehension was too ghastly to contemplate. To keep from his mind a child he had not seen, a child he had exchanged for an ideal that was showing the seams of another agenda, one that had nothing to do with Luke Mbeki, he asked to be reattached to ZIPRA, the military wing of ZAPU, where he would fight the monster he truly hated, the South African police. To bolster a deteriorating military situation in Rhodesia, the Pretoria regime had sent in troops and paramilitary police, and at the same time the Smith government had called up all white residents who had been in the country for more than three years. Jonathan Holland and James Bell fell swiftly into the net.

For Madge Holland, otherwise happy in her new country, it was all happening again. She could hear the air-raid sirens, the German bombers, the ack-ack, the fearful drone of the V1 flying bombs. She prayed to her God and, while she prayed, the World Council of Churches in Geneva allocated funds to the forces of communism, to ZANU and ZAPU, in the name of Jesus Christ. Liberation theology had finally gone to war.

Three weeks after, a baby girl named Peace was born in the tranquillity of Port St Johns, to which the black car had not returned, Jonathan Holland received his commission in the Rhodesian Light Infantry. James Bell had refused a commission, and the partners requested a posting that would keep them together. As their business increased, the roles had reversed, with Jonathan taking the lead and making most of the decisions.

The bush, once so alien, had become his second home. The night sky of Africa, seen for the first time four years earlier, was a map he read as easily as the streets of London. Establishing due south from the four stars of the Southern Cross and the two pointers was to him no more than a glance at the heavens. The change in the cricket song was equal to a stop in the London traffic. Lean, tanned, confident, he led his men into the bush.

Jonathan had finally come home. Africa, his Africa, was worth every ounce of his energy.

WITH THE PATRIOTIC FRONT now established and ZIPRA and ZANLA warfare directed against the whites and not themselves, Luke walked into the compound of a farm on the northeast border of Rhodesia, the soft underbelly that enabled the guerrillas to attack a white farmhouse and slip back into the protection of Frelimo's Mozambique before the night gave way to daylight.

As regional commander, Luke wished to visit the area in which his troops were having so much difficulty. He was dressed in old clothes, the cast-offs of a white farmer, and he looked like any of the farm labourers. There were three hundred blacks in the compound, mud huts clustered together next to a river that served as bath and drinking water. The white farmer never went into his compound, preferring to hit a plough disc to summon his gang to work. Life on the farm was regulated by the sound of the clanging *simbi*.

To overcome the problem of language, Luke spoke in Fanagalo, the language of the farms and mines where different tribes joined from all over central Africa. Luke spent a night and a day in the compound before walking back over the border, a distance of twenty kilometres, back into the sanctuary of Mozambique. As he travelled in the night, he passed across the gun-sight of Jonathan Holland, lying in ambush across the path known to the security forces as the terrorist route out of the area.

"Let him go," whispered Jonathan. "There's only one, and he's old. That one's a farm labourer, even if he's breaking curfew." Jonathan had not yet reached the stage where he could fire on civilians without provocation.

The ambush waited in place until dawn washed the sky in the east, and then they picked themselves up from their cramped positions to begin the long slog back to base camp at Sipolilo. There were seven men in the stick, and all but Jonathan had seen action.

"You should have shot 'im," said Major Calucci.

"He was old and bent. Sort of dejected. How could I ...?"

"He broke curfew. Anyone break curfew, you shoot. Terrs look like old men when they want. You watch careful, Jonathan. No gentlemen in war. They kill you quick, too. You tell me next man go past in curfew and I kick your arse."

"I'm sorry, Major."

"Now you bugger off, Jonathan. Maybe it better you stay in England with that insurance company. Go up to London on train. You too soft."

"Next time I'll shoot."

"Good. You 'ave lunch and go right back. They hit three farmhouses last night."

"Anyone killed?"

"What you think? Eleven terrorists. Soon we go hot pursuit. Politicians! The UNO, it say all right for terrs to come over our border, but international border violation if we chase them home. Bull bloody shit."

Luke reached his base camp about the time Jonathan was preparing his ambush, determined to let nothing move in the night. Luke was bone-weary tired, and the last thing he needed was the commissar asking questions. He hated the commissar, who had not once put his foot over the Rhodesian border. The fact was, he hated communists, but without them there would be no guns and no war of liberation.

"You'll not go over without asking me," the commissar instructed Luke. They spoke in Xhosa, as both of them were ANC and had been born in the Transkei.

"Look, you little rat. I am regional commander."

"And I am political commissar, and if you go again, I tell them to send you to a training camp. You go against me again and maybe I send you to a different camp. I know a good one outside Dar es Salaam, comrade."

"I'm not your bloody comrade!" snapped Luke, in English. The man did not speak English, having spent only three years at primary school.

"What you say?"

"Fuck off! I'm tired and hungry, and those farms are like fortresses. Big wire fences all round, with claymore mines on top of the fence poles. Lights, big lights, on the corners of the houses. Dogs inside the wire and men in those houses who know how to shoot straight. Eleven minutes after our attack and the bloody police arrive on motorcycles. How many did we lose last night?"

"I don't know."

"You do, but you won't admit it's a bloody fiasco. You tell those kids the whites are all running away. Well, I've got some news for you. Not only haven't they run away, but they're still ploughing at night with big bloody headlights on the tractors."

Luke strode off to call a meeting of his commanders. First he would eat, and then he would tell them what they were going to do. Next time, when the police came roaring up the driveways, they'd blow themselves to pieces on a land mine. First job before an attack was to mine the farmer's bloody road. If the police missed it going in, the farmer would hit it going out. And they needed grenade launchers, rockets to hit the homes from a distance, to give his men a chance of living through the night.

HECTOR FORTESCUE-SMYTHE WAS at last doing the work he wanted to do: directing the surge of communism. They controlled North Africa after ejecting the French from Algeria and Morocco. The horn of Africa was theirs after the old emperor had been thrown out of Ethiopia. West Africa with its oil owed allegiance to Moscow and, with the bases in Zambia, Mozambique and Angola, all of central and southern Africa with its minerals and sea route would shortly fall to the power of Russia. And now he was at the heart of it, out in the open, no longer wearing the horns Helena gave to him three times a week, no longer doing what he was told by a man he hated.

Minister Kloss was going to pay for his arrogance. A tribunal. A quick, public trial, and execution by 'necklace'. A big, lovely Dunlop tyre shoved over his arrogant head to pin down his arms. Covered in petrol. Touched off by a match. Flames of agony. The necklace. For pigs and traitors. For the right-wing fascist bastards who stood in the way of the world hegemony. Russian hegemony. World communism. Peace and order for a thousand years. Total world empire. Total control. Discipline. The end of war and opposition. The world's resources channelled into an upsurge of living standards for all the peoples of the earth.

Hector drummed his fingers on the old desk in his sweaty office in Maputo, the capital of Mozambique. It was hot even in April, with the humidity drenching his clothing. But he was happy, co-ordinating the flood of Russian arms to the liberation movements, giving them the tools to do the job. He had been back in Africa for a month, gone to war with his mother's blessing to fulfil the dream she had dreamt for fifty years. To fulfil his destiny.

The light bulb over his desk dimmed, and for a moment left him in darkness. Then the power surged again, and he was sitting in a pool of light and able to carry on checking the inventory of the boat in the harbour, ostensibly bringing machinery to power the new, free Mozambique. The guns were still coming in from the end of the Vietnam War, and the result of which had convinced Hector that guerrilla warfare was unstoppable.

The door to his office began to move. When it opened Luke Mbeki stepped round to find himself looking at a British service revolver pointed at his belly. He was dressed in his old clothes, had not had a bath for a month and stank, a stench he had not noticed after the first week. Travelling like the rest of the peasants made it easier and much less conspicuous, especially in Maputo, where the Pretoria regime had eyes all over the place.

"Evening, Hector," Luke greeted him, as Hector put the revolver away. "They told me you were running supplies. You need to watch security. That little thing won't help you against South African automatics, and when your father-in-law finds out how close you are to his guns it will give him pleasure."

"Ex-father-in-law. She can screw who she likes without bothering me anymore."

"White men stick out in Mozambique. Me, nobody notices. You got any whisky?"

"Of course, Luke; it comes with the job. How are you? Those meetings in London seem a long time ago."

"They were, and we've come a long way.... The Rhodesians are proving far more of a problem than we imagined."

"Sit down and tell me," invited Hector. "Maybe I can help. Drink it neat. The water's full of shit. Seems the waterworks don't purify any more. You should ask your fellow blacks to be more efficient. Quite frankly, they're making a bit of a mess of things. We're sending in East German advisors that'll sort it out. The Germans are always most efficient."

"I want to put land mines up every farmer's driveway. I want mines under all the roads. RPG rockets to fire a kilometre into the farm houses, penetrate the walls and then explode. I want to burn their tractors in the sheds and chase them out."

"Cheers, Luke. You're in luck. The boat in the harbour is from Indo-China with forty-seven thousand land mines, limpet mines and personnel mines. How many do you want?"

"All of them!" exclaimed Luke, looking suddenly hopeful.

"I don't know about all of them, but I'll make sure you have a real pile of them, Luke. Please sit down. You seem tired and nervous. How's Chelsea?"

"She ran away."

"Oh, Luke. I'm sorry."

"We were going to have a baby. She must have had my son by now."

"Where is she?"

"I wish I knew." Luke spread out his hands in a gesture of despair.

"Maybe I can help."

"Please Hector. I want to know where she is. I miss Chelsea. Didn't know how much I relied on her being there."

"Do you know, it's five years since your friend Matthew Gray disappeared. Now that was a victory for communism. Chased the capitalist right out of business." The light dimmed again.

Luke looked up at the fading light before making comment. "Like they did here. Where do you think Matt went?"

"South America. People always go to South America when they want to get away from things. The Great Train robbers went to Brazil."

"I miss him, too."

"You sentimental old boy. Have another whisky. I have three cases locked in the cupboard. When I was a boy scout they told us always to be prepared."

IT WAS NOT OFTEN that Archie Fletcher-Wood had the chance of taking a drink in public on his own. He was still known as Archie, despite his mother's insistence that he call himself Archibald to measure up to his wealth. It was his fiftieth birthday, a secret he kept with his mother, who now lived in South Africa, supported by her son. It was a situation with which Archie had no quarrel: it was a son's responsibility and pleasure.

The snag was she still treated him as a child and wanted to mother him. Her memory was going and, though he had sent her a bunch of flowers, a custom on his birthday started by his father to thank his mother for the pain she had suffered in giving him birth, she had not realised the significance. And Archie, turned fifty, wanted to be on his own to think back on his life and wonder where he had gone wrong and where he had gone right.

He had chosen the small, dark bar in the old Rosebank Hotel on Oxford Road, a one-star establishment that would not expect to entertain the joint CEO of the seventeenth largest conglomerate in the country. He had gone home to his Sandown flat, changed into old clothes and sat at the bar without a tie to hamper his momentary freedom. It was a Friday night, and he was not going into the office in the morning; he was going to get a little drunk and enjoy himself like he had done in the old days before circumstances made him a big shot and it became a social and business crime to be found in a bar on his own. He had left his money on the bar for the barman to pick up.

"Put in another, Mister Barman."

"You celebrating?"

"Matter of fact, I am... You always so quiet in here?"

"This old hotel's going to fall down round my head."

"You been here a long time?"

"Twenty-seven years. Since nineteen fifty. We were a smart place in those days. You visiting?"

"Yes... It's my birthday. You want to have a drink with a man of fifty?"

"Why not? Let's get started." The man had a broad southern Irish accent, even after so many years. He was short, very short, but Archie suspected it would not be anyone's good idea to pick a fight or misbehave in this man's bar. "A touch of the Mist. Charge you the same as whisky. Irish Mist You want to try one?"

"Why not?"

"One Mist, one Scotch. Your good health." The barman downed his drink that he had soaked in cubes of ice, and began to polish the bar. The third round, the barman announced, was on him, and Archie let it go, not wanting to break the spell. It was like drinking with a very old friend, the best kind of drinking companion who never had a memory the following morning, never told you how much rubbish you had been talking with so much affected wisdom.

When a woman on her own walked into the bar, they were both disappointed, but the professional in the barman brightened up for the customer.

"What'll it be?" he asked her.

"What are you drinking?"

"Irish Mist and then a whisky. Kind of ring the changes."

"Then give me the same," she ordered.

"A Mist or a whisky?"

"Both." She was probably in her late forties; and might have been good looking in her youth. She had green eyes with yellow flecks in them, and she did not look as if she could afford a cheap drink, let alone the most expensive.

"Have them on me,,,. it's my birthday," Archie offered. The woman was looking at him with soft eyes, the yellow flecks dull and warm.

"That'll be kind of you. Am I interrupting anything?"

"I was thinking of getting a little drunk and the barman was helping me out. It's my fiftieth birthday."

"Fifty must be a real bitch... Cheers. Two years and I'm forty."

Both the barman and Archie tried not to look surprised. The third member of the bar looked as if a few years had gone by since she had turned forty. Archie pushed himself round to give her a better look.

"It may sound a silly line at fifty, but don't I know you from somewhere?"

"Yes, you do."

Archie waited but the woman lifted her whisky glass. She had put down the Mist in three gulps. Looked as if she needed a drink.

"I didn't ..."

"No, you didn't even take me out."

"Well; that's something. A friend of a friend, so to speak."

"So to speak." The woman was smiling at him – almost laughing it seemed to the barman.

"Give us all another round, Mister Barman," requested Archie.

"Let's get started," said the barman for the second time.

Archie was halfway to being nicely drunk and he stopped exercising his brain to work out when he had seen the lady before... what did it matter?

It was his birthday and he did not have to stand on ceremony. He and the barman continued their reminiscences and new drinks, by which time both Archie and the barman were drunk but did not show it. The woman broke into their confidences.

"I'd buy you both a drink but I don't have no money." With the drink inside the woman, Archie made out a strong cockney accent but was too drunk to give it a care in the world. More interestingly, the woman was beginning to look pretty.

"My name's Archie."

"I know," she replied.

"Then you know who I am?"

"If you mean, I know you can afford to buy drinks... you can afford to buy the hotel, for that matter, but I don't see anyone wanting to do that with two customers, even if they are drinking two at a time."

"Mister Barman, be kind enough to order me a taxi." Archie turned back to the woman. "Would you care to have dinner with me?"

"Where do you wish to dine, sir?" asked the barman, enjoying the joke.

"I think the Balalaika. The food isn't what it was in Firth's day, but it'll do. And it's close to my flat and I can walk home. My good buddy, please keep the keys to my car and take off the Yale so I can get in to my flat ..." He turned to the woman again. "What is your name?"

"Poppy."

"Well, Poppy. How about celebrating a birthday with an old man of fifty?"

The barman chipped in again. "They won't let you in without a tie."

"Then lend me a tie and look after my car."

"Which one is your car, sir?"

"It's the Rolls Royce parked outside your front door in the loading zone. Better move it in the morning before the cops give it a ticket," Archie added.

"You mean the one parked next to my Cadillac?"

"Didn't see a Caddy when I came in. You always park in the loading zone?"

"Always. Now let's all have one on me," smiled the barman.

"You are a gentleman and a scholar."

"Make mine a single," said the woman. "I've got out of the drinking habit... you don't know who I am, do you, Archie? Have I really changed that much?"

"Doesn't matter," Archie assured her. "We'll have a night on the town two spare bedrooms. You won't have to worry if you don't want to worry…Mister Barman, why don't you close the bar and come with us? It's been a wonderful evening, wonderful."

"Two's company... You can watch the bar while I go to the John."

"Will be my pleasure... and hurry up with the taxi. I've decided I'm hungry."

The woman was now looking at him with sad eyes. "You sure you can make it, Archie? Don't want me to take you home?"

"Have it your own way."

"Be Jesus," said the barman, coming back into the bar.

"There's a bloody great roller parked outside the front door."

"I told you. It's my car. You've got the keys in your pocket."

"Who wants a taxi?" called a man from reception.

"Come along, Poppy. The night is but a pup."

When the barman closed his mouth and his two customers had left his bar, he found a fifty rand note tucked under his glass. It made him feel sad, old and lonely. He waited another half an hour but no one else came into the bar.

It was only in the morning when the sun was streaming through his bedroom window, waking him up, that Archie realised who was lying naked in the bed next to him, fast asleep.

"Sunny. Sunny Tupper. Poppit Tupper. I'll be damned. And I haven't enjoyed an evening as much for years."

"Neither have I," said the lady next to him. She was smiling, the yellow flecks in her green eyes less prominent in the sunlight.

"Do you have anywhere else to stay?"

"No."

"Then you'd better stay here."

"I'd like that, Archie. And not just 'cause you drive a roller."

"You didn't even mention Matt all evening."

"He's dead?" A vacant look came over Poppy's face, as if she were trying to forget.

"I'm not so sure. Not so sure. Fact is, I think I know where he is. Have for some months. But I don't see why I should blow his cover if that's how he wants it. I've had to come to terms with my own life... You want some coffee? Then you can tell me what really happened after Matt walked out on you, and I'll tell you what happened after he walked out on me and Lucky. Do you miss him?"

"Yes."

"So do I," admitted Archie. "He was quite a man, Matthew Gray. Maybe he still is."

"Why don t we go and ask him?"

"He's married, Sunny. Has a daughter: They called her Peace."

"Does he love his wife?" asked Poppy unable to keep the wistfulness from her voice.

"Very much so."

"Then we'd better leave all of them in peace. We can't always rely on Matt to make us happy." She gently pulled him down to her and kissed him on the lips.

"You knew I was in that bar."

"I followed you. My last few rands went into an old mini."

"It's twenty years since you walked into Gray's. We had some real laughs in those days." Now it was Archie's turn to look wistful.

"We will again."

"Maybe. But not the same. Youth is very special." Archie's eyes were looking a long way back into the past.

FRIKKIE SWART FOUND out about his wife's sexual habits six weeks after they were married. Unlike her first husband he did not take kindly to his wife screwing around. He beat her up.

"This marriage (BANG!) was a marriage (BANG!) of your father's convenience (BANG!), but it also included me (BANG!)." The slaps had turned to fists and the pain had increased with each successive blow releasing in Helena a sexual excitement far greater than she had ever felt before.

"Make love to me Frik. Do it for God s sake." Between blows she pulled off his trousers and grabbed at his genitals. When she got off her own pants, it was too much for Frik and he gave it to her with all the pent-up frustration of too many years. When he had finished, she lay bleeding from the nose and mouth, but she was satisfied for the first time in her life.

"Frik darling that was marvellous."

"You'd better go and wash up in the bathroom."

"Yes."

"And if I catch you screwing that tennis player, I'll kill you."

"Please," gasped Helena, shuddering in masochistic delight.

"I mean it."

"That's what's so exciting."

WHILST HELENA WAS WASHING up in the bathroom Hector was looking at his ex-wife's handwriting. The letter reached him at his office in Maputo delivered to the mail box and collected by a member of his staff. The envelope was thick and had been registered in Pretoria.

"What does the bitch want now? She's not getting any money out of me." He took the letter opener off his desk and ripped open the envelope causing his desk to explode and making his right hand come away from his arm. The blast shattered the windows in the office across the road. Hector stared at the stump of his arm, blood gushing.

"The bitch tried to kill me." They were the last words he spoke for a week, and would have been his last on earth without the genius of an East German surgeon who operated on the stump of his arm half an hour after the blast. The effects of the letter bomb were devastating.

THE AGRIC-ALERT WENT off in the police station, but there was no one left to react. The army were eighty kilometres away at Sipolilo; the elderly sergeant cranked the hand phone and ten minutes later got a call through to Major Calucci at the army base.

"Eleven contacts tonight. Can't cope. Latest Horseshoe Block," and he gave the major the co-ordinates. "They're still calling for help."

"Take an hour but we go... Lieutenant Holland, get your arse into gear. Farm attack. Take two trucks and ten men. Go. The farmer's kept them off so far. Dawn light in seven hours. Someone's co-ordinating these bastards."

They could hear the gunfire half an hour later and see the enemy tracer.

The farm's compound was on fire and a row of tobacco barns was burning with the farmer's bulk shed and half his tobacco crop. At full speed, Jonathan took his men down the dirt road that led off the tar. Corporal James Bell was driving the lead Land Rover, and the friends were racing each other.

"Get ahead of him," ordered Jonathan.

"I can't," said his driver. "He won't let me."

"Faster, man."

"This bloody road's got more potholes than road." They were bouncing half out of the open vehicle. "Farmhouse is still returning fire. Someone's firing back from the compound."

They could see the tracer from automatic FN rifle fire. A rocket exploded somewhere inside the house and blew off a part of the roof, sending the thatch into a gush of white flames. "Shit!"

They drove on at full speed, the lead vehicle thirty metres ahead and kicking up a wall of dust as it slewed into the road leading to the farm buildings. Then a violent explosion shot the Land Rover into the air, scattering pieces into the farmer's ploughed land through the avenue of jacaranda trees, and Jonathan's driver careered from side to side before slamming sideways into one of the tree trunks.

"Driver! Look to Jim's Landy. Come on. Open the door. The terrs are on this side." Heading his five men, three of his own and two from the destroyed Land Rover, Jonathan went on the attack across the ploughed field. They worked their way forward under darkness, picking out the flashpoints of the terrorists attacking the house.

Nearer the house, Jonathan shot off a Very light, turning the night into day. "RLI!" he shouted to the farmer, and opened fire. The terrorists were caught between the farmhouse and the road, and were shot down as they ran. All the time, Jonathan was desperate to get back to the Land Rover, hoping against hope that Jim had somehow survived. But he had his duties to do first.

By the time the flare went out, the contact was over. The farmer, his wife and their ten-year-old daughter were alive and unhurt inside the burning house. There were two dead terrorists on the wire, blown up by a claymore, exploded by the farmer from inside the farmhouse in the initial attack. Two more were dead on the lawn next to the swimming pool.

Back in the avenue of jacaranda trees, James Bell was dead, killed instantly by the land mine that had been triggered by the right-hand wheel just in front of him. In the compound, the guard force of blacks armed by the farmer to protect themselves had killed a fifth terrorist.

Inside the compound of thatched huts, most of them burning, it was carnage. The terrorists had vent most of their firepower on their fellow blacks, the sell-outs who worked for whites. The young and innocent had taken the brunt of the agony.

Jonathan waited with his friend until dawn, when a helicopter arrived to take the body to Salisbury for burial. He felt a lot older than his twenty-three years, and utterly hollow inside. Maybe, he thought, they should have stayed in England. During a brief moment in the middle of the night, he had lost his friend and his youth.

"GROUND CONTROL, this is green leader. Do not allow aircraft to take off or land. I repeat: do not allow aircraft to take off or land. We are in control of your air space." The air traffic controller at Lusaka airport stared at his radar console control that was showing more bleeps on the screen than it had ever done before, when no aircraft were scheduled for landing. Above, the scream of jets could be heard outside the tower and helicopters were landing on the runway, troops disgorging before the choppers had touched the tarmac. Then the land phones began to ring.

"Ground control, this is green leader. Do you hear me?'

"I hear you, green leader. There's an aircraft due from Luanda in half an hour. What do I do?"

"Send him back or we will shoot down the aircraft. I repeat no aircraft to take off or land. Do I make myself clear?"

Luke heard the aircraft in the night sky from the flat he had shared with Chelsea for so many years and went to the window, throwing it wide. Two storeys below, cars were being stopped by men in military uniform, and armoured cars were parked alongside the road, with more military vehicles turning into the road. Taking three big strides, he was back in the room with the phone in his hand, dialling the police station, cold fear clearing his brain with the surge of adrenaline.

"What the hell's going on?" he asked when the phone was answered.

"This is Luke Mbeki."

"Rhodesian air force have taken the airport, that we do know."

"There are troops in the street outside my window."

"Not ours, sir. Must be Rhodesian."

"What the hell are you doing about them?"

"Nothing, sir. What can we do? They have helicopter gunships. Armoured cars. You do something." Luke put down the phone. Back at the window, he looked down on an armoured car parked outside the entrance to the block of flats. Then he understood.

Back at the phone, he dialled another number, the number known only to the Zambian president, the ZIPRA commander and himself. "Mister Nkomo. Get out of your house. Through the back. The Rhodesian army have invaded to take out our leaders. GET OUT!"

Three more strides took him back to the window. When the Selous Scout kicked open the door and threw a grenade into the lounge, Luke was on the roof lying flat next to the water tank. He could see the Hunter and Vampire jets circling the city. It was a long night for Luke Mbeki.

Only with the dawn did the Rhodesians withdraw, the aircraft cover being replaced twice during the night. When Luke climbed back into his flat, he found their double bed had been punctured by gunfire. The framed picture of Chelsea stood on the bedside table untouched. Luke began to shake and then he cried. If she had not run away, they would both have been killed, Chelsea and his son. The war of liberation had come right into his bedroom.

Outside the city the guerrilla training camp had been devastated. Nearer to Luke the house of Joshua Nkomo had been destroyed, only Luke's call allowing the big man to be pushed through the bathroom window at the back as the Rhodesians came in the front.

Three days later Luke caught an aircraft for Moscow and was met at the airport by Hector Fortescue-Smythe who had spent six months in hospital while the doctors repaired his face and fitted an artificial hand to the stump of his arm. Luke shook his left hand.

"Congratulations," said Hector, "You were luckier than me. I have a meeting set up with the Russian air force tomorrow. Never again will those clapped-out old Hunters have control of the air."

"And the South African defence force? They have Mirage jets."

"Still out of date."

"But we don't have any pilots," protested Luke.

"But the Cubans do. Some of the best in the world. You and I are going to make sure the liberation armies have control of the air. Armscor's Achilles heel is aircraft, despite help from the Israelis. They have a gun in development, a field gun that can fire forty-five kilometres and knock out your front door. But no aircraft. We must convince our communist friends to give the Cubans state-of the-art combat aircraft and send them to Angola. Otherwise there is a chance we may lose. The United Nations is shouting from the top of the building in New York at Smith's blatant aggression, blatant transgression of international borders. But we still need aircraft... And I have some good news for you, Luke. Chelsea is in Lisbon. She called the boy John. He was one years old in September. Congratulations. You have a Portuguese son by the name of John de la Cruz. It's a crazy world."

Luke looked at the man for a moment and shook his head again. Hector could see none of the irony of what he was saying.

"Was it painful, Hector?"

"All the time. Still is. Makes me hate a lot better. I'm going to kill that bitch Helena and her father... You can fly from here to Lisbon when we are finished. I made the arrangements. Oh, and your friend Matthew Gray. He's in Port St Johns. We dropped a large consignment of arms down the coast. Quite a coincidence. Been there for years, living like a hippie. Big-shot Gray living like a hippie! Makes you laugh, doesn't it? Our friend Ben Munroe did a better job than he ever imagined."

Des Donelly met Bishop Porterstone at a fund-raising event for the anti-apartheid movement, and was impressed by the cleric's sincerity. As an Irishman, he knew what it was like to have been ruled by outsiders, and his sympathy was firmly in the court of the oppressed blacks living under the jackboot of a racist government that did not allow them to vote, live where they liked, or even go to bed with whom they wished, if the cause of the urge to procreate was white, semi-white, Indian or Chinese.

There were laws which stopped them joining a union, eating in a white restaurant, bathing in the sea or getting into a bus. And if they wished to leave the country with a passport, there was no guarantee that a black man would be allowed to return to the country of his birth. As for starting a business in a white area, it was better to kill a fellow black, the chances of receiving the immediate attention of the police being far less. The way Bishop Porterstone put it, Des had never heard of such repression since Adolf Hitler. Fortunately he had not heard of Joseph Stalin's agricultural programme that had slaughtered millions more than Adolf, or he may not have been so quick to join his talents to a movement that was said to have communist backing. Des Donelly's career had reached its peak in the early seventies when he measured up in the top ten rock stars in the world. His name was still a household word but his new records were not selling, and no one wished to send him on tour to hear the shouts and screams of an adoring public. Des Donelly needed applause more than drugs or booze. His addiction was fame. The bishop had used him to draw a crowd and the idea seeped into his craving that just possibly the bishop could be used to draw the crowds for Des Donelly. In England there were dozens of bands and artists who had made a little fame for themselves, and all of them would give more than their talent to appear on a live stage with Des Donelly under the glare of the TV cameras and with a pre-publicity that would match the best of Elton John.

It took Andrew Porterstone less than five minutes to work out what the rock star was after but he did not care. The idea suited his purpose. The idea was superb. A concert at the Royal Albert Hall, hosted by Des Donelly, with the cream of English and American talent who felt strongly for the cause would attract the television cameras and imagination of the world. It would make all the on-going demonstrations in Trafalgar Square of so little consequence and, best of all, it would raise funds for the cause that was always in need of money.

A grand, anti-apartheid concert would take off the proverbial rafters. Big black names in the USA would find it impossible to keep away and all of them would give their time and talent free of charge. They would make a record of the concert. They would sell a million copies to the people who hated racism. It was a truly wonderful idea.

Ben Munroe received a phone call from the bishop at eleven o'clock at night, as the bishop had no idea what time it was in Washington DC. He listened carefully to the laconic bishop.

"You've got Des Donelly!"

"He came up with the idea."

"He's big over here."

"Can you get us the publicity, and two or three big black names?"

"If you had gone into business, Andrew, you would have made a fortune."

"When are you doing another piece on that man Gray?"

"Tomorrow morning if I could find him."

"You do this one for me and I'll give you his address," promised the bishop.

THE BLACK CAR returned to Port St Johns two months after Peace turned one year's old, when Hector was back in London organising the biggest rock concert in the history of music. It was exactly a year since Hector had lost his right hand and his face the ability to smile. The plastic surgery had been good but left his face static, as if he was wearing a mask.

Lorna was at the end of the beach by the rocks, the autumn sun playing gently on the bare bottom of her daughter which stuck out of a hole in the sand next to the tail of their dog. They had dug a deep hole and there was not much left of either of them above the ground. Lorna was as content as any mother in the flush of youth could be. Her figure was back to perfection, and she was sure that another child would soon be on its way, the boy they both wanted.

There was a slight berg wind bringing in warm air from the interior and the sea was rolling in from a kilometre out to sea, where behind the first rollers a small sailing yacht was beating up against the wind. It was late in the afternoon and time for her to pick up the child and return to their hut to cook the evening meal. She wrapped a piece of material around her waist and called the dog, causing another spray of sand to come out of the hole.

Her hair was almost bleached white by the sun and the surf, the constant play of sun on salt water. Her body, like that of her daughter, was brown as a hazel nut and just as smooth. She picked Peace out of the hole that was filling up with water and put the child on her hip, a wide, comfortable hip that gave Peace a gentle ride back across the length of the beach. The cross-bred, fifty-seven variety small dog followed behind, occasionally breaking off to chase the sandpipers and the black-backed gulls that were feeding off the flotsam washed in from the sea, a mix of oysters, mussels and red bait. The sea was rich and beautiful.

When she reached the path up to their hut, she stopped for a rest, putting Peace down on the sand to crawl away with the scampering dog. A spent wave washed the child and dog, making Peace shriek with delight. The black car was still parked in the open space next to the Vuya restaurant, but there was no one inside or near the vehicle. The car left a false note in the air, mixing the warm, salty breeze with a tinge of unease.

She walked down to Peace, seeing that a bigger wave was on its way, picked her up and walked back to the path that led up through the wild banana trees to the hut on its flat piece of land cut into the hill, the big rondavel open in the front, gaping out across the sea and surrounded by the wild banana. As she walked, she could hear birds searching the trumpet flowers for nectar, singing as they worked. There were flashes of colour as the sunbirds moved from tree to tree above the girl's head. At the top of the patch, where it reached the front of the hut, she stopped to catch her breath and enjoy the view of beach down below and the vastness of the sea.

From inside the rondavel, she heard the voice of a man, and checked herself from turning to go inside the house and see how Mark was getting along with his painting. He had learnt so much in a year that it would not be long before the tourists were buying his paintings.

"Matt, you've got to understand! There can be criminal proceedings, and now we've found out we must report it to the police. You set up the deal with Smythe-Wilberforce, so I had to come and see you. You can't have expected to hide away down here for ever. Millions have been channelled out by the investment manager and he insists it was on the instructions of Hector, with your full knowledge. You did give them carte blanche on investing policyholders' funds.

"I didn't know Hector was still a communist. Where have the funds gone?"

"We think to the SA communist party and the ANC. Don t you see? Both the parties are banned. I'll end up in bloody jail. I'm joint CEO."

"Sit down Archie. We've had a lot worse than this in our time."

"Thank God you said 'we'," returned Archie, sitting down heavily. "Now I feel a lot better. When are you coming back? Teddie says we can form another pyramid company and sell it our shares. Then we issue more shares to you to give you control. Back where we were."

"I can offer the colony special. Strong as hell. Carel van Tonder makes it when he's not smuggling dagga. You can have a smoke if that will calm you down?"

"I don't smoke," replied Archie missing the point in his agitation. "What are we going to do?"

"Personally, I would do nothing. Make the money a donation to charity. Tiny Rowland of Lonrho has been giving money to the liberation movements for years. A bit of insurance. After all, you are in the insurance business."

"When are you coming back to Johannesburg?" Archie asked insistently.

"I'm not."

"But you must."

"I gave up the musts in my life when I gave away my money... What do you think of my painting? Not in the class of what we walked out of the Congo, but not bad for a beginner. Lorna's teaching me. She'll be back from the beach, and then you can meet her and see why there's no way I'm leaving Port St Johns."

Archie looked up to see a woman silhouetted against the rays of the setting sun, her profile stark against the sun. She had a child resting on her hip and a small inquisitive dog at her feet.

"Lorna, this is an old friend. Archie Fletcher-Wood. Ignore the suit. Underneath he's the same as us."

"Why did he call you 'Matt'?"

"Let's all have a good drink of Carel's special outside in the last of the sun," suggested her husband. "It's been a beautiful day. You'll stay the night with us, Archie? Not the most luxurious hotel, but the food's good and we'll put a mat on the floor. Then you can tell my wife what I did before I walked up the coast to Port St Johns. I have nothing to hide or be ashamed of. But I want it clear that Mark/Matt came home and is staying home, and if Luke Mbeki had any sense he'd do the same. Poor old Luke and poor old Chelsea. Her kid must be the same age as Peace."

TWO WEEKS LATER, a second black car was parked in the open space next to the Vuya restaurant. The colony was already abuzz with the story of Matthew Gray, a story which the man they called Mark neither confirmed nor denied. Now the world was coming back to Second Beach, Port St Johns, and their reclusion and safety was being disturbed.

A man had emerged from the car and seemed to know where he was going. He walked across the end of the beach and took the path up to the hut on the hill. It was another beautiful day, balmy with the warm berg-wind and the sea was gentle as a lamb, the colony's fishing boat having gone out early in the morning to try for mussel-crackers, copper steenbras and seventy-fours.

"Good morning, Teddie. Have you come to buy one of my paintings?"

"Not really, Matt. It's good to see you."

"Your mother told you how to find the way?"

"She did, as a matter of fact. Archie is in England, talking to Smythe-Wilberforce. They were horrified to hear what was being done to our investments. Hector said he knew nothing about any such arrangement and, if any of the staff were doing anything wrong, the police should put them in jail. The legal brains have pushed aside Hector's posturing and agreed to disinvest... You really think we should give the ANC a donation every year? You forget, Matt, that I was fighting the communists in Angola. They're all tarred with the same brush; they want power, not justice. And their kind of power will be a lot more oppressive than ours. The KGB have been instructing the MPLA in Luanda exactly how to go about their business... I like the painting. How much do you want for it?"

"You can have it as a present and hang it on the wall so you won't forget me. Do you know which was your grandfather's house? Come outside and we can just see the green roof at the other end of the beach. Looks better from a very long distance. What can I do for you, Teddie? I presume you have not driven so far to buy a painting."

"I want you to see sense and stop this nonsense. There's a real world out there, and you were part of it. A big part of it."

"I question which world is real. This one was made by the gods," replied Matt, staring out towards the sea.

"Is the water problem as bad as they say? A casino holiday resort will make a lot of money."

"The gods must have felt a swift shot of pain!... Yes, water is a problem. Ask your mother. Maybe there isn't another paradise like this for me, but I know enough of your real world to know it will only last for a while and then be destroyed. The black government here is despotic. What is new? Africa was run by despots for all its history. A few years of white rule hasn't changed that. Just given them some new ideas. No, I would not put my money, if I had any, into Port St Johns. The salt river's too silted and no way is there enough drinking water. You staying for lunch?"

"Thought I would buy you a beer in the restaurant I passed. Does it make any money?"

"No. You can ask the owner. How can anyone make money out of a restaurant in the middle of nowhere? None of us have any money. No, he likes the place. Some people prefer the quieter life, so please don't buy the restaurant. Why is it everything you look at has a dollar sign on top? Lorna's out visiting. We'll drink alone. She keeps laughing at the idea of my being a big tycoon. She thinks it's all very funny."

"She doesn't like the idea of wealth?" queried Teddie.

"She never mentions it."

"Maybe when the children are older. A little girl and another one on the way?"

"Are you married, Teddie?"

"Never had time."

"That was my problem. That and a lot of money-grabbing women."

"You know who's living with Archie?" Teddie asked, changing his tone.

"He didn't say."

"Sunny Tupper that was."

"Stop stirring, Teddie; it doesn't suit you. Stay the day with us. The night. You'll see what I mean."

"I don't have the time; I'm seeing the paramount chief and the mayor. They find our investment a lot more interesting than you do."

"Water, Teddie. I'm not giving you a bum steer. You can't run what you want to do without a massive amount of water. Don't let them con you. They're pretty good at fleecing white men with bright ideas. Stick to what you know. The insurance business. I believe the company has grown very well."

"You won't come back?"

"What do any of you need from me?" asked Matt, dismissing the question as if it were ridiculous.

"May we ask your opinion?"

"Anytime. But here. And please, all of you, come down in an old bakkie and old clothes. You stick out like a pork chop in a synagogue."

"Dress casual." Teddie gave a forced laugh.

"You got it, Teddie Botha. You got it. You don't want the painting, do you?"

"Not really."

"Good. At least there's some part of me you don't want."

THE FISHING BOAT landed long after Teddie Botha had gone tearing up the dirt road to Umtata to invest his money the best way he thought fit. The sun was slipping into the sea, making the water shimmer with the rays of the setting sun, shooting its colour at the heavens. A small moon was visible in the sky and the wind had dropped to nothing. Soon they were all coming down to the shore, some to help beach the boat and some to wonder at the catch gleaming in the sun as it was tossed, fish by fish, to the wet sand. Matthew Gray strode down the path to the beach, woken from his reverie by the noise of excitement. When he reached the boat with its old outboard motor serviced meticulously by Carel van Tonder, three fires were already being lit above the high-tide mark, just down from the Vuya restaurant that would buy enough fish to refuel the boat. The beach was filling up with everyone from the colony and the black village. For the first time that year, there was enough fish for everyone, and if it was not eaten fresh it would go off in the morning sun. When Matt looked into the boat, his arm around Lorna who was holding an excited Peace, there were still some on the bottom.

"Found the reef, Mark. Found the reef. We're going to dance on the beach all night." Mark or Matt; it made no difference. They did not care about his past. All that mattered was the moment, the excitement, the abundance of fish. What anybody did to them afterwards was outside their control. For the moment there was peace on earth and joy to all men. He was happy and so were his friends.

MAJOR ANTONIO VAN Perreira dos Santos Cassero of the Cuban Air Force paradoxically believed in God, Castro and socialism, and he had arrived in Angola to spread the word of communism to his black brothers. He was a dedicated revolutionary who would use any means and justify them in his pursuit of world communism.

Without Castro and communism, he would have been nothing. He would still have been in the slums of Havana without an education and the skill to fly the most sophisticated aircraft in the world. He was the product of equal opportunity, the proof that a boy could be taken from Third World poverty and propelled in a few years into the First. Greed and capitalism had no place in his life, only dedication and gratitude. He was as high as a kite on the dreams of Utopia, the belief that man could at last be saved, turned from an animal of self-destruction to an altruist who enjoyed the happiness of his fellow men and would not constantly be demanding something in return.

A swift wind and a predilection for coloured women had seen his grandfather lose his sugar estate and his son. Antonio's father had been left with no means of fending for himself in the slime left by Batista, the dictator who had broadened the gap between rich and poor to the point where most of Cuba would have been better off not having been born. To add to his woes under Batista, Antonio's father had married a black woman, the descendant of a man torn from the highveld of Monomatapa, the kingdom of Zimbabwe, by an Arab who sold him to an American slaver, who sold him to a mean son-of-a-bitch Spaniard who enjoyed inflicting the pain of slavery.

Antonio had been born of both worlds, and his job in Angola was to create an air force that was powerful enough to terminate the air superiority of the Ian Smith government of Rhodesia and the apartheid government in South Africa. There was more than aircraft and pilots to be procured. A whole infrastructure of airfields, ground staff and missile protection had to be placed across Angola to challenge the white, racist capitalists. It was going to take him many years.

• • •

LUKE MBEKI KNOCKED on the door in Lisbon. The two stood looking at each other in silence, the years of their lives shared together flowing between them. There was no sign of his son.

"How did you find me, Luke?"

"You can find anyone if you look long enough... I have to go to London. They tracked our flat, and I thought of you there and I cried, Chelsea.

"You cried!" She opened the door wide.

"They bombed the lounge and machine-gunned the bedroom."

"Where were you?"

"On the roof."

"And you're going to ask me to go back with you to Lusaka!"

"Where is he?" asked Luke, looking past her inside the house.

"Asleep."

"You don't have a lover?"

"Not just now."

"I love you, Chelsea." She shut the door carefully so as not to wake the child, and crushed herself against his body. They were both crying and kissing. Laughter and tears mingled, and flowed down their faces.

DOWN RIVER FROM CHIRUNDU, all was quiet in the Zambezi Valley. Jonathan had not crossed enemy spoor since the air force paralysed Lusaka.

The midwinter sun was hot but pleasant, and with the cold at night the flies were not breeding, giving respite from tsetse and mosquitoes. The river was clean and cool, and they had camped above a bend in the river where the water was calm. There were beers cooling in old orange bags in the water. The fire was smokeless, ready for the meat, and the men were smoking under the great spread of an acacia tree.

They had been in the valley for a week, following ten days' leave. His mother had bought a small house in Avondale, putting in a swimming pool and starting a rose garden among the cannas and agapanthus. She had been troubled. She could not shake from her mind the thought that, if Jonathan's driver had been faster, her son would have been buried in the grave where they had placed James Bell so far from the roots of his life.

She pleaded with her son. "Africa is beautiful but deadly. Why don't we go home? If you don't want to go into insurance, we can buy you a business. Sell those shares Matthew made worth so much. I can't live with the thought of you in danger. I don't have a lot since your father died, and what I have is all wrapped up in you. Why can't we go back to England where you can meet a nice girl and settle down?"

"I'm alive in Africa. In England it's all the same. There has to be excitement to make life worth living. Jim was yelling his head off when he hit that mine. He had life. Short, but a life. He didn't dribble it out year after year, going up to the city and sitting behind a desk. You have to do something with your life. I don't want to reach the end of it and look back on a boring job, a boring house and a boring wife who's worried about the neighbours. I don't want to compete in the popularity stakes. I want to live. Have space. Breathe clean air. Feel the brush of danger. Then I feel alive, and life is great, wonderful, exciting.

"Ma, look what Jim and I have done. Could we ever have done that in England? 'I say, old chap. Are you really in the empty bottle business? I mean, really.' Dear Mother. Relax. I'm not going to get myself hurt. Only the good die young and I was told at school day after day that I wasn't any damn good. When we win the war, I'm going to buy a tobacco farm and put on a manager so I don't get caught up in the boring parts. I'm going to start a safari company like Aldo, to entertain rich Americans. I'm going to learn to fly. There's so much out here to do, it boggles the mind. And you want to go back to England. Sorry, Mother, not me. I don't think I'm ever going to live back in England. I just can't see what for."

An hour later, the patrol came back from further downriver. "Come on, guys. Put out the fire. We're back in business. The terrs have crossed the river eleven kilometres downstream."

They had just finished lunch.

THE BALMY SKY revealed the ghostly silhouettes of trees, the fingers of the wild fig above the banana fronds. The Gap became visible, the shoreline, the smooth sea-washed beach and the rolling waves. The sky paled more, and the colourless light moved into the shadows of the trees, looking for life on earth, trying to rouse the birds to wake the world. Colour bleached the sky above the distant sea, far away across the ocean, bringing to earth the clouds while turning out the stars and banishing the moon.

Slowly, the sun reached up from the sea, blood-red, full of fire, shooting rays to herald day and spread the real dawn across the white tipped waves, pure, fleecy white, un-dirtied by an older day, reaching for the shore and the beach, the untouched, wave washed sand pure from the footprints of man or beast or the lighter touch of bird. The sun reached the tops of the trees with the wild fig, the wild banana fronds, waving back at the distant sun, alive and coloured by the ray of sun. Now it was reaching lower, down to the bottom of the trees, running back down the hills to the shadowed beach and yellowing the sand, picking out lines of flotsam on the shore and the first brave sandpiper in the morning. And then the birds began to sing, the fingers of the wild fig pointing the birds to song. God's symphony of life.

A shaft of pure sunlight crept through the open window of the hut, searching slowly down the wall, flooding the room with light and taking focus on the painting on its stand. The bright colours were smiling, reflecting the warmth of the sun, the sea, the rolling waves, the gulls circling a shoal of fish, the clouds of morning under-touched, blood-red, with the shooting rays of the sunrise red and warming, giving the signs of hope and danger, the strength and warming of the universe.

The light touched Matthew Gray awake, the delicious slow awakening from a well-slept night. He watched the sun reach the face of Lorna sleeping gently next to him, and then the sun found Peace, the small pure face asleep below her mother's on the pillow where she slept between the lives that gave her life reflecting their own, and giving the future for them all. Here in the morning sun was peace and Peace; and he smiled softly, soft blue eyes surrounded by warmth of laughter lines. Lorna's eyes flickered, bathed in sunlight, opened, snuggled and woke and smiled back at him in dawning knowledge of the day and sun.

"Good morning, my darling." The baby's eyes came open at the sound and the tiny mouth pursed out a yawn. Matt took the fingers of the child in his own.

"It's a beautiful day." He spoke again, gently, so as not to chase away the magic of the sun. They lay still, smiling at each other, enjoying their closeness and the child, rare human harmony.

"Let's go down and swim."

Naked, they rose from their bed and let the warmth of the sun enjoy their flesh, the tall, bearded, still-lithe body of Matt and the smooth arms of Lorna, her breasts proud and pointing at the day. Matt took up the gurgling child and woke the dog. Outside he stopped to breathe the fresh salt air and look across the ocean to the new-born sun. Below, the rocks were throwing long shadows on the beach and the waves were beating on the shore, spreading a pure white lacework, broken by pools of blue, dark blue, almost green.

They went down to the sea. Putting Peace on the sand with the dog sitting on its haunches, they ran across the wet sand and into the waves, going deeper, feeling the tingling salt high up between their legs, washing them clean. Matt dived a big wave; Lorna lunged and fell headlong on the water, spreading her long hair. The dog barked from the dry sand, and she turned on her back to check on her baby, found her foot on the sand and pushed back into the wave The Mozambique current had reached right to the shore and the water was salt-soft and warm. When they came out of the sea, they ran up the beach, Matt lifting Peace above his head, squealing, the dog barking, and raced up the path.

"The coals are still hot." Ignoring the chill while the water clinging to his body evaporated, Matt boiled water over the fire, sitting on his haunches with the dog, feeding lemon-grass into the open kettle. Behind the hut a bantam hen cackled, and from the top of the green roof, right across the beach a peacock called, the wild descendant of the birds brought down by David Todd. With the remains of last night's fish, they breakfasted with the dawn, Peace chewing on a flake of fish and drinking the warm, lemon-grass-tainted water. There was no hurry for anything.

Low tide was four and a quarter hours after sunrise, and Matt strapped on his catch bag over his loin cloth and walked down to the beach. The sea was just calm enough to take black mussels off the rocks but the water in the gully was churned by the running sea. Lorna watched him stride away across the beach, a tall man in the prime of his life. They had weeded the vegetable garden and planted the new tomato seedlings, nurtured from pips dried in the sun. The fruit would be small but sweet.

The header tank from which they had watered the garden by gravity was empty and, while Matt walked out onto the black, wet rocks, pounded on one side by the waves, she went to the hand pump and pushed the wooden handle from side to side, drawing the stored rainwater from the reservoir Matt had cut out of the natural rock under the house, up to the high tank, roofed with wooden planks he had saved from the sea. Their water supply was an epitaph for a drowned sailor, his teak-built yacht smashed on the shores of the Wild Coast in a winter storm. From the header tank, scrounged plastic pipes led the water into the kitchen and the outside 'throne'. The storms that lashed the Transkei coast gushed water down the roof into the big gutters and down the side pipes into the reservoir.

When the header tank slopped over, she sat Peace in the kitchen and began cutting the fruit for the tomato to join the rhubarb chutney, the pickled onions and the pickled fish in her store cupboard. On the thatched roof, pumpkins were stored, and salted meat from a wild boar lay out in strips to dry, away from the dog. Beside the hut on an old plough disc, plugged to be leak-proof, was evaporating sea water to leave the sediment of salt, which was used to cover the meat and strips of fish that hung like a tethered line of washing under the tall beams of the hut.

Next to the pickle jars were bunches of dried herbs and dried pine-ring mushrooms from the forest. Jars of dried fruit, banana, apricot and wild fig took up three of Lorna's shelves, and hanging on strings among the rows were clusters of chillies, rich reds and yellows. Today and for the three days of the spring tide, they would pickle mussels in the cheap vinegar for which Matt had walked seven kilometres back from the store in Port St Johns, giving the storekeeper a painting of hers to sell to the tourists in exchange. She liked to watch him stride back, his curved pipe, long since out, clenched in his mouth, carrying fifty kilograms on his shoulders like a bag of feathers, his blue eyes smiling with pleasure. His other life was so far away, picked over by the vultures.

He had smiled at her when he said, "I prefer the name Matt. Mark was just in case. After a few years, the press gave up. I'll have the paramount chief change our marriage certificate to Gray. For Peace. That much I still remember of the outside world."

"Lorna Gray. It sounds so nice."

"I'm glad you like it." She smiled as she worked. Teddie was more wrong than he ever knew. She had no more wish for the new world than Matt. Her mother and father refused to visit them. She had married a goy. To them she was dead. Gone for ever. Never to be mentioned. She wondered how her father would react if he knew she was married to the man who was once Matthew Gray, man of business, man of property, wealthy to the extreme of their wildest dreams. "One day in Jerusalem. Mazel tov."

Anyway, she would teach the child her religion. If God had found her so much happiness, it was fitting for her to be grateful, to praise her God with joy and faith, without which there could never have been existence. What else was man? For Lorna it was simple. They were the children of God.

# 3

Jonathan Holland woke regularly during the night, checking the silhouette of his sentry and listening to the night sounds of Africa. Without a fire, the danger from wild animals was greater than that from the terrorists. There were six terrorists, whose spoor they had been following for three days, but there were more lions, leopards, hyenas, wild dogs, jackals, hippopotamuses, crocodiles, snakes, elephant and buffalo. The men slept strapped into trees; they were young, healthy men who had followed the spoor all day and now slept through exhaustion, with their food hard rations, water that they carried and their FN rifles.

The rains had not broken, and away from the river the water-holes had dried up. In late October, it was debatable whether terrorists could cross the Zambezi Valley and climb up the escarpment into the highveld to the farms and water. The night before, the path of the terrorists had begun to curve. When the Southern Cross had become visible at three fifteen in the morning, a cloud base, the prelude to the rains, having hitherto obscured the heavens, Jonathan was able to climb down from his tree and take a true south position. The terrs were going back to the big river. Their water supply was low and they had probably cut an old track from his section's earlier patrol.

The dawn, the prelude to the heat and humidity, woke him in his tree, his eyes full of the grit of spasmodic sleep. There was not enough water to wash them out and, as soon as the light was good enough to see the spoor, the hunt continued. At eleven o'clock, when the power of the sun was taking water from their bodies as fast as they put it back from their water bottles, Jonathan found the spoor obliterated by the pounding hooves of buffalo. Something had gone wrong for the buffalo to stampede.

An hour later, they found the body of the first terrorist. The lion was still at the kill, with two lionesses back in the grass waiting for the male to finish feeding. The lion was crouched on the ground with its head burrowed into the man's entrails, its tufted tail twitching. Three hundred metres away in the thorn thickets below the kopje, three jackals waited their turn and, in the lone tree on the kopje with a full view of the kill, sat the vultures, hunched and shaggy, nursing their patience. The hyenas would wait until nightfall.

"Poor sod," said Clem Bartley. "No water, no food. That lion hasn't eaten properly for weeks." Jonathan was staring at the kill. The man's AK47 was next to him with the remnants of his pack.

"Are we going to bury him?"

"His friends ran." Jonathan's eyes were drawn to the tail of a lioness, twitching in the grass. "She hasn't eaten for a week. If we shoot the lions, the terrs will hear. Try and chase him. Get the terr's rifle."

"You're the lieutenant. All yours, sir."

Jonathan walked across the open ground, the grass brushing his thighs just below his shorts, his lightweight canvas boots making no sound on the earth, and his FN rifle ready on automatic. He was upwind of the lion, but the animal took no notice. The need for food was greater than the need for caution.

"Look out, Jon," called Clem. Two females and three cubs had stood up in the grass and, if they moved forward, they would cut off his retreat. Jonathan stopped in his tracks and turned to look into the eyes of the nearest lioness. There was no fear, or even concern. An impala would have made her react in the same way. She stood still and watched, only her tail twitching erratically, signalling the danger of a pointed gun. The lion did not remove its head from searching the dead man's belly for food and moisture. Slowly, watching the lion and its family, Jonathan pulled back from the kill, abandoning the AK47, and led his men away, to split up and look for the direction of the spoor.

Clem Barkley picked up the running spoor close to the kopje. He gave a brief shout; the RLI stick came back into formation and the hunt continued.

"They were unsure last night. Now they've run for the river." Jonathan broke into a steady jog, despite the heat and the flies. Above the running men, the thousands of tsetse fly sounded like an engine. They were following the spoor of four men, the dead man and one other having dropped out of the war.

Just before nightfall, they found another terrorist. He was unable to walk and he was clutching his gun as his only protection. He had been abandoned, left by the others to die in the night. As he heard the stick approaching, he swung the Russian gun up from the ground and Jonathan shot him in the head.

"These poor sods are committing suicide. Who the hell sent them into the valley with water bottles that size? Probably twisted his ankle running from the buffalo that were spooked by the lions. I'd like to get the bloody commissar in Lusaka, not the other three, poor sods. We're heading straight for the river; they want water more than they want to cover their tracks. The moon comes up at ten twelve and there isn't any cloud. We'll move ten degrees off the cross and be at the river to wait for his friends. We'll cover this gook with stones. Get his ID. Someone somewhere loves him. Why the hell did he want to come playing around in my back yard?"

Jonathan reached the river six hours later and set the trap along two kilometres of the Zambezi. The false dawn had enabled him to position his men on high ground, giving them an interlocking field of fire. If the terrs had reached the river ahead of him, they would be safe in Zambia. He waited in the shade of a tree, chewing a stick of biltong and imbibing regular sips of water. When they had taken out the terrs, they would make a fire and catch themselves a fat bream each. There was nothing in the world Jonathan wanted more at that moment than a nice piece of fish.

The sun rose higher in the sky, subduing the sounds of the bush, pushing the crickets to silence. A hundred metres up the river on the Zambian side, a fish eagle waited patiently and, from behind him, a lonely dove called for a lover. The day grew brutally hot and the Mopani flies crawled into the moisture around his eyes. Methodically, he scratched at his crotch where it itched like a bastard. Under his woollen socks, his athlete's foot was giving him as many problems as his itch, but he could not take off his boots.

Forcing his ears to listen intently and ignoring the irritations of his skin, he listened for the sounds of the terrs. He was the middle man in the man-trap he had set along the river bank. Down in front from his high-ground tree, some seventy metres away, two Nile crocodiles basked in the sun. He could even smell their fetid breath. In the middle of the river, a family of hippo, only their eyes and noses above the surface of the dark-flowing river, was watching him on his bank, dappled by the shade of the almost leafless acacia tree, its thorns giving more shade than its leaves.

At midday, a small buck was somewhere behind where he was sitting, probably a kilometre away behind, and Jonathan concentrated on the sound. The dove had stopped calling at the sound of flight and the big eagle moved a centimetre or two on his perch, giving Jonathan a better view of his white feathers and a perfect silhouette of the hooked beak of the predator. Ten minutes later, a flock of sand grouse broke cover, and Jonathan was sure they were coming straight at him, the broken twigs sending small, brief reports into the noonday sun.

The eagle moved its wings, dropping in a flash to glide and clutch the river, snatching a bream in its claws and planing with the fish across the water to the sand in front of the crocodiles. The bird stood and looked at Jonathan, the fish struggling helplessly in the power of the talons. Methodically, the bird began to tear its prey apart with its beak, feeding hungrily. The crocodiles ignored so small a parcel of food.

Jonathan was watching the exact spot when a terrorist, dressed in a similar camouflage to himself, broke cover and ran to the river, startling the crocodiles onto their feet, before they moved with violent speed towards the food they saw running towards the water of the river. Jonathan's FN came up and fired in the same movement. The bullet took the crocodile behind its head as it swept its lethal tail at the drinking man. Water gushing out of his open month, the terrorist turned to face the danger and screamed.

The second crocodile and the fish eagle made off across the river, alarmed by the noise. The thrashing crocodile, now half in the water, was over four metres long and still snapping. Jonathan fired at it again. The terrorist, waiting to die, gaped at him horrified. The dying crocodile floated slowly away into deeper water and the two men were left alone, looking at each other.

"The others?" asked Jonathan, in English.

"Don't know." He was shaking from fear. His English was intelligible. "How old are you?"

"Why?"

"I'm not going to fire," Jonathan assured him.

"Fifteen."

"Drink your water... ONLY ONE!" shouted Jonathan to his hidden companions. Wearily they joined him, and then took the boy back to the tree and gave him a stick of biltong to chew while they waited. It was a long, hot afternoon for all of them and, when dusk came, the boy described how all his friends had died. They lit a fire and cooked the fish they had caught in the river, the boy far too frightened and grateful to have told them a lie.

The boy had been abducted from a Church of England mission six months earlier. The terrorists had attacked the mission, seventy kilometres from Sinoia, at dusk, and ordered the pupils to join the glorious struggle to kill the white people and free their country. Not all the children wanted to go, and the boy claimed he was one of them, but he was led into the bush with the others. For three days, they avoided the security forces, leaving some of the younger girls behind to fend for themselves in the bush. He never knew what had happened to them.

They crossed the river in motorboats sent across by the Zambian police, making the crossing at night. They were then made to train as soldiers and go back, over the river to kill the white farmers. Their people would give them food and hide their guns and uniforms during the day, so at night they could attack the farmhouses. He had lost his rifle when the buffalo charged, and only because he knew how to find south from the Southern Cross had he led the others back to the river.

"Who was your leader?" asked Jonathan.

"I was the leader."

"The others were older?"

"Younger."

"Do you want to go back to Zambia?" asked Jonathan, causing his men to look up in surprise.

"I want to go back to the mission."

"They killed your teachers and burnt down the school."

"Why?"

"You'd better ask the Russians and the World Council of Churches," suggested Jonathan. "The people who give your people money to fight the war. The people who think we are wrong to try and give Rhodesia a better life than the rest of Africa."

"If I go to police, they kill me. Maybe army torture me. Information, they say. Cut off my balls. Sharp knife, they say. I go back, they send me back… We are the sheep."

They ate round the fire, feeling the comfort of the flickering flames that shot light into the trees and kept the animals away during the dark of the night. The smoke repelled mosquitoes. They were seven men alone in the middle of nowhere – six white and one black.

"Where you from?" asked the boy, his English and curiosity the product of five years' good schooling.

"London... that's in England."

"I know... what are you doing here?"

"I don't know, really. I like Africa. Want to live here. We all want to live here."

"It's my country."

"Maybe. But all of us need help. You help me and I help you."

"Maybe. But my country. I don't want help."

"You wanted a lot of help from the crocodile."

"Why you kill the crocodile, not me?"

"Instinct. We're all human. Against the crocodile, we fight together."

"I want Zambia. War over soon."

"We'll shoot up the water on either side so you can swim across. What's your name?"

"Jamba Sithole."

"I'm Jonathan Holland."

The next morning, they watched the boy reach the far side of the river, turn to them from the top of the Zambian bank and wave.

"Don't look at me like that, Clem. Did you want to shoot him? I shot one young boy because he was going to shoot me. The balls I'd like to cut off belong to the do-gooder sods in armchairs who send those kids to the slaughterhouse. One day I hope they'll all be very proud of themselves. The report will say six dead terrorists, all under sixteen years old. Are you all agreed?"

"Yes, sir," they replied in unison.

"You think he'll get back to Lusaka alive?" asked Clem.

"He has a chance, probably a good one if he meets a Zambian patrol. I'm going to take my boots off and scratch my athlete's foot."

Within a minute, the whole stick was scratching with deep satisfaction. This was followed by a wash in the river, powder and clean socks. Jonathan's feeling of bliss was equal to a cold Lion Lager. He was glad the boy had made it across. Jamba Sithole. He would remember the name.

It took them two days to walk across the Zambezi Valley, where the clouds were building up all day with the oppressive heat. There was thunder but no rain, and the nights were as hot as the days. At the foot of the escarpment, they camped next to a giant baobab tree that was as wide as an elephant. Clem was pushed up into the stunted branches of the big tree until he could pull himself into the bowl where the giant arms converged.

"About two litres in this one," he called down.

"Looks bigger." The taste would be tainted from the sap in the tree, but a man dying of thirst who was still able to climb the giant tree would survive.

The six men sat down with their backs to the tree. They were all tired but Jonathan stopped them making a fire to eat the snake that Harry Simlet had caught and skinned. They ate from tins and drank the tainted water to conserve the little that remained in their water bottles.

"Let it rain. Just let it rain," said Harry, who was nineteen years old and a clerk in a bottle store when at home in Salisbury. When he entered the army, he knew more about French wines than rifle drills and land mines.

"A cold frosty," said Clem.

As the dusk turned to night, the great pre-rain clouds obscuring the moon and the stars shrank visibility to the distance of a man's arm. Their voices came out of the darkness. There were no mosquitoes as there was no water for kilometres around. The animal calls that were heard during the night were from further back by the river, and now there was no need to sleep in a tree. Jonathan arranged the guard roster and the conversation gave way to snores and the sounds of sleep.

They had been in the valley a month. The immediate bush, the tangled thorn thicket and long, straw-coloured, sun-dried elephant grass were ominously quiet, even the insects waiting silently for the blessing of rain. Not a drop had fallen in the valley for six months. The surface earth had turned to dust, making it easy to follow a spoor. Thunder rumbled from across the great escarpment as Jonathan fell asleep, wedged comfortably against the tree, his rifle resting under the crook of his left hand. By three in the morning, all six men were sound asleep.

Jonathan was the first to wake with the dawn. It was cooler, but still hot and humid.

"Make a fire, Harry," he ordered. By the time the terrs found his camp, they would have long since departed. Dusk had been different.

The climb up the escarpment taxed every muscle in their bodies as they scrambled round boulders and through crevices washed out by the rains, using stunted trees rooted deep in the crevices to haul themselves up. The view looking back was spectacular all the way to the river, which was now shrouded in heat, the Zambian escarpment barely visible. They looked over the tops of the trees, the landscape dotted with baobabs, with not a trace of colour in the sea of brown. They climbed on upwards, spurred by the thought of food and beers, the comforts of civilisation. No one spoke.

At the top, Jonathan looked back over the heat-crushed valley far below. It was like standing in the heavens above the earth. Not a sound reached them from the valley, not a whiff of smoke as the sun dipped blood-red into the heat-haze, a great ball of molten red fire. When the light had almost gone, a bat began to circle them, dipping down almost at their heads, its keening coming and going, but the bat itself was invisible. They scanned the treetops looking for it.

"I hate bats," said Petrus Krobler, the one Afrikaner in the stick. "Hell, man, they sound like ghosts. Disembodied. I once shot one with an air gun. A fluke man. Right through the bloody head. I was drunk, waving my kid brother's gun, and down came the bat, shot between the little devil's radar. Don't have eyes, bats... give me the creeps, man... When's it going to bloody rain?"

Jonathan was glad to lead his men out of the valley. The air was cooler and less oppressive, and his feeling of isolation lifted with the highveld plateau and the first msasa tree. Somewhere far away he could hear the distant sound of a tractor ploughing the lands at night. It was as if he had re-joined the human world and the sound was deeply comforting.

The gunfire when it came was just as distant, but further to his right than the tractor sound, some fifteen kilometres from the top of the escarpment. The explosion was more distant, and Jonathan was able to pinpoint the direction of the sound. Softly, he took a compass bearing.

"That's a farmhouse under attack." They were all listening.

"Too far to be sure it's AK47 fire."

"The bang was an RPG rocket," said Clem.

"Some of the sods must have got round us down in the valley," said Petrus. "There are too many bloody terrs, man."

Every man in the stick was buckling on his webbing and, without any word of command, Jonathan led his men in the direction of the gunfire. By the time they had covered the first kilometre, the gunfire had stopped and the last of the day had faded into darkness.

"Terrs," said Jonathan. "Hit at dusk and run for the valley. They'll be coming towards us, away from the police going to help that farm. In half an hour we're going to set an ambush. They'll be running, not concerned with noise, wanting to get as far from the police as possible before the dawn sends in the choppers." Adrenaline was pumping through his body as he pushed his way through the bush, the darkness enfolding them.

He set the trap in an arc, his men lying flat in the dark, well-spaced but each knowing the exact whereabouts of his companions. They waited and listened and, when the moon began its game of hide and seek among the clouds of black cumulus, they heard the terrorists running from their pursuers, blundering through the bush and making a noise that could be heard three kilometres away. They were halfway between the farm and the escarpment.

Petrus Krobler opened the contact, killing two men he could see by the light of the moon. Jonathan saw nothing, but heard the gunfire from his men on either side of him. They waited in position for the dawn, and then waited four further hours, baked by the sun, awaiting any of the terrorists who had gone to ground, looking for movement. The vultures were flying lazily on the winds when he finally gave the command to advance. If any terrorists had survived the ambush, they would be well on their way down into the valley.

"Boys," called Clem, studying the corpses. "Kids. Just bloody kids." They left the bodies of the children for the vultures and advanced in open formation towards the farmhouse they could identify on a low kopje amid a grove of gum trees, surrounded by tobacco barns and grading sheds.

The rocket had gone over the defence wire, through the wire cage that protected the window, and exploded when it hit the wall of the bedroom, showering the two sleeping children with deadly shrapnel and punching a two metre hole in the wall into the bathroom behind. The police had arrived within thirty-seven minutes of Raleen Urbach calling the police station on the agric-alert. There had not been a chopper available for the follow-up operation as the terrorists were attacking farmhouses throughout Rhodesia, escalating the air defence and disseminating the security forces.

"Kids they might have been," said Clem. "Now are you glad you let that terr go home so he can come back again?"

"It seemed right at the time," said Jonathan.

"We got to go and hit their camps in Zambia."

"We got to stop this war, that's for sure." Jonathan Holland felt a long way from Charterhouse and the petty search for popularity.

"The woman won't leave," the police constable said to Jonathan. "Will you try, sir? Her husband was killed three months ago by a land mine on the road into Karoi."

There was blood on her skirt, blood on her hands and blood down one side of her face. "Are you hurt?" Jonathan asked her.

"Not me. Oh, for God's sake. Now the kids."

"I'll take you into Karoi."

"Why didn't they kill me as well?"

"My name is Jonathan Holland. Maybe you had better come to Salisbury. You have relations?"

"In South Africa."

"Then you'll stay with my mother."

"What for?"

"Because I can't think of anything else right now and you can't stay here," Jonathan told her firmly but kindly.

"What does it matter? Take me where you like. I want to kill those bastards."

"We did. All of them. One of them wasn't old enough to carry a rifle. He had the last rocket on his shoulder. He was probably twelve."

She looked at him with an expression of horror. Then she was sick; the vomit spurted out, covering the blood of her children.

THE CROWD STOOD on their feet to applaud at the Royal Albert Hall with the same feeling of indignation and self-righteousness that the World Council of Churches had felt when they diverted parishioners' offerings to God to freedom fighters in Southern Africa, money ostensibly for medical supplies but in reality used for the waging of revolutionary war. Des Donelly onstage felt the waves of applause at the end of his concert in support of the anti-apartheid movement and was sure they were clapping for him, his music and his great generosity.

The fund-raising success had been staggering, and in the audience Hector Fortescue-Smythe banged his claw on the chair in front of him while the noise and acclaim fed his overwhelming desire for revenge. If he could raise a similar amount of money every week, he would kill every Afrikaner from the Limpopo to the Cape and from the Cunene to the shores of the Indian Ocean. With so much money pouring into the war chest of the ANC, the liberation movements of Southern Africa, co-ordinated by the KGB, would sweep the colonial, racist, capitalist pigs into their graves or into the sea, and the Soviet Union would raise the red flag over the whole of Africa.

His unsmiling face bore no testimony to the feeling of savage joy that coursed through his body as the brilliance of communist propaganda made the capitalists of London contribute so willingly, proudly, with such beneficence, to the detriment of their own pampered existence. What was ten pounds if it atoned for the guilt of the past, the horrors of colonialism?

Some of them stood on their chairs to shout to the roof-top, the Victorian dome built at the zenith of the empire, a testament to the colonial past. It felt so good to shout at the past, to vilify their race and cry foul at the memory of their ancestors. Television cameras took the riot of acclaim around the world, making millions feel benevolent in the chairs round the hearths, fired with the self-righteous feeling of doing something to eliminate the horror of apartheid, the sin against humanity, the reincarnation of Nazi Germany, man at his worst. Here was a way the man in his chair could contribute tangibly, to participate in the tearing down of apartheid structures which made a man a slave in his own country. And it was all so comfortable, so right and the problem so far away from hearth and home.

A hundred years previously, their great-grandfathers had poured money into the coffers of the missionary societies to send Livingstone and Moffat to bring God to the savages. Now that God had found the savages, they cried freedom, freedom for Africa, tore down the colonial pillars and threw Africa and its godless millions back into their past, into the glories of anarchy and savagery in the name of human rights. And they all felt pious as they clapped and stood on their chairs, and the message of so much hope flew round the world and burst out of the screens to mesmerise the civilised world.

Gilly Bowles was thirteen years old when she realised that what men wanted was between her legs, not between her ears. It was during the same year that she decided to be a journalist. She wanted to be able to get her own back for being sent to boarding school, and she wanted her family to stop telling her to pipe down. She wanted to pipe up and be noticed. The sexual awakening was a revelation, but there had to be more to her life than a rich husband and babies and limiting her power to telling them to pipe down. By the time she met Ben Munroe, she was a second-class reporter but a first-class whore, in the sense that she used her body as leverage. Journalism wasn't writing good or even brilliant English; it was being at the centre of things, the confidant, the owners of other people's secrets, ones they did not wish other people to know. The secrets of ordinary people were of little consequence, so she slept with the rich and famous, mostly older men in business or politics. Three of them were trade union leaders, and she knew it gave them a delicious sense of inverted snobbery to sleep with a girl who had spent four years at an exclusive girls' boarding school before being shipped off to Switzerland for the finishing touches. She was not a particularly pretty girl, but her eyes worked up a story for every man she looked into, and the pert, high breasts, the small tight buttocks and the long legs did the rest. She was the most successful flirt of her class and she had honed her skill to perfection.

By the time she attended Bishop Porterstone's celebratory cocktail party, she was twenty-three, and had made sure she had never been in love, an impediment that she was sure would be boring, counter-productive and prone to give the man in question power over her. She was the one person in the room, the one outsider in England, who was certain that the bishop was a veritable fraud, and the idea of defrocking the minister was delicious.

She had slept with Ben twice before going cold on the man in a technique she found charmingly simple. Men always wanted to consume their women and to be the one to do the throwing away. Once they had sex with her, they thought of her as their personal property. There was nothing like a good flash, a good bedding and a well-locked chastity belt to have the most rampant male chauvinist, and he was manifesting all the tendencies of a love-sick puppy. Gilly thought a lot in clichés and spent much of her time trying to keep them out of her writing.

The party for Des Donelly and his band of international artists was full of the type of men with whom she liked to associate, men with power and influence and, with Ben as her mentor, the man who had drummed up so many of the black American artists of fame, she was indulged by any man she chose in the room. She chose to find out why a man with a claw hand, a man she had never heard of, was being treated as an equal by so many men who were usually either condescending or fawning. She sensed in the man with the claw a power that turned her on. She had learned the reason, though she had not yet pinpointed the cause why powerful men responded so readily to her sexual power, power that neither, usually, found able to bring to a lasting, all-consuming climax. She was the receptacle for their phallic urge, the place to plant their lasting seed, this power coming second only to immortality.

Gilly was dark, with a short, elfin haircut, the colour and sheen of a raven. Her eyes were wide apart and her mouth was large and always slightly open when she was talking to men. Her irises were a dark brown in a sea of pure white, and her perfect white teeth matched the pureness of the whites of her eyes. She wore clothes that spoke firmly of her breasts and buttocks, and her often dark stockings had a pattern of big holes accentuating the texture of her smooth legs. At special functions like the party of the anti-apartheid movement, she wore black lace mittens that made her fingers, red-nailed and long, an invitation to the central parts of a man's body. When she took an olive out of a dry martini, smoothly polished and dripping in gin on the end of a thin stick held between long, slim fingers, it was a sensual masterpiece as the olive was sucked between her lips, the red of the lips matching the flawless red of her nails.

Gilly worked her way round the room, and had no difficulty in catching the eye of her ex-lover.

"Who's the man with no smile and one hand?"

"Why?'

"I find him very sexy." She smiled knowingly at Ben.

"Hector Fortescue-Smythe. Could be a dollar billionaire by inheritance, but went off to Africa and now he's here at a political party. Take your pick … you want a Manhattan?"

"Dry martini, darling. And please tell the man one part Vermouth to five parts gin. Noilly Pratt. French, not Italian. Gin and French, darling, with a large, juicy olive... you look very pleased with yourself."

"I made a lot of friends helping the bishop."

"Is he married?" asked Gilly.

"Who'd marry the bishop? He's so fat ..."

"Fortescue-Smythe, darling."

"No. Divorced. They don't talk about him."

"Introduce... please." She was standing very close to him in the crush and rubbed her thigh over his crotch. "Then you can go over and ask that nice Italian barman – the one that looks like a real wop. How on earth did they ever create an empire?"

They eased their way through the crowded, exuberant room chock-full of familiar faces.

"Hector, meet my girl. Gilly Bowles." Gilly winced at the patronage and pulled a small face for Hector's benefit, leaving no doubt in his mind that she was no man's girl.

"They make a proper dry Martini, if that's any consolation." She knew she had Hector's full attention, having caught his eye twice during the evening. "Are you an altruist, a communist or a man who genuinely believes in the dignity of the human race? And, yes, I'm a journalist. *Daily Telegraph*. Nice and conservative."

"And Ben?"

"Ben invited me here. We're just good friends. Who invited you?"

"The bishop. We met in South Africa," Hector informed her.

"What were you doing in South Africa?"

"Working for the apartheid government. I think it's terrible."

"This party or the South African government?"

"Both."

"So you joined the AAM. Very noble. And what happened?" She waved at his arm.

"There are risks in opposing oppression. They sent me a letter bomb."

"Nasty... They really are pigs."

"Yes, they are." A picture of Helena flashed into Hector's mind.

"Are you alone?"

"Yes."

"Why don't you join us for supper?" suggested Gilly. "Ben knows all the good restaurants in London. Do you think they'll give him an OBE?"

"Probably." They were both watching Des Donelly holding court. "Even a knighthood."

"The Beatles gave back their MBEs."

"Probably because they were only MBEs. They don't return knighthoods and baronies quite so quickly."

"I want to write a big article about the AAM. From the intellectual point of view. Try to turn our conservative readers. Will you help?" asked Gilly.

"Of course. It's a just cause. You can't have governments going around separating people on account of their race."

"Maybe we can get Ben to go home early."

"That would be nice."

Outside, while Hector was waving his rolled umbrella for a taxi, Gilly held back under Ben's umbrella. It was just beginning to rain.

"Soon as you've eaten, darling, make an excuse about filing your story. Go on home and I'll join you as soon as I've found out what I want to know. And don't ring up another girl while you're waiting. I'll see you in bed." She smiled deeply into his eyes, her mouth just parted, her lips moist and rich red, and Ben felt a need so powerful his wits were dulled. It took Gilly just an hour to dump Ben and have Hector all to herself.

"You never answered my question. Are you a communist?"

Hector gave her a warm, gentle smile. "I don't think there are any communists in the Cavalry Club."

"You a member?"

"Tanks, national service. Quite a hoot, actually."

"Why the AAM?" Gilly wanted to know.

"I told you. Just cause. I'm a pure socialist. Cambridge did that. Father never understood. The old firm's run by mater, really. Didn't want to spoil my principles by joining the ranks of the capitalists. Professional managers do so much better. I went to South Africa to find out what on earth they were up to... If they don't like a man's politics, they put him in jail for up to ninety days without trial, and give him a tie to hang himself with in his cell. If that doesn't work, they methodically beat him to death. Bunch of bloody sadists?'

"Are you ANC?"

"Anyone in the AAM is pro-ANC," stated Hector. "Anyone who opposes apartheid supports the ANC. One day we'll get Mandela out of jail and march on Pretoria."

"A lot of people will get killed."

"A lot of people are being killed, Miss Bowles."

"Call me Gilly."

"Are you going to see Ben later?"

"No... I'm yours for as long as you like."

"You have me confused," Hector confessed, "I thought you were after a story."

"Maybe I was .. I love iced Polish vodka." The slim glass in front of her was heavily frosted. "French brandy in a large glass is old-fashioned. Does it hurt?"

"Yes, as a matter of fact," admitted Hector. "There's a raw nerve in my face that hurts like hell. It reminds me... Sanctions will get to the Boer eventually. My ex-father-in-law is the minister in charge of their bureau of state security. 'BOSS' is such an evocative acronym."

"Did he send you the letter?"

"No. His daughter. I thought she was after my family money. We were getting a divorce. I was a fool."

"Sounds more like a capitalist protecting his wealth... I'm sorry," Gilly apologised. "In any normal society they would hang her for attempted murder ... Why did you want a divorce? Did you throw her out? A woman scorned can be very dangerous."

He lifted the claw to acknowledge the truth. "They found out I was working for the opposition."

"Wow! That put the shit on the fan" Gilly began to laugh, a low, husky laugh both musical and genuine. "I would have given anything to see the face of the boss when he found out his son-in-law was an admirer of the ANC."

"Not an admirer. Fully-fledged member." He was also laughing, which made the blank expression of his face a menacing contradiction. "I got out of the country a few hours ahead of the police. Drove out through Botswana. She was screwing around."

"The minister's daughter? Did you love her?"

"Probably not. There isn't much of a story for you in me."

"Depends which way you look at it... What do you do in London?"

"Some family business. Mother makes me do that. And the AAM. I'm trying to get onto the committee."

"Ask the bishop," suggested Gilly.

"He's chairman. That's the one that puzzles me. What's a clergyman doing in a liberation movement? You don't fool me. The AAM is the British front for the ANC."

"Liberation theology. There are some good Catholics in South America. Jesus believed in mercy. In peace to all men."

"You sound a very sincere man. I'd like to help. I want to bring the readers of the *Daily Telegraph* behind the AAM."

"We need all the help we can get, Gilly."

THE MEETING of the South African communist party took place in London on Christmas Eve, 1977. The only person of consequence missing was Bishop Porterstone who had to attend to other duties. Hector Fortescue-Smythe chaired the meeting.

"I have some very good news to report. The Smith regime wants to talk. They've approached the British government to set up a meeting between Nkomo, Mugabe and Smith. The puppet Muzorewa will do the handing over of power. Hitting them all over the country spread their security forces too thinly and sanctions are biting hard. We must concentrate on South West Africa. Swapo need all your help and, when we have forced South Africa to give independence to the new Namibia, we will have all our resources available to concentrate on South Africa itself.

"We must instruct our friends in the ANC to start a low-intensity guerrilla war. Limpet mines in shopping centres, at railway stations. Easy to place and difficult to detect until they go off. I have some expertise in this matter. We have total control of the new trade union movement that Botha was stupid enough to sanction. Our friends in the TUC here in London did a great job pressuring the British government to pressurise Botha. It may take us years, but in the end we will paralyse their mines, and that's the way to collapse the Boers. Low-scale warfare in South Africa and total onslaught in southern Angola against the puppet Savimbi and his South African supporters. Draw the South African army away from their air bases and hit them with the Cuban air force.

"Today, we have the privilege of listening to Colonel Antonio van Perreira dos Santos Cassero of the Cuban air force. He will brief you about the new MIG aircraft being sent to Angola from the Soviet Union. The communist revolution is entering its final phase. The next decade will give us total victory. Africa, to all intents and purposes, is now ours."

SUNNY TUPPER KNEW BETTER than anyone else that Archie was her last chance. In another three months, she would be forty years old. Living with a man was as temporary as the next day, and gone as quickly. Sunny was desperate. Her figure had been forced back with rigorous exercise and willpower over her love of food, but it was not enough. Archie was past fifty and, after the first flurry of excitement, sex was not the dominating factor. If there was going to be a marriage she had to make him so damn comfortable that the inconvenience of losing her was greater than the implications of taking a wife.

From the moment he woke in the morning with Sunny bringing his first cup of tea, to the time she turned out the light for him over their queen-sized bed, she concentrated on smoothing the path for her lover. Whatever he had to say, she heeded attentively. She joined in the conversation intelligently and, though she suggested and gave him ideas, she never contradicted. She was the balm for his business worries and his honour of growing old.

For Archie at fifty-two, it was as well that he was wealthy, as most of his hair had fallen out and his paunch was testimony to too many rich business luncheons. The muscles of his youth had gone to fat, and even his voice had slowed down to a more sonorous, slightly boring monotone. His personal wealth exceeded the one hundred million mark and everyone paid him the attention his wealth deserved.

Archie was a successful businessman in the old tradition, and he never mentioned his earlier days in Mongu or the old Belgian Congo, though his leg did twinge regularly to remind him in the privacy of his mind. With Teddie Botha playing an ever-increasing role in decision-making, Archie was happy to fill the role of company representative. It was Archie's job to entertain, and he entertained while Teddie got along with the business. It was a little like the British monarchy and it worked very well.

During the day, Sunny took herself off to catering courses and classes that taught her how to arrange bowls of flowers. She dressed expensively and well, and read the newspaper thoroughly so as to be able to join in any general conversation. Realising the inadequacy of her education, she began to read avidly, from classical fiction to Plato and Aristotle, and she had herself understand what the philosophers were saying. She was going to make herself indispensable to Archie Fletcher-Wood who was going to marry her and she was going to live in the luxury she craved for the rest of her life.

Her plans would have worked out very well if Archie had not had a memory, if they had met without Archie knowing her history. But they had not. Archie remembered only too well the night Sunny Tupper had made a fool of his best friend, a best friend with an engagement ring in his pocket. Housekeepers came a lot more expensively than Sunny and were a lot less pleasant, and Archie still enjoyed a little sex every now and again without having to go to the slightest trouble.

For Archie, the arrangement was ideal. He had what he wanted without having to take the slightest risk. In business they had always known him as the bachelor with a long line of girlfriends. Cohabitation was as common as marriage; almost no one cared any more. Such a trivial matter as morality had long since been laughed away in the circles in which Archie moved. Commitment, truth and integrity had given way to lawyers circumventing the most meticulous agreements, advertising which never told the truth, and the size of a bank balance carrying greater weight than the magnitude of a man's integrity — or so it seemed. Everybody lied to get what he could. It was a new world.

BEN MUNROE HAD FOUND it difficult to have another shot at Matthew Gray but, with an eye to knowing what his public wished to read, he managed to turn a penniless recluse into a mass exploiter of the blacks in South Africa for the second time.

The story and pictures became another Munroe sensation, read and believed by millions across the world. The photographs of a man at play with his young girl 'wife' had been taken with a telephoto lens, with Lorna generally topless and Matt in his loincloth surrounded by good-looking, young and seemingly carefree people. The pictures of the colony were like the pictures of paradise, but the words that went with the pictures were as far removed from the truth as the two extremities of right and wrong. But it did not matter. The trick was to sell newspapers and magazines.

After Ben had been tipped off as to where Matt was hiding, he made a trip to Africa and quickly uncovered the fact that only a small portion of Matt's original wealth had been distributed to the poor, as very few blacks, the majority of whom valued their dignity more than a free lunch, had come forward to the banks to claim their right to a day's free food. Ninety per cent of the wealth remained in the trust account, earning compound interest and, as the banks had received only one instruction as to its distribution, it stayed where it was, with the banks making a nice ten per cent return on what they were paying the trust and charging their clients. According to the banks, the only signature that could change the situation was that of Matthew Gray. If it was ever proved that he was dead, the money would devolve to the state.

Ben's story centred on Matt living off the fat of the land at the expense of the starving masses, and that his disappearance was a gimmick to get him away from the press to enjoy this ill-gotten wealth that he had wrung from the blacks of South Africa and now refused to return to them, despite the sanctimonious illusion of altruism displayed at the man's final press conference. Once again Ben Munroe wiped the floor with Matthew Gray and made himself a huge profit in the process. The fact that the local newspapers rushed down to Port St Johns and photographed the colony with all its arts and asked how rich a man could be who lived a hand-to-mouth existence made no difference.

The following week's editions of the world's magazines carried another set of stories. Fortunately for the colony, the administration of the independent state of Transkei was so bad and corrupt that money for mending roads never figured in their spending, and the road from Umtata to Port St Johns was a test of skill and courage – the courage being needed when a bus came round the corner of the twisting mountain road on the wrong side of the broken down track. Only tourists who enjoyed the beauty of the Wild Coast with its rock fishing chanced the dangers of the road, most with four-wheel drive vehicles.

After a three week flurry, life returned to normal at Second Beach, but the colony had now become famous for what it really was, a sanctuary from the modern world, and a steady flow of happy-go-lucky drifters found their way down the Umtata road and up the coast to Second Beach.

The big problem for Matt was his wealth. After thinking he had thrown the whole lot away, he discovered that after all, the monster was still very much alive, and the visit from the bank manager, who was also the trustee, with Matt's lawyer, came as no surprise. The bank wanted him to tell them what to do with his money. The sight of the top banker in a dark suit being deferential to Matt in a pair of shorts, no shirt and hair down his back, sent Lorna into a fit of giggles, earning her a rare frown from her husband and a "Please take Peace down to the beach."

"Give it away," he said, turning back to the bank manager.

"But to whom?"

The bank manager had drawn up a list of charities, but Matt knew the fund raising business was a business like any other and that most of his money would be siphoned off by the fund raisers to cover their expenses. His grand gesture had not been so simple after all, to do the job properly so that the right people benefited from it required Matt as well as his money. Even giving it away was an exercise in good management. For the first time since he had walked up the coast, he was truly stumped. The thought of returning to the world he had left was out of the question.

"Gentlemen, leave the money as it is in the trust," he decided eventually. "Maybe one day I will have cause to give it away properly."

"Do you wish to sue the overseas newspapers and Ben Munroe?"

"Whatever for? All that would do is make him copy. The problem is his, not mine; his and the poor people he purports to champion. You can't exploit a man who has nothing to be exploited."

"Mister Gray, there is one more thing I would like to ask. A favour."

"So long as it does not require me to leave the Transkei."

"The painting. May I buy that painting? I presume it was done by your wife. My only hobby is art and that is very good. Where does she exhibit?"

"She doesn't. She sells her paintings to the local tourists. It's what we live off. That and odd building jobs I do in Port St Johns."

They were both looking at the large canvas hanging on the wall opposite the window, where the afternoon sun was playing on the rich colours of the flamingos foraging in the wetland at Umgazi Bay. The birds were tall and beautiful, the third dimension so deep in its execution that they looked as if they were walking right out of the picture into the room.

"Then how much does she want for the flamingos?"

"That one's not hers."

"You have another painter in the colony?"

"Yes," answered Matt, laconically.

"Will she sell me the painting?"

"No, but he'll give it to you. I'll have to take it off the frame to get it into your car." Matt went over to the wall and busied himself.

"You can't give away a painting like that. It's worth a lot of money."

"Of course I can. It's mine."

"But who painted the picture?"

"I did," answered Matt, shortly.

The bank manager looked from the painting to Matt and back again. Matt went onto explain, as he carefully rolled up the painting two metres by two metres in size. "My mother was an artist. She taught me to draw as a child. I get more enjoyment out of painting than business, and I give it away but only to people who understand. And none of them are ever signed. I don't have the ego for signatures."

• • •

Frikkie Swart had followed his wife across Pretoria to the house of a mutual friend, whose husband also worked for the bureau of state security. The man's wife had often given him the eye. Helena was on the fat side, but still voluptuous, and the baby blue eyes focused on some other male made him jealous, violently jealous, which led to the best sex, even if it meant that his wife was bruised for a week afterwards.

His friend's wife turned him on not at all. She was far too fat. He had known that whatever was going on was going on during the day, and it was not with the tennis professional. At night, when he came home, Helena was the dutiful wife and only made the rare mistake of looking at another man in his company, the subsequent pleasure of sex being tempered by the progressively more violent beatings.

Frikkie arrived at his friend's house at two in the afternoon, just after lunch. The house had high walls and good security, befitting a man who fingered activists as part of his job.

"This is state business," he told the guard on the gate, and pushed past him, striding up the tree lined driveway to the house. Silently he walked through the rooms, checking each one as he went, until he came to the back and the patio with the pool, hidden from anyone's view. Frikkie's friend was in Cape Town, attending to business at Frikkie's request. He opened the door into the back of the changing room that opened up onto the pool and its grass surround.

On the lawn, naked, spread out in the sun, were his wife and his friend's wife. She looked worse with her clothes off, her flabby breasts hanging to her waist. In the tableau, one next to each woman lay two coloured boys, young, free of fat and full of erection. Frikkie watched half an hour in the cool and the dark of the dressing room, and when he had taken his pictures he left as silently as he had come.

"If I hear you've mentioned my visit, you're fired, and I'll stop you getting another job in South Africa." He spoke to the guard on the gate in Afrikaans, and enjoyed the fear in the man's eyes. Then he returned to his office at the Union Building.

Judging his time carefully, he returned home half an hour earlier than usual and, when Helena opened the front door to their home he shot her three times in the face and one in the pudenda. Then he drove with the polaroid photographs to the house of his father-in-law and showed him the prints.

"What are you going to do?" asked the minister, looking quite ashen. In apartheid-ruled South Africa this was the ultimate scandal. Frikkie must be placated at all costs.

"Your daughter shot herself, Mr Kloss, when I showed her these pictures." They looked at each other for some time in silence.

"Very well. I will have the police return a verdict of suicide."

The only surprise for Frikkie Swart was the tears in the minister's eyes.

AT THE END of the year, while Hector was watching the triumphant march of communism through the talks at Lancaster House in London that were paving the way for Marxist rule in Rhodesia, the weather in Port St Johns was perfect. The warm balm of summer was brushing the Indian Ocean and the long white beaches, disturbing the fronds of the wild banana and the feathers of the peacocks with the gentlest touch.

Matt had taken his fishing rod to the rock below their hut soon after the sun had set behind the colony, touching the sky with red and orange, a triumphant fanfare to a perfect day. It was too hot to lie in bed, and the breeze that came from the sea cooled his naked body as he stood with feet firmly planted on the smooth rock, to cast far out in front of the short reef for the deep, sea fish of the ocean. Reeling back the slack, and with five hooks waving from his line deep in the ocean, he sat back on the rock to enjoy the stars and the sea. Tied to the hooks were juicy limpets he had cut from the rocks and expertly fastened to the big hooks with cotton. He had the certainty of a big, fat fish. Life was good to him. He had never been better. He was happy. He was in love. His wife loved him. What else could a man ever want?

The fact that, by midnight when the half-moon rode high in the darkness of the sky, the fish had ignored his baited hooks mattered not at all. Obviously the fish had better things to do than eat dead limpets tied up in cotton thread. He had placed the handle of the rod in a holder wedged into the crevice of a rock, and only if an unwise fish swallowed a hook would he know what was going on down in the deep in front of the reef. Twice Lorna had come down with a pot of lemon-grass tea and they had sat and enjoyed the night together, silent but in perfect harmony with each other and the balmy warmth of the night. Each time, when the tea was finished, they climbed off the big rock to the soft sand and swam in the sea and the slow, gentle waves.

After the third pot of tea, brewed in an old coffee jug a tourist had tossed out with the garbage, Matt carried down two old mattresses from the hut and they went to sleep next to the phallic rod, a piece of string attached to Matt's big toe and the taut line that gently moved to the swell of the sea. Peace was fast asleep in the hut and there were no sounds from the colony; only the sucking noise from the sea and an owl back in the forest.

They would have slept through the night and woken with the dawn, had a fish not swallowed a limpet, swum up over the reef and headed out to sea, yanking Matt awake with a yell of pain that continued after the string broke, as he grabbed the rod and tried to apply the drag. By the time he had finished bellowing his pain and excitement, the whole colony was awake and the dogs were barking. The moon had gone, but two layers of stars were so bright that they showed the line tight and running.

Lorna tried hard to strap on the leather rod holder, for the reel was running out of line, when the fish turned back to shore, Matt wound the line in furiously while Lorna fitted the handle into the hole in the leather holder now tied around his waist, and the fish came under control. Matt walked down off the rock to fight the fish from the beach, where he could sink his feet into the wet sand and hold when the fish turned back out to sea.

The day of the copper steenbras saw the arrival of a young girl at Second Beach. The whole colony had emerged with the dawn to watch Matt land a sixteen kilogram fish with a big, fat head, a wide mouth and an oval body that shone in the wet with the colour of copper. When the girl arrived, walking from First Beach where she had slept the night under a tree in the campsite, the fish had been eaten. She was carrying a backpacker and wearing shorts that displayed a good pair of legs which contrasted with a sturdy pair of brown leather boots and short grey socks. Her hair was black, her skin well-tanned and smooth, and Lorna knew she was Jewish.

Matt was standing by the fire on the high water mark, picking at the bones of the big fish with his fingers. He was smiling at everyone else's happiness. It was going to be a beautiful day, the sky cloudless, the sea calm and the wind still a gentle breeze from the sea.

"Are you Matt? I'm looking for somewhere to stay. My name is Raleen Urbach... I lost my kids and husband in the war in Rhodesia, and I'm looking for some peace. I don't have money. All I have's in the pack... I sold the farm but you can't take anything out of the country." They were all looking at the stranger.

"You've found your sanctuary, Raleen," smiled Matt. "Welcome to the colony. There's a bit of fish left on the bones, so help yourself."

"Are you Jewish?" asked Lorna.

"Yes, I am."

"So am I."

"Good," said Matt. "Now we can build a synagogue."

For Lorna, it was to be her first true friend, a friendship that was to last them the rest of their lives.

# PART 4

# 1

Sven Hylan watched the demonstration from his fourth-floor office window that looked down Hamngatan, a major street in the city of Stockholm, Sweden. It was a cold winter day in early 1981. All the placards were in English for the benefit of the television crews that fed off the demonstration like a pack of barracuda feeding off a shoal of sardines.

The placards were crude and handmade, and priceless for the cause, the struggle. 'Viva Mandela', 'Viva ANC', 'One settler, one bullet', 'Apartheid is a crime against humanity'. He and the Russian watched the well-orchestrated crowd cross Malmskillnadsgatan. A flurry of snow floated past the double-glazed window and added to the picture for the cameras.

Sven sighed. Another cause. Another demonstration. Anita was always anti something. He could not pick her out but under one of the fur hats in the cold street below his window, his daughter would be shouting with the best of them.

The Swedes were great demonstrators who believed that man needs laws and discipline in order to live. The current butt of the jokes among the likes of Sven, taken very seriously by everyone else, was the Swedish parliament, which had already passed one thousand new laws that year – one law for every eight hours of the day and night. He wondered if there was a law telling him how to go to the toilet. He did not have time even to read the new laws, let alone debate them and pass them through parliament. Were it not for the Russian connection, he would have left Sweden and gone to live somewhere else where he did not pay ninety-three per cent of his income in tax. His pile of untaxed money outside the country was all very well, but he could not spend it in Sweden.

"You know the big black nigger?" asked the Russian, who was looking through the window next to him. He had relearnt his English in America.

"One black man and five hundred Swedes," responded Sven.

"They've run out of ideas to interfere with the lives of their own people. What do they know about Africa?"

"You think they don't believe it?"

'Passionately – for the moment. The house has rung with the horrors of white rule in South Africa for the past week."

"Only a week?" The Russian smiled to himself.

Sven moved from the window and sat behind his desk. He had wanted a few minutes to think. Buying a mainframe computer from America and shipping it to Russia was a lot more difficult than stealing blueprints and formulas.

"We'll have to find a company that needs the technology," he said.

"Or a government."

"Can't we get you the know-how?"

"Take too long, buddy boy. By the time we build a replica, our weapons would be out of date."

"You don't mention the price," Sven reminded him. The Russian shrugged and went on looking out of the window.

The Swede rose and re-joined him. The Russian made him nervous. He was thinking of Taiwan. Maybe his Chinese friends could buy the computer and sell it to a South African firm, who would tranship the container at Cape Town and ship it through to Russia. Everyone would blame the racist South Africans and say they wanted the mainframe for their own weapons programme. He could tip off the Americans when it landed in Cape Town, tell them they would buy it back and then simply make it disappear. The more bizarre, the more-likely it was that the Americans would believe his story.

He would blame the communist Chinese and the apartheid government. He would sign the American document which guaranteed that he would not allow the computer to be sold to a country on the American list of unfriendly countries. By the time he had changed the certified invoice three times and the back-to-back letters of credit, he would leave three million kronor in his overseas accounts.

"Must be a head taller than anyone down there... How long will it take?" the Russian continued.

"Six months."

"You think they know anything about all that crap on the placards?"

"People like telling other people what to do. We Swedes are a nation of busybodies. We like poking our noses into other people's business."

The Russian took a final, careful look at the demonstration he had orchestrated, and wondered at the gullibility of his fellow man. Making the Swedes the conduit for aid to the ANC gave the guerrilla movement international legitimacy. The anti-apartheid lobby in America would not be jibed for aiding a Russian-supplied guerrilla army. And the money raised by the industrious Swedes would return to mother Russia to pay for the AK47s, the RPG7 rockets and the limpet mines that so easily terrorised a civilian population into changing its power structure. Manipulating Anita Hylan had been the easiest part of the exercise. She was twenty-seven, a big strong Swede with an insatiable appetite.

"His name's Luke Mbeki," said Sven. The demonstration was going off down Malmskillnadsgatan. It would be dark in half an hour. Snow was coating the fur hats and shoulders of the demonstrators.

At fifteen, Anita Hylan had lived with a man of thirty whilst demonstrating against the laws prohibiting juvenile sex. At nineteen, she had a surprisingly satisfying affair with a girl of her own age while demonstrating the rights of men to have anal sex with each other and women to play games with other women. At twenty, she had blown her mind while demonstrating the right to smoke pot and swallow LSD. At twenty-one, she had fallen in love but was unable to convince the man that monogamy had been invented by the establishment to enslave the people into neat little families that could then be told what to do. She had forced him into group sex when she had ground hashish into a cake she had baked for his birthday, and was still unsure why he had walked out on her the following day. They had all enjoyed themselves so much.

At twenty-two, she started a box card system so she could remind herself with whom she had slept. These records proved valuable the following year when she caught a dose of gonorrhoea and had to phone her lovers of the previous two months to tell them to go and have a jab and tell their friends, or the damn thing would be all over Sweden.

She had had it off with a Spaniard, doggy fashion behind a bush during a beach party while on holiday in the south of Spain. She had not even removed her shorts, which had demonstrated nicely at the time what a nice, dark Spaniard would do to a tall blonde goddess from the north. She would have phoned him had she known his name: she certainly did not blame him for the pox. By the time she walked down Hamngatan holding the 'One settler, one bullet' placard, she had had three legal abortions and had tried everything but a black man. Which was why she had agreed so quickly to the Russian's suggestion to organise the anti-apartheid demonstration.

Luke Mbeki was the first African she had met, and the colour of his skin turned her on more than group sex and young boys. She had listened to him with bated breath as he told her of what the likes of Minister Kloss were doing to his people. At forty-eight, Luke knew exactly what was going through the girl's mind when her eyes kept straying towards his trousers and, with Chelsea again refusing to move out of Lisbon and follow him round the world in his new capacity as head of fund-raising, he was prepared to play along for the sake of the struggle. Hector Fortescue-Smythe's handler, who was also Sven Hylan's partner, had warned him and explained the girl's real interest in the anti-apartheid movement.

"She's been in the business a long time. Give her what she wants. She'll have the Swedish government matching donations krona for krona and I'll take a bet we get a Nobel Peace Prize out of them." The Russian had known not to laugh at the lunacy of a guerrilla movement or its surrogates receiving a prize for furthering the cause of peace.

When he arrived at the Hylan manor house the day following the demonstration, which had been shown on seventeen networks across Europe and America, Luke was not surprised to find the father and the Russian had stayed in Stockholm for the long weekend. He and Anita had taken the train into the chateau country to the old city of Ystad, from where they took a taxi to Knutstorp Manor.

Someone had come in and lit the log fire to supplement the central heating. It was too cold to enjoy the countryside, so they spent hours around the log fire talking about Africa and the rights of man: the right to free medical care, free pensions, free pay for the unemployed, free theatre – always something free from the state. She never once mentioned that the state was the people, and the ones who demanded everything free were freeloading. Luke asked where the money came from, but was told that was a silly question; the state always had money.

When the weekend was over, he took a hot bath in his cheap hotel in Stockholm, and scrubbed himself all over for half an hour. Doubts were again creeping into his mind, and he began to question the means that justified the end. It was a breath of uncertainty, an uncertainty born from the possibility that he was being used, that the rightness of the struggle had been hijacked by the likes of Anita Hylan. Was the Russian sincere in his concern for the black people of Africa? Why was Hector so dedicated to the cause? The girl's blatant demand for payment had sown the doubt.

Could a black government in South Africa fulfil its promises to the people? Where was the money going to come from, year after year, once the first deluge of aid came to an end? How was the black man going to make enough money to provide a welfare state? His friends said they would redistribute the wealth of the white state – or, more simply, take away the assets and jobs of the whites and give them to the blacks. The years of study which led up to his doctorate told him the plan would only work once.

What did any of his friends know about running Security Lion, about running anything other than the type of liberation movement that shouted the frustration of the illiterate Third World? He was not even sure how long the Swedes could maintain their own benevolent state without going bankrupt, or without the few who made the money saying they had had enough.

Very few men were altruists, people who gave away the fruit of their labour. The white skills in South Africa would leave a lot quicker than they came. In his search for funds, he met the white South African liberal all over Europe and America, and he had the feeling that very few of them, if any, would return to a new, socialist, just society in the land of their birth. They did a lot of talking but gave little money. To them it was a game to be encouraged from their new positions of security and privilege.

Where would the ANC find the skills to run a modern industrialised country if the skilled whites took a short journey to the airport, like the whites in Zimbabwe, where the white population had dropped by half in the first year of black government? Twenty per cent of the white population in South Africa had the right of residence in the United Kingdom alone. Sweden and Anita with all her talk and blatant sexuality had brought a new focus to his own struggle for freedom.

Lying back in the hot bath, he thought of Matt; Matt who had simply withdrawn his labour, hurt to the quick by a journalist who wanted to sell newspapers. The likes of Matthew Gray created wealth. The likes of Ben Munroe were the jackals and hyenas that waited for the lion to kill before they could eat. The need to talk to Matt, to explain, to ask, to question, took his thoughts to a higher plane, away from the animal greed of the grunting, screaming Swede desperate for the climax that never came and never would. He thought of Chelsea and young John.

Eventually, he fell asleep in the bath and dreamt he was back in Port St Johns, walking the beach close to the gentle waves under a clear blue sky. The air was clean and he smelt the tang of the sea; and then he was running, running as fast as his legs would go. When he woke in the lukewarm water, he had still not caught up with Matthew Gray.

WHILE LUKE WAS TURNING on the hot water tap, Matthew was furiously adding paint to a picture that came from his mind, and the shape and colours grew with the feeling of understanding. The pain of rejection was evident, along with the weight of a monumental responsibility.

There were vague shapes of black miners hacking the rock face, distorted lamplight and teeth, eyes protruding, showing the pain and fear of manual labour deep underground. Fists clutched thorns below a brooding, tangled sky. Away from the agonised mine workers, a mass of movement looked like the surge of a turbulent sea. In the centre bottom of the large canvas was a cave leading out of the back of the picture, giving the promise of light and warmth and the feeling of joy.

Matt had been working for fifteen hours a day without sitting down, eating with hands covered in paint, the food Lorna left on the table, drinking the tea when it was cold and collapsing on the mattress next to the unfinished canvas when the lack of light in the great rondavel stopped him painting the urgency in his mind. Then he slept like the dead until the sun's rays touched the back of the hut and the frenzy to paint began all over again.

Peace had been left with Melissa and Martin with the black beard when the frenzy began, and everyone in the colony knew better than to walk up the path to the hut that bestrode the cliff overlooking the sea. The frenzy lasted ten days, and when it was over Matt sat down in the wooden chair he had made for himself from driftwood and smiled at the canvas.

"Lorna," he called softly. "Come and have a look."

She came to the doorway and stood a metre behind her husband, looking at the canvas on the easel, the sun bathing the horror and joy.

"Not bad for an amateur... What do you think? Where's Peace?"

"With Melissa," she said, without taking her eyes from the picture. Then she began to cry, and tears flowed down the perfect smoothness of her skin. She waited until she could speak, while the dog got up and scratched itself before going back to sleep. "Are you going to sign this one?" she managed.

"I'm never going to sign a painting. I'm not good enough. Frankly, half the time I don't know what I'm doing. I just do what my feeling dictates, and there it is. What do you think?'

"That you're probably the best painter in Southern Africa."

"Don't talk rubbish. I took it up for something to do."

"You can't believe that," insisted Lorna, looking up at him intently.

"Why not? I'm a business man who was thrown on the garbage heap."

"What are you going to do with it? Can't I sell this one? Matt, I can get a thousand rand for that canvas even without a signature, and Peace needs some shoes."

"No one would pay a thousand rand for the nightmare of an amateur."

"I want to send it to Everard Read," Lorna told him. "You've given away dozens of paintings, but this one we need. Please, Matt, sign that painting. For me. Trust me. You always trust me in everything but your painting."

"And who's going to pay for a frame?"

"Let me worry about the details. Please, Matt, just sign."

"For you, my love, how can I refuse? First I want a kiss, and then you can tell that little girl of mine to come and see her daddy. I'm starving. Have we got any food?"

"Raleen baked bread this morning and Carel brought in a pig. How that truck of his doesn't fall apart, I'll never know."

"Have you looked under the bonnet? He's a crook, darling," smiled Matt. "A sometime benevolent thief and he will most likely land up in jail. Or he may just become very rich and go to America, but I think that idea's fading a bit. Either the dagga business is in recession or he likes it here."

"He likes Raleen."

"I hope you told her he deals in drugs."

"I told her," Lorna assured him. "She seems to think pot is no worse than whisky or cigarettes. Like everything else in life, she says it has to be taken in moderation. A joint or two clears the brain. Something like that. This brush will do. Blue paint. Blue for Gray. Come on, my giant, sign it or I will do something very dangerous with the other end of the brush. Then we can swim on the way to Melissa. You must make the right noises about her tarot cards. She really believes she has the second sight."

Very slowly, Matt wrote his name in full in the right-hand corner of the painting, put down the brush and took his wife's hand. There was no one on the beach within a hundred metres, so Matt dropped his loin-cloth and ran into the sea as naked as on the day that he was born. A big wave curled up and he dived into the centre, coming out at the back and shaking the sea from his hair and beard. He had never felt so good in all his life.

The minstrel boy watched them from the cover of his hide through the hole where the milkwood tree allowed a narrow view of the beach and the sea. The foliage was thick and the small one-man tent he had put up was invisible to even the closest scrutiny.

He had been at Second Beach for a week, coming out at night, making sure that the refuge they had told him about in Johannesburg was secure. He had been on the run for five years, ever since the Soweto riots when the black children had revolted against being taught in the language of their oppressors, Afrikaans.

"Try the Transkei, boy. They're meant to be independent. There's a hippie colony outside Port St Johns. Blend into the scenery. Jo'burg's too hot. PW Botha thinks the total onslaught is directed at his chosen people and any white man deserting the army should be shot. Why don't you get out of the country and join the ANC? They welcome white recruits."

"I don't want to shoot whites any more than I wanted to shoot black kids who wanted a better education," protested the boy.

"Try the Transkei. If the MPs find you, you're dead meat. They don't treat political deserters kindly in the defence force. When you crossed the line five years ago, the rule of law went out of the window. Better still, get out of Africa."

"I don't have any money and I don't have a passport."

"Can't help you there. Best of luck, boy, but you can't stay here any longer and, as you say, you don't have money."

Back at the start of his odyssey, he had changed his name and grown an apology for a beard, and after six months had relaxed, taking jobs in bars and working in restaurants. Then he had begun to sing, which was fine until he made a name for himself and they printed posters of John Marais. Someone told the newspapers his real name was Wilhelm Pretorius Marais, that his great-grandfather was old Oom Paul Marais, the Boer general who had run the Brits a dance for two years, the last of the Bittereinders; that Wilhelm Marais was a deserter from the South African defence force whilst doing his national service and that the police could pick him up at the Tulbach Hotel where he was singing on Tuesdays and Fridays.

Luckily, there were three entrances to the hotel and the minstrel boy was having a break, taking a pee. When he emerged from the toilet, he knew that the red-capped men in uniform could only have been after him.

He went through the coffee bar and to his friend in Hillbrow. That had been a month ago, and he was still scared. They had retrieved his eight string guitar, given him the tent and told him to hitch a ride to Umtata and then to Port St Johns. All the time he was terrified, his vision of the detention prison worse with each day of the panic. His only hope was the big man swimming in the nude in the giant breakers, the Wild Coast living up to its name. Above all, the minstrel boy needed food and a friend.

He watched them come out of the sea, the great rollers coming in from a kilometre from the shore. He longed to catch the waves on his board, the way he had lived before the army reached out and plucked him from the beach at Geoffrey's Bay. When they were fifty metres from his hide deep in the milkwood and the tall wild fig trees, he began to play one of his own compositions. He sang, and the notes were pure, the words were sweet and the sound was the magic that heaven was meant to be.

Matt stopped in his giant stride, his loin-cloth in place. He listened to the music and looked from whence it came. Lorna took his hand and they waited in the hot sun.

When it was over, they walked towards the bushes. They were almost there when a ragged man with unkempt hair and the smile of an angel stepped out of the thick bush, the guitar on his back but no shoes on his feet.

"You are Matthew Gray." said the boy as a statement.

"Yes."

"I'm the minstrel boy and I need your help."

"What's the problem?"

"I'm on the run."

"Criminals are not welcome in the colony."

"From the military police," the boy added.

"That's different. You'd better come with us and meet Black Martin. Then we'll find some food."

Martin with the black beard, Black Martin, gave them food. The afternoon became evening, and the colony came one by one to the new sweet sound of the minstrel boy's guitar. He sang till the dusk brought the people closer to the fire for the light of company; then the stars came out and a joint was passed. The crash of the waves on the shore, the rolling stones as the sea withdrew, the call of the gulls and a dove, a brave dove, heard softly between the bolder sounds, became one with a soft warm wind and the scent of night-blown flowers.

Raleen watched the minstrel boy, thin, gaunt and innocent; Carel van Tonder watched them both and knew she was gone. He sighed, listening to the words and the poetry he could never write and he looked up at the stars from where he sat on his haunches, away from the light of the fire: two layers of crystal, perfect stars studding the black sky with diamonds. Maybe it did not matter; maybe he would not go to Fort Lauderdale; and maybe the soft night, the powerful sea, the music of the man and the people around him of gentle persuasion would go on for ever. Matt and Lorna, holding hands as they so often did, seemed spellbound by the music, and young Peace was curled up and fast asleep on a rug at their feet, like a puppy-dog exhausted by a day of joy well spent, and happy in her dreams, her mother stroking her sleeping brow as gently as a butterfly.

Raleen had been kind to him, thought Carel. That was good. He had listened to her tell about her children. That was good. He had heard about her husband. All dead. He was the listener, never could have been the lover.

He rose from his haunches and walked down to the beach and along the shore. A sliver of moon came up and he watched from a rock as the tops of the distant curling waves frothed white in the light of the moon. A ship was due to flash its distant light in three days' time, and that would be the last. If he stayed in the colony, fixing the motor of the fishing boat and doing odd jobs on tourists' cars, he could live, and the money in America could stay and grow and be there for his winter's day. The old man he would pension. Keep him in food and tobacco for the rest of his years.

Carel's last dreams of wealth, the life of the other world, had gone out with the boy's guitar. He belonged in the colony, after so many years. He and the boy would surf the big waves. She had never really been for him.

He looked up at the stars and, faint but visible, above the second layer of the stars, was the third, so precious a layer, and the night was clear and pure. Strange, he thought; I am happy, and happiness is worth all the jewels on earth.

A week after the minstrel boy had made his bed in the lean-to next to the two-roomed brick house of Black Martin, a beautiful dark girl appeared on Second Beach and rented a small, thatched rondavel in the municipal campsite that bordered the colony. This was home to the tourists that gave the small living to the waifs and strays, the drifters who made up the ebb and flow of the colony. She was dark of complexion and her hair was long, shining with the same blue-black of a raven's wing.

She was Malay of ancient lineage, and the fifth generation of the flotsam left behind by the Dutch who had transported trouble-makers from their rich spice colony of Batavia to the Cape, the halfway station for sailing ships to replenish their stores with fresh fruit and vegetables for the onward voyage round the Cape from the Indies. She was pure Malay of aristocratic heritage, her great-great-grandfather having been a sheik of the island, and she was Muslim. Under the strange, cruel laws of apartheid, she and her family were classified as coloured.

They lived in District Six in Cape Town, until the government tore the coloured from their homes and deposited them in the new suburb of Mitchells Plain, many kilometres from their work and in clean, sterile rows of neat houses that lacked the pulse and life of the Malay quarter. It was like throwing a fish above the high-water mark. The Malays were stranded and miserable and their old homes were torn down to make way for a new white suburb.

Apartheid, separate development, had separated the races that little bit further at the whim of the autocrats in Pretoria. Sophia's great-great-grandfather had taken a Dutch name, as he was not allowed to use his own, the Dutch not wishing to remind anyone he was a sheik in Batavia, but Sophia van Hock looked nothing like a Hollander.

When she arrived, the people of the colony noticed that she was always smiling, laughing with herself, hugging herself with joy and what looked like a great expectation. After three days the smile began to fade, and at the end of a week she was dying, so Matt sent Lorna across to help and find out what could be so much the matter with so beautiful a girl. Lorna was gone all morning and most of the afternoon, Peace and the dog staying with Matt while he fished from the big rock down in front of their house.

Somewhat like pulling teeth, Lorna dragged out the story and convinced the girl to move out of the thatched hut she was renting daily, ever thinking only a day was necessary, and moved her into the big rondavel above the sea. Matt heard the story that night when the girl was finally asleep, exhausted by emotion, on a mattress next to Peace.

Sophia had committed the worst sin in apartheid South Africa. She had fallen in love with a boy who was not of her racial classification. Under the law she was only allowed to marry or bed a coloured, a person of mixed race. Forbidden were Asians, blacks and, above all, whites; the penalty, jail, the chances of circumvention in the Republic of South Africa nil. Their only chance was to leave the country or live in one of the strange homelands, such as Transkei, recognised by South Africa and no one else in the world as independent, where the laws of apartheid did not apply.

Sophia and her young lover were to have fled together to Port St Johns, where they would marry and live happily ever after. They had left separately, but her white lover had not arrived. When, at the end of the week of waiting for him, she had phoned his house in the rich white suburb of Constantia, his mother had told her their boy had seen sense, that to throw away his career at the age of nineteen and not finish his degree at the University of Cape Town where they had met was senseless, and would Sophia please keep away from her son or she would call the police.

Matt had listened in silence as they walked along the beach, and then he spoke quietly. "There are aspects of the human race I find so disgusting I am amazed we have survived so long. I am ashamed to be part of that race... poor child. What are we to do?"

"Look after her. Hearts can mend. The colony may be her salvation."

"Let her stay?"

"She won't go back to university. He is there ... maybe the boy?"

"You'd better ask Raleen about that." Matt gave a deep chuckle. "I thought good friends confided in each other."

"You think ... she's three years older than the boy ... maybe the sand, sea and sun will heal, thrown in with a little wisdom. She can't even talk to her own mother. For a Malay to spoil her bloodline is a worse sin than for a white. Parents can be so silly ... Peace wants to meet her grandparents. Everyone makes the simplest things so stupidly complicated."

"Your parents will come around in time," Matt assured her. "Peace is nearly four years old."

"And absolutely gorgeous."

"That she is." They walked on in happy silence. "We're very lucky, Matt."

"That we are."

The early morning sun pushing up from the sea found the minstrel boy astride Carel van Tonder's surfboard out where the big waves formed, waiting for the swell to lift, watching each formation building out to sea. He had paddled out in the first light of dawn, having paddled in the previous night in the dusk. The sharks, the theory went, were well fed on the Wild Coast, the sea teeming in fish with only the colony's old ski-boat to catch the occasional fish. He was alone on the water, his borrowed wetsuit keeping his body warm, and there was nowhere on earth he would rather have been.

He had been at the colony a month, and today was Christmas Day. When they asked, he would sing them carols around the big fire on the beach. An ox was being cooked, had been started the previous day, and everyone on Second Beach had been invited for Christmas, including the paramount chief of the Ponda at Matt's personal invitation.

On shore, looking out to sea and the lone small figure waiting out there for the big wave and the hope of running the Tube, Sophia watched the sun rise and the day begin. To her Muslim faith, a faith she believed in and loved, Christ was a prophet and, as some of the others at Second Beach were Muslim and all were invited, the bull had been specially butchered according to the Muslim religion. The colony, according to Matt, was for all people and no one should be precluded from a day of joy and celebration. Sophia smiled at the thought of the man's constant consideration and, though the emptiness was deep in her stomach, a pit of hopelessness, she no longer cried.

Out to sea, the minstrel boy paddled furiously with his hands, looking back, judging the building wave. As he caught the curling crest he stood up on his board and rode the wave rushing down the side of the green-blue water as it curled over his head, holding the water with one hand as he crouched and looked down the tunnel of sea, riding the tube. His moment of ecstasy seemed to be suspended in time as the great wave thundered in to the shore, throwing him out like a cork from a bottle.

He was shouting his joy at the top of his voice as the board slipped over, landing him back on his feet. After a moment, savouring the perfect wave, the minstrel boy began to paddle out to sea, to wait again for another few moments of pure exhilaration that left the South African army so far away that it might as well have never existed.

Sophia drew up her knees and hugged them tight, happy for the boy but, on her own little seat on the sand, sad in comparison. The wave looked so big and strong, so very important to the boy. It was a tower of beauty that made petty her thoughts of loneliness and the aching void that would never be filled. That life was over, the promised land seen and lost, found so wondrously and lost so fast; gone for ever that brief moment of a pure, beautiful life that made the rest a mundane worthlessness that was utterly futile.

She sat for an hour watching the boy as he studied the waves astride his board, but the big one never came again. Then the sea calmed with the new day and the ski-boat went out to fish, dodging the diminishing breakers until it found a way to the open sea. It was expertly gunned by Carel van Tonder, who waved to the lonely boy out on the sea.

The life of the colony picked up around her as the visitors came down to the beach and Matt took up his job as life-saver, warning the unwary swimmers. Always they called out, "Happy Christmas!" and she thanked them too.

As the minstrel boy came into the shore, paddling along with the waves, she rose and walked away down the long white beach towards the Gap and the big rondavel. She waved to Matt on his perch atop the lifesaver's stand, the megaphone next to his feet. The wind had changed, and the tang of the sea was strong and fresh. The big wave had gladdened her heart, and she looked around at the beach and the sea, the wild banana trees running riot on the hills, the wild fig higher than the fronds of the banana tree and the lush green of the milkwood down on the shore.

The smell of roasting ox reached her from the small, private beach away from the crowd, and she knew the pain would leave her in the end. Lorna and Raleen were tending the giant spit, basting the carcass, and Peace and the dog were getting in the way. Two of the men were moving the hot coals from the secondary fire, and all of them waved as she walked through the small space between the giant boulders that guarded their private beach.

"The minstrel boy caught the perfect wave," she called, giving them the smallest of smiles.

"There's life after a broken heart," whispered Lorna to Raleen.

"Yes, there is. A different life. But life." She was thinking of her dead family, and for a moment she saw the farm and heard the guns. Jonathan Holland was there in her mind, along with the wide sweep of land to the great escarpment. It was all so far away and gone forever. She turned, and through the passage between the boulders watched the boy stride along the beach carrying the surfboard under his arm, and she smiled.

"It's going to be a beautiful day," said Lorna.

"Mummy, can I have a piece of meat?"

"Not yet, darling."

And the dog barked for the joy of it, and there was peace on a small part of earth and joy in the heavens.

From his perch on the life-saver's tower, Matt watched over them all. He was happier than at any other time in his life as the future unfolded around him, seemingly going on forever. He was home where he was born, and the spirits of his mother and father were close and they, too, were happy.

"You would have loved my little girl," he said aloud. "Happy Christmas," he whispered to them. "Happy Christmas."

. . .

# Part 4

AT THE END OF JANUARY, when most of the tourists had returned to their cities, a young man appeared by the side of the road, dropped by one of the recent tourists who had given him a lift from First Beach, seven kilometres back down the coast. He looked bewildered, uncertain what to do. He carried a single suitcase instead of a backpack, wore long trousers instead of shorts, and was so white of complexion that it was doubtful he had ever seen the sun. Dumped at the side of an African road, he looked both ludicrous and a little bizarre.

Carel saw him on his way back from the beach after an hour stolen from the boy on the surfboard. Carel looked, and then looked again when he saw the young man open up his walking stick so that the top formed a seat, and sit down. The suitcase was just off the main road, and the man's perch was comfortably in the shade of the big wild fig at the entrance to the campsite. The young man seemed to have no intention of entering and booking himself a hut. He was tall, well-built with good shoulders, and his hair was sandy red. The soft blue eyes that watched Carel approaching him were somehow familiar.

The young man sat on his stick and did not move, though the eyes watched Carel coming closer with a nod of satisfaction. It was as if the young man was used to people coming to him. The eyes were scarcely curious and gave the lie to the man's appearance. However he might have looked, he was perfectly at home under the tree out of the sun, sitting on his shooting stick.

Carel inclined his head as he passed, and received in return a quizzical smile and a look which revealed that Carel van Tonder amused the young man immensely.

"What's so funny?" demanded Carel in English, turning back. It was that obvious that the man was not an Afrikaner.

"You won't go far on that boat."

"It's a surfboard, not a boat." The man was still smiling at him. "You looking for someone?" Carel continued sarcastically. He had taken an instant dislike to the man.

"Actually, yes, as a matter of fact." His accent was plummy English. "Is it always so hot? Man called Gray … You know a man called Gray? Pater said he was very tall. Never met 'im myself."

"Matthew Gray?" The man probably belonged to Matt's other life. "Big rondavel at the end of the beach, this side of the gap." Carel moved off again, and had walked on a few paces when the man continued the conversation.

"Could you show me, old chap?"

"No." In reply, there was a deep chuckle from beneath the fig tree, and Carel stopped and turned again. The man was looking at him with apparent pleasure.

"You must be one of the dreaded Boers... He's a distant relation of mine. Maybe you could go and tell him the earl of Lothianmore is sitting under a big tree and requests the pleasure of his company."

"Are you serious?" Carel demanded rather than asked.

"Quite. Absolutely. Tell Mister Gray that Charles Farquhar, twelfth earl of Lothianmore in the county of Lothian, requests the pleasure of his company under the big tree. Being unfamiliar with the types of trees you have here, I am unable to be more specific. There's a good chap. I haven't had my breakfast. You could mention that as well."

"I could, could I?"

"Very kind of you, old chap."

Carel swore at him in Afrikaans and left him sitting under the tree where he remained all morning, until word reached Matt that someone wanted to see him under the big tree outside the entrance to the campsite.

To Charles Farquhar, the apparition that confronted him just before noon bore no resemblance to the young man described by his late father, but then it had been a long time ago.

"My name is Matthew Gray. I believe you are looking for me." Charles had read the stories but still could not imagine how the freak in front of him was going to solve his problems.

For the first time since his arrival, he rose from his shooting stick and extended his hand. "Hello, Gray. Charles Farquhar. When you visited the castle, I wasn't born, I'm afraid. My father mentioned your grandmother. I need a little favour, old chap. Would you be a good fellow and buy the castle. Keep it in the family. Death duties. Pater died a year ago, and inland revenue say that, if I don't come up with half a million pounds, they'll take the castle. I mean, that's quite ridiculous, as I barely had enough money to fly to Johannesburg. Do you think you could run to lunch? Jolly silly of me, but fact is, I don't have a bean in the world, as inland revenue have frozen the bank account. How they valued that old pile of stone beats me, but you can't argue with the tax man. They won't budge a penny from the half-million."

"Who's the funny man?" asked Peace, looking up at the whitest man she had ever seen.

"This is my daughter, Peace," Matt introduced her.

"Then she must be some kind of relation to me."

"It would seem so. You'd better give me that case. You'll be able to carry the shooting stick, I suppose?"

"I should be able to manage if it isn't too far."

They had gone halfway to the rondavel before the Scotsman spoke again. "Point is, my father said before he died that, if your ancestor had been a male and mine a female, I'd be you and I'd be carrying the suitcase, if you see what I mean. There was some other talk about charity beginning at home, but I won't bore you with all that, if you know what I mean, old chap."

"Good."

"I say, who's that positively gorgeous girl over there? She's absolutely ravishing."

"Sophia van Hoek,"

"Does she live here?"

"Yes."

"Good. I'm going to like it after all."

"Are you staying long?" Matt looked at him quizzically.

"I don't have any money. Rather like your grandmother when she arrived at the castle. If you see what I mean, old chap."

"I think I get the drift."

"Jolly good. Could you make the introduction, old chap?"

"Not just now, Charles. Not just now. We don't allow people to chase young girls before they have had their breakfast."

"So you did keep me waiting." It was spoken happily, as if they were old friends sharing a joke.

"I was painting. And, if you're going to stay, I suggest you lighten up a little, or it will be my pleasure to box your ears." Matt was finding it a little difficult to keep his patience. They walked across the beach in silence, Matt carrying the surprisingly heavy suitcase and his distant cousin following five paces behind, swinging the shooting stick.

At the bottom of the path up to his rondavel, Matt put down the case.

"What the hell have you got in here?"

"Best of the family heirlooms. Damned if I'd let inland revenue have everything. They're for you to take your pick. Sort of an olive branch in adversity. Why do you live in the back of beyond when you have so much money?"

"The money is in a charitable trust."

"But you can control the trust."

"How do you know?" demanded Matt.

"I made it my business. Desperate people search every avenue and you, Gray, are the family's last hope."

"Why don't you sell the castle for the death-duty valuation?"

"No one wants to buy. Living in a house full of ogling tourists isn't everyone's cup of tea, old chap."

"Then give it to the tax man."

"After all those years of history? Over my dead body! This is obviously going to be more difficult than I imagined. You'd better give me the suitcase to carry, old chap."

The entire wall space of the big rondavel was covered with paintings, only the bookshelves Matt had carved into the rock face being spared the riot of colour and movement that spread around the home. Charles Farquhar, Earl of Lothianmore, took Lorna's hand in silence and kissed it correctly, but kept his eyes on the walls of the thatched room, as sunlight poured in through the big windows from three sides. He had put down the heavy suitcase, but still carried his shooting stick as he went from canvas to canvas. The soft blue eyes lost their lazy humour and showed intense interest and understanding. He stopped at the large unfinished painting on the first easel, and then at the second easel, floral and foliage in pastel with lighter colours that Lorna had worked on for a month.

"This one's yours and that one's his." It was a statement, and the eyes were now full of excitement. "Both have the third dimension and you taught him how to paint, Missus Gray. I pronounce you both to be great painters, and I thank the day that rude journalist wrote such a slanted article about your husband."

"You know something about painting?" Lorna was finding it difficult not to laugh.

"Oh yes. I studied fine arts at Edinburgh and visited every gallery in England before I was fifteen. Kind of a hobby. Well, more of an obsession... How do you sell your art?" he asked, turning to Matt.

"I don't. I give it away. Lorna sells to the tourists. What we live off"

"Amazing. Quite amazing. Do you mind if I take off my jacket?"

"In this heat you'd be quite mad not to," laughed Lorna. "Matt's the talented one, not me. His mother was an artist."

"My ancestors had a strange habit of marrying artists, Gray. Where you get from, probably. Genes are strange carriers of disease and genius. You have to be born to anything, Gray."

"Please call me Matt" He was being sarcastic.

"You may think I'm patronising, but I'm not … I have lived a life cut off from people, except when I went to varsity. I want to become an art critic, you see. Or an art dealer. I could sell these paintings in Edinburgh for a lot of money."

"Before we get too carried away, there's some leftover fish from yesterday that shouldn't have gone off, and Raleen baked this morning and left us some bread... Matt, for goodness sake, lend the young earl some clothes. He looks quite ridiculous. And keep out of the sun, Charles, except in the early morning and late afternoon. You can have the mattress on the other side of the room from Sophia."

"She lives here?"

"Yes, she does."

"That goddess. I have arrived in heaven." Matthew Gray shook his head and then he began to laugh.

WHILST CHARLES FARQUHAR was changing into a pair of Matthew's shorts and exposing the knobbiest knees Lorna had ever seen, a thousand kilometres away in Johannesburg the manager of Everard Read gallery was facing a dilemma. The third exhibition of paintings by Bernard Strover was taking place, and the man from London to whom Matthew had sold the old Dutch masters in another life had bought eleven of the paintings. The money paid in pounds sterling, pleased Bernard Strover, as it circumvented South African exchange control and, when he sold the pounds on the black market, they would be worth double the official commercial rand rate of exchange.

Bernard Strover's financial background had been invaluable and, coupled with his knowledge of modern paintings, was making him a pleasant income to supplement his substantial salary as an investment consultant for Teddie Botha. On his visits to Port St Johns to evaluate the casino and recreation complex, still envisaged for Second Beach when the political climate was more favourable, he had found the unsigned paintings in the restaurant, the mayor's office, and one of the best in the butcher's, all of which he had purchased for a few rand and shipped to Johannesburg. Here he signed them with his own name to give them authenticity and himself the fillip of fame that came with being an artist.

Bernard had a predilection for female artists of the young and hippie variety, and liked to live the bohemian life during the weekends down by the Vaal River, away from the pressures of big business and Teddie Botha, a man who considered a day was created for work and nothing else, grudgingly granting six hours' sleep every night as a necessary evil.

The first exhibition had been to impress his artist friends but, when the canvases sold out in three hours at an average price of nine hundred rand, Bernard became an instant celebrity in the world of art. For the second exhibition, the paintings having been tracked down with careful dedication to those who had received Matt's gifts, the gallery had doubled the price, and for the third they had invited the man from London.

Bernard Strover, dressed in arty gear that would have greatly surprised Teddie Botha, was attending his own exhibition, surrounded by arty young girls, when the painting sent by Lorna from Port St Johns arrived from the picture framer. It was the largest and best canvas Matt had painted and was welcomed by the manager and the man from London, until both of them noted the signature in the bottom right-hand corner. Bernard Strover went cold all over. The painting belonged like a brother to the Bernard Strover exhibition.

The gallery was full and, as the unwitting staff of the gallery hung what they knew was a Bernard Strover without looking in the bottom corner, a crowd gathered around the painting of Hope. All but two of the remaining paintings carried red stars. The man from London caught sight of Bernard Strover looking at the painting of Hope, and knew that something was wrong.

"Better take that one back into your office," he said but before anyone was able to do anything about it, one of Bernard's young girls asked the question.

"Who is Matthew Gray?"

"Where did this one come from?" the Englishman asked the gallery attendant.

"Port St Johns. Special delivery. We had to have it framed."

"Who's the painter, Mister Strover? You or Matthew Gray?" They looked at each other without speaking for a moment.

"I've never painted a picture in my life," Bernard eventually admitted, having the intelligence to know that, when caught, the truth is usually easier to explain.

"Then you had better go down to Port St Johns and come back with a document saying Matthew Gray gave you permission to sign his paintings," said the gallery manager. "Otherwise the fraud squad will put you in jail. Furthermore, I require a statement in writing protecting this gallery which exhibited your work in good faith. And while you are in Port St Johns, please ask Mister Gray if he wishes to exhibit with Everard Read. I am very curious as to why he signed this one painting and not the others. Most artists have an ego bigger than a house."

"Maybe he thought this was the only one worth signing," suggested the man from London. "He sold me paintings once. I think I will come with you, Mister Strover. Together we can save your neck."

The man from London had also read the deluge of unfavourable press reports directed at Matthew Gray.

WHEN THE CONTRITE Bernard Strover stated his case, Matthew listened carefully, while the man from London continued to circle the rondavel accompanied by a not-so-pale Charles Farquhar, who was by now looking a little less like a ghost from the highlands. Sophia was watching them closely, though still determined not to have anything to do with another man in her life.

"I am flattered to hear that the paintings sold so well," said Matt. "Lorna was worried about a pair of shoes for our daughter. The simple answer is for you to carry on signing the paintings, subject to two conditions. First you convince my old company that Second Beach, Port St Johns, is not the place for a casino and, if my wife wishes formally to educate our daughter, you undertake to pay the fees. That way we all get what we want.

"And one more thing. The Englishman you brought with you once did me a favour. He is honest. Any paintings he wants, he can have for nothing, provided they carry the name Bernard Strover. The one you brought with you, I will paint over my signature. That way I can live in peace, you can play artist with the young ladies, and Ben Munroe hears nothing. And if you would be kind enough to take back another young man in your car, you would be doing us all a favour. And if he asks you to buy a castle, take him seriously.

"Now, gentlemen, if you would be so kind, I have work to do. My wife will show you the local restaurant. My old friend from London can discuss the shipment with Lorna. There are three hours' light left in the day, and every one of them is precious when I feel in this mood."

For Matthew, a brief glance back into his previous life was enough. He was content as he was, and wished for nothing to disturb his tranquillity. He was briefly surprised when Sophia agreed to go with them, and then he was left alone. Even the dog had gone, yapping happily down the path to the beach.

But the spell had been broken. Despite the intense wish to disappear into the world of his painting, no such thing would happen. He had a feeling of heaviness in the pit of his stomach. His mind was drifting far away to other days and other places. For the first time since walking up the beach from Cape Town, he felt the need to get drunk. Whatever he produced in life, there was always someone ready to take it away. Even his painting.

The Vuya restaurant nestled among the milkwood trees. The building was low-thatched and spacious, and the tables set generously apart from each other. At the back, the wild banana trees rustled in the breeze and the long stoep was set with tables.

The owner, who was his friend, had given up a career in the circus as a catcher on the high wire, and any money that was made from the spasmodic throngs of tourists was lost to the colony, who used the restaurant as a side-walk cafe that overlooked the beach instead of the street The owner's rationale was that artists and drifters attracted the paying customers, but the truth was something else. Profit was not the motive, survival and lifestyle being the prerogative. The food was superb, the beer cold and served with fresh cooked mussels from the sea, and the minstrel boy sang during the evenings for his supper and the pleasure of trying out his songs.

Surprised at the double-damask dinner napkins, the pure white table cloths, the exotic flower arrangements and the smell of French cooking in the back of beyond. the man from London became expansive and asked everyone to join him for lunch. His second surprise was when the minstrel boy, Raleen and Black Martin eagerly took up the over-generous offer and, before he knew it, three tables had been joined together, as the word drifted out to the colony. When he looked up from studying the menu, he found himself host to a round dozen for lunch. His third and happiest surprise was to realise, on converting the price into pounds, that the Dorchester would charge more for one lunch than the Vuya for twelve.

By the second serving of chilled white wine, it was obvious that the party would last for some time, so he sent a message to the Cape Hermes Hotel at First Beach to reserve him a room for the night. Then he settled back to enjoy himself and remember his youth, while the minstrel boy sang and Lorna went up to fetch Matt from the rondavel. A singsong shook the rafters and food kept arriving from the kitchen.

Charles Farquhar performed every trick he knew to gain the attention of Sophia, but to no avail. Belted earls figured for nothing in her life and his title made not the slightest impression. Tales of his own days at Edinburgh University made her cry, and she then drifted off into a world of her own, oblivious to Charles or the joy that had taken over the restaurant. Some of the boy's words made her cry again; Matt, singing badly in a deep, tuneless bass, failed to erase the tears, and with each small glass of wine her sadness grew.

The dancing began after the food, with the kitchen staff joining the guests. The man from London wrote out a cheque in sterling instead of in rand, which cost him four times more than was necessary, but by then he did not care, giving a flourish to his signature that was going to give his bank manager, an old friend, a good smile on a bleak winter's morning in London.

The luncheon finished long after the sun went down, and when Bernard Strover drove them to First Beach, erratically but safely, Charles was in the car. During the days when he played centre for his school first fifteen, Charles had always been able to see the gap, and he had seen one as large as a house that suited his purpose. He had tried selling the castle to a happily drunk Bernard Strover and bequeathed the problem to the office of the inland revenue. No one wanted to buy his castle but, having a one-track mind, his problem was Sophia rather than the old pile of stones left him by his ancestors.

By the time they reached the Cape Hermes Hotel, he had convinced Bernard to set him up with a camper, a lift to Johannesburg to buy the camper, and a small salary of three hundred rand every month. In exchange, Charles would save Bernard the trouble of chasing up the Gray paintings that Matt gave away at a whim. Charles would follow each painting's progress from the easel until it rested in the Everard Read gallery in Sandton.

"He is my cousin, old chap, and I am the earl with or without a bloody castle." Bernard, being the epitome of a snob, knew that an old kombi camper and three hundred rand a month to employ an earl was worth every cent. The name dropping that would follow would earn him great respect from some of the Inanda set who produced as much manure from their mouths as they did from their horses.

The next day, when the fumes from the party had receded, Matt was delighted to find his cousin had departed. Life in the rondavel returned to normal; Sophia moved into the tiny cottage with Raleen, and together they set up a small bakery making exotic breads and sweet cakes and all the lovely things that make people fat.

Matt and Lorna sat alone in the cool evening air, looking out across the sweep of the sea, holding hands and talking of their day. Peace and the dog were fast asleep in the rondavel as the lap of the waves mixed with the calling gulls and the sweet scent of blossom drifted down from the trees.

"It's frightening to be so happy." said Lorna.

"No, it's wonderful" After a long pause, Matt took his pipe from his mouth. "Material things they can always take away, but they can never take away your soul."

Ten days later, Matt was striding along the road to First Beach, his backpack ready for the supplies he would buy. The day was nicely overcast for the seven kilometre walk to the shops. The pipe in his mouth was cold and his feet were bare, his only clothing being a pair of shorts designed by Lorna from an old black curtain. The backpack rested easily on his sinewed back, tanned to mahogany by the sun. Doves sang from the hills and the sea breeze was fresh.

When the kombi stopped and the apparition of a driver offered him a lift, even though they were travelling in opposite directions, Matt smiled, creasing the deep crow's feet around his soft blue eyes, took his pipe from his mouth and made a gesture to the scenery that made it clear he was happy to walk. The man inside the driver's cab wore a green felt hat with a feather on one side, and when he got out to pursue an unwanted conversation he carried a shooting stick which he tapped on the tarmac to gain the attention of Matt, who was by now ten metres further down the road.

"I say, old chap. Don't you recognise your cousin?" Matt stopped, inwardly groaning, and turned to look back. Charles Farquhar was dressed in a caftan, there was a green silk scarf around his neck which matched the hat, and sandals on his feet. The kombi was painted with weird, arty symbols in all the colours of the rainbow.

"Is Sophia at home?"

"She doesn't stay with us anymore."

"Still in the colony?"

"Still in the colony."

"Wonderful news. Toodle-loo, then... Sure you don't want a lift?"

"Quite certain, thank you, Charles."

"Toodle-loo old chap."

The minstrel boy saw the apparition outside the Vuya and recognised the shooting stick. "Come to stay with us?" he called.

"Have you seen Sophia, old chap?"

"Down on the beach."

"Wonderful news."

Carel van Tonder, in his new job of Mr Fixit, heard the tuneless whistling and looked up from the old engine that still kept the colony's fishing boat out to sea. It was beached above the high water mark. Having realised that Raleen and the minstrel boy were an item, he had turned his attention to Sophia, with even less success. On the other side of the boat, Black Martin was gutting fish. Under a tree some metres away, Lorna and Raleen were deep in one of their long conversations.

The sea had risen with the overcast conditions and the swells could not be surfed. Scattered groups of tourists were walking the long beach and Sophia was the only one swimming in the warm water, her long black hair streaming down her smooth back, the perfect oval of her face accentuated by the wet hair. Charles stopped in mid-beach, caught by the perfection of her face and body.

"Hello, old girl ... it's me. The belted bloody earl. Back again. Fancy a cup of tea in my kombi? Guarantee the cups have not seen alcohol. You look positively wonderful, old girl."

Sophia looked around to see to whom the man sitting on the shooting stick was talking, while the tourists gaped at the caftan and the green hat with the feather. Then she dived into a wave and swam a little way out to sea. The feel of the warm water and salt was a soft caress.

In the trough between waves, she floated on her back, thinking of the bay she loved, mingling salt tears with the salt water. The pain was hopeless, her body and soul empty of everything but the loss of her love. He was not going to return to her but she hoped, would always hope; a hope she would take from her youth to the ugliness of her old age. That much was part of her forever. When she emerged from the water, he was still waiting.

"Please go away," she said.

"I've come back to you."

"You're the wrong man, Charles, and you always will be."

The cliffs above the Wild Coast in autumn were brown from the lack of rain, Port St Johns receiving most of its rainfall in the spring and the early summer. For Matt, May was the month for walking. Peace had just turned four and was able to walk some of the way, and for the rest she would view the majesty of the crashing waves on the rich black rocks from high up on the cliff path, sitting on the bare shoulders of her father, her favourite position from which to see the world,

Garlanded with wild flowers and with a banana frond for Peace to beat her father into a regular gallop, the family took its annual walk down the coast, with the dog following, chasing butterflies. Above, the red-winged starlings sang in the sky, trilling the pure sound of nature. The path wound down the gullies, where small streams joined waters with the sea, among the richer foliage, and the path made tunnels through the trees where the sun-birds lived. There the high cliffs faced the great ocean.

When the sun dipped into the sea each night, they found a cove and camped on the shore. Matt dived for crayfish and octopus, mussels and oysters, bringing with him the green seaweed that they stewed with the mussels, crayfish and the wild sage Lorna had picked on their journey. They carried blankets for the cold nights and dug their beds in the dry sand of the caves, small dugouts in the base of the cliffs made by the wildest seas.

The old man from his hut watched the fire down below on the beach. Peace's shouts of joy floated up to his old ears and his old, wrinkled face smiled in the night. He joined with them in their happiness and was sad in the morning to find them gone. With a thousand-metre stare, he looked out over the empty ocean and remembered the joy of his own children. For the whole day he lived with them in his mind, and when he cooked a little of the maize meal brought to him regularly by Carel van Tonder he was happy.

For a week, Matt and Lorna lived off the sea, making love when the child was fast asleep. And under the cool stars and a waxing moon, Lorna conceived again. When the night was quiet of crickets, and frogs in the river near their camp had stopped the clicking of a thousand castanets, she leaned upon the rug-strewn earth and looked at her big bear of a husband bathed in the silvery light of the moon.

"Darling, I'm going to have another baby."

"When?" His hand came out to touch her stomach.

"In nine months' time." She knew. She was absolutely positive.

THE LETTER from Madge Holland came into Matt's hands through a Zimbabwean tourist, as the Grays had no postal address. It was addressed to Matthew Gray in an educated hand.

---

*Dear Mr Gray*

*I am going to worry you once again about Jonathan, as, ever since the war and the death of his friend James Bell, he has been unable to concentrate on anything, work or people. The bush war has left many scars. Raleen Urbach was brought to me after her children were murdered by terrorists. Her husband died in a landmine blast three months earlier. She writes to me, which is how I know where you are. Since many years ago, when you saved my husband's insurance company and educated Jonathan, life has led us in the strangest paths. Who, then, would have thought I would be living in Central Africa?*

*I read that American's articles that made you look like a monster. You should have fought the man. Why did you run away? People will think he is right, that you exploited the blacks in your pursuit of money. You must always fight for what you believe.*

*Half the whites have left this country. They have gone leaving behind their wealth (exchange control allows them $200 out of the country) but taking with them the skills that bring men out of the mud hut away from the flies, the disease and the poverty. When governments change so fundamentally, the poor people pay such a terrible price. Here, they all thought they were going to be rich like the white men but it is turning out so sadly different. Once again, the world is turning its back on Africa and it makes me very sad. As I grow older, I wonder how many of man's dreams are not based on the whims of the greedy few? Everything is always going to be better if they knock down what is already there. For them, maybe, for the very few, some well-meaning, some the political predators who have stalked the long sad history of man.*

*Being alone, I have time to think. Too much time. I am fifty-eight and have had my life, and my only real concern is Jonathan. He is a young man who has seen too much of the truth too soon and finds the purpose of his life in question. He says the promises of happiness and peace are a figment of man's warped imagination, that man is only interested in taking and all the promises are a smoke screen for that desire. He does not seem to like the world in which he lives and drifts aimlessly from job to job, person to person and worse, from bar to bar. I think he takes drugs, though I can't be certain.*

*He knows Raleen is living in a colony on the coast and talks of joining her, away from the crowd. I have told him you have withdrawn from society and live with your wife and child in the simplest way. That sparkled his eye for the first time since James was killed. I have told Jonathan to go down to Port St Johns and see if he can make some sense out of his life. He is twenty-seven and should be married with a good job. Maybe you and Raleen can help.*

*I always remember you as such a wise, sensible man.*

*Yours sincerely,*

*Madge Holland*

---

Anita Hylan was admitted to one of the best equipped maternity hospitals in the world, everything paid for by the benevolent Swedish government. The fact that there was no husband waiting in reception made no difference to the Swedes, some of whom were convinced that children should be brought up by the state, which was better equipped for the job than young and often unstable parents. The fact that she was with child came as a surprise, as she was four months into her pregnancy before she realised the pill she had taken so faithfully had let her down.

"Anita, my dear," said her doctor, "this time, if you abort, it will be the last. Do you know the father?" She had never known before, so the doctor was on safe ground to ask such an unprofessional question. Anita laughed and gave him a quizzical smile, one of speculation mixed with mild amusement. She shook her pretty head.

"I'm going to have this one. It might be fun. Something new. Tell me what I have to do."

"I think you have done what was necessary." They both laughed.

If Anita had known that she would be in labour for sixteen hours, she would have aborted her little bastard without another thought. But by the time the agony began, it was too late, and the doctors could see no reason to perform a Caesarean section. When the young man finally fought his way into the world, he instantly howled at the cold air and the doctor's slap on the bottom.

Anita was too exhausted to pay any attention, and the child was cleaned and checked by the doctors. The quiet surprise in the delivery room quickly overcome and all the right clichés were spoken for the benefit of the mother. Then the child was brought to Anita and laid in the crook of her right arm.

Smiling, she brought her face round to look at the child, the pain of giving birth drifting away as it was overwhelmed by the tenderness of motherhood. As her eyes rested on the child, she screamed, and went on screaming until the doctors removed the child.

The child was black.

# 2

By 1982, the power of apartheid was at its greatest. The surrounding countries of Mozambique, Angola and Zimbabwe were destabilised by the intrigues of the South African defence force, Doctor Jonas Savimbi's UNITA in Angola, Joshua Nkomo's ZAPU dissidents in Zimbabwe and the warlords of Renamo in Mozambique.

The total onslaught of communism was being met with the same methods used so successfully by the communists around the world themselves. In Pretoria, Hector Fortescue-Smythe's old employers, Armscor, had developed a gun capable of knocking the handle from a door at a distance of forty-four kilometres, The G5, a 155 mm howitzer, was the best artillery piece in the world, and it was one of the many high-technology weapons perfected by South African scientists under the pressure of the world arms embargo, along with the Olifant main battle tank, the Seeker anti-tank missile and the cactus SAM.

The PW Botha nationalist government totally ignored world opinion, locking up anyone, with or without trial, who disagreed with their policy of separate development. The pass laws kept every black in his kraal, trade unions were illegal and every fit young white man was trained efficiently to maintain the status quo. There was not an army in Africa that could match the power of the South Africans.

Russia poured Cuban troops into Angola and South Africa armed Savimbi, helped, curiously, by the Americans, who could not make up their minds whether it was better to fight their old bête noire, Cuba, or to keep the South Africans as something to beat to satisfy the local civil rights movement. Savimbi received the most sophisticated ground-to-air missiles to counter the Cuban flown Russian jets. Minister Kloss was well satisfied with the way in which the Americans squirmed, and Savimbi, after power like every other leader in Africa, accepted guns and help from wherever it came.

THE BUREAU of state security had changed its name on a regular basis, but the intention was always the same. White rule or, more exactly, white Afrikaner rule, was to be maintained. Having shot the minister's daughter to death for a crime the minister considered worse than treason, Frikkie Swart was in charge of all clandestine operation, which included the elimination of people living outside South Africa who were working to overthrow the apartheid government. Many young activists disappeared, lost between leaving and arriving, and what appealed to Frikkie Swart most was his lack of accountability. The funds to run the operations were freely available, but no one in the government had any wish to know how they were being spent.

Being one of the few people in the country with a true oversight, Frikkie was convinced the days of the Afrikaner nationalists were numbered, with Rhodesia gone and the pressure building up in South West Africa. So he did the sensible thing and channelled some of the funds into bank accounts around the world, upon which he would draw when the ANC came to power. With money, Frikkie Swart had learnt he could do whatever he chose. He was a man well content with his life. He, unlike so many others, knew exactly where he was going.

HECTOR FORTESCUE-SMYTHE DINED REGULARLY at the Cavalry Club, 126 Piccadilly, finding the food very much to his liking. It was the perfect haven for him when he wished for peace and quiet, as women were not allowed in the club and there was not a communist with whom he did business who would have the slightest chance of getting past the doorman.

In the club, members rarely spoke to each other. The claw hand was an obvious testimony to his military service and, at forty-five, Hector looked like any other retired tank colonel in his dark, pin-striped suit. The club staff were good at cutting up his meat and making sure that no one from the outside penetrated his sanctuary. It gave him time to think and contemplate the culmination of his life's work, the collapse of capitalism, America in particular, and the organised worldwide rule of a communist government, creating the perfect society where energy was channelled into progress rather than the constant bickering that made up the present world

Monday evening, the 19 August 1982, found Hector alone in the dining room. It being a week after the opening of the grouse season, he had ordered the game bird stuffed and broiled, then grilled for three minutes and covered in rashers of thick, well-cured bacon. Plain roast grouse he found tough and dry. The side dish was a well tossed salad for which he had made the dressing himself, liking one part vinegar to four parts olive oil, mixed with salt, pepper, sugar and dry Colman's mustard. For once his left hand did not hurt.

His mind compassed the day and came back, as it usually did when he was alone, to Gilly Bowles. They had been seeing each other for four years and, under normal circumstances, Hector would have considered a second marriage. The girl satisfied his physical needs and was almost as good at sexual excitement as Helena Kloss, but a second mental effort in living with someone who thought he was somebody else was no longer possible as the party took up most of his working day. He and his mother had finally left the daily running of Smythe-Wilberforce to professional managers.

To give the curious a handle by which to understand what he did with his days, he had bought a small estate in the Surrey countryside where he purported to breed Sussex cows that would provide the best beef in the country. There was a price to pay for everything, and the comfort of a good wife and children was the one he had to pay; until the revolution, and then all the subterfuge would joyfully come to an end. Smiling to himself, he wondered what Gilly Bowles would think of him as an arch-communist rather than a pillar of the conservative establishment. One day, he was going to enjoy her look of shock and, with the Americans plunged into a vast deficit to fund their star wars and the burgeoning arms race, he was sure that day was close.

While Hector was enjoying his grouse, Gilly Bowles was on a Pan-Am flight to New York with the careful research of four years filling the large briefcase she had pushed under the seat, not even trusting the airline to look after the dynamite contained in the neatly typed pages. They were all there in catalogued order, with Hector, her erstwhile lover, heading the list. With the decision taken and her own by-line in *Newsweek* assured, she was content to sacrifice any feeling she might have had for Hector to further her career.

She was twenty-seven, and there were a lot of men in the world to satisfy a news woman of fame. She would probably move to America, take an apartment in Manhattan, survey the scene and take her pick. Thirty was a good time for marriage, when her career was assured, and nobody would be able to dictate to Gilly Bowles for the rest of her life. Her 'get lost' money was in the briefcase under the seat in front and her stocking feet had a comforting toe on the handle.

She had wired Ben Munroe to meet her at the airport. For the first big one, she still needed Ben. She might still have to sleep with him to get what she wanted, but after that she would be on her own, her own woman, and they could all take a running jump at themselves. With her large mouth slightly apart, she considered the joys of living, the excitement to come. There was a lot of living to be done in Gilly Bowles' life. Her excitement was physically tangible.

Ben Munroe's hormones had given a sharp lurch when he opened the cable. Gilly Bowles had been one of the few women to get away from Ben before he was satisfied, before he was finished with her. Some women took a night, some a week, but Gilly had taken a lot longer. She had always kept something back; she was not available every time he wanted her and, had he not been such a male chauvinist, he would have realised that the girl was using him.

When Gilly met him after passing through immigration, she saw the lust in his eyes, and decided that sex came first and business afterwards when the man was still panting for more. With the kinky side of Hector to draw from, she had some tricks to show Ben that he had never even dreamt of.

"Ben, you look wonderful."

"Where are you staying?"

"With you, I hope." The slightly open mouth, the long legs cased in white stockings, the short black hair with the hint of blue and her blouse just open enough to flash brought Ben's hormones to a peak.

"Are you going to carry my bag?" she asked sweetly. "This one's mine," and she picked up her briefcase.

Even in the cab, he had his hand up her leg. For three hours she kept him at bay and, when she let him take her from behind while she held onto the back of the couch, her feet splayed, her mouth open and her eyes lasciviously watching him in the mirror, it was all over in seconds, leaving her as high as a kite with nowhere to go. Gilly Bowles remembered. Ben

Munroe was a lousy selfish lover. When he wanted it again in half an hour, she told him once a day was more than enough and changed the subject. When Ben finally fell asleep, he was more frustrated than when he had started, and Gilly was content with her power.

Gilly Bowles had come from a family which believed that achievement was the only reason for coming into the world. Success. You had to be a visible success. If behind the facade you beat your wife, that was your business and, provided it remained in the family, it did not matter.

Her brother was two years older and a sportsman of promise from an early age. Her father basked in the boy's success which culminated in his opening the batting for Surrey and proceeding to make his debut memorable by scoring a century. Her younger sister had married into the minor aristocracy when she was eighteen, and was now the mother in a family that stretched back gloriously for three hundred years to a freebooter who had sold his sword to Charles I. Whenever Gilly went home to the stockbroker belt, thirty kilometres south of London, something she did as little as possible and only if she had something to show, her mother gave her the look which said quite clearly that it was a pity she could not be like her brother and sister. It had begun when she changed her degree from English literature to journalism and proposed the move from Oxford to London University.

"My dear, don't be silly. Only common people are journalists. They are vulgar and rude, pointing their cameras where they have no business. I mean, look at the Royal Family. Really. Every Tom, Dick and Harry poking their noses in. If you ask me, this freedom of speech has gone too far. Isn't one's privacy worth more than another man's freedom to speak? Your father won't approve of journalism. I don't think he'll pay for that kind of degree."

"He won't have to; I won a grant."

"You don't have to be rude, Gillian. You find yourself a nice young man and have some children. Oxford is the perfect place. You're attractive, and sometimes I think you may have brains. You go back and finish your English degree. You could easily find a young man with a title and money. Money and position are the only things that count in this world, despite what all these socialists have to say for themselves. Thank goodness for Margaret Thatcher. Now she doesn't stand any nonsense."

Ben Munroe had been giving the public the news they wanted to read for twenty years. He had a nose for it, a communication with the millions of people who read his words and agreed with what he said. Ben liked to be in agreement with people and talking to the readers was no different from talking in a bar. Once you understood the other man's point of view, you brought up subjects that fed his opinion and everybody had the kind of evening they most enjoyed. Many times Ben changed his opinion in mid-sentence to coincide with the popular thought.

Among people, Ben was a regular man, popular, sought after and always listened to with respect. The few people he attacked in his articles were the fools who were out of tune with popular opinion, and they were the best ones to rip apart, the small minority, the ones who would not affect the circulation of a newspaper. He was forty-two years old, had married twice with no children, and at the top of his profession where he intended to stay for as long as possible. If he was a cynic, he never admitted it to himself.

His father had left his mother when he was two years old, married again and forgotten the kid. There had been neither love nor money from his father, so his mother married again, three more times, alienating Ben more each time. The kid was a nuisance, a mistake; the stepfathers had no time for him and neither had his mother, who was too busy ingratiating herself with her lovers.

Where his mother went wrong, and Ben saw the lesson, was to agree with what the men were saying. Ben worked out at an early age that you had to feed new ideas, ideas that instinctively you knew would be agreeable, making the other person feel good. The sweetest sound to young Ben's ears was someone saying just within earshot, "I like that Ben Munroe. He's a real nice guy." Making other people feel good about themselves was the secret, not fawning at their feet.

At fifteen, he left home and joined a newspaper, but it took years for them to take him seriously as a writer. Young Ben was there to fetch and carry. Young Ben was there to tickle their fancy. No one ever thought he could write articles and have them taken seriously. One needed a good school to be a journalist. The days of starting at the bottom without a qualification were long gone in America.

It had been slow, but persistence had brought its rewards, and with it a journalist with the genuine common touch. He knew what the public wanted to hear and when, on the third day of chasing Gilly around his flat, she had come to the point and shown him what she had spent the previous four years investigating, he was horrified. Out of sheer amazement, he read it right through and then he did the last thing Gilly Bowles ever expected. He laughed.

"Are you serious?"

"Why ever not?" she flashed at him.

"You want to go for the anti-apartheid movement, and you want me to help?"

"It's a communist front."

"You don't understand, lady," Ben exclaimed, amazed at her naivety. "It's the anti-apartheid movement. They can all be red, including your bishop, which I doubt, but it doesn't..."

"The KGB have infiltrated the Russian Orthodox Church. The top monks and priests are communists. I think they've done the same with the Church of England and it controls the biggest church in Africa. That's the best bit of investigative journalism you've ever seen, and you know it. That's the truth ..."

"Maybe. But one swallow doesn't make a summer. Some of the AAM may be communists."

"Then it should be reported," she insisted.

"You got to grow up if you want to be a journalist," Ben informed her, a little condescendingly. "You can prove our Ted Kennedy's a sex maniac, but no one will print the story. He's a Kennedy and a democrat. Both his brothers got knocked off fulfilling the American dream. Everyone seems to think the brothers were banging Marilyn Monroe, but nobody cares except their wives. Even the kids probably think Daddy was a sport. I'll tell you one thing for sure; *Newsweek* won't touch it, and neither will *Private Eye*."

"The whole thing's a fraud. A communist plot to take over Africa," stated Gilly strongly, beginning to feel indignant.

"They take over a bit of Africa for ten minutes, and we take it back again. We've got the bucks they don't have. But what stays in Africa and in America is the black man, and no journalist with any feel for self-preservation insults that wave of consciousness. Was that what you came for?"

"Yes."

"You're honest ... if you want to be a journalist, best thing you can do is move in here and listen. Maybe, five years down the line, you'll know what I'm talking about. Then, with your other talents, you'll get a story the people want to hear. What you got here is journalistic suicide."

Luke Mbeki had come to the same conclusion as Gilly Bowles but, having the same instinct for self-preservation as Ben Munroe, he kept his thoughts to himself. And, if the communist influence over the ANC suggested a hidden agenda, they paid the bills, and when the revolution was over the true believers in the welfare of the people would take control and taxpayers' money would take the place of Russian patrimony and charity. But who would actually be left to pay the taxes? Even Ben didn't want to think about that.

But Luke did, and he wasn't too sure. If those who created the wealth were rendered impotent or driven out, who was left to take up those skills? The black man was, by and large, incapable of doing so, thanks to the racial system which saw him as no more than a hewer of wood and drawer of water. The black man had never been taught the skills required to build wealth; it would take many years to learn – and what was the point if a communist government was to take all his wealth from him in the end, anyway? Was it a vain hope that, when the ANC was confronted with the realities of running a country, communism and command control would give way to pragmatism?

Luke often smiled at all the rhetoric and, having been into Russia, Angola, Mozambique and East Germany, he knew that the system of controlled capitalism was the only one that created lasting wealth, a sustainable and growing standard of living. Political freedom without economic freedom, he told himself, was as much use as a vote of thanks to the board of directors. Money controlled destiny. Money controlled the ANC. And it was his job to go around the world telling the ANC story and looking for funds.

Chelsea refused to move out of Lisbon, and the distance between them was more than mere kilometres. She had her job in the First World where everyone bought insurance to provide for a comfortable old age. The wealth was prodigious. Luke dealt with poverty and the way to drag his people out of the quagmire. Abject poverty was a condition only of man. Nature took care of the animal population, except for man in Africa, where Western influence had interfered with the nature of things. The black man had to gain the same knowledge and means of production if he was to feed the exploding population. They had to catch up to join the clean world of plenty. With his education, he was able to see quite clearly what had to be done.

The only place that Luke could call home was a one-roomed flat in the southeast of London, where he shared a bathroom with six black families. His few possessions were in the room and he cooked on a small gas stove built into an alcove opposite his bed. The walls he had painted himself, and on one was a big, beautiful photograph of John de la Cruz, his son. The boy had turned six in September, two months earlier.

The Portuguese were more interested in their new democracy and their own problems, and to them the ANC was merely another liberation movement, no better than Frelimo or the MPLA. The Portuguese had been physically thrown out of their colonies after four hundred years and they were not inclined to give away money to an organisation that they considered would reduce another part of Africa to anarchy.

Over most of former Portuguese east and west Africa, Mozambique and Angola, the AK47 assault rifle ruled. The coffee and sugar estates, the mines and factories were overgrown with weeds, and any crops that were grown were stolen by the warlords. Luke had not been to Portugal for over a year. There were no funds for him to raise there and he had no money for private journeys. Anita Hylan found Luke through the AAM and, when he opened the door to his room, she immediately put the baby straight in his arms. It took a moment to recognise the woman he had met while fund-raising in Stockholm. He looked from the baby to the blonde woman in amazement.

"This one's yours. No mistaking that" She put a small bag on the ground and turned to leave.

"What's all this about? ... Do you want to come in?"

"No, thanks. If you don't want him, get him adopted in England. In Sweden no one seems to want him."

"But he's your baby!" Luke's face was horrified, and the baby's bottom was wet and smelly.

"I'm too selfish. The idea seemed good, but the practice is no fun. You've got that lady in Portugal. Maybe she'll look after 'im. I'd make a lousy mother."

"And your father?"

"The child's black, Luke. He belongs with you. I've signed some papers. He won't have any kind of life in Sweden. Believe me. Whatever they say about racism, they don't mean a word. Funding the AAM is great fun so long as they don't have a racial problem of their own."

"Are you sure it's mine?" demanded Luke, aghast

"You're the only black man I ever slept with. There's an affidavit to that effect, too. You work out the dates. Perfect. You're the father all right." She turned and ran off down the cold corridor. Her high heels clattered down the stairs to the ground floor while Luke stood alone with the child, listening to her sobs as she went.

"They don't want nothing to do with us, Luke," said a black woman emerging from the next room. For a change, August in England was hot, and she had kept her door open to cool down the room. "Whatever they say. That lady's right. Better you look after that boy. She said 'he' so I presume that baby a boy. Poor mite, not even three months old. Bring 'im here, Luke Mbeki. That's a woman's job. You wouldn't even know how to heat the bottle but you don't need much of that in this heat. Worse than Trinidad. There we had the sea. First let me clean 'im and feed 'im, then you think. Give me that bag. She didn't look the type to breast-feed. You be more careful where you put that thing of yours, Luke." They went back into Luke's room and the woman began to change the nappy.

"It was kind of a condition," Luke began to explain, rather weakly.

"Tried everything but never had a black man?"

"Something like that ... Poor little fellow. He never did anything wrong."

"Your woman in Portugal?" suggested his neighbour.

"She wouldn't take him."

"You can't take a baby on your travels. What you going to do?"

"Send him home."

"To South Africa? That's where every damn one's a racist."

By the time the British Airways Boeing 747 landed at Heathrow airport, Gilly Bowles had faced the realities of her life. The briefcase was still under the seat but her toes had not once touched the handle. Her days as an investigative journalist had come to a shattering end. She was not going to see her name in *Time* or *Newsweek*. She was probably going no further in journalism than she had already gone. Personal fame was not to be a reality, and the alternative was very simple.

Once again her mother was right. A woman's place was in the home looking after children, not proving a bishop was a communist. She knew that Hector was a communist; she even knew the name of his handler and had some good photographs of the two together. But he did not know that she knew, and life in the Surrey countryside, bringing up a son who would play cricket and a daughter who would ride horses, was not unattractive. She felt resigned to her fate, rather than bitter.

The man was rich; she had no doubt about that. Every man had the need to leave a son behind and, if she played on the prospect of a son and heir, she just might convince Hector to propose marriage. Their backgrounds were similar, both enjoying the privileges of British upper middle class, even if Hector wished to change the world into a one party state. His dream, like hers, had no chance of success. People were too greedy. They wanted more than the next man, not simply the same, however much the same might be. Man was always trying to prove he was better. Women, too. What was the women's liberation movement all about?

"You may disembark, madam." said the air hostess, bringing her back to the real world.

Gilly looked at her brightly. "No point in standing to let the others off. Thank you for a nice flight."

"You're welcome."

Gilly waited until the weekend before travelling down to Surrey. She would give her lover a surprise. The train arrived at Godalming and she took a taxi to the Fortescue-Smythe estate. Even if Hector was away, she had the key, and the servants treated her almost like the mistress of the house.

The summer fields were full of butterflies flitting over rich yellow buttercups, and the thought of living the rest of her life in the country was made easier by the rare sunshine and the beauty of a perfect summer's day. She let the taxi drive up to the front door, and for the first time looked at the old house as a prospective home.

She would join the local hunt and have a tennis party every Wednesday in the summer, and if it rained they would talk and exchange the local gossip.

The children would enjoy being brought up in the country and, when the Soviet empire collapsed, Hector would forget about a world government and accept the realities of an imperfect but workable British democracy. It was Winston Churchill, she thought, who said that democracy was the worst form of government except for all the other forms of government that had been tried.

England was all right. It had survived the war and the peace, and as part of Europe the island would prosper, if not quite as much as the Germans. She gave the taxi driver a good tip and rang the front-door bell.

"He's coming back tomorrow. Been away a week. Come in, Miss Gilly. He'll like to find you're here when he comes home." Gilly smiled at the housekeeper. "Can I make you a nice cup of tea?"

The rooms were large and full of light from the sash windows, and throughout the house were bowls of flowers.

"He likes flowers. But you know that. Wouldn't have time to do it tomorrow."

There was a large parcel on the hall table as Gilly looked through the mail. Sometimes her own mail came to the house, along with her *Newsweek*. She had time to read only in the country. London was too hectic.

"Who's the parcel from?"

"Addressed to the occupier. One of those free samples, I should think."

"Big for a free sample... Where are the dogs?

"My husband took them for a walk. Full of energy, those dogs. If they don't get a walk, they tear the place to pieces. You want a scone with your tea? ... We had a calf on Wednesday. Lovely little thing. I like cows when they're small."

Gilly picked up the parcel and two copies of *Newsweek*, and took them through the lounge out onto the terrace, where she put the parcel on the white wrought-iron table. She went back into the house, collected the chair cushions, and made herself comfortable in the shade of the great oak that made the lawn and the terrace so pleasant in the summer.

She looked out over the Surrey countryside and could hear in the far distance a lone motorcycle. It was a sleepy, hot late afternoon, and when the tea came with the scones and fresh farm cream and a large bowl of strawberry jam it all looked delicious. The contents of the briefcase back in her flat in Kensington were as far away as the moon. The sound of bees and occasional birdsong high in the afternoon sky was a perfect surround.

She poured a cup of Hector's mother's blend of tea, half Indian and half China that was made up by Fortnum and Mason, the same blend that the family had been drinking for fifty years. When taken with a thin slice of lemon, Gilly found the tea perfect. She flipped through the earlier *Newsweek* but found the whole thing boring. After all, she was not going to be in one of them.

Then she unwrapped the brown paper parcel and found inside a Walkman with a tape and a letter. She had not looked at the postmark or she would have seen the Johannesburg date stamp. The letter said the company had a magnificent offer for a time-share in the most exclusive private game park outside the Kruger National Park. To give the carefully selected prospective buyers a taste of the sounds of Africa, the enclosed would enable them to play the tape through the headphones, close their eyes and imagine dusk falling across the bush, the sun blood-red behind the mopani trees and hear the roar of the lions, the laugh of the hyenas and the sound of game drinking at the waterhole close to the thatched chalets that the lucky few could buy on time-share.

Curious and never having been to Africa, Gilly put the tape into the machine and fitted the headphones comfortably over her ears. On pressing the start button, she received a blast through her head that killed her instantly, bringing the housekeeper running out onto the terrace to see the horror.

Inside each of the tiny earphones, Frikkie Swart had installed a wedge of plastic explosive that was wired to detonate from the electricity generated by the small batteries in the Walkman. Her whole face had exploded like a pumpkin hurled at a solid brick wall.

Hector had parked his Jaguar in the lock-up garage at Heathrow airport and, having returned from Mozambique via Sweden in the best of spirits, he drove down to Surrey.

The seminar had been in the Ukraine, in a delightful dacha on the shores of the Black Sea. The weather had been perfect, the food good and the conversation stimulating, the only dark cloud being the war in Afghanistan where the Soviets had sent in their own troops. The next few yards of communism's long journey were about to be taken and the green fields of England looked greener than ever before. The days of chaos, dissension and poverty were almost over. There would be a world fit for the nobler conditions of man, where no one would grovel in the dirt. There would be order, discipline and plenty.

He turned into his driveway on the Saturday afternoon to find the courtyard in front of his house cluttered with cars. His annoyance at his housekeeper welled up instantly and, when he parked at the end of the jumble of vehicles, he slammed the door, something he never did to a car. The front door was half open and he pushed his way through, to find his house full of strangers.

"What the hell's going on here?" he shouted over the chatter of people's voices. No one took the slightest notice. At the end of the hall was a large brass gong that his grandfather had brought back from China, which was used at Christmas time to announce to the children it was time to open the presents. A large stick with a hard leather ball on the end was attached by a thong to the gong, and after a few sonorous notes the conversation tailed off and the people looked over to see who was making the noise.

"I said what the hell's going on in my house? Where's my housekeeper?"

"She's locked in her bedroom with her husband holding her hand," said a uniformed man, detaching himself from the crowd. "You must be Fortescue-Smythe."

"Too bloody right I am. Who the hell are you?" demanded Hector, unusually emotional.

"Chief Inspector Holliday metropolitan police. Your girlfriend has been killed by a letter bomb."

"Gilly! Who'd ever want to kill Gilly"

"Maybe you can help us find that out."

The two policemen questioned Hector for four hours, long before the end of which he realised the police thought he had murdered Gilly Bowles. They left him alone under the oak tree the blood of his mistress still visible on the crazy paving. First bewilderment and then pain overwhelmed him. Tears oozed from the corners of his eyes and he tried to wipe them away with the claw, forgetting his left hand was buried in Maputo. Then he staggered to his feet and was violently sick over the terrace wall onto the lupins.

For the first time, Hector wondered if the cause was worth all the pain. He knew perfectly well who had killed Gilly Bowles, but for some reason the police would not see it so clearly. Once again, his ex-father-in-law had tried to kill him. This time they had tried to blow off his head, not just his arm.

The policemen were watching him from the lounge, through a long sash window, while reporters asked an avalanche of questions and long-range cameras photographed the vomit spraying over the terrace to land on the flowers. There was an international feeding frenzy of the media.

The chief inspector nodded to his off-sider and together they left the house. In the unmarked police car, they sat quietly for a few moments.

"What you think Fred?"

"Don't know George. Don t bloody know. You really think the South Africans would try and kill a British national on British soil? Not likely. We're their third biggest trading partner, and though Thatcher let the commies take control in Rhodesia she's still the best friend they've got."

"Unless the South Africans knew that Miss Bowles was about to blow the whistle on our friend under the oak."

"Then why the bomb? A discredited Fortescue-Smythe would have been worth more to the South Africans … Maybe the bomb was meant for the girl, that's what I think. Sent from Johannesburg to look like their bureau of state security. Kill the girl, stop the story and still blame apartheid South Africa. Perfect commie hallmark, if you ask me."

"Except you don't vomit on your flowers when you've pulled off a double bluff. I say that bloke knew nothing about it."

"I hate bloody commies."

"So do I, Fred, but there's no law in England that says you can't be one."

• • •

Ben Munroe had flown over on the Concorde. A mutual friend in Gilly's office had phoned him the news. He had arrived at the country estate an hour before Hector keeping well in the background while he made his own assessment.

Within a short while, it was clear that the police had found Gilly's briefcase in her Kensington flat, but he did not bother to tell them he was the only person other than Gilly who knew about the expositions. Or was he? To obtain her information she must have left a trail of some sort he argued with himself.

Then he thought for a while, and decided it did not matter. A public outrage could only be fuelled by blaming apartheid and the evil South African government. Gilly would have her name in *Newsweek* after all, the victim of an apartheid bomb sent to her boyfriend, the famous anti-apartheid activist. The story had all the benefits of racist-bashing. With luck he could find out enough to cover four columns. Special report by Ben Munroe.

Watching Hector, he was convinced the man under the oak knew nothing of the contents of the briefcase. But there were others. If exposed, Hector would say, so what? The South African communist party had always backed the African National Congress and Nelson Mandela. But what would the bishop say to the press? What would the bishop say to the Archbishop of Canterbury? That he was an atheistic communist, but still believed in God? His duties as a committee member of the anti-apartheid movement would not stand him in good stead with the squad of bishops in the Anglican Church. Without his power exercised through his position in the church, the Very Reverend Andrew Porterstone would be washed up in the garbage heap, no use to the communists, the AAM, the church or himself.

The black churchmen in South Africa would claim a South African government smear campaign and continue their work in Soweto and Guguletu. The man most affected by the briefcase was the fat bishop, and to take some of the piss and wind out of the pompous ass would give Ben great pleasure. He was a staunch Episcopalian, the American offshoot of the Anglicans. And he believed in God, which was more than the bishop did.

He looked again through the window at Hector on the lawn under the oak and decided to leave him alone. Pictures of Gilly leaning over a settee were not what the man wanted right now. Nor the treachery of a lady who had been part of his life for four years. Anyway, Hector would want to know how he had come to pitch up so quickly. God would take care of the bishop, of that Ben Munroe was certain. It never occurred to him that God might also want to take care of Ben Munroe. Ben would file his anti-apartheid story and leave it at that.

Then he laughed as he left the home through the backdoor and came round to his Hertz car. *Newsweek* would not print an expose of the bishop any more than they would have exposed the AAM to a communist plot. However it went, his story had to blame apartheid.

George Holliday arrived at the bishop's palatial residence as dusk was falling, to find the bishop at home, and quite overbearing in manner. Even if the policeman had not known the man was a fraud, he would have disliked the pompous sanctimony of the man. George Holliday believed in the Church of England in the same way that he believed in the laws of England. They were the best available, and God was well served by his church in England.

"Come in, dear man, come in. Late it may be, but God's work is never done. What can we do for you?"

"Police work, my Lord Bishop, not God's."

"Oh, my dear. What's gone wrong in the diocese now?"

"Not the diocese. A woman you may have known was killed by a parcel bomb."

"Terrible," declared the bishop shaking his head in pious hypocrisy. "I heard it on the news. As a member of the AAM committee, I can tell you ..."

'We would prefer to have your views as a member of the communist party Bishop Porterstone." The bishop paused for a split second too long and glanced over George Holliday's head.

"What nonsense are you talking?" demanded the bishop, recovering the smile of being in the know with God back on his face.

"The young lady was about to expose you, my Lord Bishop. She quoted chapter and verse so meticulously that even you would find it impossible to refute her statements, to say nothing of your fellow bishops. But being both a member of an atheistic organisation and a member of the church is not against the law of this country, though it probably should be. We are investigating a murder, and you had a very strong motive to kill the young lady. That does break the law, and having you locked up with a bunch of thugs for the rest of your natural life would give me the greatest pleasure. I want you to promise me you knew nothing about the details we found in the lady reporter's briefcase."

The only satisfaction that day for George Holliday was the slow but total deflation of the man who called himself a bishop. "And don't give me any crap about the wonders of communism," said the policeman.

THE PRESSURE from the African lobby and the anti-apartheid movement reached George Holliday on the Monday week, after he had interviewed the twenty-third person mentioned in the exposés by Gilly Bowles.

"I might have used the AAM to get my name back in lights," said Sir Desmond Donelly, "but I am no bloody communist."

"Your name has a question mark in her notes, but what can you tell us about the others? Particularly Bishop Porterstone?"

"Andrew's not a communist. He's a good man. Does a lot for the poor and needy. Together we have raised millions of pounds. It was the South Africans. All the papers say so. There should be a Nuremburg trial when apartheid falls. You're not trying to tell me Andrew had something to do with this girl's death? That's crazy ... Poor Gilly. Hector was lucky, but poor Gilly. We'll have a Gilly Bowles concert at Festival Hall ... I'll sing for her ... compose a special song ... raise money ... the Gilly Bowles benevolent fund. Everyone will come."

George Holliday and Fred, his sergeant, had left the man sitting on the telephone, building up a storm.

"Never could sing," said Fred with a certain amount of contempt, as they reached the police station.

"Sir Desmond bloody Donelly. Next they'll give Boy George a knighthood."

"He can sing."

"You've got to be joking."

The memo on George Holliday's desk was quite clear. "Stop investigating the AAM." He put down the memo and smiled. "It wasn't them, was it, Fred?"

Fred shook his head. "What beats me is why they posted the bomb in Johannesburg."

FRIKKIE SWART WAS furious to hear that the bomb had killed Gilly Bowles instead of Hector Fortescue-Smythe.

"Worse than an own goal, man. Did their work. But I want that man." They were speaking in Afrikaans.

"Wasn't he married to your late wife?"

"He's a bloody communist," asserted Frikkie.

"What were you going to do about the Jo'burg postmark if we'd got him?"

"Leak the information she'd collected. Make her come out of the closet. Make it seem as though the bishop or one of his friends wanted her taken out. Muddy the water."

"No comeback from the British, which is a surprise."

"They found her notes," Frikkie explained. "At least now they know that the bishop is a communist. You go away and have your team come up with another way to assassinate Fortescue-Smythe."

"Does this come from the minister?"

"Minister Kloss knows nothing. That's how they sound so righteous when they are interviewed on TV."

"How did you know about Gilly Bowles?"

"I was paying the bitch," Frikkie revealed. "Telling her where to go. How do you think she could have found out so much without my help?"

A WEEK LATER, Hector's mother died and was buried. When he returned to his lonely estate, he walked into his fields and down to the river, a sluggish water of leaves, twigs and minnows in the backwaters.

There was no sound of man down by the River Mole, and Hector let the loneliness engulf his spirit. She had led him in so many paths and guided his way. Her belief in equality was as real as her wrinkled smile, her calling his name, and her love of the dogs and cats that ruled her home. She had been a good mother to him but had he been the son he should have been?

Reminiscing over the years he had lived with her again, her wrinkles dropped away and she was once again a youthful mother thumping a tennis ball around the family court, exhorting him, her doubles partner, to play harder, to win. The flood of memories flowed as surely as the river, and the pain of loss ran away to the bigger Thames and the sea ... And here he was. Alone by the banks of a river, quiet in the summer's day. But alone.

His ex-wife had been shot to death, murdered he knew – Helena would never have killed herself. Her appetite for living was far too strong. He had used her and she had used him. How else could it ever have been? Her love for him had never been more than a flutter in the breeze. And Gilly Bowles, blown to death by a force that was meant for him; and prepared and ready to sacrifice their fraction of life together to make her fame. Why else the police questions and lack of British government pressure on the South Africans? She had been his Trojan horse. What irony.

Hector threw a pebble into the water, and watched the ripples vanish into the flow. Staring at the water, seeing deeper than his soul, he was no longer sure. Whatever doubts there had been before, there had been his mother to put him right, to keep him firmly on the track of the one last revolution that would make it worth the living. But were men ever right? They never had been before. They squabbled and fought and savaged the prize and, when the frenzy of change had gone, so had the prize. He was forty-five. No wife, no family and, if he asked himself honestly, no friends.

He stood up, stiff from squatting during his reverie, and traced the path through his fields, past the big, brown cows that meant nothing in his life, through the formal garden of flowers and sundials, lily ponds and roses that also meant nothing in his life, walking always towards the ideal that he now questioned would ever exist.

There was a man on the terrace, seated at the wrought iron table, in the same chair they had cleaned of Gilly's blood. The floor had been washed clean, and the seated man was unaware of the memory. No one would leave him alone any more, the world press seeming to sense something deeper than the obvious; jackals, circling hyenas waiting for the lions to feed and leave them the carcass.

He remembered the lions of Africa from whence the blast had come, attached to the long arm of Minister Kloss. They wanted him dead and soon, maybe, he would go the way of Gilly, his mother and Helena. Did it matter? He doubted it … After all, he was not going to make the slightest difference. A normal life tossed away on the dreams of a cause!

The man rose to his feet as Hector approached; he was a middle aged man, but the eyes that searched for his own had nothing of the predator. They were soft brown laughing eyes, with a depth of understanding.

"You're not the press, are you?"

"No … Forgive my presumption. No, goodness, I'm not the press. Those people I find always want something. I'm your neighbour, Richard Makepeace Williams."

"You're the priest!"

"A parish priest is all things to all men, even to atheists. I believe you are a communist, Mister Fortescue-Smythe?"

"Hector, please."

"Well, Hector, come and talk to me. That's why I'm here. I heard about your mother. You've had a bad time by all reports and need an ear to bend.

I always try in circumstances to do what Christ would have done. He would have come to give a sad man comfort. To listen. To show that not everything in life is loss ... she was a good woman, your mother."

"And a communist."

"Does that make any difference?" The Reverend Williams laughed, a rich, mellow laugh, and Hector sat down at the table under the oak.

"Would you like some tea?"

"Why do Englishmen always offer each other tea?"

"It's what's expected ... I don't believe in God," stated Hector, firmly.

"Would it come as a shock if I said I'm not sure if I do, either?" the minister replied. "But I believe in Christ. Jesus Christ. He was a good man, and I say I believe in God because He said that God was His Father and He never lied. Do the communists never lie?"

The soft brown eyes watched Hector for a long moment, and then lifted to look out over the lawns and through to the distant landscape pressed down by the heat of the day. "It's a beautiful world," he said at last. "If you want me to go ...?"

"No, please stay. It was kind of you to come."

"Good. I like to be welcome. Why don't you start and tell me what kind of a communist you are," and he spread out his hand to indicate the house, the garden and the fields of the estate.

Hector did his best to answer the question sincerely. It seemed an inadequate set of reasons to account for so many years of his life, but that was how it was. He had done what he could for the struggle.

"Those ideas won't work without the fundamentals being in place," the priest replied. "And Christ understood those. They are simpler than we make them. Some of the churchmen attach a far greater meaning, far more complicated, and in the process interfere detrimentally with the running of men's lives. I wonder if some of them read the Bible? ... now that is being disloyal, isn't it? To my simple way of thinking, the only striving we have to do is to live our lives as closely as possible to the teachings of Christ, and if His promise of God comes true we will be part of His miracle. All we have to be is good. Be right, not wrong. To tell the truth. To love without motive. To give without being asked. To be good, like Him. That is my faith. If we were all good and lived as Christ taught us to live, we would not need your communism to solve our secular problems. Christ taught us how to behave.

"The pity is that no one listens any more. Even many in the church are too busy with man's politics. Some of the world's great religions have given it a word. Fundamentalism. But now even that slogan has political connotations. We must read the Bible and live by God's word, not by the words of man who too often has a hidden motive for his exhortations. Let us be good first and, when we are truly good, we will have earned the love of Christ and then, maybe, we will have the true faith for which I yearn."

Hector looked at the man for some time, the sun having gone down behind the elms. They had talked for a long time. It was a beautiful evening with the swallows flying high.

"Would you join me for supper? I don't want to be alone."

"That's why I'm here," smiled the Reverend Williams.

"She died right there in your chair."

"I know."

"Who told you?"

"No one. I just know. There are so many things we don't understand and there is so little time to find out … throughout my fifty years, I have found it easier to live by following Christ. He, you see, was a good man. It is that example that is the great comfort for my life, without which it would have no meaning. Maybe, just maybe, if I live long enough, I will be blessed with the truth of God. It is my hope and should be yours."

"Now you are selling me your religion." But Hector was smiling.

"Maybe just a little. Shall we be friends?"

"I could do with a friend … A glass of wine with the cold beef?"

"A game of chess?" suggested the minister.

"Have you read Plato?"

"All of him. He reads closely with Christ. Socrates was also a good man and they made him drink the hemlock."

Together they rose and went into the house. The parish priest left at one o'clock in the morning. Hector finally slept as the sun was rising in the east. The birds were singing. God's overture to the new born day.

Luke's situation was impossible. The baby had been his to feed and look after for over a month, and twice he was forced to postpone a trip to Angola where the ANC were building up their military forces to help the South West African People's Organisation force South Africa out of what they preferred to call Namibia. With Cuban air cover, military equipment and logistical troops from the Marxist MPLA, there was a good chance of forcing PW Botha into his first military defeat. And Luke wished to visit the war zone so that, when he asked for funds, his pleas for help were authentic and up to date.

But he could not move from his flat with the baby. After Angola, he was scheduled to tour America as a guest of Jesse Jackson and there was a substantial amount of money to be gleaned from that source. But what could he do with the baby he asked himself. Even had he wished to put his son up for adoption, there were complications, as the child had not been born in England. And adoption for Luke was not an option. A son had a right to his real father, and how would he know what strangers would do for the boy?

Luke's mother and father were dead, the kraal behind Second Beach, Port St Johns, long eaten by the termites, and any relations he might have had were unknown to him. The party, quite rightly, just laughed. Told him to find a wife and give the boy to her to look after, and in the meantime get on with the job. There was a war to be fought and won, and the day of the great liberation was upon them, with half the black townships in South Africa ungovernable and sanctions forcing the white economy to crack. The black kids were boycotting school, no one was paying rent to the white controlled municipalities, garbage was not being collected and bombs going off in white supermarkets.

South Africa was spiralling downwards towards chaos and revolution, when the only people who would be able to restore order, like Robert Mugabe's Zanu in Zimbabwe, would be Mandela's ANC. They were winning, and would Luke Mbeki please get on with the job, and fast, and stop worrying about a baby. There were a lot more babies in South Africa with a lot more problems than the one he was complaining about. When the struggle was won, they would all have time to worry about minor problems.

"Don't you have anyone you can trust to look after the boy?" His neighbour worked during the day and had her own children to look after, two of them in the same sized one roomed flat – 'flat' being the polite word for a hole in the wall.

"Yes, there is, but he's white."

"You revolutionaries make me laugh, babe," chuckled the woman. "Make me laugh. All those people out there doing good and all you got's a white to trust. Oh, I see, one of them commies. Don't go for commies. Had a friend from Cuba and she didn't talk too well about commies. If you ask me, best you can do is give up this revolution and use that degree you have to get a job. English university, you say. Get a job, Luke. Revolutions never got nobody nowhere. You look at where I come from and mark my words. That Caribbean they're always revolting about something. Don't feed nobody. Where's this white man live so we can get this little child a home while you throw bombs around?"

"In South Africa."

"Now I've heard it all. You spend all your days finding ways to kick them whites clear out of Africa and you tell me that."

"We don't want all the whites to go."

"Sounds like it to me and them. Ones who stay won't be no good to you. Just the poor and lazy. No man worth a day's pay stays in a place he ain't wanted. Why should he? By the time you lot win your revolution, there won't be a brain left in the country, black, or white, if you ask me."

"I hope you're wrong."

"I'm never wrong, Luke Mbeki, which is why you got to do something about this child. I can't help no more and you sure can't. You got to do something, and fast."

The letter to Matthew Gray took a month to arrive, through the hands of the paramount chief. The cable was waiting under Luke's door when he came back from the day care centre that looked after the boy during the day. "MY WIFE AND I WILL ALWAYS HAVE A ROOM FOR A CHILD OF YOURS. HAVE BOY SIMILAR AGE. LIKE OLD TIMES. MATT"

When Luke Mbeki had read the cable, he sat down in the solitary chair and cried. Chelsea de la Cruz had refused to have anything to do with the boy. Matthew Gray had been the little boy's last chance and, as Luke thought of the long beach and the wild bananas, the giant wild figs, the river with mullet, the gully and oysters and the green slopes rising from the Gap, he knew the boy would be safe for him when he finally went home, when the struggle was over and they could all live as men should live, in harmony, without oppression, without apartheid.

The next day, Luke flew to Luanda with the child, and from Luanda in Angola the boy was taken to Botswana. From there he was smuggled into South Africa, wrapped in a blanket across the back of a black girl who was trained to place limpet mines in street dustbins and who would work out of Umtata in the Transkei.

This was how Sipho Mbeki, named after his grandfather, came to the land of his forefathers, to the very place where they had lived for two centuries, and he howled his lungs out with delight. The boy was five months old and arrived just in time for Christmas.

After touring Angola for a week, Luke knew the total onslaught being prepared for South Africa was real. Antonio van Perreira dos Santos Cassero had flown him from one MPLA stronghold to another, and within a year the push to remove Jonas Savimbi and his Unita movement from the face of Angola would begin. To ensure the South Africans were kept busy, there would be major incursions by SWAPO guerrillas, backed by the ANC, into Ovamboland in northern South West Africa. The Marxist MPLA were backed by Cuban troops and the Cuban air force, and in overall command was a Russian general.

"By the end of this year," said Antonio, "our forward base at Cuito Cuanavale will be ready and our MIG 23s will dominate the South African Mirages and Buccaneers. We will shoot them out of the sky and control the air space over northern South West Africa. On the ground, our T54 and T55 tanks will push the South African army into the sea. Then I will have a nice piece of land and grow coffee in the land of my mother's people. I will be home."

They were walking in part of a military complex, the Cubans wishing to impress the ANC with their power. Luke looked at the man and wondered why it always ended up the same way. You conquered a land under whatever pretext and took the land for yourself, the conquered working the land as serfs. A cold shiver ran through his body at a premonition of what was really going to happen to Africa when communism won the revolution. The agenda of the black nationalists, like himself, was very different from those of the communists, but each were using the other with the smug certainty that when the battle was won they could control the other party.

It had never occurred to Luke that the Cubans intended to farm Angola. He had thought they were crusaders. Russia gave them five billion US dollars a year to prop up their economy and, in exchange, they fought the capitalists in Africa. There was a price for freedom. Would the ANC freedom be a communist dictatorship with an economy in tatters like Cuba, backed up by Russia and doing exactly what the Russians told them to do? Puppets of the Russians! Was he spending the best years of his life to replace the Boer with the Russian?

Except for a very few blacks, would it make any difference? What they wanted to control would have gone. The great wealth of South Africa would have trickled away. He knew better than most that the most difficult quality to find was good management. Would they inherit the mines and the industries, only to find they had no one left to make them work? That a piece of economic sanctions that they heralded in the ANC as the big weapon for change would have changed so much that there was nothing worth having? What would the people do to those who made so many promises? The only freedom they would have would be the freedom to starve, and the predators like Colonel Cassero would own their land.

Even his friend Matthew Gray had withdrawn his management, not interested in being labelled a white settler/exploiter. And the withdrawal of Matt's skills was far more devastating than all his workers going on strike. Matt could survive wherever he went, but could the workers survive without jobs?

"How are you going to get land?" Luke asked innocently.

"These people will need someone to organise them. They won't do it alone. They'll be only too pleased to give me land to provide employment. It's a beautiful country. I'm so very excited. What you do when we win, hey, Luke?"

"I don't know."

"They make you minister. Then you get rich, hey. Ministers always get rich. Me, I grow coffee and get rich. Big house on the hill. Sell the coffee to the Russians. You come and visit."

"It wasn't what I had in mind."

"What then? What it all about? You think it all about a new philosophy? Poof! It all about money. You see, Minister Mbeki. You get rich. We drink beer together."

# 3

Teddie Botha was harassed. Security Lion in England was launching a retirement annuity product for 'top-hat' executives. The new Security Life building in which he sat, on the twenty second floor, was only seventy per cent let. Lucky Kuchinski, the best general sales manager a CEO could have, was drinking too much and would listen to not one word of advice, and Archie Fletcher-Wood was spending half his day on the luncheon circuit, which was not helping the running of a company that controlled seven billion rand in assets and had to find a weekly home for thirty million rand that came into the company through corporate pension funds, single premiums, and everybody and his dog paying fifty rand a month for thirty years.

The company was saturated with other people's money and the only place to put it each week was on the stock exchange, as the rate of inflation was running higher than the short or long-term interest rates. To attract potential customers and satisfy the old who looked to the Security group for their pension money, the company had to show a growth in their investment funds in excess of the rate of inflation.

Money could not legally be transferred outside South Africa, and the British and South African companies were kept at arm's length for fear of breaching the stringent South African exchange control regulations. Anybody with money wanted it outside the country, as sanctions bit and overseas companies disinvested under pressure from the ANC. Local money caught in the trap chased itself in a spiral, pushing up the share prices but doing nothing else for the economy or the people. And, to add to his troubles, he was due to report to the army in four days' time to run around the arid north of South West Africa to demonstrate to the Russians that, if their tanks came any nearer to the border, the South Africans would go in to knock them out, using hot pursuit of Swapo and ANC guerrillas as the excuse.

And then there was Tilda, a charming girl who had every right to desire marriage – but how could he ever find the time to consider the consequences of a wife and children when half the day was spent trying to find ten minutes to have a crap? Tilda was twenty-three, very pretty, and made him think of her far too frequently when he had other matters that required his concentration.

The predators in the corporate world were snapping at his door, looking for the first mistake, and while everything was going well he kept them away. Every year the actuaries analysed the company's commitments to its policyholders and told him his solvency rate. The drop in the property and share market in England in 1973 had caused two big life insurance companies to collapse through very little fault of their own, and as it had been shortly after he had joined the company and then been forced to do his two years' national service before returning to find out what running a company was all about, the memory of their fate had stuck in his mind. Archie had done a fairly adequate job in his absence, but the man preferred to implement business policies personally rather than calculate what had to be done and give instructions to others.

Tilda had moved into his penthouse in Sandown piece by piece. First a toothbrush, followed by a set of clean underwear, then an evening dress, and something to wear in the morning. Then she cancelled the rent on her own flat and moved in with him. In some ways, this arrangement did have its advantages, as it saved the travelling time required to pick up a date and take her home after dinner. Never once had Teddie thought of living with Tilda, but he had insufficient energy to fight the reality when it had taken place. He wondered what she did during his trips round the branches and overseas but, when he asked, she said that she merely watched television and waited for him to come home. She was very pretty, so Teddie left the matter as it was and proceeded with the mammoth task of running his business.

When he returned home with the army call-up phone call still ringing in his ear, she was already in bed, tucked up and looking smug.

"I'm pregnant," she informed him.

Teddie looked at her, then at the door, then at the window.

"My mother thinks it's wonderful," she continued, patting the soft cover of the bed. "Edward, aren't you pleased? I mean, we do live together, which is almost the same as being married. How was your day?"

"I'm in the army, Monday," Teddie replied flatly.

"What do you think about the baby?"

"I have a lot more pressing problems at the moment."

"You should be pleased. I'm pleased."

"Is there any food?"

"There's cold chicken in the fridge ... Mother wants to meet you."

WHILE TEDDIE WAS IN JOHANNESBURG, wondering how sure he could ever be that he was indeed the father of the child, a storm was raging along the Wild Coast a thousand kilometres to the southeast. Winds rushing at one hundred and sixty kilometres an hour were thrashing huge waves onto the shore and the fronds were being torn from the wild banana trees all along the coast. The August storms were the same each year and the colony's fishing boat had been hauled well out of the way of the sea, driftwood had been stored for weeks, and wooden shutters placed firmly across the face of the hut on the hill. Giant sprays from the Gap threw salt water over the thatch and dripped it down the shutters when the wind finally stopped throwing it further up the hill.

Inside the big rondavel, a fire warmed the hearth and a large fish stew bubbled in its three-legged pot in one corner of the fireplace over its own small pile of coals. The minstrel boy was playing to himself with his back to the stone wall next to the bookshelves, his bare feet towards the warmth of the fire. He had been watching the food for some time while he sang. At the side away from the fire, Raleen snuggled against his hip and smiled at the words of the old English ballad that sang of a farmer's boy who to the wars had gone. Sophie and Charles Farquhar were at opposite ends of the room, and Jonathan Holland, as high as a kite on dagga was watching Raleen, watching the minstrel boy.

Stretched out on a rush carpet in front of the fire, oblivious to the storm raging across the ocean outside, Matthew Gray was fast asleep, his length quite remarkable at full stretch. Lorna stirred the iron pot with a piece of driftwood and waggled her finger at Peace, who was about to tickle her father's bare foot with a chicken feather. Robert Gray, one and a half years old, lay flat on his back on a mattress and, like his father, was fast asleep. Next to him, the year old Sipho Mbeki had just had his nappy changed and was watching the flames rise and fall from the fire, his coal black eyes accentuated by the pure whites of the surrounds.

In front of the fire, Carel van Tonder was whittling a piece of wood to make a hand line for fishing. In front of Sophia, a pile of children's homework was being read and corrected, her school now teaching fifteen pupils, ranging from six and a half year old Peace to a Xhosa man of nineteen who wanted to learn how to read. Charles Farquhar was resigned to Sophia's rejection of him, having discovered the reason, and was giving thought to his next move. Matt had completed eleven paintings, all of which had found their way to Bernard Strover and thence to the man in London or the Everard Read gallery in Johannesburg.

The castle had still not been sold, the tax men finding themselves in a quandary. In reality, the old pile of stones was a liability, the upkeep being greater than the value of the land. The taxman and the earl were at a standoff, but content with the status quo. Charles tried again to catch Sophia's eye, without any success. He really was wasting his time.

"You want a joint, old son?" asked Jonathan. "Good for the blues and I should know. Why suffer when pot can blow your mind away?"

"Why not?" said Charles, taking the joint carefully, pulling in a drag and handing it back. They passed the joint back and forth until it was finished. "What are you going to do with the rest of your life?" Charles then asked Jonathan.

"Get stoned ... get beautifully, totally stoned. Old Ding-dong always believed in getting stoned. First time we met. Stoned. That was booze. Too expensive. Too much tax … and I hate hangovers. She's beautiful, isn't she?"

"Very, old chap."

"I mean Raleen, not Sophia. You're looking at the wrong woman … he can sing, I'll give him that," referring to the minstrel boy. "Best thing I ever did was coming to Port St Johns; cheapest place in the world to get stoned." He lay back and smiled at the patterns in the thatch high above his head, flashed to him by the flickering flames of the fire.

TWO WEEKS AFTER THE STORM, when September rode the first days of an African spring, the sea was calm and gentle, giving sanctuary to the battered seabirds who rode the gentle swells, feathers preened, letting the sun warm their exhausted bodies that had fought the winds and rain. It was the period of renewal.

Carel van Tonder had launched their boat at first light, and stretched in the prow was Matthew Gray in his loin cloth, the salt crusting the lower part of his body from the time when they had pushed the boat out into the water from the beach. Charles Farquhar was watching his cousin, whose eyes were almost closed against the glare of the morning sun.

The minstrel boy was perched on the back bench, behind the big fish box, his hair tied up neatly, his eight string guitar left behind in the small school they had all helped to build. Sophia was happier on her own and spent hours of her leisure time walking the cliffs and the beach, reliving the hopes in her mind. Black Martin was making a hand line with one of the sticks whittled by Carel during the storm. No one had spoken for half an hour while the small ski boat motored slowly to the reef, where the fish were big and the mountain from the bottom of the deep blue sea rose to within ten metres of the surface.

Jonathan Holland had been left on shore under a wild banana tree, smoking his first joint of the day and talking quite happily to Ding-dong Bell as if his dead friend was alive and well; this morning they were collecting bottles to take down to the Salisbury industrial sites to exchange for money. A young African by the name of Jamba Sithole was recruiting the blacks to go out on the Street tricycles to collect empty beer bottles. Matt had written to Jonathan's mother, saying the boy was fine and well, which in a way was true.

They anchored over the subterranean mountain peak and let their lines down into the water, all except Charles, who pulled out of the empty fish box a picnic basket of gargantuan size. From the basket he took four bottles of excellent Cape white wine and a canvas bag to which was attached a long length of rope. Carefully, Charles let the wine filled bag down over the gunwale. When he felt it finally touch the bottom, he pulled it up a metre and firmly tied the end of the rope to a rowlock.

Matt leant up and looked into the hamper. There were neat rows of wine glasses attached by leather thongs to one side, a corkscrew with an ivory handle emblazoned with the family crest, and a number of interesting plastic containers of varying sizes all tied down to stop them moving around. On the other side from the glasses were leather straps which held the picnic plates, and attached to the short sides were plastic teacups and two large, red thermos flasks. Matt could see a wooden salad bowl with a long pronged fork, a fat wooden spoon and a small row of condiments. Each compartment was full of something.

"There was a delightful character in a Howard Spring book I read as a youngster," said Charles, by way of explanation. "His name was Septimus Pordage, and he firmly believed that no civilised person should go further than fifty metres from his own front door without victuals, which always included a bottle of hock wrapped in a double damask dinner napkin as white as the driven snow. I could not find a suitable napkin nor the hock, but I did find a delightful bottle or two of Bellingham Premier Grand Cru (PGC to the initiated), which I hope will suffice. I mean, it was an emergency, old chap.

"Now, if one of you fine gentlemen will put the bait on the end of my hook please? The picnic hamper was a present from Bernard Strover and the corkscrew was one of the heirlooms I salvaged from the department of inland revenue. In a manner of speaking, 'tis all I have of the castle right now, but who would want more than a gentle sea and a ship and the deep blue sky of heaven? Thank you, dear boy," he said, as Black Martin handed him a line with baited hooks. "Most kind. Should I be so bold as to catch a fish, you will have the honour of removing it as well. I was always squeamish, old boy. Do you think you could sing a fishing song, old chap?" He was smiling at the minstrel boy. "Something rather enticing. The wine should be chilled in an hour. If you don't sing, old chap, I shall have a go at 'A life on the ocean wave', and my voice is even worse than my cousin's."

"What food did you bring, man?" asked Carel.

"All manner of things to delight the most discerning palate."

"Where did you get the money, man?"

"That is for me to know and for you, if you wish to be a bore, to find out. No pun intended, good Carel van Tonder. No pun intended."

"Two blerrie lunatics," muttered Black Martin. "One in the boat and one on the shore."

"When you have supped the cool wine and eaten the perfect crayfish mayonnaise, you will wish for a world full of lunatics."

Instead of singing, the minstrel boy took a harmonica from the deep pocket of his shirt and began to play, with the end of his fishing line hooked around the big toe of his right foot. When he had finished, he took up the line and looked out over the sea.

"If there be a place called heaven, then this be it," he said quietly.

They came ashore ten minutes after the fiery sun had gone down, sending red shafts of light to the heavens. The fires had been lit on shore and the whole community of Second Beach had come down to watch the beaching of the fish. Using his great strength to its limit, Matt helped pull the laden boat from the gentle surf; and the hatch was opened for all to see. Everyone was waiting his turn to look over the side of the boat at the great catch that had almost filled the ski boat.

Charles stepped off onto the sand carrying the picnic basket, light as a feather, full of empty flasks and bottles, with not a morsel of food uneaten. Matt hugged Lorna first, then Peace, then little Robert, and finally tossed the baby Sipho up onto his shoulders. All the fish had to be gutted and cleaned, the offal being thrown into the sea as food for the scavenging crayfish. Raleen kissed the minstrel boy, while Melissa took the hand of Black Martin. Charles looked for Sophia and Jonathan offered his help with the gutting of the fish.

"Best bream gutter in the Zambezi Valley ... who wants a joint?" said Jonathan.

A moonless darkness had gripped the beach by the time the last fish had been gutted and all who needed had taken a fish home to their huts. The Vuya restaurant bought seven copper steenbras, which paid for the petrol for the next seven trips. The fish were so large that even the smallest weighed nineteen kilograms. On each of the driftwood fires on the beach, they grilled a black steenbras, with all the people of Second Beach and its surrounds mingling around the great fish, children rushing between legs, skipping in the darkness and laughing with the joy of plenty. Many were hungry as, with the storm, nothing else had come out of the sea.

The fishermen tried their best to carry on with the party after the first serving of cooked fish but wearily, they climbed to their huts, washing the salt water from their tired bodies before falling face down onto their mattresses. Matt was still smiling as he fell asleep, and still holding Lorna's hand.

"Come, Peace," she said. "Your daddy has earned his sleep," and, pulling a thin blanket over his long body, they tiptoed out of the big rondavel, leaving Sipho asleep in his cot next to Robert. Just far enough away from the hut, Peace squealed and ran down the path to join her friends on the beach.

The stars had begun to appear, bright and clean. Lorna stopped at the bottom of the patch and looked up at the heavens. "Thank you," she whispered, and, hugging herself, knowing her man was safe, she went out on the beach to join her friends.

"Hey," she called. "Is there any of that fish left?"

"Plenty," came back the chorus in English, Afrikaans and Xhosa.

BEING unable to leap in and out of the open cars without using the doors any more, Lucky Kuchinski had resorted to dyeing his hair the original dark brown and lying about his age. He frequented the most upmarket boutiques and wore clothes that would have suited a man of thirty. The gymnasiums did their best but a fifty-four year old body is still a fifty-four year old body, and a good chest had declined to around the waist, making belts or braces essential. Bending down and rising again most often produced a jerk in the action and a pain in the back.

Lucky was hysterically determined not to fall prey to the beckoning hand of old age. Once his virility had gone, Lucky knew he was dead, and he pursued the company of young girls like a man in the desert pursues water. The cleft in his chin was still there, but no longer clean and square, having joined the crags and crevices that now made up the pattern of his face.

Instead of showing his grandchildren how to fish or catch a ball, Lucky was still trying to be the man-about-town. The Aston Martin DB4 had given way to an imported Porsche, with the highest number in the catalogue that could travel up to two hundred and thirty kilometres an hour, but he now rarely drove outside the built-up area of Johannesburg. Lucky, to prove he was still the life and soul of the party, was permanently travelling somewhere, and always by aeroplane. If he met a new girl in Cape Town, he wanted to fly her to a party in Johannesburg, and a Johannesburg girl to a beach party at the Cape.

Lucky was too terrified to stop for a moment and accept the truth that it was all over. He had never married, preferring to flit from one woman to the other, finding physical satisfaction in the chase rather than consummation. The only thing that kept the young girls from laughing at him was the money, and money in the quantities lavished on them by Lucky is the strongest aphrodisiac known to certain types in the world of women.

Lucky was never short of the wrong kind of girl. They were the type of women who had a body and nothing else, and their years of cashing the chips were a lot shorter than Lucky Kuchinski's. The idea of marrying, relaxing and living in luxury with an old rich man was highly attractive. Who wanted to work when one good effort could solve the biggest problem of life once and for all?

But, like most opportunities in life that seem too good to be true, they rarely came true. Trapping Lucky in a church or even a registry office was quite impossible. The man was a butterfly and, when he saw what young Tilda was doing to his boss, he took off from his mighty pursuits to warn the younger man he was in danger. Lucky had known Tilda's mother intimately many years before, and knew her for a first-class scheming bitch.

"Have you met the mother?" Lucky inquired.

"Not yet."

"Meet her. Always check the mothers. Remember one thing, Teddie: daughters always, without exception, end up like their mothers. Do you really want a whingeing wife and three whingeing kids to make you wish you never had to go home at night? You might get three girls just like their mother."

"She's pregnant."

"With all your travelling, how do you know it's yours?"

"I trust the girl," stated Teddie, with more conviction than he felt.

"That's the first mistake of life. Never trust anyone, and certainly not an unmarried girl who tells you she's pregnant. Tell me something, Edward Botha. Would you take over another insurance company without checking every fact and weighing all the possibilities?"

"Of course not."

"And yet you meet a young girl in the bar, let her move in with you, get her pregnant, and you're thinking of marriage and you haven't even had a glance at the balance sheet"

"But, if the kid's mine, he must have a father."

"Give the kid support, maybe, after a blood test, but don't enter into a lifelong contract with a total stranger. You've only known her three months. When's the baby due?"

"She doesn't know."

"Find out from someone you can trust" insisted Lucky. "Send her to your doctor."

"She has her own gynaecologist."

"Then have your doctor find out from him. Believe me. And if you don't believe me, meet the mother. Theodora Blaze won't have changed. Once a scheming bitch, always a scheming bitch. And I should know. I lived with her twenty years ago."

"You mean Tilda is ...?"

"No, Tilda was two. And I'll tell you something else. Theo was never sure who the father was, whatever story she has made up since. Believe me, please believe me. Those two women saw you coming from the other side of Johannesburg. I swear it on the grave of my Polish mother."

"She's a lovely girl," protested Teddie, weakly.

"They all are at twenty-three."

. . .

THEODORA BLAZE KNEW the one weak link in her plan was Lucky Kuchinski. They had met in London soon after Lucky and Archie had walked out of the Congo with the few Kruger Rands strapped to their waists. Theo had made up her mind to marry a rich man and, though Lucky swept her off her feet, showing her places most girls of modest means read about only in newspapers, she knew the source of his wealth was short-lived, if she had only known Matthew Gray was going to take him back into the jungle and bring him out richer than any man she had ever known, she would not have dropped Lucky for what she thought at the time was a better long-term proposition.

A fact she did not know was that she had been to Lucky the only girl he would ever have married. They were the same type. Prospectors, predators, maybe. They liked to live off other people. They were both good at banging the drum for other people's ideas and they made making friends a purpose in life. Knowing their own inadequacies, they were insecure. By the time Lucky had returned three years later and Lion Life had blossomed, it was too late. Deliberately, Lucky had started the relationship again, waited until she thought he was going to propose, and then dumped her the way she had dumped him. When he returned to South Africa, she had followed, hoping he would turn to her again, but by then the overflow of money had gone to his head.

Theo had watched her daughter grow into the rarity that all men seemed to want and she had schooled the girl to wait until the real money came along. It was very much a case of like mother, like daughter. Tilda knew, as her mother had known, that a girl's looks do not last and that a man's great prize in life is possession of a woman that all other men want.

She had first gone to bed with Teddie before she knew who he was, Teddie having borrowed a car from the garage while his was being serviced. On the first Friday night, they had met in the Balalaika along with the rest of the crowd, and he had given her a lift home, on the way buying her a steak at the Bonanza. They had spent the weekend in her bachelor flat, returning to the Balalaika at Saturday lunchtime to join the crowd and the rest of the hedonists. She would have left it as a pleasant but unproductive weekend had her mother not picked up the name in conversation.

"Teddie Botha? What does he do?" asked Theo sharply. The combination of an Afrikaans surname and an English Christian name was rare. They were all known as Koos, Naas or Pik.

"Something to do with insurance."

"Did he say which insurance company?"

"No, but someone in the pub on Saturday asked him how it was going at Security Lion. He's a salesman. Sells life insurance. Ugh! Forget him. Nice enough guy, I suppose ... How was your date?"

"When you start going for the thirty year olds at my age, you know you're reaching menopause. Now, young lady, just you come over here and sit down. Did you sleep with him?"

"Mother, please!"

"Good. Now, is this the man you met?" The magazine was the Financial Mail which Theo read as part of her job in the advertising agency.

"That's Teddie. Was he salesman of the year or something?" The face from that weekend was looking at her from the cover page of the magazine.

"No. He's chairman of Security Lion."

"Doesn't drive much of a car."

"Very rich men don't have to. You go and read the article on Teddie Botha, and when you're finished we'll make a plan." Her one track mind had gone into overdrive; she had nurtured her daughter through the months that had led to the pregnancy.

AN HOUR after making the phone call, Teddie's doctor phoned him back. The doctor had had his secretary phone all over Johannesburg to track down Tilda's gynaecologist.

"Miss Matilda Blaze is ten weeks pregnant, Teddie."

"She could not be over three months?"

"Definitely not. I specifically asked him that question."

"I owe you one." With the receiver back in its place, Teddie clasped his hands together on his desk and pressed the palms together. They were sweating with excitement. He was going to be a daddy and all the ancestors in his genes were tingling with joy. He rose and walked round the large office, hugging himself with happiness. Then he dashed back to his desk and dialled Lucky Kuchinski on the intercom.

"You're wrong, Lucky. You're wrong."

"I'm glad, Teddie," Lucky responded, after taking a moment to grasp what Teddie was talking about. "Hope you're not mad at me."

"Better to know now than think later. Have a cigar."

"Your son's not born yet, Teddie."

"But he will be. That's the point."

"Congratulations."

When Lucky replaced the receiver he looked at the phone for a long time. Then he shook his head.

"Some of them just get lucky," he said to himself. He was certain a lot more had gone into that pregnancy than met the eye.

THE WEDDING WAS A WILD AFFAIR. Not wishing to have the newspapers involved, they used the garden of Archie Fletcher-Woods's house, erecting a marquee for two hundred guests. The magistrate came to the house as Teddie had not been able to tell the minister that his wife-to-be was three and a half months pregnant. The Dutch Reformed Church, which believed so strongly that God made the Afrikaners his chosen people who should never mix their blood with the blacks, thought just as strongly about marrying pregnant brides. Each was a sin before God.

Teddie had met the mother in his euphoria at becoming a prospective father and found her charming. Before the ceremony, Theo avoided Lucky but, when the deed was done and signed, she feigned suddenly to recognise his presence. The bride's mother was more blooming than the bride.

"Well, if it isn't Lucky Kuchinski!"

"Dear old Theo. You really must be whooping with joy."

"Why you've lost most of that lovely Polish accent. Just a little still maybe. What are you doing these days?"

Lucky just looked at her and shook his head but, when she walked away to find the bride and groom, his eyes followed her through the milling crowd. Then the band started to play and Lucky felt every one of his fifty-four years.

"What's the matter, Lucky; you seen a ghost?" asked Archie, coming up to chat.

"You could say that, Arch."

"Matt didn't come."

"Did you think he would?"

"Not really. You know," Archie said, turning to his live-in lover, "maybe we should get married."

"Yes, dear," Sunny, clinging to Archie's arm, as usual agreed with whatever he said, as within ten minutes she knew he would change his mind.

She had cried at the wedding ceremony, as much for herself as for Tilda Botha. She had been living with Archie for four years, which was better than working as a middle-aged secretary. At forty-four, life could have been worse, even if Archie did threaten to kick her out every six months. The man had more moods than hours in the day, and the wound in his leg gave him hell every time it rained. But they did have their softer moments; not many, but some. All through the day she had hoped Matt would come to the wedding. The older she became, the fewer of her hopes ever came to fruition. She had learnt to live from day to day … and her life had started off with such promise. She was day dreaming again.

"It's going to rain later, dear," she said.

"I can feel it in my leg."

"Tell me when you want to go."

THE DAY AFTER THE WEDDING, Teddie put on his uniform. They had postponed his call-up for three weeks, the expected incursions by SWAPO into the white farming area south of Ovamboland not having happened at the end of the dry season. Teddie looked in the mirror and shook his head.

"What's the matter darling?" asked Tilda.

"It's going to be hot in Ovamboland. Just before the rains "

"You will be careful."

"Only the Cubans can give us any real trouble, and they're hundreds of kilometres further north. We'll go down to Cape Town when I get back."

When she kissed him goodbye downstairs and watched him drive away she really did hope the child in her womb would be a boy and that the boy's father was indeed Teddie Botha. He had been so thrilled at the idea of fatherhood.

Her only fear was that her husband would discover that she had not slept on her own every night he was away. She had slept away from the penthouse, but Johannesburg was still a mining camp and everyone talked. She should be able to know when the baby was born; know for herself. She had told no one, least of all her mother. Teddie's chances of being the father were one against four. Every time Tilda Blaze had had a few too many drinks, she had never been able to say no. She smiled wanly to herself as the car disappeared. She wondered how many people really knew who their fathers were. She for one did not know hers.

She turned back to the block of flats and rode up in the lift to the penthouse. Nothing mattered, provided that Teddie Botha never found out she had slept with other men after she had spent the weekend with him in her flat. Deliberately and firmly, she put the problem out of her mind; it was Teddie's baby and she was going to make sure of that. Then she laughed out loud and sat down on the big couch that looked out through the French doors to the patio and the small plunge swimming pool.

"Got the best and richest and still don't know what I want," she said out loud to herself. Everything bad happened so quickly.

THE FOLLOWING SUNDAY, while Teddie was suffering forty-five degree heat and thinking through his role as father, Archie rang the door-bell of the flat Lucky had occupied for seven years, and was surprised to find Lucky on his own. It was twelve o'clock in the morning and already thunder clouds were building, along with the humidity.

"Where's Sunny?" asked Lucky, letting in his friend of so many years.

"I left her alone."

"Want a beer?"

"Sure. Why not ... You and I see each other in the office most days, but ever since Sunny moved in we never seem to talk."

Lucky went to the fridge and came back with two cans of beer, the frost dripping softly down the sides. They 'kissed' open the cans in unison and drank. Neither of them ever used a glass for beer.

"You're a married man, Arch. Life changes between bachelors when one of them marries or lives with a chick... Let's sit on the stoep. Should be cooler. What's the occasion, Arch?"

They sat down on the swing couch and looked out over the blocks of flats. Rosebank was overcrowded like so much else of Johannesburg.

"You ever hear from Aldo?" said Archie.

"Not for years."

"I did ...He's married. Running his safari camp again. Mugabe seems to have that country under control. Tourists coming back. Aldo's a father twice over."

"Who'd he marry?"

"Didn't say ...You think we've been right? No real wives and no kids?"

"You got to add it all together. Could have got a safe job in London all those years ago. You could, anyway. We didn't, Arch. Kept on running. There's a price for everything. But add it all up and we're okay. You and I did a lot of living. Just now we feel old. Happens to everyone. You see, Arch, it's all coming to an end. Few more years. I try to put a brave face on it. But we're rich. Wouldn't like to be old and poor. No regrets. Better to regret what you haven't done than what you have."

"What I mean is we missed out on a family."

"Can you think of any of the women you should have married?" asked Lucky.

"None, really."

"That's the point. You and I married women in the plural."

"You think we'll get lonely as we get older?"

"Probably ... But would it be any better with a wife? Kids pushed off. You know many married at our age who'd do the same again? Half are too scared to argue with their wives."

"Matt's happy," said Archie.

"Matt's always been happy. Only all-together man I ever met. You think I should take out Theo again?"

"Why are you asking me?"

"She's well over forty."

"You think me and Sunny ... Maybe. You sick of young girls, Lucky?"

"You know, Arch, I just can't be bothered to chase any more ... You want another beer?"

"Whisky, man, whisky. This is serious. Jo'burg's oldest teenager has gone senile ... Fact is, I was thinking of marrying Sunny. Make her happy. Poor kid's helluva insecure."

"Shit, Arch, I'd better join you with the Scotch."

"We've known each other so long, me and Sunny. That means a lot. Memories together. We know the same people. We can sit for hours without talking. Maybe that's all it's about at our age. You don't want to have to get up and start performing."

"Good to see you, you old bugger."

"Likewise, Lucky. We've come a long way together and friends are important. Most important of all, I should think. If I marry Sunny, would you be my best man?"

"Be an honour, Archie."

EXCEPT IN VERY BAD WEATHER, Matt never closed both stable doors to his rondavel, the top part always being left open on the catch. The cats and dogs could get in and out, and if anyone wished to steal anything badly enough they were welcome. The rafters were used as clothes hangers for the few clothes owned by the family, and without a refrigerator there was little food in the house apart from bottles of pickles, dried fish or pumpkins on the roof of the small shed that had been built to serve the growing family and which housed an interesting adaption of Mr Crapper's ingenious invention.

The three young black children had appeared on the beach a week earlier but they were shyer than a duiker from the forest. They lived in a small cave on the other side of the Gap, which Matt knew to be dangerous when the seas were high and the crashing waves inundated the cove. No one had been able to get near enough to warn them of the danger. They were living off raw mussels and anything else washed up on the shore, and it was quickly clear that they did not belong on the Wild Coast. The black families who lived in the fresh clearings behind the colony were as much in the dark as Matt. Even a word through to the paramount chief threw no light on where the children were from and what they were doing scavenging on the beach. They were too young to be known to the police in South Africa or the Transkei. All three were thin and badly fed.

Lorna became certain that, whenever they left the rondavel unattended, some of the bread that Raleen brought to them every morning, fresh from the oven, was gone when they returned. Not all the bread, but some; and it was the first time anything had gone missing, as waifs and strays who drifted into Second Beach were fed anyway and, if they stayed, found something productive to do that would pay for their board and lodging. The path from the rondavel led down to the beach in full sight of everyone and, as the big hut had its back to the rock on the slope of the steep hill, it was not possible to approach from any other direction

The Heath Robinson affair that Matt had set up to slam shut the top half of the stable door was a masterpiece of unconventional invention, but it worked; and when the door shut, it could not be opened from the inside.

Leaving for the full morning after the bread was delivered to ensure that the trap worked properly, Matt was not surprised to find that, when he opened the door, a child of ten was looking at him with coal-black, terrified eyes. His thin arms were clutched across his bare chest and his tatty trousers that had once reached all the way down to the ground were at half-mast and just about to fall off completely.

Very politely Matt wished him good morning in Xhosa but, to stop the lad dashing for an uncertain freedom, he shut the stable doors, knowing that Lorna would let them out when he had got to the bottom of the situation. Moving across to the area they used as a kitchen, past the big canvas he was almost ready to say was complete, Matt found a breakfast fish that had only been half-eaten and offered it to the terrified child.

"You eat that," he said, again in Xhosa, "and then we talk." He noticed that the piece of bread that had been detached from the morning's loaf had not been eaten. The child was foraging for his friends. Matt sat on his home-made wooden chair with the single-shaft wooden back that was surprisingly comfortable when tried out by visitors, and kept his eyes on the waif who was holding the food, too scared to eat.

"Eat it," commanded Matt in a very loud voice, which did the trick.

The story that came out was far worse than anything Matt could have imagined. He had been a long time living on his island in the sun, and what the child told him brought Soweto with all its cruelty and hardships into his home, a cold wind of agonising horror that Matt found impossible to imagine had been inflicted by man. It was a story of greed, double standards and the stupendous heights of manipulation by man in his struggle for power to have and to take, to hold or to rip out of the hands of those holding. It was blind, terminal self-destruction, a whole nation killing itself. There was no past or future, only the blind fury of the disembowelling moment.

Ever since the earliest days of the white colonialism of Africa, which pre-dated the slave trade, a colour bar had been created to keep the whites from mingling their blood with the blacks. The situation had been little different in the East where the brown people were looked down upon as inferior.

The manifestation of man's self-importance had reached its pinnacle when the National Party came to power in South Africa in 1948 and enacted by parliamentary law the separation of the races. As the years of their total power progressed, they became ever more fanatical in their determination to keep the white tribe of Africa, the Afrikaner of Dutch, German and French origin, pure. They even created a new race out of their policy: the coloured, those who had been mingled, the tangible result of the sins of their forefathers. They made laws which forbade any social contact between black, white or coloured. They created areas for each of them to live apart from each other and forced pockets of the black and the coloured peoples to move out from among the whites to places far from the homes of their fathers.

They created homelands for the blacks which represented a tiny portion of the land of South Africa and, even if the black lived and worked outside his designated homeland, a place he had mostly never seen or heard of, he was a citizen of the homeland with no rights in white South Africa, other than to work for the white man with minimal education and no trade unions. Trade unions were banned, along with anyone who disagreed with the apartheid system. The minority white English population talked liberalism, voted for the progressive party or whatever name it had at the moment, and secretly thanked their lucky stars for the National Party which maintained their privilege and wealth.

But power corrupted, and absolute power finally corrupted absolutely. The progressively more regressive national governments became totally unaccountable to anyone, even to the whites-only parliament. The communist onslaught was their manna from heaven, and they used it to justify their total oppression of the black and coloured peoples of the country. Jail without trial, deaths in custody, forced removals, banning and jailing of any opposition, political murder, stirring up the opposition in neighbouring states: the litany continued, with the civilised world howling with frustration, but frightened of the real power of the South African defence force.

America, in its blind and deadly fight with its own total onslaught from the 'evil empire', did not know what physically to do with South Africa, so it chose to talk tough and do very little. But what it did agree to do, along with the rest of the United Nations, was to impoverish the whites with trade sanctions, something they could do without getting hurt: though cynically they did make exceptions of strategic minerals that they could not buy elsewhere. Like small boys at school, they sent South Africa to Coventry, stopping sport, culture and carefully selected trade. Probably, without an armed invasion, there was nothing else for them to have done. And black opposition leaders from exile or jail could only call down the wrath of sanctions on the heads of the white government, hoping it would force it to change. But, like the white man with his separate development, his apartheid which prevented blacks from gaining a proper education or wealth, the body that made up South Africa was one, and the pain inflicted on the white bank account was felt far more painfully in the black man's belly. The nation was inseparably joined by an inseverable umbilical cord. Apartheid threw the baby out with the bathwater, and so did sanctions. Everyone suffered, but a rich man lowering his standard of living was nothing compared to a poor man going without food.

The children's story told of fathers with no jobs, shacks being bulldozed by the whites for being where they should not be, according to the apartheid law, and of the black nationalists' determination to make the townships ungovernable and bring the people in their desperate poverty to open revolution, which would ultimately bring Nelson Mandela to power.

The boycott syndrome prevailed. Rents were not paid for housing owned by the white government. Schools were boycotted, by pupils and teachers. White shops were boycotted, even though black shops charged more than white. Comrades roamed the black townships in the name of the banned ANC, and were infiltrated by self-seeking thugs. To add to the misery, the world refused to buy South African, and many of those who had had jobs were retrenched.

A whole generation of schoolchildren were not receiving an education. Some ran away to Botswana to join the ANC and to be trained in military skills, and three boys ran away to Second Beach to get away from the anarchy, poverty and constant fear for their lives. They told Matt that anything would be better than the slums of Soweto. All three children said their fathers were in jail for contravening the pass laws, which stopped them moving elsewhere to look for a job. Their mothers had more children than they could afford to feed, each boy coming from a family where there were six or more brothers and sisters. They had been trapped without food, schooling or shelter and, if they died of starvation on the coast, at least they had escaped. The country, Matt's country, was dying for lack of hope.

The day the children were found a hut to live in, given daily food and told to go and spend their days with Sophia in her school, a storm arose that battered the inside of the children's cave and would have drowned them without trace, sending their bodies to feed the sharks and the barracudas that scavenged the waters of the Indian Ocean. The colony returned to normal, except for the powerful images that remained in Matt's and Lorna's minds. It was the first chill wind that suggested their sanctuary was vulnerable after all.

The three boys took to the school as hungrily as they had taken to the food, doing any jobs after school with a willingness born from the hot flames of adversity. The year finished with the annual influx of Transvaal tourists who bought the hand-made crafts and pickled foods that kept the colony in just enough money to buy the necessities they were unable to produce themselves. After a 'whip-round', one of the boys was sent back to Soweto by bus to tell the mothers that their boys had found a home which suggested the small glimmer of hope that they would now be allowed to grasp an education without which they would live and die in poverty.

The January school term in Soweto was a non-starter, the children and teachers politicised to the point where they were high on the promises of liberation theologists and the liberation movements in exile. They believed the struggle was almost over and that, if they rampaged through the streets burning tyres and attacking government property, which included their schools, they would reach up and grasp the magic of 'one man, one vote', and vote themselves rich. Instead of instant freedom, the piles of uncollected garbage grew, sanitation broke down, the repair crews refused to enter the troubled townships, and the comrades ran riot, beating up any child who attended school.

At the end of January when the tourists had all returned home to their safe white suburbs, small black children began to appear on the beach, all of them without visible signs of support. The three boys greeted their friends and marched them off to Matthew Gray. To ensure that he did not make the wrong decision he asked Lorna to park their own three children with Raleen and together they set off to walk the cliff-tops and think through the problem that was changing the face of their colony. When they returned to the rondavel on the third day, they had made up their minds.

"What I'm suggesting is that I use some of the money I placed in a trust to give these children a proper education," Matt said to Sophia van Hoek. "I can pay for you to go to England to obtain a degree in education. I want nothing to do with the department of education in Pretoria or Umtata. I once tried using my money to give away food. It did not work. In two years, when you come back, you can set up a proper school. Charles can't stay here for ever. He can take you over. That is, unless any of you can think of a better idea." His eyes were soft and smiling, the crow's feet deep at the corners.

"You see, the moment we do something for people, we become responsible. In the end, no one will give us any thanks. Or else we can close down our school. It's early days. No change has yet been made. Now, I haven't painted for three days. It's for you all to make up your minds. Talk about it and let me know."

They were all sitting on the stoep of the Vuya restaurant, spending a little of the money they had earned from the tourists on cold beers. The weather was hot again and the sky out to sea a deep indigo, tinged with purple. No one said anything and, looking from one to another, Matt realised it had been easier to theorise on the top of the cliff in the moonlight with a small wood fire to give them comfort.

"It won't work," said Charles. "Much as I'd like to take Sophia to England, old chap. Won't work. You'd be flooded. Couldn't cope. You see, the apartheid state is no different from a lot of others. Trying to keep a white or First World ship watertight. If the Western democracies opened their doors to everyone, they'd also sink. None of their welfare or education systems could survive the flood of poor people who would try and climb on board, old chap.

"South Africa is a whole lot of little bits of First World floating in a sea of Third World, and it's protecting itself through the laws of apartheid in the way the British clamped down on immigration to keep out the West Indians and the other darker citizens of our erstwhile empire. Australia no longer has a white Australia policy, but instead brings in immigration laws that require an education or wealth in its new Australians that only the Western democracies or white South Africa could offer. America doesn't welcome everyone anymore, only the people they want to improve their economy … You offer a First World education to the Third World without restrictive laws and you'll sink with everyone, leaving nothing. Too many of them, not enough of you.

"Take it up at the United Nations, old chap. Try and tell them the rich and wise must educate the poor, and every rich country on the Security Council will use its veto. Open up the world to a free flow of its peoples, offering everyone equal opportunities, and Western wealth will collapse in five years. They like to talk about race relations, but they should talk about wealth relations. Your idea, noble as it is, won't work, old chap. Either the First World sets about educating everyone, or no one. This crap about giving them democracy first is passing the buck for someone else to find the solution.

"'One man one vote and a Westminster constitution did no one any good in the Third World. Now the poor sods are free it's their fault they are starving. India has a caste system to keep the poor off the backs of the rich and didn't they howl about apartheid. Morality! The Western democracies don't know how to spell the word … won't work, old chap. Brave idea. Once they kick out apartheid as they must, we will all come down to the same level, except for a few politicians who'll transfer whatever they can get their hands onto a safe, white controlled ship of state like Switzerland.

"To solve the problem you walked the paths to think about, it needs everyone with education and wealth to contribute, but the most difficult thing in a democracy is for the elected government to increase taxes. Trying to tax an Englishman or an American to pay for African education would create a laugh right across Europe and North America. Two per cent of the gross national product for aid is about the mark. Bit of feel good charity the loose change of the rich. But, my word do they make their hypocrisy sound righteous! Over there they are safe; over here, the whites are not, because the problems are physically closer. And you can't try and educate the blacks of South Africa from Second Beach, even with the best will in the world."

There was complete silence as everyone shuffled in their seats.

"That's the first time I've ever heard you being, serious," said Sophia, looking at Charles for the first time since he had arrived at Second Beach.

"There aren't many serious subjects that interest me. International hypocrisy is one of them. Cousin Matt, you're on the right track, but you'll never get enough people to help. Now can I buy you all a beer? You think we might have enough money to run to supper? Only Jesus was able to feed the five thousand with a handful of fish. Starving ourselves won't change anything. That's the reality of Western thinking. All this human rights for everyone are words to make them think they are offering a difference.

"It's the human condition, good people. Some are rich and some are poor. You can even ask the Russians. Communism is their way to empire. Religion and trade was the British way to do it. Fascism was Hitler's. Apartheid is the brain-child of the Afrikaner. The Americans invented the power of the dollar to make them rich and howl for free trade, not the free movement of people."

THE WORD REACHED Matthew Gray from the paramount chief. The Transkei police were about to arrest the minstrel boy and extradite him back over the South African border. The pressure from Pretoria, from where the money came to balance the Transkei budget, was too great.

Matt put down his paintbrush and moved out of the rondavel more quickly than Lorna had seen him move in months. He was down the patch and across the beach before the police truck arrived. Raleen was baking.

"Where's boy?"

"Surfing."

"We've got to get him out. Police. They'll have him in an army detention camp within a week if we don't move fast. Pack food, clothing and a sleeping bag. Bring it to Third Beach. We'll meet you in the milkwood trees. They won't be able to follow over the cliff path in a truck."

The police arrived at the bakery hut an hour after Raleen and Lorna had left with the boy's rucksack packed with essentials. The local police were happy to find the man gone, and Black Martin told them he had left a month ago.

When all but the minstrel boy returned to Second Beach that afternoon, Matt sent word that he wished to see the paramount chief, and returned to his painting as if nothing had changed.

"We must get him out of Southern Africa," he said to Raleen, who was in tears. "I'm sorry ... a tourist must have seen him."

"How are you going to get him out? The airports will be watched." Her life was repeating itself and there was nothing she could do.

"Luke. He owes me one. The ANC have got to get your boyfriend out of the country. We'll hide him until we can send him to a safe house."

"He's white, Matt. How do you hide a white man in a black man's house in South Africa? They'll kill him. Say he had an accident. Why won't they let people be happy? Anyone that's happy they want to hurt. They always get you. They hate the white liberals more than the blacks. They'll kill him. Then what do I do? I can't go through that again ... not again." She was crying, sobbing, her world having crashed around her again.

THERE WAS an old hut high above on the cliff, over the cave the minstrel boy found, in the base of the rock face where the igneous rock had left a soft cove the sea had gouged out over the millennia. It was dry and smelt of old fungus, but the worst storm would not reach that far back.

He groped his way in the dark, carrying his rucksack and guitar until he could go no further, and sat on a flat ledge of rock to rummage through his few possessions for a box of matches. He had felt dry wood with his bare feet and yesteryear's seaweed was drier than paper. Ten minutes later, he had a small fire burning, which he plied with old wood from a ship lost during the last voyage of Bartholomew Dias in the fifteenth century.

The flames caught quickly and revealed an Aladdin's cave. The flat rock he sat on was a box and around the fire were case after neatly stacked case, the markings in a language and characters that were unintelligible to the minstrel boy. He tried again to open one of the wooden crates, but there was nothing his hands could move.

With the fire burning brightly, he took his guitar from its soft leather case and sang a shanty of the sea, an old song for which the dead sailors would have yearned when washed up on that lonely shore. He had endured worse accommodation in the years he had been on the run. If Matthew Gray had walked up the coast, he would walk down, and the gods would take care of the minstrel boy. He had known the day he deserted the army that he had no future in South Africa.

He picked up the guitar to sing again, a song for the love of the girl he had left behind. The song was a song of parting, the inevitable, and where love ran out at the sweet moment of its beauty. It was a song of joy, as the lovers had not died; the love kept living all the years of their mortal lives, even beyond to the world where all the lovers go, where love is always true.

The morning sun was glorious from the sea, the gulls high in the sky, the salt sea air a change from the fetid cave. And with one last look back along the shore, the minstrel boy, singing as he went, was gone on his way. When the tide came in, the sea washed the sand and even the trace of his feet was gone.

LUKE MBEKI WOKE on the morning of his fifty-first birthday, and was unable to recollect where he was. It was dark and bitterly cold. He had slept with the window open, and snow had collected on the window sill and left a wet mush at the end of his bed. Between closing the window and returning to bed, he worked out that he was in America, and lay back in the dark, deep inside the blankets, to try and trace where his third visit to the United States had deposited him the previous night.

Under the blankets, he looked at his watch and caught the time at just after five in the morning. Even that was no certainty, as in his travels through the States he was constantly readjusting his watch. Then he saw the date, and pushed his head up from the blankets and spoke the first Xhosa that room ever heard. "It's my birthday," he said. Then he sat up, thinking hard. "I'm Luke Mbeki, I'm fifty-one today, but I have no definite idea of where I am." He was not even sure whether to get up and try to find out, as the street outside had been empty and the real time could be the middle of the night.

Luke tried to go back to sleep, but his mind was working, and images flashed through his thoughts, ending in a sharp, vivid picture of Chelsea. From Chelsea his mind moved to his job and why he was not with his woman and his sons. With the progress came the dreary swing through America, telling his hosts of the atrocities, to which they listened in silence and then talked joyfully all about America. The night before had been quite typical … and then ping! He knew where he was! This was some kind of relief, but he would have preferred to be anywhere else with Chelsea. Congressman Rian O'Rorke of Boston, the spawning ground of the Kennedys and the Fitzgeralds, the birthplace of manipulative politics, of which he and the ANC were now a part. He was in Boston, Massachusetts.

The congressman had not been the slightest bit interested in South Africa, but only in how he could help the ANC and please his black constituents. The struggle in South Africa was a tool that the congressman wished to use to maintain his black support. To be vociferously anti-apartheid was a win-win situation for the congressman, unlike gay rights or gay-bashing, which both had supporters who voted for congressmen. The outward face for the cameras said the congressman was deeply concerned about the rights of black South Africans, but Luke was sure the man's concern was with the votes of black Americans. A few dollars for the 'Release Mandela Fund' were cheap at the price

And as Luke walked out of the door, the congressman would ingratiate himself with somebody else. The morning, anti-apartheid; the afternoon, protect the spotted owl; and in the evening, duck out of the lesbian dinner, with last minute words of pain at just not being able to get across Boston in time. The congressman, to Luke's way of thinking, juggled a hundred ping pong balls in the air all at the same time. The man's job belonged to the people and he was trying to be all things to all men for as long as the ping pong balls stayed in the air. Behind the big expansive smile lurked, for Luke, "what can I get out of this one?" Sincerity and honesty were dead, gone with the popular vote.

Luke believed a one-party state was the only way for those who wished to govern effectively. Not every action of a government could possibly be popular. The nation had to be run by the elders, by the wise, by the men of experience, not by the whims and greed of the people. The tribal laws, adapted to a one-party democracy, where everyone voted, but for the same party, in the way they had always followed the hereditary paramount chief. That was the way to struggle for consensus, for harmony, with the party listening to the voice of the people.

Having the people tell the government what to do on a daily basis through the opinion polls was something Luke found difficult to comprehend. Yes he was all for a multi-party, one-man-one-vote, but only to rescue his people from under the foot of the Afrikaner. The constant interchange of favours necessary to have anything done in the legislature was something beyond his understanding. To Luke, the American system was political anarchy, which was why the discipline and control of communism, was better suited to the African tradition.

He lay back in the bed his feet still ice cold and tried to smile. Who was he to complain about their system if, by giving him desperately needed dollars, it helped a man keep his seat in congress? His last thought before he drifted back to sleep was that his feet were too far away from his head. If he was a lot shorter they would not be nearly so cold.

. . .

Every year on his birthday, Matt tried to do something that he had never done before. On his fiftieth, he had made and flown a kite, which pleased Peace, who screamed with excitement when the contraption rose into the air and flew for all of three seconds before crashing to smithereens on the beach, narrowly missing the dog. The crazy dog had barked right underneath it until the thing had come down at its head. This year, Matt's fifty-first, he was going to get up on a surfboard and let a wave bring him swiftly in to the shore.

As luck would have it, the waves were perfect by eleven o'clock in the morning, and the beach was infested by the colony, the village folk and a few tourists who had wanted to know what was going on. To maintain the proprieties of life, Matt wore a pair of trousers firmly tied to his waist with a piece of string, not wishing to arrive on the beach standing loftily on a wave with his loin-cloth way back in the sea. For days he had cajoled Carel van Tonder to give him the theory of surfing, and Matt now knew the right wave, the right way to point the board and the right way to rise from his knees and stand his almost two-metre frame so that he and the board would ride the wave to shore in perfect unison.

"If you get dumped, you can break your neck," argued Carel, right up to the time when Matt was striding down the beach, the puny surfboard, borrowed from Carel, tucked under his arm.

"I will not break my neck."

"You have not surfed before."

"That is the whole point. Today is my birthday."

"People start surfing when they are kids."

"There was a granny who high-dived at seventy-three," pointed out Matt.

"You're too tall for surfing. You probably need a very long special board."

"This one will do. I only have to do it once."

"Daddy, are you going to shoot the tube?" broke in Peace.

"Probably not, darling."

"Oh dear. I told all my friends you would."

Matt walked into the surf and, when the sea came up to his waist, he floated the board, mounted from the left-hand side and fell off the right. He then looked back to ensure that no one had laughed. Pushing the board down between his long legs, he let it come up under his seat, adjusting the board until they were both floating nicely, and then began to paddle out to sea as he had seen Carel and the minstrel boy do on most days of the year.

Faced with a big, curling wave, Matt paddled for it furiously. He found the front of his small craft lifting alarmingly in the air and himself sliding back into the sea, where he was tumbled over and over by the force of the wave, popping up at the end of the rope which was attached to his ankle at one end and the surfboard at the other.

The initial laughter from the beach turned to silence as the seconds passed without a sign of the surfer. Matt had successfully held his breath for ninety seconds, the years of diving for crayfish preventing him from taking down a lungful of warm, salty sea-water.

"Well, that didn't work," he said aloud. The surf was three hundred metres from the swells where he needed to be. Shaking the sea from his long hair and his beard, he began to swim, towing the board behind and diving through the breaking waves, until he reached the calmer sea where, after a lot of trouble, he finally climbed astride the board and waved to his friends on the shore, before turning to study the swells for the perfect wave that would rush him in to the white, far-distant sands.

The ninth wave was perfect, and he pointed his board with the flow, paddling furiously without falling off, until he found the sea was taking him fast with the crest of the wave. With concentrated power, Matt lifted himself onto his knees, then, with a last desperate heave, up on one foot, where he hung for the longest half-second of his life, until he toppled into the mouth of the onrushing wave. It pushed him down and down and down, until he hit a rock which knocked him senseless.

On shore, Lorna waited in anguish, while Carel with powerful help pushed the ski-board into the sea. When they reached the surfboard, Matt had risen from the bottom of the sea, and was floating face down in the water. It took four men to heave him up into the boat and then they took it in turns to pumps his chest and breathe air into his mouth. With the boat turned around and racing up and down the breakers to find the gaps, like a greyhound searching out a maze, they finally pulled him ashore, head down, and planted him on the sand, where they pumped again and again.

"Daddy's playing tricks," said Peace, quite sure nothing was wrong.

Slowly his breathing started again, water stopped flowing up from his lungs, and he choked. When they hauled him to his feet, he felt as weak as a kitten and his face was the colour of putty.

"Should have tried that one a good few birthdays ago," he gasped, weakly.

"You got up on the board, Daddy."

"Not for very long."

"The kite didn't fly long last year." She was very excited and thought it all part of the fun, despite the blood trickling down her father's face from the gash that had opened when his head hit the rock. "What are you going to do next year?"

He hated the idea but, for the first time, he knew he was growing old. Taking his wife's hand and with his arm over his daughter's shoulders, he walked up the beach, followed by the colony.

"I owe you one, Carel," he said.

"We all owe you, man, a lot more than you owe us," replied Carel van Tonder.

"It's good to have friends," said Matt.

# PART 5

# 1

Raleen Urbach had taken to smoking dagga with a determination to self-destruct that bordered on madness. She had had enough of the real world and, if the weed did keep her 'goofed' all day, then it was the solution to her life. The struggle had killed her husband with a land mine, her children with an RPG7 rocket and taken away the love that had started to heal her wounds. She was not strong enough to fight any longer, and was content to sit under the wild fig tree and listen to Jonathan rambling on about Ding-dong Bell and the great business they were building for their future.

After the fifth joint of the day, when the sun was only a metre above the wild banana trees that fringed the coastline, she would tell him about her children and how well they were doing in school. She talked to her husband, blasted to pieces on the Karoi road eight years earlier, as if he was sitting with them on the ground. They had both gone out of their minds to a friendlier world, unable to give them any more pain. Neither of them ate very much and most nights slept under the trees on sheets of old cardboard, curled up in individual balls under blankets, oblivious of each other as they were of anyone else. They had left the world to soar in the clouds of the drug-induced euphoria, and all the coaxing in the colony would not take them from the path of their own oblivion.

Lorna cried for her friend and watched to see that she came to no physical harm. The talks they had enjoyed had blown away in the wind. They were strangers now. And as the weeks went by without the minstrel boy, the two addicts were left alone, watched carefully but left alone to live in the new world they had chosen. Jonathan was not even aware of the passing of his thirtieth birthday. His habit was fed by the small allowance that reached the post office in Port St Johns every month from the trust setup by his mother. He would have been better in the lead vehicle with his friend, destroyed by a single explosion.

Every time the outside world reached into the colony, it destroyed their happiness, an insidious beast hovering behind the great white clouds to poison them. The world outside was bigger than all their tiny lives, wanting even the little they had, searching for their souls, the virus of man more deadly than a bomb. The two creatures under the tree outside the campsite entrance had only delayed the time of their burial. They were the living dead.

Sophia's school stabilised at sixty pupils, the word having reached Soweto that the small sanctuary on the Wild Coast was full. Charles helped with the teaching and found deep satisfaction in the yearning for knowledge he saw in the mostly forgotten children from the slums outside Johannesburg. The dawning excitement of understanding on a small black face when the meaning of the printed word became intelligible was all the reward he would ever ask. Passing on his knowledge was an experience of joy that he grew to cherish, and he used this as his excuse to stay washed up on the shores of nowhere, at the base of Africa, looking out on untold kilometres of open sea and the wilderness, on a shore containing not one monument to man's so glorious past.

He had waxed philosophical at Sophia's lack of interest in his person. It was given to some the magnetism to draw to them the opposite sex. It was the way of things, and nothing he could do would change her mind or cause her to look at him as a man, other than a person to talk to about the school and what they could do for the children. It was his destiny to wait and watch, to hope, to dream of a future day when all the understanding in his heart would be seen by her. Then he would live. There was happiness if he waited.

Whenever the light was good enough, Matthew painted, and the world around him was re-recreated on the big canvases he slashed at with the brushes day after day. All the joy and harmony of the colony spoke from the paintings, surrounded by the beauty of their island in the sun. Lorna watched him with growing pride, and kept the physical world around him a perfect setting for his work. She herself painted for the tourists, but most of her waking life was spent keeping the home and creating the ongoing happiness for her children. There was much laughter in the rondavel, and the wonderful pleasure of each other's company.

When Matt had finished his work for the day, Sipho was hoisted onto his right shoulder and Robert on his left. With Peace skipping behind and running in front and Lorna at his side, Matt and his family walked down the beach for their evening stroll, the curling pipe in Matt's mouth out of fire but unable to be lit, and the colony smiling at the happiness of their ritual walk to see how the day had been spent.

ISIDORE SOCRATES SALVADORI, the man from London, had been born plain Jack Kemp in lower Ashtead, a favourite commuter spot as it is near the railway station. His father had been a bank clerk, catching the seven-ten to Waterloo for forty-eight years. He retired on a Barclays DCO pension and lived another three weeks. Young Jack had watched his father's daily journey to and from the city, and determined there must be a better way of life.

The break in his life came during the war, after he was called up in the army to fight for King and Country against the Hun. His father had spent three years in the trenches, the likes of the Kemps being fodder for the cannons of the politicians. Old man Kemp's death, so soon after his sixty-fifth birthday, had been brought on by forty-seven years of coughing, the result of mustard gas in his lungs. The Huns had got him in the end.

Jack had been the skipper's mascot. So long as the young voice of Sergeant Jack Kemp came back through the intercom, the skipper knew they would be one of those to return to RAF Boscombe Down. It was a regular occurrence for the four engine bombers to return from Germany with a dead gunner in the turret, gunners being the prime target for the German night fighters.

It was the skipper who introduced Jack to the world of art, and indirectly caused him to change his name by deed poll. Whoever could imagine a man with a great knowledge of the arts having the plebeian name of Jack Kemp! Darling, be serious! The public needs to know! At the age of twenty-four, Sergeant Jack Kemp died, giving way to the metamorphosis of Isidore Socrates Salvadori, a man steeped in literature and the arts. By the time Matthew Gray came along to sell the masters he had salvaged from the jungles of Zaire, Jack Kemp, the tail gunner, had long been forgotten.

Duncan Grenville Fox had taught Isidore everything he knew about the appreciation of art, and had watched his pupil grow and pass him with the inborn pleasure of a creator. There was something deep in the genes from lower Ashtead that recognised good art, and knew how to present it to the public in a way that made the buyer feel good and satisfied with the great work of art about which he knew nothing at all.

"Do you know, old boy, I paid ten thousand pounds for that! Marvellous, isn't it? Isidore says it'll be worth a fortune in twenty years' time. Jolly good investment." Looking at the two old men inspecting each of the Strovers in proper detail, no one in the gallery could ever have imagined where the two had met.

They had been going round together for an hour. "Do I have a blind spot or is this really good, Skipper?" asked Isidore, a deliberate rhetorical question.

"It'll last a lot longer than Campbell's soup cans painted one on top of the other. Or junk stuck together from a council grant. Who is he?"

"A recluse. The bloke Strover's a front. Between you and me. You need the artist to sell a living painter."

"The one in the caftan looks the part."

"Would have made money on the stage," speculated Isidore.

"Where's the background?"

"There's another rub. I dare not say."

"And Strover? Where is he from?"

"Holland, Amsterdam. The home of the great painters."

"I have not seen so much joy and happiness in an exhibition in London. Not from a living artist. Time will tell, my friend. So you think the days of the art world pulling the legs of the rich are over?"

"I do. It's why the real painters – Van Gogh, Cezanne, Monet – are selling to the Japanese for numbers neither of us would ever have imagined."

"Is he well-known in his own country?" asked Duncan.

"Very. But not as a painter."

"I will come back here over the next week. Then I will say, maybe; don't let them out until then. Have you sold many?"

"All but four, and those I am keeping for myself."

"You want to tell me the story?" Duncan prompted him. "That Polish restaurant in Hay Street? We have a lot more secrets from the public than a painter without a name ... Do you know, I still dream about those burning cities we destroyed."

"So do I Skipper. But art like this does something to balance the horror."

There were twelve tables in the restaurant, each of them in its own private alcove. The owner knew Duncan Fox and had responded positively to the phone call for a table. The Bernard Strover exhibition was in a hired gallery, as the canvases had been too large to exhibit in the small Bond Street gallery that had been home to Isidore for twenty-seven years. The vodka came from a freezer chest and was poured at their table into small, thin glasses. They drank slowly, savouring each drop of the delicious liquid, while Isidore told Duncan the story of Matthew Gray and how he was living on the Wild Coast of South Africa.

The food was brought in seven courses, each a small portion, and the old friends enjoyed the victuals, the perfect service and the ambience of a truly civilised restaurant. The tablecloth was white and reached down to the floor, the tableware was solid silver from Mappin and Webb, the flowers from Covent Garden, the soft music Chopin, and the paintings on the walls had been carefully selected by Duncan for the owner over three decades. The light was soft, but sufficient to let them see what they were eating and to appreciate the ruby colour of the Polish red wine.

"They even have a restaurant at Second Beach that produces excellent seafood. And the wine is good," said Isidore. "If I told the world those paintings came from a homeland within the borders of South Africa, I would have the demonstrators from Trafalgar Square tearing down the canvases."

"He sounds the richest of men … What a wonderful quality of life. And it's the politics that preserve the isolation. If it were politically acceptable, life in such a paradise at so low a cost would bring the hordes trying to be artists. And he can paint without interference. Wonderful way of life. They all go that way, of course. Through jealousy or imitation. Would probably paint nothing worthwhile in a normal setting. Gauguin. Same style of living. Life in a hut with the natives. Extraordinary to have so much money and give it up. And then find a talent to paint. You wonder what else he could do … Churchill could paint and lay bricks. Nobel prize for literature. So many gifts in one man … Is this Gray conceited?"

"He certainly doesn't think he can paint," Isidore informed him. "His wife knows. And Charles Farquhar. We all hope nothing ever happens to stop him from working. Money comes and goes between men in history. Art lives forever. Good art. I think he will last."

"You mind if I smoke a cigar?"

"I'll have one with you, Duncan … We've had such a good life."

"It has been blessed. Except that bit at the beginning. I much prefer to create than knock things down. They want to put up a statue to Bomber

Harris. I really don't know … We had to do it, of course, or Gerry would have done it to us. For me, I prefer to forget. How are the wife and children?"

"Not exactly children any more. Beth's as well as can be expected … six grandchildren."

"I still miss Marjorie," mused Duncan. "The children and grandchildren are scattered all over the world. We British are breaking up. As always, the best leave this little island … You really wonder what it was all about."

NOT FAR AWAY, in a flat in Soho to which he had been called by his controller, Hector Fortescue-Smythe was listening to a litany of woes that was turning his life upside-down. The flat was above a Greek restaurant and the smell of rich food permeated the room, despite the windows being closed against the winter.

"Afghanistan is a disaster," repeated the Russian. "No one has ever won a war against fanatical guerrillas. The helicopter gunships don't help. We are drowning ourselves like the Americans in Vietnam. Reagan is forcing us to spend vast amounts of money on an arms race, money we don't have. Unlike the Americans, we can't borrow it from the Japanese. All our foreign adventures are costing us money, and none of them is giving us anything material in return. Some of these people in Africa change sides, milking first us and then the Americans. Reagan talks of six hundred ships in his fleet and, if we are to compete with his Star Wars project, we go broke, and, if we don't, the Americans control the skies. Control the world.

"We are telling our Cuban friends that, if they are unable to finish the Angolan war this year or next, we will be unable to support them anymore. And we say the same to you and your friends in South Africa. You must topple the white pariah government and let Mandela out of jail, or you will have no support, no military strength, and you will be forced to deal with the Afrikaners. The South Africans must be forced into a conventional war to support Savimbi in southern Angola, in their effort to stop SWAPO taking over Namibia. They must be defeated on the battlefield. The talk in Moscow is of perestroika, restructuring. Gorbachev is trying to make an arms deal with the Americans."

"You can't be telling me communism is not going to win? That we are not going to achieve our world government?"

"The one thing about being on the inside, Hector, is being able to take precautions to protect yourself. Go back to Smythe-Wilberforce and run the business. You never know, I may need a job." The man's laugh was hollow and made the smell of stale food even worse. "The Soviet Union is broke, Hector. We make old machinery bring up oil, but even the flow of oil is decreasing and we don't have the money to install modern machinery. The money goes to the arms race. Our industry is old, run into the ground to compete with the Americans. Even our scientists are lagging behind in the space race. Win fast in Africa, or make a deal, if you can't topple the government by force."

"I'm glad my mother did not live to hear what you are saying. Surely, you are wrong," almost pleaded Hector.

"Believe me."

"Was it all for nothing? That I can't believe."

"This was just a talk between old friends. Life is always full of surprises. I wish you luck, Hector. Tell Luke to look to the West for money. What is in the pipeline will come to him, but very little else. There will be one last battle in Angola. Make sure you win. The MIG 23s can out fly the South African Mirages. The Cuban pilots are good. If you can flush the South Africans out of Namibia, you may flush them out of Pretoria."

LUKE MBEKI HAD BEEN MOVED from fund-raising to co-ordinating the world press and television to focus on the greatest black leader in the world after Martin Luther King, Nelson Mandela. In jail for twenty-three years following the Rivonia treason that broke the leaders of the ANC, the groundswell for his release was rumbling across the world, and it was Luke's job to orchestrate the 'Release Mandela Campaign'. To give him a better profile for the mass media, the liberation movement had provided him with sufficient income to lease a one-bedroomed flat in London.

In yet another effort to bring Chelsea back into his life he had travelled to Lisbon and explained his new job and his belief that victory and a return home for all the exiles was a realistic possibility. He had taken the opportunity of Christmas to make his point hoping the season of goodwill would work in his favour. His son John had turned ten in September.

"I'm quite happy with my life," she had told him not even willing to let him stay with her and his son in her small villa. "I am forty, I have a career in insurance, a pension when I need it, and John goes to a school where he will grow up as a middle-class Portuguese with all the benefits of an ancient civilisation. Running around putting bombs in supermarkets has nothing to do with John de la Cruz. If you wish to see the boy, you are welcome. I hope you speak Portuguese. What the great liberation movement has done in Mozambique leaves me cold to your cause. You all talk of making a better life in Africa, and reduce each country to poverty and civil war. You are even strangling the great South African economy in the name of the struggle. I suggest you stay in a hotel, Luke Mbeki. Despite what I once felt, you are not welcome in this home. There is blood on your hands, and there will be a lot more before you have finished destroying Africa."

"Apartheid is totally unacceptable to any civilised man," Luke stated with a degree of indignation.

"So is your alternative. Look at Mozambique, with a million dead and everyone starving not even ten years after the great liberation. Ask my mother and father. You are a good man Luke, but there are others who are using you. The communist may need you now, but wait until later ... And what happened to that other little fellow you brought into the world."

"Matt's looking after him in Port St Johns."

"Now I've heard everything ... we're Portuguese, Luke. First World. And we wish to stay that way for generations. Please leave us alone." Her eyes had been cold. It was over. The loneliness had swept over him and left a void in the pit of his stomach. But she was wrong. The struggle was worth the pain. They would get Mandela out of jail, and then he would show this woman what a real liberation struggle had all been about.

Instead of turning him away from the cause she sent him back with renewed energy and determination to win. They were going to make the difference for the blacks in South Africa, whatever the mistakes to the north. There was just no alternative.

THE HEIR to David Todd's empire, his great-granddaughter, had been born in March, and it had not taken Theo Blaze two weeks to move into the mansion her daughter had persuaded Teddie Botha to buy soon after they were married. The penthouse rattled skeletons in her cupboard and made her nervous.

The house was in Sandhurst, a Johannesburg suburb where it was said no one lived who was not a millionaire, other than the servants. Theo, judging this to be her only chance of finally living in luxury, had chosen the house, as there was a sweet granny flat with its own swimming pool that suited her image of the glamorous grandmother. The technique used by her daughter to move into the old penthouse was used again, Granny claiming the right to baby-sit so the proud parents could dine in the best restaurant in Rivonia, The Fiddler.

When Teddie went to work the next day to battle with the mounting volume of administration that daily seemed poised to overwhelm him, his mother-in-law was having breakfast, and when he came home at eight o'clock she was sitting at the dinner table ordering the servants around as if she were paying their wages. Teddie was just too tired to argue; he ate his supper and went to bed.

There were far bigger problems than Theo Blaze on his mind, the biggest problem being his inability to decide which was the biggest problem under the pile of paper that he was never able to diminish. The problems of the administration of Security Lion and its subsidiaries landed on Teddie's desk and if any of them arrived on Archie Fletcher-Wood's, he soon moved them across to the CEO. Archie had never liked taking important decisions, though he carried out his CEO directives with enthusiasm.

All through their lives Archie and Lucky Kuchinski had passed the buck. They were superb number twos, but had never wished to be the boss. They preferred to enjoy their days in business, not worry about them, and most of all not wake in the middle of the night and think about what they had not been able to do during the day. Teddie had employed a flock of accountants and financial advisers, but all of them deferred to the executive chairman and in many ways made more work for Teddie than they solved. They fitted their job descriptions and collected their salaries, but they were employees, people who did what they were told but rarely thought for themselves. For them, the right decision was always the safe decision, which normally meant doing nothing without a written instruction.

Business was definitely not fun for Teddie Botha and when a good Samaritan let drop that he knew of a man who had slept with Tilda Botha nine weeks before the wedding, the situation in the office almost collapsed. Teddie stopped functioning. The one thing he wished to do most of all was to go away and never think of another insurance company in his life. Teddie sulked for a week, and then told his wife he wanted a blood test.

"Why, darling?" she asked sweetly, feeling anything but confident inside.

"Why not? How do I know there was only me? Why not? We were sharing a flat. Not married. You caught me, Tilda, and I have enough problems at work not to worry about this. I want to know and I want to know quickly. I can't even think straight."

As luck would have it, the baby began to cry, and Tilda left the room to find out what was going on. Only then did she tell her mother.

"Life is full of gambles. Have the test. You've a fifty-fifty chance."

"One in five, Mother. Like mother like daughter they say."

"Don't infer things you know nothing about," retorted Theo, tartly.

"What do I do?"

Her mother gave the predicament a search for alternatives and shook her head. "Have the test. What else?" She was a gambler by nature.

When Tilda told Teddie she would take the baby to the doctor, he said he wanted the man named by his friend to go as well. "And we can all have a test for Aids. It's my own fault for marrying someone I knew nothing about. Trouble is, I always take people at face value."

Two days later, Teddie's doctor phoned him at the office. "The good news is none of you are HIV-positive."

"Who's the father?" Teddie had a sinking feeling in his stomach.

"Neither of you. The man was rather relieved when I told him. There is no chance whatsoever of either of you being the biological father of the child."

"Poor kid … Poor, bloody kid."

"By the way Teddie, do you know your wife is pregnant?"

COLONEL ANTONIO VAN PERREIRA DOS SANTOS CASSERO was still the youngest colonel in the Cuban air force, but it did not stop the tsetse flies attacking him at first light every morning. He was stationed at Cuito Cuanavale. The newly built air base in the southern part of Angola, a base which gave the Cuban air force and its MPLA allies command of all the air space in Angola.

The offensive against the rebel Unita movement had swept out of the Angolan capital of Luanda and crushed everything in its path, the control of the joint forces falling to a senior Russian general and his staff. The rains had been over for two months and the tracks through the bush were able to take the Russian T55 and T54 tanks which massacred Jonas Savimbi's troops, who had not been supplied with armour by his mentors, the American CIA and the South African defence force. Heavy machine guns but not TOW anti-tank missiles, which made it clear to Antonio, who flew five strafing missions every day to add to the misery of the Unita troops, that the communists would soon be on the border with Namibia, which the South Africans still called South West Africa and administered under a post-First-World-War mandate from the League of Nations, which the United Nations had revoked without the South Africans taking the slightest bit of notice.

Another week would see the combined Cuban and Angolan MPLA army sweep Jonas Savimbi out of his bush stronghold at Jamba and Antonio's MIG 23s posing a lethal threat to South African air space in both South West Africa and South Africa itself, when the Cuban air force moved in behind the advancing SWAPO and ANC troops to conquer what they would then call Namibia. The very sovereignty of South Africa, with its inferior aircraft, would be at stake, bringing a swift collapse of apartheid rule and a communist takeover of the whole of South Africa, with its strategic minerals, the lack of some of which would threaten the Star Wars programme of Ronald Reagan.

The excitement of the advance with its stupendous possibilities, kept the adrenaline flowing through Antonio's veins. Soon he would be master of a vast coffee estate and, if he was not too far mistaken, Russia and her allies would rule the world. The victory in Southern Africa would counter all the problems in Afghanistan. The descendant of the third son of the fourth wife of the king of Monomatapa (or so he thought of himself) was coming home for good.

Minister Kloss, acutely aware of the problems that a Cuban victory in Angola would pose for South Africa, had secretly called up the South African reserve, intending to go to the aid of Jonas Savimbi with tanks and the South African air force. Unknown to the Cubans, they had been equipped with new weaponry developed by Armscor, the erstwhile employer of Hector Fortescue-Smythe, who, had he still been under cover, would have warned his masters in Moscow. He would also have told them that the T55s and T54s were no match for the South African main battle tanks, the Olifants that had been developed by Armscor from the base of the British Centurion tank. He would also have mentioned that G5 howitzer, the best in the world. But Hector had blown his cover.

In the previous dry season, in 1987, when Teddie was trying to keep his mind from blowing to pieces, the UNITA troops had stopped the MPLA forces without the help of South African troops, but the consequences of the new situation were too terrible to contemplate. Pretoria and its generals were fully aware that a Cuban advance into South West Africa would put their own country at risk. With the tacit nod from the Americans, the South Africans were moving out of the Caprivi Strip and over the Angolan border to the help of their surrogate friend, mortally threatened by the advancing columns of Russian tanks.

Colonel Edward Botha was a part-time soldier who believed in leading his troops from the front. When the South Africans reached the Lomba River at the beginning of October, he was in the forefront of his tanks which totally destroyed the MPLA's 47th Brigade. The Cuban/Angola advance was stopped dead in its tracks. For three days, Teddie revelled in the battle not once thinking of Tilda's second child or the mess he had left behind at the office.

The rebels advanced behind the tanks and the Mirages gave the ground troops air cover. The controlled discipline of the South African defence force was awesome and, when the G5s came within range of Cuito Cuanavale, Antonio saw his dreams crashing with the finely-tuned direction of the shells. Even when he was up in the air for his last mission out of Cuito, he could not detect the G5s camouflaged in the mopani bush and he could not see the South African commandos with their binoculars calmly trained on his air base, directing the guns in their hideouts scattered through the bush.

What he did see was a column of South African tanks, and he banked his MIG 23 to attack, hurtling down and releasing a deadly air-to-ground missile at the lead tank, which disintegrated in a gratifying ball of fire and smoke. With just enough fuel, Antonio left the battle zone, returning control of the air to the Mirages based in Caprivi. Without his forward air base, his MIG 23s could no longer influence the ground battle.

Even though the South Africans won the battle and saved southern Angola for Jonas Savimbi, they had received a fright from which their old illusion of invincibility was never to recover. Minister Kloss had come face to face with the possibility of a Russian aircraft over Pretoria, and it made him acutely nervous. Backing down from strident arrogance, South Africa let it be known to the rest of the world that they would sacrifice South West Africa for a Cuban withdrawal from South Africa.

The generals, pointing out the consequences of a second confrontation with even more sophisticated Russian weaponry operated by Cubans, had lost their nerve and led the South Africans into four-cornered negotiations with Russia, America and Angola. At the very edge of the precipice, they had seen the light and the Russians, at the end of their financial resources, were willing to withdraw their surrogate Cuban military and claim a victory which they would lead to independence for a communist-inclined Namibia.

It was to be the last African battle of the Cold War, and Teddie Botha was one of the last tank commanders to die as a direct result of the superpower confrontation. He had been yelling his head off with excitement when the rocket hit the turret, his head and shoulders, out of the tank, directing his armoured column in hot pursuit.

WITHIN A WEEK, the predators among the insurance companies had sensed there was something wrong. With the chairman dead and the world stock markets taking a sharp dive, the shares of Security Lion dropped thirty per cent in Johannesburg and London, and Archie Fletcher-Wood lost control of the situation. The pile of unfinished business on Teddie's desk would have daunted the best administrator and, to add to the problem, Lucky Kuchinski was no help at all.

The company was suddenly coming apart, and the registrar of insurance turned his attention to the solvency rate of the third largest insurer in the country. With all shares on the Johannesburg stock exchange diving twenty-one per cent in one day, the actuarial conversion of assets against future liabilities of policyholders was badly affected, causing the red light to flash at Security Lion. Teddie Botha could not have chosen a worse time to get himself killed.

A rumour started in the market that the investment manager in charge of the huge funds flowing into the company had been buying and selling shares in the name of seven companies, of which he was the sole shareholder. Before the fraud squad could catch up with him, he drove to the airport and caught the plane to London, leaving his car in the parking lot. Bernard Strover had left the country in his artist's gear and, when he reached London, he collected every pound owed to him by Isidore Salvadori and kept running. A large amount of the money he had made was safely invested in Asuncion in Paraguay, where there was no extradition agreement with South Africa. He was even smiling when he arrived in the middle of South America, as he considered the way he had made his own money a legitimate part of his position at Security Lion Holdings.

First he had bought a small parcel of shares for one of his dummy companies, then he had forced up the price by using Security Lion money to buy a large parcel of the same shares, finally buying the shares from the dummy company with Security money at the newly inflated price. The reality was that Security Lion bought shares for its policyholder fund at a three per cent premium overall as, when the heavy-buy signal stopped, the shares sank back to their true market value.

If Teddie Botha had been on top of the pile of paper in his office, he would have seen the scam. Archie and Lucky, both directors, never looked at the buy-and-sell sheets but, under the Companies Act relating to responsibilities of directors, they could be found negligent in the carrying out of their duties. There was a lot more to being a director of a company than having a name on the letterhead, especially when things started to go wrong.

Three weeks after the destruction of Teddie's Olifant tank, both friends wished they had been in the tank with the chairman. As executive directors, they found themselves held fully responsible for the running of the company during their stewardship. There was a good chance of their not only losing the value of their shareholdings in Security Lion, but also of their going to jail. When the savings of the ordinary man in the street was at stake, there had to be a scapegoat, and Bernard Strover was well beyond the reach of the law.

Even if they had wanted to, it was too late to leave the country. If the mess in Teddie's office had been decipherable and a clear financial position calculable, the run on the Security Lion shares would have stopped but, when an outside firm of auditors was appointed by the registrar of insurance, they announced it would take them weeks, if not months to ascertain the financial strength of the company.

From outside the country, the ANC shouted to the world that here was another example of white misrule and that, when they took over the country, they would sort out the problem by nationalising the insurance companies. This resulted in massive off-shore dumping of South African shares by overseas shareholders, which depressed the market further, making the actuarial calculations of the Security Lion companies' solvency rate even worse.

THEN THE CUBAN air force struck the dam wall at the Cunene River on the border between South West Africa and Angola, killing a platoon of South African soldiers in the process. Antonio had led his squadron on a long raid behind the South African ground forces, totally outflanking them and proving the sophistication of his MIG 23s and the speed that took them so quickly away from the dam wall of the vast water scheme that fed the parched area of Ovamboland.

There was panic in more places than the glass tower of the stock exchange. Minister Kloss, as a result of the shock, found himself quite constipated. Frikkie Swart discreetly checked his overseas bank accounts but decided in the panic-induced confusion that even larger amounts of taxpayers' money could be plundered from the fund for clandestine operations. To make his minister a little happier, he had his men take out four prominent political activists, two of whom were white, one shot to death by a shotgun blast right outside his front door.

Tilda and Theo were left in the massive Sandhurst house with no servants and two dirty swimming pools, all Teddie's assets being frozen. When the family lawyer came up with the will, there was a recent codicil explaining the parentage of his daughter and leaving all his money to the small son who had luckily tested positively with Teddie's blood. Like everything at the office, Teddie had left behind a mess.

Theodora Blaze had never felt more frustrated in her life, shouting at Lucky Kuchinski to do something.

"What the hell can I do?"

"I don't know, but do something. There must be someone who can sort out the mess. The bloody man bought and sold shares; he didn't run off with the company's money. You're all running around like chickens with your heads chopped off … oh, hell, I wish I was a man."

Sunny Tupper saw her man disintegrate and decided her mask of subservience had better slip. She had worked at the company for a number of years and quickly realised that the problem was confidence – a run on the bank, so to speak, and not an inherent defect in the financial position of Security Lion Holdings. The demise of the third-largest life assurer was in the interests of the remaining insurance companies, despite their pained posturing to the press. The big boys were delighted and, business being competitive, no one could have blamed them for their hand-in-front-of-their-mouth jubilation. When the Security Lion shares had dropped forty per cent, she put her few saved rand in the market. The company was far too important to the country to crash, she reasoned, and then she went to work on Archie.

"I want the car and I want to go away for a few days," she told him.

"That really is bloody marvellous at a time like this. Even you think the ship's going to sink." Looking at the woman who had been for so many years part of his life, he wondered if marrying her would have made any difference after all.

"It's quite clear you and Lucky can't stop the rot," said Sunny.

"Where are you going?"

"That's my business."

"It's my car." He said it in the way a petulant child says, "It's my toy and you are not going to have it to play with." She looked at him and shook her head. The king really had lost his clothes.

"Then I'll hire one from Hertz," she said, breaking the silence.

"Take the damn car ... see if I care."

"Have you ever thought of all those policyholders who could go without a pension if all this nonsense is not knocked on the head?" Sunny tackled him, trying to persuade him to see further than the end of his own nose.

"I've got enough problems of my own ... Matt got us into all this mess. If he'd let us invest our own money when we came out of the Congo, we would never have heard of Security Lion."

"I seem to remember it was a precondition before he financed and led you into the jungle."

"I don't remember the details," muttered Archie, sulkily.

"You should, Archie. You were broke, remember. Your friendship with Matt was the one sensible thing you have done in your life."

"If you are going to be abusive, you can leave my house right now."

Sunny, remembering very clearly from whence he had come, slapped his face hard. "Give me your car keys," she demanded.

"How do I get to the office?"

"With the amount of good you've been doing lately, you're better off staying at home."

Archie listened to the clunk of the automatic garage door and heard his car going off down the drive. The thought of being penniless at the age of sixty-one was worse than being sent to jail. He had done nothing wrong. He had never stolen a cent from anyone in his life. It was the prospect of being fat, half-bald and poor that shattered him. His only armour of late had been his money and, once that had gone, even Sunny had walked out of his life.

His mother and father were dead; he had no children, no wife, and lunches would come to an end. People would not want to listen to his jokes when they proved him negligent, as everyone was saying they would, the press mentioning his name at the top of the list of those responsible for the debacle. They would make him put every cent he owned into the liquidation. They would take his house and leave him a few clothes to go and stand in the street. There was no welfare in South Africa and, even when he reached sixty-five, the government pension did not apply to him as he was still British. He had left England because he thought the socialists would bankrupt the country and, after so many years overseas, they would also find a way to put him out in the street.

If he had the guts, he would go into the bedroom and put his gun to his head, but he no longer had the guts. The soft living had left him an old man, a crushing bore. Even he knew that, in his heart of hearts, without the trapping of his wealth, no one would even bother to give him the time of day.

Then he looked up from the floor. "They won't call him Lucky any longer," he said aloud. It almost gave him some kind of satisfaction.

LUCKY KUCHINSKI WAS a fatalist who never worried about anything he could do nothing about. He had just had a visit from his old flame, who had left, banging the front door to his Rosebank flat. Theo even made him smile. There was nothing worse than a woman like Theo parted from her money. The thought of jail, preceded by a long-winded trial, was the possibility that bored him most. He was a salesman and there was always something someone wanted to sell. Many people in business thought selling things was somewhat beneath them.

Lucky rose and went to the window to look out at the Old Mutual building that stood on the site that had once been the George. He could still remember two of the girls he had met at the George, and that had been twenty-five years ago. He smiled at being able to remember both their names. They had had a good time; he remembered that, too. Good, carefree days when people were not talking politics every five minutes in South Africa and ten rand bought dinner for two in the best restaurant in town.

He and the girls had driven down to Cape Town for a week on the beach. They had stayed at the Clifton Hotel which had been turned into sectional title flats a good many years ago … they had been good days and, whatever they took away from him now, they would never take his memories: memories of when he was young, of laughter, a zest for life and all that life could give. He had had a better innings than most, but he was not going to end up in jail. He sold the policies. What they did with the money afterwards was their business. Then he laughed aloud and began to whistle as he picked up the phone.

"That you, Archie? Lucky. Pack a suitcase and a passport, and I'll pick you up, old buddy.

"I'll tell you where we are not going. We are not going to jail, old buddy."

"You sound as cheerful as a cricket."

"I am."

Back in the house, Archie returned the gun to its drawer next to his bed, below the telephone. Then he gave a bellow of joy. He was not on his own after all.

Heading north, the two friends were over the Zimbabwe border before the sun went down, and drinking beer out of the bottle in the Lion and Elephant. The most remarkable surprise came in the person of Aldo Calucci, who greeted them the following day, not in the least surprised himself. Whenever Aldo had had a problem he had taken refuge in the bush to live with the animals. He understood the news of Security Lion, which had even penetrated to his bush camp on the banks of the big river.

While the three friends sat on the stoep drinking cold beer from frosty cans, they could hear the lions roar on the Zambian side of the Zambezi River, not far from where Jonathan Holland had let the young Jamba Sithole escape over the water. And since Robert Mugabe had taken over Rhodesia and called it Zimbabwe, the only gunfire in the valley had been the shooting parties culling the game or the game rangers keeping the poachers away from the dwindling herd of rhinoceros. There was peace in the Zambezi Valley and goodwill to all men, except for all the poachers.

"How long can we stay, Aldo?"

"You can stay long you like." His Italian accent was still as thick as treacle. "It always good to have old friends. Old friends, most important. My wife, she best cook in Africa. Good Italian wife. Two boys. She give me good food and two boys. Hey, why you always come when in shit?" Aldo pronounced the word like something that is put on the blankets of a bed.

For the first time since he heard Teddie had been killed, Archie Fletcher- Wood relaxed. Maybe there was life after death.

THE NEWS WAS SPLASHED across the top of every newspaper 'DIRECTORS ABSCOND'. The shares for Security Lion Holdings, Security Life and Security Lion (UK) were suspended and Ben Munroe arrived in the country from Washington, sensing there was an anti-white story for *Newsweek* that would make the earlier stories pale. The collapse of a major South African institution was better than General Motors being forced by American public opinion to disinvest from white-ruled, apartheid, racist South Africa.

In London, Smythe-Wilberforce were delighted they had been forced to sell their Lion Life and Security Life shares. Hector read about it in the *Economist*, which took delight in pointing out once again that the old empire was falling to bits. The UK company then divorced itself from its parent, its own books being exemplary and up to date, the shares being reinstated on the London exchange. The English directors promptly looked around for a buyer, and the brave who bought the shares before the suspension made a happy, unworked-for capital gain of fifty per cent.

Among them was Hector Fortescue-Smythe who bought in London and Johannesburg. He may have inherited his communist instincts from his mother, but the genes of his grandfather were strong in his DNA. Being a man of clear thinking, he was hedging his bets and testing his nerve. There was only one way to make money under the capitalist system and that was by speculation. The rich in Europe, America and Japan were those who made money on the telephone, hard work having long since given way to the rise or fall of the financial markets, a system that Hector was convinced would one day take them all to financial hell. Alone in his splendid country estate, sometimes playing chess with the parson, he watched the markets: share, currency and commodities. Socially, he was a recluse, and the condition was suiting his temperament.

In an attempt to find the clue to the imminent collapse of communism, he was rereading the Greek and Roman philosophers, though all of them seemed to confirm that man's condition never improved, that reform rarely solved anything in the long term; that the flaw was man himself, not his systems.

Hector celebrated his fiftieth birthday all alone in front of the fire. The party he had was only in his head, with all the people he had known through his life: revisiting his Cambridge tutor, and his mother and father, all dead; his wife dead; his woman dead; his hope for the future of humankind being, according to one who should know, his controller, mortally wounded. It was the beginning of the eccentric, the end of the communist, and he saw it all in the leaping flames of the fire, a half-bottle of very old port mellow in his belly, the rest of the bottle ready beside him, ready to go.

The same day he had heard that they had made Porterstone an archbishop, and he had laughed. Sometime before, the man had returned his communist party card, saying that if anyone suggested he had ever had anything to do with the party, he would say it was a communist plot to undermine the church. Personally, Hector thought it a great pity the bomb had not killed the bishop. Gilly Bowles had been worth ten Andrew Porterstones. He missed her more than he would ever have imagined.

. . .

THE ONE THING Ben Munroe wanted more than anything else was to be deported from racist South Africa. His entry visa said he was a *Newsweek* reporter. The man he brought in with the camera came as a tourist. With the help of the underground ANC, they were going to make a one-hour documentary that would show every white in the country sitting pretty at the expense of the blacks. It would show the white voting population to have abdicated their right to know what the police were doing to the blacks, as none of them wished to know.

If the police raided a man's hut in the middle of the night to demand his pass, the document that told him where he could live in his own country and nowhere else and abused the man because he was black, whether he had or had not the discriminatory piece of paper, the white public did not wish to know. If a man accused of being a terrorist, but with no legal proof, was forced out of a third floor window and landed on his head, the whites did not want to know. If the police took a village of people and dumped them in the bush hundreds of kilometres away, the white public did not want to know. If the white army reserve was called up and sent into battle in a foreign country, the whites did not want to know. The sordid application of apartheid was left to the bullies and thugs, paid for from taxes collected from everyone in the country, black and white.

The whites wanted a whites-only suburb, a swimming pool and the sun. They did not even want to see the blacks, except as servants, servants who would have to behave or they would call the police. For forty years, a progressively more corrupt National Party government had been maintaining their privileges, and it was quite satisfactory to them, the privileged white public. The means justified the end. The few living like kings, the many grovelling in the dirt of poverty, hoping for a few crumbs from the white man's table.

Ben Munroe was going to condense the abuse and the hate into sixty minutes of prime-time viewing, and it would take him from the written reporter to the small screen where he now wanted to be. He was going to expose the worst system of terror government since Hitler let the Gestapo loose on the world. He was going to make everyone who saw his documentary scream for the release of Nelson Mandela. He was going to help make South Africa explode.

SIR DESMOND DONELLY was in his element. They wanted him. The audience at the Royal Albert Hall were on their feet giving him a standing ovation, and he had not yet begun to sing. The 'RELEASE MANDELA' banners were strung across the stage, draping the boxes lining the foyer outside. The people were standing in the aisle, in contravention of the fire regulations, and in the wings stood the greatest names in the world of pop music.

Sir Desmond held up both his long arms, palms to his audience, and the noise subsided. There were tears in his eyes. It had been a long time since they had wanted him and, with the microphone firmly in his right hand, he began to sing the song that had made him famous twenty years before. His old band gave the same backing they had done at the time of his triumphs; he felt the true power of his lungs and sang like he had never sung before. Coming to his finale and throwing his arms to the heavens, he waited for the cascade of applause that would eclipse even the ovation they had given him when he first appeared on the stage. With his arms heavenwards, he waited.

Luke, sitting in the front row as co-sponsor with Sir Desmond Donelly of the release Mandela concert, realised the horror of the moment. Before the terrible silence had lasted longer than a second, he stood up to his full height of one hundred and ninety-eight centimetres, dressed in the hired tuxedo Moss Brothers had found so difficult to fit, turned to the audience behind and clapped like he had never clapped before. He willed them to clap, willed them with all his mind to rise and give the man onstage what he wanted.

The television cameras of the world took this moment in time into a hundred million households across the globe where the great population of the world was helping the ANC to carry on the struggle. The song did not matter. It was the singer they must clap … and then the tide broke, and he turned back to clap towards the man who had helped to raise so much money for the cause. But he had gone, fleeing into the wings, away from what he understood at last. The singing career of Des Donelly was over. It had been for many years. He had just made the perfect fool of himself.

During the standing ovation, while the people were still expecting the singer to come back onstage, Luke Mbeki made his way round the orchestra pit and up to the stage. When he raised his arms for silence, a tall giant of a black man in the heart of British culture, the crowd sank back into their seats.

"My name is Luke Mbeki. On behalf of Nelson Mandela, I want you all to rise once more and thank Sir Desmond Donelly, without whom there would be no concert. I CHALLENGE THE WORLD! RELEASE OUR LEADER! RELEASE MANDELA!"

Outside in the street, the police contingent looked round to see what had happened in the hall. The shout for freedom had been proclaimed around the world. Inside the concert, without Des Donelly, continued to its climax, the great names of modern pop wooing the crowd to hysteria.

For Luke, it was the greatest fund-raising platform he had ever created. For the first time in his life, he really knew they were going to win. They had the sympathy of the world. The roll of thunder had crashed around the globe. No one could stop them now. When the paying public had left, the jam session started. The artists had donated their time, but they were going to have a party and Luke wanted to join in the fun. He went off-stage to change out of his immaculate black dinner-jacket, white starched shirt and black tie.

The party was turning into a riot, and not one person recognised him when he landed perfectly, barefoot, from two metres off-stage, the drums having taken over from the electric guitars at his instigation. The lion skin had a few more moth holes, but the rest of his tribal regalia had survived the years since he was a student playing the jazz clubs to help put himself through university. Two black bands from Soweto followed him onstage and the result was a sensation, which ended with Luke playing the bongo drums in a frenzy of sweat and adrenaline. Somehow, he half expected Matt to leap up on the stage in the hour of his greatest triumph but, instead, the greatest names in music gave him thunderous applause, word having gone round that the savage on the drums was the same man who had saved Des Donelly's bacon.

There were screams of 'AMANDLA!' to end the dance, and Luke fell back exhausted, almost passing out from the exertion, blackness overwhelming him. A member of the band threw a glass of water in his face and revived him just as he felt he would faint.¶

"When you're over fifty you shouldn't do things like that," he muttered in Xhosa to himself.

"Sometimes it is good for the soul," said the black man with the empty glass. "Today is a great day for South Africa." When Luke left the Albert Hall at three in the morning, he was again dressed in his evening clothes under a thick overcoat. Three policemen were still outside and one of them tipped his hand to his hat.

"Quite a party, sir." It was the first time Luke had been called 'sir' by a policeman and, as he turned back to smile at the man, someone caught at his elbow. The woman looked old and drawn from the cold and he heard her say his name, but still there was no recognition.

"I want my son back," the woman asked.

"What are you talking about?"

"I WANT MY SON!" she shouted.

"Bit of trouble, sir?" asked the policeman, moving forward.

"I'm not sure … This woman thinks I have her son."

"You do, Luke. I'm Anita, remember. Our son."

"I have no idea what you are talking about," Luke told her coldly.

"We had a son."

Luke looked down at her from his full height, directly into her eyes.

"Where is he?" she whimpered. "I can't have any more. I tried."

Luke shook his head and turned away, leaving Anita Hylan on the steps of the Albert Hall. He should have done, but he did not feel sorry for the wreck of a woman he had not seen for six years. When he climbed into the taxi that would take him home, his heart was as cold as the English weather.

In his pocket was a photograph of his son trotting behind Matthew Gray and holding hands with Robert Gray. The picture had come in the post a month earlier, and the happiness of Matt and his family had spoken to Luke from all the distance that kept them apart. When he turned to look back at the woman who had given birth to the child, she was sitting on the step, three up from the pavement. Not even the policeman was taking any notice. Her figure grew smaller as the taxi drove further away.

IT HAD TAKEN Ben Munroe six weeks to compile the most damning indictment of the white man's stewardship in South Africa. The misery of the poor, the hopelessness of the ignorant, the generations of poverty to come unless the world of money and power came forward to stop the human degradation was in every shot, every movement of his film and he knew it was the best reporting he had ever done in his life.

He and his cameraman had gone into seven of the black townships across the country without the required permission from the government. Under the laws of apartheid, no white man was allowed into the sprawling poverty of the townships across the country without a permit, which was only given to journalists under strict police supervision, the regime deciding where the reporters would be taken.

Every day of his odyssey, he had expected the police to arrest him and deport him from the country but, as he passed through customs with his cameraman, the excitement of having made the scoop of his life made him want to shout with joy and raise two fingers at the government of the country he was about to leave. There was no longer a direct flight to

America, sanctions having stopped American airlines from flying to South Africa and South African Airways from landing in America. Still treading on eggs, he climbed up the steps to the first-class section of the British Airways Boeing 747 and found his seat.

Ten minutes later the great plane moved out and away from the terminal with Ben Munroe still clutching the video tapes that would make him more famous then he had ever been before.

"Champagne, sir?" asked the hostess, whom he noticed was pretty.

"Scotch for both of us," and he looked up into her eyes, glowing in triumph.

"You had a good trip," she laughed.

"You can bet your life on it."

FRIKKIE SWART HAD WATCHED his man for six weeks and, when the plane came off the end of the runway on flight for Nairobi and London, he spoke into his two-way radio and set the police on a series of swoops that would net them some of the ANC sleepers they had been hunting for years. There was a sneering smile on his face that had been there all the time as he had watched Ben Munroe move through the airport procedures.

At Heathrow airport, London, Ben changed planes and took the first flight to New York without waiting to catch upon any sleep. A taxi at JF Kennedy airport took him straight to the television station where they were waiting for his expose, having sold it to networks across America and around the world. The head of the network shook his head, and the news editor took the videos, pressed one into the player, and they all looked up at the screen.

"This one's blank, Ben. You put in a blank?" He flipped out the cassette, pushed in another and pressed the button.

"This one's also blank, Ben," he exclaimed, puzzled, after half a minute.

"The bastards." Ben was white with anger.

"What about your contacts? They're still in South Africa." The head of the network had understood.

"I've blown every one of their covers and there's not a damn thing I can do ... when it's too good to be true it usually is. They set me up! Those bloody bastards set me up." Ben rang across the room to a telephone and dialled rapidly. He waited. The phone at the other end rang for a long time, but no one answered.

The man he was phoning was already dead, dropped on his head from the fourth floor window at John Vorster Square police station. After twenty-four hours of interrogation, exquisitely enjoyed by three white policemen who had tortured the terrorist for information from the moment they had him in the back of the truck in Soweto, they had allowed the man to run at the open, beckoning window. "Bloody kaffirs can't take it," one of them had said in Afrikaans, as he closed the window.

"Man, you'd better go down and see he's properly dead."

"You think he told us anything Koos."

"How the hell would I know? Check it out, man. Bloody kaffirs are nothing but trouble."

## 2

Two months earlier, Sunny Tupper had arrived in Port St Johns, on the same day that she drove Archie's car out of the garage, taking the terrible dirt road from Umtata down to the coast along the winding path that leads through the Transkei hills.

She had never been more frightened in her life. But there was nowhere to turn round and the nightmare had continued into the night, her car tilting at angles that threatened to drop her down into the gorge, hundreds of metres below, in the dark. The money to repair the road had long been embezzled by the Transkei administration who treated the South African government cheque accounts as their own.

Sunny had booked into the Cape Hermes Hotel, where she spent an exhausted night. The following morning her courage failed, and she wanted to drive back home, but the dirt road was too terrible to contemplate. It was over twenty years since the night of her greatest stupidity. It was still fresh in her mind, frequently played through and twisted, haunting her nights. The man and their subsequent marriage had been more of a fiasco than the night when Matt had come home to the Halfway House smallholding and found her in bed with the driver of the Mercedes 450SLC parked in the driveway.

At lunchtime, she sat beside the pool, looking out over the silted estuary which prevented Port St Johns from operating as a port any longer. She drank a stiff gin to calm her nerves and give her the courage she needed to drive on down to Second Beach, to the colony and Matthew Gray.

If anything was clear in her life, looking back, it was that he had been her only love; the twenty-two years that followed the night of the fiasco had been empty. Nothing of any importance had happened since. She had gone on living her life, but the brilliance had gone. Life after Matt had been dull and leaden. She had never felt vibrantly alive again and the man just down the road from her now was the cause of it.

She looked around the pool bar at the young men, not one of them interested in catching her eye. There was nothing in her to attract men any longer. She wondered if life was only for the young, that modern man with all his medicine made people live too long, until they were of little further use to anyone else, or even to themselves. Sitting alone under an umbrella, close to the bar for replenishment, she drank steadily throughout the afternoon, trying to remember and trying to forget. They brought her sausage rolls and the day wore on relentlessly, with the great Wild Coast sea rolling in to the shore, a kilometre of white-topped breakers.

She had supper alone in the near-empty dining room keeping her maudlin thoughts to herself and wondering why old people on their own seemed so ridiculous, while the young were so full of potential. At eight o'clock, a little drunk but still in full command of her faculties, she went up to her room to be on her own, and slept the night through. Her dreams were beautiful and she was young again, the laughter ringing and everyone calling her name.

Somehow, she could not think why, it made her feel better in the warm light of the new-born day. The morning sun was streaming through her open window, with the smell of the salty sea air and the tumbling roar of the waves. She had a bath and fixed her face as well as she could. She prepared her mind for the job ahead, as job it was, and all the past pain in her mind had nothing to do with the desperate task in hand.

She went down to Archie's car and drove the seven kilometres to the Vuya restaurant, where she parked it and prepared to walk across the beach to Matt's rondavel.

Everyone she spoke to knew Matt and everyone smiled at the mention of his name. Nothing had changed. She always smiled at his name herself. Sitting under the tall trees in front of the Vuya, she looked across the beach that had been his home for sixteen years, trying to summon up her courage for the long walk back into the past of her life.

And then she saw her giant man, striding down the beach, coming straight towards where she sat as if he had expected her to be there. Some ten paces behind came two young boys, one white, one black. A tall colt of a girl was part of the family and she ran back into the warm sea, calling to her father to join her in the water. But the person Sunny watched was not the children, or even Matt himself after the first lurch that turned her stomach upside down, but the woman holding his hand and walking so comfortably at his side, her long, light-brown hair down a well-tanned back and with the figure of a girl. Sunny could feel their love from where she sat on the beach, watching the tableau sweeping into her sanctuary under the trees.

She rose, as the family approached, and nervously emerged into the sunlight.

"Hello, Matt," she volunteered with a tremulous smile.

"Good gracious! It's Sunny! Lorna, this is Sunny Tupper! Sunny, what on earth are you doing in Port St Johns?"

"There's a terrible problem at Security Lion, Matt, and you're the only person who can sort it out. I've come to plead with you."

"Come off it, Sunny, I've forgotten what an insurance policy looks like. How are Archie and Lucky? How's Teddie?"

"Teddie's dead, and Arch and Lucky have every chance of going to jail."

Matt sank down on the bench on the other side of the wooden table, patting the seat next to him for Lorna as Sunny returned to her seat.

"You had better tell me what this is all about." He was as white as a sheet, and the fear that stabbed Lorna was greater than that she had felt when she had seen the surfboard disappearing with him into the giant wave on his birthday.

The children drifted off on their own as Sunny began the story from the time when she had realised Teddie Botha and Archie had lost control of the company, some years before the tank exploded in the Angolan bush.

They sat under the trees for an hour, the life of the colony continuing around them unnoticed. The geese were being fed on the pathway; Jonathan and Raleen wandered past, happy in their cocoon; Carel was taking out the boat with Charles and the hamper; tourists were helping to push the ski-boat into the surf. Children were playing in the warm Indian Ocean, children of all races, laughing, chasing and enjoying each other's company. It was a place of joy and sunshine, in deep contrast to the world of the big city, the way of war, the ways of confrontation.

Sunny refused their offer to visit them in the rondavel, not wishing to see his paintings or the trinkets of his love for Lorna, the small things that would have made her cry for the life she had lost. There were no secrets between these two, and she was sure that he had long ago told her all about Sunny Tupper, the girl from London who had blown it all for one brief orgasm. Lorna looked at her with sympathy; not jealousy, the type of jealousy some women have for their men's past.

"Is there any other way out of here other than that terrible road?" asked Sunny.

"Through Lusikisiki. Longer, but the road surface is better and there are not so many suicidal buses driving along the road. You really want to go now, Sunny? No food? Nothing?" He had risen from the beach when she rose to go.

"Bad news doesn't eat well," replied Sunny dully. "You must talk to your wife. Unless you come to Johannesburg, a lot of people are going to lose their pensions and your two best friends are going to jail. You made them, you made the company, you started the public paying monthly to protect their children and their old age. You are the only person who can stop the registrar declaring the company insolvent, and you are the only person who can put all the systems you created back on the track. But, most important, I know and you know that you are the only person who can instantly restore confidence in Security Lion."

"They told me I was exploiting the public."

"They were wrong," insisted Sunny. "You don't exploit a country when you create wealth, jobs and stability for people in their old age. If you had not created the vehicle for the people to save, they would become a burden on the state when they are unable to work. There would have been more orphaned children with no money and the loss of their pride. The challenge will be greater now than when you started your companies and took over Security Life. You see, Matt, the likes of you and Luke are never able to be torn away from their responsibilities especially when everything, is going wrong. Then the real leaders have to stand up and be counted, when the tin-pot dictators and the manipulators have been destroyed by their own greed.

"I'll leave it with you, Matt, you and Lorna … I love your kids. I never had any children … If I don't go now, Archie will do something silly. Despite all the hail-fellow-well-met, he's not very strong. But you know that, you are his friend. Lusikisiki, you said? I'll find my way. You look well, Matt … You look well."

They both watched her go in silence, embarrassed by the tears, both terrified to contemplate the decision that had to be made. The dog found them and jumped up on Lorna's lap, trying to lick her face.

Lorna stood up and walked out to the beach and the sunshine. She was wearing a bikini she had made herself from soft, yellow leather. It was nice to be able to wear a bikini after bearing two children. The sand was hot under her feet and she moved quickly to the wet sand where the sea-snails were making tracks in the film of water left behind by the flow of the tide. A pair of sandpipers was rushing in and out with the ebb and flow of the waves, picking at food and ignoring Lorna and the dog. A black-backed gull with its large yellow beak was hovering above the patch of flat rocks and bombing the ground with a black mussel that cracked open on impact. Lorna watched the satisfied gull land in a welter of flapping wings and eat the flesh exposed inside the cracked shell.

A small cloud passed over the sun and patterned a shadow on the beach. The children were playing away from the dangerous backwash of the gully, Sipho and Robert throwing smooth flat pebbles at the surface of the sea, skipping them along into the face of the tumbling waves and competing with each other to see who could skip the stones the farthest before they sank. Peace was flirting with a young boy, an innocent prey to her instincts. Away towards the Gap, the rondavel looked across at them, the home of all their happiness. She had left him to think, knowing when it was time to talk and when to leave him alone.

She knew he would have to go. There were too many people involved, the great mass of dependants who relied on the likes of Matt to keep it safe for them. He had kept it safe for her and her children. So many precious years, and now they would have to go. They would all go; she made up her mind on that point, even though the thought of leaving the colony made her feel physically sick. There were just too many families involved, and she knew Matt well enough to know he would never allow his friends to go to jail for negligent management. Not if he could help it.

She began to think of how she would pack and what she could wear. Matt's long beard would have to go and they would clothe his wonderfully tanned body in a suit. He would have to cut his hair. They could stay with her mother and father until they found a home. Matt would say the job would be short, but they never were when other people were involved. Other people never allow you to come and go as you wish. They want part of you in the big new world and never let you go twice – rarely even once – eating you up for their pleasure, their need, exercising their rights.

Lorna shuddered at the thoughts, feeling cold in the hot sun. She wondered how her children would react to the children of the other world, the world that by a miracle they had left behind for so many years. She wondered how Sipho would understand the taunts of racism, where he would go to school as the system prevented him from going to school with Robert … There were just too many problems, but the bigger disaster overwhelmed them all. If they stayed and thousands upon thousands of families lost their savings, Matt's happiness would be shattered anyway. Maybe, just maybe, he would solve the problem quickly and they could go home. Just maybe. It was her only hope.

Then she looked up from the waves and shouted, "NO!" The black-backed gull, too engrossed in eating the mussel, had not seen the dog slink up behind, and the shout of warning came only just in time. Her dog looked back with a clear expression that told her he had nearly gotten away with that one. The gull flew off, the broken mussel in its beak, looking back and downwards at the dog wagging its tail.

SUNNY HAD ARRIVED back at the house to find it empty. The servants knew nothing. The drive through Lusikisiki had been almost as bad as the journey through the hills from Umtata, one oncoming bus crammed with people forcing her into the ditch to avoid a head-on collision. She had only relaxed after leaving the Transkei, a state that had retrogressed back into the Third World: goats and chickens all over the road, fences broken, acute soil erosion and too many cattle to the hectare. Leaving a barren earth, stripped as cleanly as though by a plague of locusts. So much for black self-government, she told herself, even with aid from Pretoria paying half the Transkei national budget. She felt there was some similarity between the Transkei and Security Lion Holdings – no visible management.

The next morning, after a night alone in the house, she phoned the office and had been told that neither Mr Fletcher-Wood nor Mr Kuchinski were to be found, and had she not read the newspapers? Typical of them, she had thought, not to face the problem. She was not an employee of Security Lion, so there was nothing more to do. She had money in her own bank account, the allowance given to her by Archie to run the house and the servants. The rates had been paid, there were no mortgages or instalments remaining and, as Archie had based his allowance to her on what he spent when he was running his own affairs, there was good money in her bank saved by prudently administering the household. Sunny sat back and awaited further developments.

MATTHEW GRAY ARRIVED in Johannesburg on the same day that Ben Munroe's ANC sponsor had landed with his head on the concrete outside

John Vorster Square, cracking open his skull and breaking his neck. There had been no enquiry or inquest, the remains of the man being simply removed and shovelled into the ground, without a mark to show for his passing.

Matt had delayed uprooting his family until he was sure he had enough votes to make him CEO at a general meeting of shareholders. Despite the telephone system from the Transkei being anything but direct dialling and because he spoke Xhosa to the switchboard operator in the Port St Johns post office he was able to arrive in the financial capital of South Africa with a majority of shareholders prepared to vote him back on the board as managing director.

The shareholders' meeting had been called for a week after his arrival, at Matt's request. He had some preconditions of his own. Before he took on the job he wished to know what was going on. So far as he could ascertain very few of his old staff still worked for the company and the names he was given of those remaining were not the ones he wished to hear.

Finding Archie and Lucky had been easy. One educated guess was the bush on the other side of the South African border, and the Harare exchange had given him Aldo Calucci's phone number.

"You got Archie or Lucky staying with you?" Matt asked after the briefest of greetings.

"Both here, Matt. Where you?"

"Port St Johns. You okay? Hear you're married. Wife. Kids. Me, too. Put Arch on the line, old friend. We drink beer again soon, you hear"

"Hello, Matt. Bit of a mess, what?" said Archie, trying to sound hale and hearty. There was little doubt as to why Matt had contacted him; it was their first phone call in sixteen years. "Bad news travels fast."

"A courier will be coming up with proxy forms for both of you. Sign them in my favour, and stay where you are."

"I'm sorry, Matt," mumbled Archie after an embarrassed silence.

"So am I."

The value of Security Lion Holdings shares were half what they had been when Teddie Botha was alive, and the next important call from his base in the Cape Hermes Hotel had gone to the lawyer who was the trustee to the money Matt had tried to give away without success, probably through the black man's ignorance not knowing how to draw money from a white man's bank, as much as his pride.

"Buy Security Lion Holdings shares through nominees and seven brokerage houses."

"But, Matt the shares are going to be suspended."

"No, they are not. Please be kind enough to do as I say. Buy slowly. You have a month to pick up as many shares as possible."

"Where are you speaking from?"

"The Transkei."

"It's a hell of a mess up here. Are you sure?" Matt replaced the receiver without answering. He had finished the conversation and other matters were on his mind. He had no time for argument. The next call had been to the registrar of insurance in Pretoria.

"If I come back, will you give me three months to find out what has gone on and another three months to put it right?"

'You will be doing me a personal favour Mister Gray. This is a mess the government can well do without"

"Frankly, I couldn't give a damn about the government." retorted Matt. "I'm worried about the policyholders. I shall want our agreement in writing, and signed by the minister of economic affairs. I don't want the Afrikaans insurance companies to use this as an opportunity to land on my head. I have enough bad memories about the insurance industry."

"Funnily enough, the shares have picked up this morning."

"I know."

"The letter will be ready for your collection."

THE FOLLOWING days were spent gleaning proxy agreements from institutional shareholders as the main block of shares. Teddie Botha's, were in limbo, with the executor of the estate refusing to make a decision preferring to wait for the courts to make the decision for him. It was a safe way out for the attorney but a major frustration for Matt. He had refused to shave off his beard, but had agreed to a good trim, which Lorna performed to perfection, still leaving a little of the painter to look back at him from the mirror. The two insurmountable problems were the effect this radical change of lifestyle would have on his family and his life as a painter. The colony would look after itself he was sure of that.

"Cousin, old chap, would you mind very much if I came with you?"

"Charles, old chap, the only good thing I could see in all this was leaving you and your shooting stick behind."

"Maybe I should make a break for it."

"Go back to Scotland and sell that damn castle," said Matt emphatically.

"Still no buyers, you see. You'll be able to paint at the weekends."

"So that's it."

"Not really. Sophia. I don't think she loves me."

"I could have told you that the day you arrived," Matt informed him, trying not to sound too curt.

"There was always hope until she heard from that man she was going to marry. That mixed-marriage act which has just been repealed allows her to marry in Cape Town. He's a doctor. Poor old Charlie's left out a bit now, old chap. Well, you see, I don't really have anywhere else to go. I thought we could fill up the old camper and drive up to Johannesburg together. The kids love travelling in the back of the kombi and there's a roof rack for the bits and pieces, if you see what I mean."

"When's Sophia leaving?"

"She's gone … You'll have to excuse me, old chap." Charles Farquhar, twelfth earl of Lothianmore, was crying.

Matt did not have the heart to ask what would happen to the school which had so relied on Sophia. He could not be in two places at once.

The entire family arrived in the floral camper at Archie's house, where they were going to stay. Matt had put his foot down about living with his in-laws. There would be enough problems without arguing about how his children should be brought up. Through the paramount chief, a letter was sent to Luke, telling him that Sipho was going to Johannesburg and giving the reasons why. The alternative raised greater problems than the ones to be faced in the future.

Surprisingly, the kombi had rattled all the way there without breaking down, the only mistake being leaving the hamper of food in the back with the children and the dog. When they stopped for lunch, the food had all been eaten and the dog and Robert had been sick on the floor. It was one of the few times Matt had ever seen his cousin get really angry.

SUNNY HAD GONE across to Tilde where the situation had normalised, the executors of Teddie's estate cashing an insurance policy where Teddie had nominated young David Botha as the beneficiary. When she heard that Sunny had dragged Matthew Gray out of the bush, Theo danced a little jig, a vision of personal wealth flashing back into focus.

"So that's why the shares are going up and not down," she said, hugging herself.

"Have you read the will, Theo?"

"The boy gets the money but it's all the same, really; I'm his grandmother." Theo sat there with an obvious smirk on her face; number one was going to be all right, and that was all that concerned her.

Sunny turned abruptly away from her, and spoke to her daughter. "Tilda," she said. "I want Teddie's office keys for Matt. He wants to make a personal investigation. If he is satisfied and takes over the management of the company, he will most probably save your son's inheritance."

Once she had the set of keys in her bag, Sunny was glad to get out of the house. Such obvious avarice made her question the laws of inheritance. It was fortunate that Matt would be dealing with the trustees of Teddie's estate until the boy turned twenty-five, rather than the two women she had left gloating around the sparkling clean swimming pool. She did not envy the children their mother or their grandmother.

MATT LET himself into the grand building, Security Lion House that had been built after his day to show how grand the company had become, the money to erect the monument to pride having come from the policyholders. He took the lift to the top floor, the executive floor.

It was six o'clock in the morning, and the man on the gate to the basement parking had recognised Archie's car and his security clearance disk with its parking bay number, and taken little interest in the bearded man driving the car. With the ANC throwing bombs around all over South Africa, it was not the kind of security which protected the building and the staff. Teddie's office was opulent, too big and too plush with carpet, in contrast to the riot of untidiness. The great expectations for the Rhodes Scholar, the man who had played rugby for Oxford, had come to a strange and sad end.

Matt looked around the mess in disgust. He would have to read everything among the litter to restore any kind of order. He had once seen a lawyer's office in the same kind of turmoil. The man had had moments of brilliance, but lost the crucial facts when they were most needed. The lawyer, Matt was happier to remember as he rummaged through the mess in Teddie's office, was on the other side, so Lion Life had won the case easily, and the lawyer's client in a-follow-on criminal case had been taken off to jail for trying to defraud an insurance company. Standing with his back to the chaos, he looked out of the twenty-first floor window on the corner of Rissik and Plein Streets, across to the railway station that Nelson Mandela had sent his men to bomb, sending him to jail so many years before.

Matt wondered vaguely what he was doing here, away from the

sanctuary of Port St Johns. There were so many wrongs and so many different ways of setting them right. He hoped the struggle for Luke would be worthwhile for all of them, and that they would not exchange one tyranny for another. There were always two sides to the same tale. Maybe the armed struggle was Mandela's only option those many years ago. How could he judge the pain from his ivory tower, his position of privilege? How could he know the burning frustration of impotence against a sea of overwhelming injustice? Maybe he too would have bombed the railway station and rationalised the civilian deaths as a small price to pay – good rationalisation except for the innocent dead and the starving poor suffering the pain of the subsequent ANC instigated sanctions that lost them their jobs. But what else could they do against omnipotent oppressors? He was not able to judge, and thanked his lucky stars that this one had not been either his decision or his responsibility.

With a big sigh that spoke of so many problems outside his control, he turned to face the mess left behind by Teddie Botha. If there was one thing that Matthew Gray detested, it was the chaos left by the incompetence of other people who professed to know what they were doing. Putting the last glorious sixteen years out of his mind, he sat down behind the desk and began to work.

By the time the door to the office opened at half past eight, there were three neat piles of paper on the large desk. One was important, the second was to be read again and the last was destined for the waste-paper basket.

The young girl who gaped at the bearded man in the ill-fitting suit was almost pretty, if a little too severe for Matt's taste. He stood up and gave her his softest smile, turning the well-tanned skin around the corners of his eyes into well-defined crow's feet. The girl backed away in apprehension at the sudden size of the man behind the desk.

"What are you doing here?" she finally managed to ask, gathering up her dignity.

"Trying to make some sense of all this," Matt explained, waving a hand at the papers. "You must be Teddie's secretary. My name is Matthew Gray. I used to be chairman of this company. I'm here to help and I am going to need a lot of yours. Maybe you could find us both a cup of coffee, and I can tell you what I want to do. At first glance it all looks a lot worse than it actually is. Teddie never used to be so untidy."

"Since that woman."

"So that was the problem," mused Matt, understanding. So his original assessment of Teddie's potential had not been completely wrong after all.

"You don't think there was anything financial worrying Mister Botha?"

"Why should there have been, sales had never been better."

"And Mister Strover?"

"He was insider-trading on his own account. The shares he bought were always good. Nothing wrong with that man's judgement. Just greedy. Did he not steal your paintings?"

"Only in a way. A way that suited me well." Matt wondered how the girl knew about his paintings. He was back in what they called the real world, the one he saw as artificial.

"I'll get some coffee."

Matt used all his charm to make the girl relax and, by the end of the day, he was instinctively sure that there was nothing fundamentally wrong with the company. There were no red lights flashing. Everything was merely six months behind where it should have been in the chief executive's office.

"I want to interview every member of the staff individually," declared Matt.

"It will take you a week."

"I have six days. Miss Tupper will interview the ladies. She is employed by me, not by Security Lion. She will not interfere with your job, but I might just mention she was my right hand when I owned this company." He was smiling again. "You may know Miss Tupper as the friend of Mister Fletcher-Wood. I know her a great deal more, especially her competence. We started the whole thing together. Sunny will reread the larger piles of paper and then we will go into the filing cabinets.

"Your job is to keep everyone else away from us, except those to be interviewed. Draw up a list, starting from the bottom, and please include the black staff including the lady who made the coffee. I like happy people to work with. Smiles. Long faces are not for me. Now you go off home and have an early night. You and I are going to sort out this place and put the smiles back on all the faces."

When the tea-girl was interviewed in Xhosa, it was the first time she had ever heard a white man speak her language and the first time she had ever sat down in any of the offices when there was a white man in the room. When she left, the beaming smile on her black face lit the corridor.

THE PRESS CONFERENCE was set up at the end of the week in the company boardroom, and Matt sat in the centre of the big table set at the back of the room, facing the cameras and the reporters. The senior partner of the company's auditors was on his right, a man who had welcomed the return of Matthew Gray with even more enthusiasm than the registrar of insurance. The modern trend with insolvent financial institutions was to go for the directors, senior management and the auditors, in that order. The era of impregnable professional accountants was over. Everyone had to be accountable.

On Matt's left was a representative of the outside auditors sent in by the registrar of insurance to protect the public. Flanking them were the outside directors, non-executive, every one of whom had offered to resign, a condition Matt was going to be happy to accept when his control of the company was confirmed at the shareholders' meeting which would follow the press conference. Archie and Lucky were still in Zimbabwe, though Matt had their letters of resignation in his pocket.

He stood up to address only the second press conference that he had called in his life. After his memories of the first, his throat was dry and he felt very tense, but he took care to make sure it didn't show.

"I am confident that my friend on my left will find nothing amiss in the books of Security Lion Holdings or its subsidiaries. I have spent a hard week finding out what was wrong around here. Mister Botha was under extreme personal pressure. The daughter that he thought was his own was not; his wife had been impregnated by another man. They would have divorced but for the fact that the blood tests which showed the impossibility of his being the father of the girl came after his wife was again pregnant. This time it was proved seven months later that he was indeed the father. The two doctors who conducted the tests are here for you to question."

"For twenty long months before his death in battle, the chairman of this company was unable to function as a man or as an executive. His wife, by her infidelity, had destroyed him and had gone a long way towards destroying this company. My two original partners, both competent salesmen and responsible for the graph of sales that shows a rise of seven per cent above the next best sales in the industry, were, by their own admission, incompetent as administrators. I have both their resignations, together with those of the rest of the board, in my pocket, along with signed proxy forms that give me control of this company once again. The mysterious buyer you gentlemen have speculated upon for seven weeks was myself, through the trust I invoked when I was forced to depart from this industry at the instigation of a colleague of yours from overseas. That was his prerogative. I have no quarrel with the methods of your reporting. Enough to say, that Ben Munroe of *Newsweek* did me the greatest favour of my life.

"I am only here to ensure that the men and women who gave me money to invest when I ran this business receive their just reward. I am back in the industry to sell Security Lion to a company that the auditors and I will judge capable of running our vast investments. It will not be a company from outside the borders of the Republic of South Africa. I also wish to report that the run on the shares of this company was carefully orchestrated by two of this company's competitors, selling Security Lion shares short after the chairman died in Angola. All is fair in legitimate business practice. I myself would not have set out to destroy a competitor in this way, but they did nothing wrong, hoping no doubt to buy us up at a cheap price at the bottom of the panic. Well, now they can compete properly and in an orderly fashion.

"The increase in the value of my trust will benefit the poor of this country in a way I have yet to implement. When the two companies were so busily selling us short, I was buying, and, if they want to cover their positions, as they must, it will be a costly affair. Some of their own shareholders may have something to say about that, but then, gambling and playing around always has its price. After this conference, I will become caretaker chief executive of this company, looking for a safe home for its assets, to allow those assets to grow without speculation and unnecessary risk. To sum up, gentlemen, this has been a cleverly orchestrated storm that I have now returned to its teacup. I will now be happy to answer any questions about the present, and none about the past other than as it relates to my earlier days with this company."

"Did you paint Bernard Strover's canvases?"

"No comment."

"Why did you run away in the first place?"

"No comment," repeated Matt, icily.

"Did you have anything to do with Mister Munroe being refused an entry permit into this country to attend this press conference?"

"No, I did not, but I would like to hear more about that after the shareholders' meeting, if the questioner would kindly visit me in my office."

"Who is the father of the coloured boy living in your house? Alternatively, who was the mother?"

"There is no secrecy about Sipho's surname. He and my son are to attend Maritz Brothers college junior school together. I am his guardian, not his father. I have stewardship, which will come to an end when this country buries the policy of apartheid and lets the exiles return and the political prisoners out of prison."

"Is the boy's father Luke Mbeki?"

"Yes." replied Matt.

"Does Mister Mbeki know his son is in Johannesburg?"

"Yes, as a matter of fact, he does."

"How do you communicate with a wanted terrorist?"

"That is my business."

"Is it not also the business of the security police?"

"Gentlemen, I am not a politician and never intend to be one," insisted Matt, rather warily. "Sipho's father has been my lifelong friend. What we do for each other is done for the sake of friendship.

"Now, please, questions about Security Lion. I want you gentlemen to be satisfied that there are no skeletons in this company's cupboard. I want to put all this nonsense about an insolvent company in the garbage can where it belongs. The Bernard Strover story is a tiny fraction of a small percentage of our investments. One day I will personally catch up with the man. Then we shall see. I don't like crooks any more than you do."

THE MEETING that took place in another part of Johannesburg shortly after the press conference was certain that, if Matthew Gray was allowed to take up his appointment as chief executive officer of Security Lion, there was a good chance that the people in the room, all Afrikaans speakers, would lose their jobs and even find criminal negligence actions brought against the two directors who had instigated the short-selling of Security Lion shares. Their scheme had worked perfectly until this man had appeared out of nowhere with a war chest they estimated at close to three hundred million rand, the amount they were able to calculate after finding out the initial stock exchange investment after Gray's abortive 'give every black a free lunch'. With the rise in Security Lion shares, they were up against a man with four hundred million to spend. There was a strong, pervasive smell of fear in the room. Big houses, expensive wives, private schools and large cars were all at stake, all threatened by Matthew Gray.

"The man's a communist," said one of the directors in Afrikaans, a man who had lost most of his confidence in the panic; in his estimation, anyone who opposed the Afrikaner establishment was a communist, and part and parcel of the total onslaught that was threatening the country."

"Can you prove that?" asked one of the younger members of the emergency meeting, in hope rather than out of any desire to challenge the assertion.

"Of course; Luke Mbeki's a communist and Gray admits to bringing up his son and having that bloody terrorist as a friend. Speaks for itself."

"Then we must get him arrested under the Suppression of Communism Act," declared the youth. "Ninety days' detention without trial and the minister can extend the ninety days for as long as he likes. Better than house arrest. Much better. I have a friend in the bureau of state security who could have this bloody communist arrested just like that, man. Take him out, if you like. Then you will see the shares of Security Lion go down, man. They'll go down, you can be bloody sure of that. Get Gray arrested and the shares will mark down twenty per cent the same day, take my word for it. A few more rumours in the market about Strover pinching money and it will cost us nothing to cover our positions."

Everyone in the room had stopped talking to look at the young man who was throwing them a lifeline. The look of the chosen few, those in command of their lives, slowly began to return as they straightened up. It was the look of power. The panic evaporated.

"Then get the bloody bastard arrested; only I never knew anything, here. Not a bloody thing. You're clever, man, I tell you." The director was again very pleased with himself. "Anyway, Gray was a bloody Englishman, kaffir-lover. Had it coming."

He picked up the phone on the table and phoned his broker. "Dump Security Lion shares, man. Sell them short. Don't argue, man. You do your job, see, and I do mine. We're going to make a killing."

THEO BLAZE WAS SCREAMING down the telephone to her lawyer to sue Matthew Gray for libel, defamation, anything to defend the honour of her daughter.

"I don't care about the blood tests. Sue him. How dare he tell those terrible lies about my daughter? And tell the newspapers anyone who prints such lies, we'll go for them too. Sue the bastards. Who the hell do they think they are, anyway?"

"They 'are', Mother. Your English!"

"Shut up. You just shut up. You got us in this mess." She turned back to the phone. "Sue, you hear? Sue!" Then she slammed the receiver down and glared at her daughter.

FOR MANY YEARS, Frikkie Swart had needed certain financial institutions to move the money he plundered from the government secret fund overseas and into the names and bank accounts of companies whose shares were owned by foreign banks on behalf of the nominee; namely Frikkie Swart. To prevent money from leaving a country in which no one had any confidence, residents of South Africa were not allowed to invest overseas. To encourage foreign investors, a separate currency had been established which enabled foreign buyers to purchase South African shares at a considerable discount. Hence a man in New York would pay sixty rand for a de Beers share, and a man in Johannesburg one hundred rand to hold exactly the same investment. The buying and selling of the shares was done by arbitrage brokers who by law made South African shareholders buy in commercial rands and overseas buyers in financial rands at the discount price.

A man wishing to move his money into a hard currency would, if he were allowed, happily pay one hundred rand for a de Beers share and sell it in New York for sixty rand, converted into American dollars. The opportunity for someone to pay sixty rand for a de Beers share in New York and sell for one hundred rand in Johannesburg, inflate an invoice for an export from New York and pay for it with the one hundred rand de Beers share was obvious to a simple minded crook and, unless every financial transaction was policed to source by the Reserve Bank of South Africa, impossible to stop. Money had been leaking out of South Africa in this way for years, adding to the misery of low commodity prices and full-scale trade and financial sanctions called for by the ANC. The phenomenal profit in that type of arbitrage made insider traders in America look petty.

When Frikkie Swart listened to his friend asking for a favour, the idea of locking up a man he was sure had once slept with his wife was not only appealing but patriotic. And Matt had been a friend of Hector's. Frikkie needed little further reason to arrest Matt as a threat to the security of the state and, when Matt returned to Archie's house after talking to the reporter about Ben Munroe's lack of an entry visa, he was arrested in the driveway and removed from the property without even Lorna knowing what had happened.

People periodically vanished and any questions were answered with a wall of denials. The security police were experts at arresting people in the dark without leaving a trace. For Lorna, Matt just did not come home. For Sunny, he had just left his office to go home. Somewhere in between, Matthew Gray had disappeared off the face of the earth.

When Sunny returned home, having finished the pile of work, they both thought Matt had been with the other.

"I sent him home to you and the kids," said Sunny. "I was reading back correspondence."

"Better call the police," said Lorna.

"Matt trod on a lot of toes today," Sunny informed her, looking apprehensive. "He accused unnamed insurance companies of deliberately trying to crash Security Lion and he told the public Tilda was a whore. He admitted Luke was a good friend. I'll get a torch. It was raining today. What happened to Matt's car, Archie's car? I've been driving one from the company pool. Matt knew the risks; when we were back in the office on the twenty-first floor, he handed me a document," Sunny handed Lorna the sheet of paper, which she read and went cold all over. The words came leaping out of the paper.

"Seeing as of today I, Matthew Gray, have retaken control of Security Lion Holdings in accordance with the extraordinary general meeting of shareholders of the same day, should I be unable to perform my duties through illness, death or incarceration, I give to Miss Poppy (Sunny) Tupper my full of power of attorney to run the company until I am able to resume my duties or she is able to sell the company to a safe and stable haven that will give all our policyholders their full rights and benefits. Held by my attorneys is a full set of suggestions as to how Miss Tupper may best achieve these goals, but she is free to exercise full control as she may see fit according to the circumstances." The brief document was witnessed and countersigned by a commissioner of oaths.

Together they walked out down the long driveway, with Sunny shining the torch on the ground.

"Those are my tyre marks," said Sunny, pointing the torch just inside the entrance gate where gum and wattle trees shielded the driveway from the public road. "Those belong to Archie's Mercedes. You can see where the Benz has been turned round by driving onto the lawn and nearly getting bogged down. There were footprints but someone has carefully scuffed them over."

"My God; he's been kidnapped!" gasped Lorna.

"Yes, and my guess is by the police. Under the emergency laws of this country, they can do what they like. Just being a friend of an ANC official is enough for them. Matt knew what he was doing, the risks he was taking Lorna. That is why he gave me his power of attorney. Typical. He was always worried about other people and never himself. Did he ever tell you about going into the Congo to look for his friends? He doesn't want one of those policyholders to accuse him of running out on them. He feels responsible. Don't call the police, Lorna. They've got him, for sure."

"Better I go to the British embassy," said Charles, who had followed them silently down the driveway to find out what was going on. Sunny shone the torch in his face as he spoke. The sardonic expression had gone and the jaw that was often a little slack had firmed up, twisting slightly, the soft blue eyes searching hard from beneath the unkept sandy hair. It was the look one of his ancestors might have given just before sweeping down on the English to drive them back over Hadrian's Wall. For a brief second, Sunny was frightened of the man.

THE INTERROGATION ROOM was on the fourth floor of the John Vorster Square police station, and the window was open. Warrant Officer Higgins of the South African police, ex-Rhodesia and Malaya, was doing what he enjoyed most: extracting information from communists.

The man strapped to the chair was naked; the neat little clamps were attached to his testicles and the wires ran to the small box next to where Warrant Officer Higgins sat on the corner of the desk. Outwardly, Matt looked the way he had when they brought him in, but the shocks had torn at the inside of his manhood and his body feared the terrible onslaught of pain more than anything else it had endured in its life. Matt was very close to the end of his tether, and the only two things in his life at this moment were the box and the open window.

"Who helped you cache the arms in the cave beyond Third Beach?" Matt had no idea what the man was talking about and could think of nothing to say, anything to say, to stop the volts of electricity that would shake his body, leaping up from his testicles. He had long stopped being able to think beyond the box and the open window. Higgins had seen the deterioration and turned down the voltage as, if the man was going to die, it would need to be by his own volition, leaping through the open window.

Watching the rich hippie with a young wife go through excruciating pain made up for being forced out of Malaya and Rhodesia, and was Higgins' personal revenge on the communists who were destroying his world and would do it again if the likes of the SAP did not stop them. Blacks, he sometimes felt sorry for. They had been coerced into communism. The brains were the Matthew Grays who were dedicated to enslaving the world in a George Orwell horror society where everyone would be ruled by the party from Moscow.

"You commie bastard," he spat, turning off the power. "Who sends your letters to Mbeki?" Again the voltage. "What were you really doing in

Port St Johns?" Again the voltage. "Why did your company give money to the communists?" Again the voltage. "Why do you bring up a little black bastard?" Again the voltage.

"Take the ropes off, Sergeant. Liberal sods like this bastard are better dead … Go on, you bleeding liberal. Get on with it. Go jump and land on your head, you miserable bastard." Increasing the voltage, he put in a quick surge, but though Matt wanted to run for the freedom of the window his body was unable to move.

"This silly sod's too old. Take him downstairs. I'll try again tomorrow … Have a nice day, Mister bloody Gray."

"NOTHING WE CAN DO, your Lordship. He's not even British. Your cousin he may be, but he's a South African. How can you be sure he's in police custody? This country's very violent, you know, your Lordship. Ransom, that kind of thing. Not like Scotland. Why don't you go to the police?"

"No wonder we British lost our empire. We deserved it … good day, sir."

"There's no reason to be rude. Just because you're an earl, you can't come in here throwing your weight around. Britain's not the same any more, you know." The assistant British Consul for Johannesburg was now on his high horse, standing on his dignity.

"Your fly's undone, old chap," said Charles, and left the man looking down between his legs. "Cheap shot, Farquhar," he said outside. "Cheap shot. Now what the hell do I do? There has to be someone with influence. Even in a police state … So much for winning the Boer War."

While Matt was regaining consciousness in a cell that was better designed for a dog, Charles had fixed the end of his shooting stick into a crack in the pavement outside the British Consul and was thinking through what he would do next. The flow of pedestrians opened up around him as he sat comfortably while racking his brains. He stood up abruptly, snatched up his shooting stick, banged the end at the concrete pavement and announced to passers-by he was going home.

As he strode towards the ticket office of British Airways, a mud-splattered car drove past him, going down Sauer Street in the opposite direction, out towards the northern suburbs.

Lucky had driven non-stop for twenty-seven hours after taking Sunny's phone call at Aldo's safari camp in the Zambezi Valley. The first of Matt's instructions to Sunny was to phone Lucky and tell him he was probably in police custody. Aldo Calucci's phone number had been neatly printed next to the request.

Close to the car and its impatient driver, who had first driven into the centre of Johannesburg to make one visit in person, the glass tower of the Diagonal Street building of the stock exchange was seeing a sharp drop in Security Lion shares. It was being said that Gray had vanished for the second time, the situation being too bad for him to salvage, and that Bernard Strover had done a lot more damage to the company than Gray had admitted at the press conference.

Every stockbroker holding Security Lion shares for his clients was trying to get through to the new CEO at Security Lion without any success, and Sunny was bringing in both firms of auditors to make a press statement that she hoped would limit the damage. She had personally driven to Pretoria and shown the registrar of insurance her power of attorney, while he had sat rigid in his seat, horrified by the possibilities that sprang to his mind with the word 'incarceration'.

"I'll speak to the state president," he said, after a brief silence. "I'll do what I can."

"I hope the state president knows what certain elements in his police force are up to."

"So do I. You don't really think someone could ..."

"Yes, I do," Sunny asserted. "It's always the very few who give the rest of us the bad reputation. Too much secrecy in government. Too many people terrified of the total communist onslaught. Too much power without accountability. They don't even tell the public where the money's spent."

"Then this country is in a lot more trouble than I thought." Sunny wasn't quite certain that the man was not being sarcastic.

The wheels began to turn, but each enquiry to the police was like eating soup with a fork. Everything dribbled through. Nothing stayed on the fork.

While Sunny was driving back to Pretoria, Charles' jumbo was landing at Nairobi airport and, when she reached home late that night, Lorna said Charles had also disappeared.

"You think the same people have run off with Charles?" she asked Lorna, as they rummaged in his room.

"Who on earth would want to do that! Anyway, his shooting stick has gone. When Matt comes home, he will think it the only good thing to have come out of this affair. The children want to know where their father is, and I said he'd gone down to Port St Johns for a few days, and they all went mad thinking he'd left them behind. They hate this place. Peace says it's the first time she's ever been bored in her life because there's nothing to do, and Sipho wants to know why everyone around here looks at him funny. He's taken to sticking out his tongue and says school is not so much fun without Sophia, poor girl. I only hope she's happily married by now.

"My mother and father have been as much use as a sick headache. Both on about 'once a hippie, always a hippie', and Dad says the rumours are that Matt's run away from his responsibilities for the second time and that leopards never change their spots. They could be some help, damn it. They won't even take the children, as they don't want Sipho in their house. And I'm so worried I can't think, and Lucky pitching up hasn't helped. If he had done what he was supposed to do and run this company properly, all this would never have happened.

"Archie's in the lounge. I just don't know what's going on. And some black man's sidled up to the cook and said if we want any help the ANC are waiting, and the cook says if the police find out he's dead, he doesn't want anything to do with anyone and has gone on the bus back to the Transkei. There's just no one I can turn to. I'm a painter and a mother and I love Matt, but I know nothing about big business and police and everyone hating everyone else.

"The place has gone mad. I grew up in Jo'burg but the place has gone mad. This is the real loony bin, not Port St Johns. Every one of them down there is sane in comparison... Damn it, I want Matt, and I want to go home and so do the children." Lorna was crying, and there was very little Sunny could do to help.

ONE HOUR and forty minutes after the British Airways Boeing 747 landed at Heathrow airport, Charles arrived in a taxi at the London office of the ANC and asked to see Luke Mbeki.

"He's not here at the moment," said the girl at reception.

"Then I'll wait." Charles opened up the shooting stick and planted the sharp end in the carpet.

"You can't do that; you'll make a hole!"

"The longer I sit, the bigger the hole." He tried the big smile to see if that would help. "And please hurry; I have to give a speech in the House of Lords at half-past two."

"I'll get Mister Mbeki, but please don't sit on that shooting stick. What is your name, sir?"

"Charles Farquhar, earl of Lothianmore."

When Charles stood up at question time, the press gallery was surprisingly full, Luke having warned reporters sensitive to the anti-apartheid cause to be ready for headline news.

Charles had been introduced in the House of Lords soon after his father died but had never returned, as he had not seen the reason. Without one note and straight from his own experience, he gave an impassioned speech to the British people, urging them not to bury their heads in their South African investments but to bring pressure to bear on the white minority government to stop a system that was a crime against humanity.

"There are almost two million of this island stock in South Africa. They must either stand up for counting or accept responsibility for apartheid, and that goes for Her Majesty's government as well. Two days ago, my cousin, Matthew Gray, was abducted in the night because he publicly admitted to having an ANC executive as a friend. It is my opinion that they want him dead. We British cannot politely ignore what is really happening in South Africa. They must be forced to change and we must help to force them.'

By the time the British newspapers were carrying the contents of his speech, Luke was able to tell Charles where Matt was being held.

"Underground in the cells at John Vorster Square. He's nearly dead, Charles. They want to kill him ... I have never felt so impotent in my life."

Charles used the phone in Luke's flat to call Sunny, and Lucky answered.

"Lucky Kuchinski."

"Charles Farquhar. I'm in London. Matt's in John Vorster Square and he's nearly dead. Tell Sunny. Tell his wife."

"We are going to tell South Africa if my plan doesn't work," gritted Lucky through his teeth.

After the second day of torture, Matt's body had again been unable to respond to the command to run for the open window and, when they dumped him back down in the bowels of the earth with a thin blanket to cover his nakedness, with water but no food, he took his mind out of his body and left the room.

He took his spirit back to Port St Johns where he heard the loud cry of the gulls, watched his children, looked at his paintings and saw the blood-red sun sink down on the horizon. All that night he stayed away from his shattered body but, when they came for him on the third day, they had to carry him up to the fourth floor to the welcoming arms of Warrant Officer Higgins.

"Strap him in the chair, Sergeant," he said in English.

"Today, this commie bastard is going to tell us all about his friends. And Sergeant, please open the window."

MINISTER KLOSS HAD BEGUN to feel the heat, but the secret of the success of the bureau of state security was that the Ministry always backed its operatives to the full. He had merely called Frikkie Swart into his office to give him a warning.

"The British press believe we are holding Gray, something I don't wish to know, one way or the other, you see. Just don't leave evidence. Make sure everything is clean. No one knows anything for sure." They were speaking in Afrikaans. The two men had not even looked at each other.

FOR THE FIRST time in years, Lucky Kuchinski was enjoying himself. He and three other ex-members of Mike Hoare's fifth commando, ex-mercenaries who had fought together against the Simba rebels in Katanga, were driving along the M1 freeway from Johannesburg to Pretoria, heading for the most expensive suburb.

They found the house they were looking for without any difficulty and Lucky drove the car just inside the driveway, where they waited until it was dark, the light fading just after half-past six. The house among the jacaranda trees would be burglar-alarmed, and Lucky smiled at the smugness of the governing establishment that considered itself so powerful that its officials only required normal household security to protect themselves. Archie, a broken reed, was not among his group. Lucky was now the one with the initiative and courage.

AFTER HIS MEETING with the minister, Frikkie Swart had spent a pleasant three hours in an illegal gambling house where the girls were both pretty and willing. He found the liquor and girls relaxed him after a hard day's work.

As he turned into his driveway, he was in a very good mood and just a little drunk from his exertions. In the warm March evening, there had been no rain that day, so he had the window down and his right elbow rested comfortably on the driver's door, a little out of the window.

Lucky took him out of the car in three swift moves – throttling him, opening the door and yanking him onto the gravel, while one of the ex-mercenaries stopped the car and turned off the engine. Within sixty seconds, they had obliterated foot-and-tyre-prints and were driving away from the house.

"There are two more of us at John Vorster Square charge office waiting to receive Matthew Gray," Lucky informed Frikkie. "And you will tell Warrant Officer Higgins to let him out, or we will repeat what Higgins has done to Gray and then hand you over to the ANC in Angola." They were driving to an ANC safe house in Glen Furness on a four-hectare smallholding.

"The police will get you bastards," snarled Frikkie, trying to cover his fear.

"Possibly, but not before you end up in an ANC detention camp."

"I don't know what you are talking about."

"That's a big shame ... guys, shall we do the stick up the rectum or break every bone in his body one by one?" Lucky was very much enjoying himself at the man's fear.

"Stick up the arse. Lasts longer," said the driver. "Took me three days to kill a Simba that way in the Congo. Bloody works, man. Only trouble is, when the bowels burst they shit all over the place."

In the safe house, they sat him down next to the telephone. "Which do you want, Swart? The stick, break your bones, or make a phone call?" Lucky's accent had broken some way back to his Polish origin.

When the phone call had been made, Lucky shook his head in disgust.

"Bullies are always the same. No guts. Nasty, weak little men."

"They're going to take Gray back to the Transkei," said Frikkie.

"Then you stay here until he arrives. We will know soon enough. If you think how I know Higgins' name, you know I know which cell. You not get him out, you're in pain, quick, you see."

Frikkie, smiling inwardly, let the threat pass. He had all the time in the world. It was his country. The police would find him soon. They had far too much at stake.

Half an hour later, the phone rang in the house and Lucky looked down on the seated Frikkie Swart after speaking on the phone. "Take off his trousers. This little man does not understand."

"You touch me and you're all dead," warned Frikkie Swart.

"You're dead meat anyway. So's Higgins. But I want you to scream a lot for what you do to my friend and too many other people. By the time I finish, you'll wish your mother had had an abortion."

. . .

THE POLICE first threw tear-gas at the crowd outside John Vorster Square, then they fired rubber bullets. Then the people began to die and all the time the cameras of the world recorded the carnage. The placards were explicit, and the message flashed round the world again: 'TORTURE', 'GRAY', and the names of seventy-four other men and women who had died in police custody that year alone.

THE MESSAGE to the police to release Gray came not from Frikkie Swart but from Minister Kloss, the first time he had ever interfered with his operatives. When they carried Matt into the ambulance, Matt was unaware of what was going on as his spirit was still in Port St Johns and his body naked in the cell. By then, Frikkie Swart was on his way to Angola and an ANC detention camp. Two days later, Warrant Officer Higgins, ex-British Malayan police, was found mutilated in his garage. Someone had cut off his genitals and left him to die.

On the Monday, Sunny, in conjunction with the auditors, sold Security Lion to a consortium of banks and financial institutions, and the shares of Security Lion Holdings were suspended on the Johannesburg stock exchange. Lucky and Archie returned to Aldo's safari camp with the ex-Congolese mercenaries who had set up an anti-poaching unit for the Zimbabwean government in a last-ditch effort to save what was left of the black rhinoceros in the Zambezi Valley.

After he had spent two weeks in hospital, Lorna and the children took Matt back to Port St Johns. But his spirit had not yet returned to his body, a body that was now a skeleton of its former self. The colony welcomed him home and went away to cry.

The most visible sign of his experience was a permanent trembling of the hands. Even if his mind had been able, he would not have had the strength to hold a paintbrush or his palette. The sun was warm on his body and Lorna fed him as she would have fed a child, half the food dribbling down the slack sides of his mouth while the sunken eyes looked out to sea with a thousand-metre stare that saw nothing. For the first time Lorna saw how old he was, and it made her sad and ever more determined.

"You are going to paint again, my husband, and you will paint in your own name and we will never again leave the harmony of Port St Johns."

Sunny, alone in her house, was wondering what to do with the rest of her life. Archie had gone without a whimper, not even helping Lucky with Frikkie Swart. She was standing in the lounge looking out of the window at a butterfly hovering over the pool, when a man came up the driveway. She heard the maid answer the door and a man ask for Miss Poppy Tupper.

The man was a policeman in plain clothes, and the deportation order was for Sunny to be out of the country within twenty-four hours. Standing looking at the back of the man walking back down the drive, she was not sure whether to laugh or cry.

WHEN THE SALE of Teddie Botha's shares in Security Lion was explained to Theo Blaze, she was at first unable to comprehend the magnitude of the money. Her grandson was super-rich and she, the grandmother, would never have to worry about money ever again. She did not even need men any longer. In the past, she had only ever needed men for their money.

Neither Theo or Tilda gave one thought to the man who had been incinerated, half in and half out of his tank. Neither of them had ever wanted the man, only his money. They brought out the best French champagne and began to celebrate.

# 3

The English spring came to Charles Farquhar with snowdrops, crocuses and an avalanche of social invitations. His speech in the House of Lords had been to help Matt and warn the British of impending disaster in South Africa, but it had also alerted every social-climbing mother in London where the affluence of Thatcherism had put fortunes into hands that wished to use the money to gain a permanent place in the way of things.

A countess in the family was a prize that many thought the epitome of social arrival, and the fact that the old pile of stones, even if it was still in hock to the inland revenue, was still in the family sent a number of rich bitches into a frenzy of desire. There was a lot more money in England than hereditary titles, the new ones mostly of life-peerages which came when the old goats had done whatever they had set out to do. Charles at thirty was a target for the nouveau riche that sent the mothers off in a hunt which made some of their daughters blush.

There were parties, flats to be borrowed (stocked with everything including the daughter), weekends in the country and prattling flattery that Charles let flow over him like so much water over the duck's proverbial back. If Sophia had ignored him, here were a number of young ladies to whom he could return the compliment while having a lot of fun. The thought of Sophia married made going back to Port St Johns as pointless as living in the damp and cold of the family castle all on his own. In the south of England, the lilac was blooming in white and purple, the trees were breaking out in leaves of the palest green and the east winds had returned to Siberia. In a perverse kind of way, Charles was enjoying himself.

ISIDORE SOCRATES SALVADORI, born Jack Kemp in an earlier life, knew the value of belted earls more than Sophia van Hoek, and was delighted to give Charles a job in his Bond Street gallery, not worrying what time he arrived in the morning or the condition of his head. With so many rich mothers out to impress, Isidore marked everything up thirty per cent and laughed at how easy it was to part fools from their husbands' money. The most that many of the wives had done in their lives was to provide the man with a daughter. The husbands more interested in other things than middle-aged women, were happy to write out the cheques.

"My wife has jolly good taste. I mean, look at this painting. The earl of Lothianmore sold it to her, you know, in that Italian's gallery in Bond Street. Don't know much about paintings myself, but this one's good. Even I can see that. Young Lothianmore's taking out my daughter – crazy about her. We'll have to fix up the castle, but what's money for, anyway, I ask you? Great speech in the Lords. Go a long way, young Charles. Best thing the British can do in South Africa is get out. Waste of time. Macmillan worked that out in the sixties.

"I'm all for the common market. Made a fortune. Bigger than America and, when the Russians collapse, there'll be a huge market in the East. You read Gorbachev's Perestroika? Man's a capitalist trying to get out. All this communism and socialism never works in the end. Can't expect something for nothing in this world. Started with nothing myself. Just goes to show. Imagine a grandson of mine being the earl of Lothianmore."

Charles was more than happy to play the game, having first discussed the morality of it all with Duncan Fox, the skipper.

"They'd waste it on something else, those women. That type are only happy flashing money. Even with you out of their lives, Charles, they'll still tell everyone who comes into the house who sold them the painting and how their daughter decided not to live in a draughty old castle in Scotland."

"Anything Isidore sells is valuable, a little over-priced for today, but valuable. The Bernard Strovers have doubled in price now the word has gone out that the painter's finished. Isidore keeps his own Strovers locked away. The paintings are what matter, not the controversy about who the painter was. Probably adds to the value; bit of mystery. Never did

Shakespeare any harm. Take the commission you make on the sales to the mothers as money well-earned and have some fun. Always have fun when you can, young Charles ... So you really think there will be a civil war in South Africa?"

"I'm convinced of it. The ANC with their 'comrades' in the townships have effectively kicked out the white government, made the place totally ungovernable. The kids can't even go to school half the time. And if the ANC comes back from exile, you think the comrades, with their kangaroo courts and the charming practice of necklacing a man with a rubber tyre, filling it with petrol and setting it on fire, will want to give up power? Power's a bigger drug than money. One of the reasons I enjoyed Port St Johns; no power, no money and the girl I loved thought old English titles quaint but irrelevant. We lived as individuals without the false face of materialism. Over here you need a fortune to live half as well, and most people are only interested in what you have got"

"Why don't you go back?" Duncan asked him.

"She married her old boyfriend." The jaw had set again, the frivolity gone. "I'll just have to stay with selling paintings to the mothers. I do have some fun. Just watching them is quite a laugh. Well, I suppose it's a laugh, I'm not sure any more where Western society has taken us. Too far from the soil. Too far from the truth. It's a very false life, Mister Fox."

"They don't think so, Charles. They think having money is all you need. Why, people fight over money! They think it the most important thing on earth: comfort, security, culture. The arts. The products of civilisation. If man had wanted to live in a cave, he would have stayed in the one he came from instead of constantly striving to better his uncomfortable lot on earth. People like clean sheets and running water, heat at the press of a switch, transport at the turn of a key. People like to be comfortable. I don't understand this Gray. Maybe it's the artist in him that goes against the grain all the time. Maybe he sees more than me."

"He says people have lost sight of how little they need to live comfortably," said Charles. "That there's too much effort required to live well in the formal sector. He says that somewhere fairly soon the graph of happiness is crossed by the graph of wealth, and thereafter the quality of life decreases with the responsibility. He says there are too many freeloaders demanding the right to take money from those who have done the work. He prefers to use his strength and intellect to look after people he knows, not the masses who demand because they are in the majority and have the majority vote. They said he was exploiting; he said he was providing. Look what happened when he went back to help! They destroyed him. He says the social democratic system, like the communist system, will eat out its own stomach and die. He says in life you can't go on taking and putting nothing back, as in the end the treasure chest is empty.

"Everyone in this urban society is marking up the price. Soon the price of the ordinary things will be too much, and down will come the stock exchange and the monetary systems and everything will collapse. You can't grow too much food on the forty-seventh floor of a Manhattan high-rise, and how do you get down when someone switches off the electricity? People here are too busy pushing around book entries and paying with pieces of paper. Everything will be fine until someone breaks the chain of confidence and asks to be paid in real money, which is a bag of grain or a kilogramme of sugar. Matt says we are living in a fool's paradise and that his paradise on Second Beach is the only one that is real. Who knows? Man's been trying to find out the answer ever since he learnt to think. All civilisations eventually fall. The question is how long will this one last?"

JONATHAN HOLLAND HAD FOUND the arms cache three months before the security police, having followed the footsteps of the minstrel boy into the cave of the ancient mariners, and it had jolted him back to life. However much he tried, war followed him. There was no escaping in a cloud of dagga smoke. War hunted him just as he had hunted the terrs in Rhodesia.

He had gone out down the coast by himself, Raleen having long left him under the wild fig tree to blow his mind out on his own. She was back baking bread and providing a vital link in the chain for the colony. The withdrawal was worse than anything else he had experienced in his life, but he had stayed with the guns and the rockets for three weeks, swimming in the sea and living off mussels, oysters and crayfish.

As the drug dwindled in his bloodstream his hunger increased to a craving and he climbed a wild fig tree to eat what the birds had left. It was the fruit of the wild fig, the small berry that countered the craving of the dagga and slowly freed his body from the drug. He knew it had eaten some of his brain and would have killed him in the end but, when he walked back to Second Beach and knocked on Carel van Tonder's door, he was sane and in full control of his faculties. His hair was lank down his back and he stank from washing in salt water, but his eyes were clear and he remembered where he went to school and the name of his mother, and had stopped talking to Ding-dong Bell as if his friend were alive and next to him. He had been a long time in the wilderness.

Together they had returned to the cave, taking the sea route in the ski-boat, and carefully carried out to the beach a selection of arms that would protect the colony and the surrounding black village against the total breakdown of law and order that had become endemic in most of sub-Saharan Africa. Carefully, they had buried their own cache of arms, and told no one.

"If he catches up with me again, I want to be ready," said Jonathan. "Ding- dong always said you had to look after number one. You think I can help out on the ski-boat and catch fish?"

"Why not, man? Maybe those guns have done some good. You had a good shock, man; I thought you were gone."

Then Carel shook his head. He had been trying hard with Raleen. It just wasn't meant for him to have a wife. "You want to stay here with me? Maybe drink beer. No pot. That stuff stinks. I should know. How I made my big living. No, man, can't do that without hurting other people, see. Never thought the time would come when old van Tonder would share a hut with an Englishman. Fishing's a good life. A man's job. Just got to make sure we don't go out when there's big holes in the sea. This is a wild coast, man."

WHEN THE AGREEMENT BETWEEN RUSSIA, America and South Africa over the independence of Namibia began to work, Hector Fortescue-Smythe knew his life's work had come to nothing. Ostensibly, a Marxist state would come into being in the old South West Africa, but the quid pro quo was the removal of all Cuban forces from Angola, leaving the real power in the hands of the anti-communists. With Afghanistan, the Russians were in full retreat, and the prophecy of Hector's handler, his warning, had come about with the speed of panic. At the age of fifty-two, Hector found himself with nothing to show for his life; his only reward was a claw hand and the memory of a girl he might have loved.

The lilacs were blooming in the garden of the country estate, the birds were chirping in the hedgerows, his Sussex cows calved down and the bulls were sold for beef, and nature went on all around as if nothing had ever changed.

There were April showers, as there always had been in all the years the island had been set in its silver sea. Young lovers went about their business in the country lanes and the day-trippers from London marvelled at the beauty of the country spring, but it was all over for Hector, alone in his mansion on the hill, his only companion, once a week, the local parson for a game of chess. He felt too old and too dejected to go and look for anything else. He had had his life.

The housekeeper kept out of his way and through the winter had laid the fire and cleaned it out in the morning, often finding Hector asleep in the chair in front of the dead fire, his claw band on the carpet. If the rain had passed over, he would tramp out into his fields and visit his bull, the father of all the Sussex calves, and he would stroke the animal's nose, his two Spaniels keeping their distance. If it was raining, he would just look out of the window and wonder what it had all been about.

No one in the movement came anywhere near him anymore, not even Luke, who had now seen his future and the future of his country move further away from Moscow. There was going to be a reward for Luke, and Hector had been glad for him as he watched so many of the others get off the communist train that they had used as much as the party intended using them in turn.

It was all part of the process of living, history changing the guard, shifting the limited wealth from one privileged group to another, often the same people dressed in different clothes, though the idea of joining the conservative party left a hollow, lonely ring that made him wonder whether all the philosophy he had attributed to his communist beliefs was no more than a blink in man's unsuccessful struggle to govern himself. A hollow dream? He wondered, isolated in his country estate. He was of the conclusion that he knew nothing any more.

THE NEWS that spread through the ANC's London office sent them all into smiles and laughter. The arrogance of the apartheid wall had split and the gap was there for all the world to see. The National Party government, the creator and the perpetrator of separate development, was talking to Nelson Mandela in his prison.

It was the beginning of the end, and all the exiles turned their minds to home and the possibility of returning to the land of their birth. The sport boycotts, the trade sanctions, the wars in Namibia and Rhodesia where the ANC had fought alongside their liberation brothers, had all been worth the pain. One man, one vote was going to be a reality in South Africa.

Luke, sitting at his desk and thinking of all the lost years of sacrifice, began to cry silently. It had all taken too long; so much of his life was now spent. And then through his tears he smiled, and rose to join the others in celebrating the historic news. For a brief moment, his mind had let him walk down the beach at Port St Johns. There would be sons for him coming home, for his old age, for his future, and his sons would be free in the land of his father's ancestors.

When the weather was good, they sat Matt on his wooden chair outside the rondavel so he could look out over the sea and feel the heat of the sun, the sun which they hoped would heal the terrible shocks his body had taken on the fourth floor of John Vorster Square. When her work was done, Lorna sat next to Matt, holding his hand and feeling the trembling.

He had begun to feed himself, albeit badly, which was all the encouragement the family needed. The old black man, whom the paramount chief had sent, had boiled barks and herbs and made him drink, and shown Lorna what to do when he returned to his kraal. It was the black man's *muti* that was bringing him round, along with the love from his family.

Six months had fled with the African winter since they had brought him home, and he could talk and smile with his eyes. When the sun was too hot, Lorna moved him beneath the fronds of the wild banana trees where he listened to the birds, the sea and the chattering of the vervet monkeys from the coastal forest behind, and tried with all his strength to bring his spirit down from the clouds, where he flew with the hawks and the eagles, back to his body.

But each time he lost his concentration and floated up again, to drift in the thermals and look down on the beach and watch his children playing in the surf, and see all around from his birds-eye view the colony at its work – the ski-boat going out, the leather work being crafted, the potter's wares out in the sun from the furnace to paint, the jewellery of the bangle man glinting in the sun, hot bread from the bakery hut, the painters painting, the gardeners' tending the vegetable patches, the family of tame pigs in the forest, geese, chickens, pumpkins, yellow-red on the roofs of the huts, clothes being embroidered with beads, sandals in the making, men carving driftwood, the sculptors facing the tower of marble from the old quarry, men with headbands, women in kaftans, children naked in the sun. From between the floating softness of the clouds, never once was there a shout of anger.

Matt enjoyed flying with the hawks and the eagles, and never really wanted to come down; he would willingly have stayed, floating close to heaven, were it not for Lorna and Peace, Robert and Sipho, who so much wanted him to come down and join them on the beach.

• • •

Antonio van Perreira dos Santos Cassero had not left Angola with the Cuban air force. He had exchanged his peaked cap for an old straw sombrero that kept the harsh African sun from his eyes. He had forsaken Castro and socialism, but not his God, and God had surely led him back to Africa, to the land of his mother's ancestors.

With his gratuity and the money he had saved as a colonel in the air force, there was money to buy an old tractor with all its implements and coffee seedlings from the only nursery left in Angola. They had let him take over the old plantation, no one being really interested in whether he did or not. The only money available was in Luanda, donated by aid programmes, the royalties the American and French oil companies paid the MPLA and diamonds, although most of the stones were smuggled out of the country. Growing coffee in the bush was definitely not the reason the MPLA elite clung to power.

No one had given Antonio title to the land, but everyone he spoke to in government said he would be welcome to the derelict farm as no one else wanted the place, and it was best he took a gun in case the UNITA rebels wanted whatever he was able to grow. They looked at the thin, gaunt man, not nearly so impressive without his uniform and his MIG23, and their look was one of puzzled curiosity as to why a man would voluntarily wish to go live in the bush, a man who could fly the best Russian jets.

Two of them had suggested he was better off joining the Angolan air force if he wished to stay. They had laughed and said there would always be pay for soldiers in Africa … He had gone anyway; he had had enough of killing people and being paid to destroy. Antonio wished to build, to own a lush estate like his Spanish ancestors, and he was going into the bush to dig a farm that his children and his children's children would inherit. He would be the founder of a new dynasty that would last a thousand years.

He had seen the old coffee estate from the air, situated in the heart of Angola in Huambo province, a hundred and sixty kilometres from the town of Huambo where there were still some supplies and also a railway to take his coffee to the coast in seven years' time. The old colonial house had half fallen down, which had saved it from the war, as there was nothing of value left on the plantation.

He drove in the tractor on the back of an army five-tonne truck that had belonged to the Cuban air force and which had been 'lost', along with its spares, on its way back to Cuba. Antonio had rationalised that there had to be some perks for a Cuban colonel. In the truck were many tools and engines and a generator, the foundation of his workshop that would force the old plantation back to life. Three Angolan members of his staff had agreed to help and had journeyed with him, two of them bringing their families. The war was over, they hoped, and a new life beckoned, which was better than nothing in Luanda. Only a few of the elite could milk the aid programmes and divert the oil revenues.

The first task was the vegetable garden, down by the crocodile-infested river, with a purloined diesel pump pulling water from the river to irrigate the parched red soil that groaned under the heat of the sun. While flying, Antonio had given a lot of thought to his project, imagining the problems of each task that would have to be completed to make his dream come true.

He had planned well, and the truck disgorged the means that would fight the bush. The seedlings had quickly been placed under eighty per cent shade cloth and watered twice a day. Part of the roof in the house had been repaired and three of the outbuildings made liveable for his staff. He was going to live alone as the planter right from the start, creating the chain of command he understood from the military. Inside the planter's clothes, under the straw sombrero, he was still the colonel, and a colonel demanded respect.

The termites had destroyed the old coffee plants, but at the end of the first year he had planted thirty hectares of new coffee, and they were pumping enough water from the river to irrigate in the dry season, though diesel fuel was difficult to buy in Huambo. Antonio bought three windmills and built a reservoir on the high ground above his lands so that he could open the tap and flood-irrigate his small coffee trees. It was the breakthrough that was going to make his plantation viable while the politicians kept fighting each other. UNITA without South Africa and America would be as strong as the MPLA without Cuba and Russia. The politicians had all talked peace and gone on killing each other, but the news for Antonio was spasmodic in his splendid isolation where he had turned the old bungalow on the hill overlooking the river into a liveable house.

The staff had grown, and Antonio was the only one without a wife. The sound of children was music to his ears, and he was happy with himself and the slow solid steps of progress. The war and Cuba were a long way away, and he thanked his God every night for his salvation and promised to build a chapel on his land the following year.

The plantation, even without a coffee crop, was self-sufficient. The days ran into nights and the weeks into months, and the small trees grew with gentle care and adequate water. The weeds and termites were kept out, along with the small buck and the wild pigs. Antonio van Perreira dos Santos Cassero was happy with his life, and so were the people around him.

WHEN JOHN DE LA CRUZ turned thirteen he was sent to boarding school, and the separation nearly broke his mother's heart, the boy having been Chelsea's sole companion for so many years. Understanding that English would be the language of European business, she had used all her savings to send him to an English public school, having kept up his English at home, despite her having told Luke that he would have to speak Portuguese to the boy if he wished to be understood. Chelsea knew what it had been like to be poor and to live in constant fear of her life in Lusaka, and her John was going to be so much part of the European establishment that nothing would ever throw him down into the pits of poverty. The winter term at Cranleigh School in the Surrey countryside was not the best time for a boy born out of Africa who lived in Lisbon to face his first English winter, but he was quite happy to be among boys of his own age and out of his female dominated environment.

Luke's son was very dark, with thick curly black hair, but the surprise was the chiselled European features of his Nordic ancestors under the black skin. He was not the only black boy at Cranleigh, and the days of bullying new boys and freezing them in heatless dormitories were over. Chelsea had chosen Cranleigh as the boy had taken to playing the piano at an early age, and it was the music scholarship that he won which earned him entry to the school and helped Chelsea pay for the fees. John was a very tall boy for his age, taking after his father in this regard, and the first rude remark about his colour had the boys calling him Cassius Clay. After the fight behind the fives courts, he settled down to receive an education his mother knew would take him onto university. What his mother did not know was that, when he arrived at Cranleigh School, he told everyone his name was John Mbeki.

"Why do you wish to change your name, young man?" asked his house tutor.

"My mother changed my name. My father is Luke Mbeki and he's going to be president of South Africa"

"We have no record of your father from when you won our scholarship."

"Would you please phone him, sir, and tell him his son John is at

Cranleigh," requested the boy. "He'll confirm who I am. Just phone the ANC office in London. Everyone knows Luke Mbeki."

"The name is familiar." The master shook his head. "What next is going to happen to England?" he asked himself but, being aware of the political implications, he made the call and confirmed the boy's story.

When the boy was told his father was coming down to the school on the first exeat weekend, John knew he was eventually going back to Africa, that he was going to be an African despite whatever his mother wanted him to be. When they showed him the music room, the first thing he played was jazz, much to the consternation of the music master who had heard the recording of Chopin's nocturnes played by the boy for his scholarship application.

PEACE GRAY WAS as wild as the sea, and she had grown up with the pounding and whispering in her ears. She could read and write and play the flute, but any attempt to extend her formal education was met with dedicated resistance, as it would take her away from her mother and father and the colony.

She had watched her father grow stronger over the eighteen months since he had returned in the ambulance and she was sure that any week now he would pick up his paintbrush and begin to paint once more. The palsy in his hands had almost gone, and Peace watched him look covetously at the paintings her mother had carefully left in the best places on the walls of the rondavel where the sun came in each day to fire the canvases to life. When she held his hand and looked out to sea, to the gulls and the shoals of pilchards, he said he was almost back on earth, that soon he would stop flying high with eagles and hawks, and she had understood.

"To stop the pain, I took my mind out of my body, darling, and it was difficult to bring it down again."

Matt was lying back with his eyes shut, speaking in little more than a whisper, but the peace was gradually returning to his face. "You're going to be a very beautiful woman, like your mother. My mother was beautiful too. Now, let me sit in the sun and you go and swim," and, as she left, she saw him leave the earth and go and fly with the eagles again. She had grown used to the sudden change and her mother had told her to be patient.

Peace was long in the leg and her skin was golden-brown, kissed by the sun and the salty sea air, and her hair was almost white. For hours she sat on Carel's surfboard, coming in with the waves, balanced perfectly, her supple body moving with the curl of the wave. She knew all the colours of the sea and all its moods and, angry or gentle, she loved whatever it gave, singing with wild abandon when the wind whipped up the wild waters into crashing waves that hurtled at the shore. When it was gentle and lapped the sun-drenched shore, she sang a lullaby she had learnt from the minstrel boy, and then she played the flute he had made and taught her how to play.

She often wondered where he was, and whether he thought of the colony. She was going to marry a minstrel boy with long lank hair and eyes full of sadness, then laughter, then all the bursting power of joy and happiness leaping from his face … Poor Raleen. So sad for her love to go away, which was why there was no way she could let them send her to that horrid Johannesburg to go to school. What for? She was going to live all her life in the colony where people loved each other, did things for each other and rarely quarrelled. Peace Gray hated quarrels that upset the harmony of the day.

Looking back at her father with a brief glance from the bottom of the path, she ran out onto the sand and into the sea, her young firm breasts giving only the slightest movement as she plunged headlong into the oncoming waves. It gave her intense pleasure to know that Matt was watching.

THE SCREAM WAS terrible and rent the still night air, waking the dogs and people. Lorna tried to wake him, but the scream grew worse, high-pitched and terrified, a tormented scream. The colony came running, but Matt lay on the mattress on the floor screaming at the night. Shaking would not stop the screams or bring him out of his nightmare, and Lorna feared for his life.

Below the heaven where he sailed, the thermal air was Africa in all its details, and Matt soared down to visit with the hawks and eagles circling in the wind, turning, changing with the wind, but always circling closer to the great plain and forests of Africa. It was a sight of great beauty, with so many birds circling in the wind, graceful, high above the verdant land where the rains were good and the rivers full. With his eyes of great vision, Matt was able to see the elephant herds, the teeming numbers of rhinoceros, the vast herds of buck, impala, springbok and kudu in the thorn thickets, a pride of lion, villages of people, the smoke of the cooking fires curling to the sky, and there was peace on earth. The great birds circled in the wind. Matt flew down to join them, circling lower, moving down the thermals, ever reaching for the earth and the great embrace of Africa and the circling birds.

As he came closer, the birds looked up, but the faces did not show the majesty of eagles or the pride of hawks, but the avarice of vultures. As he joined the birds, they were all the same: vultures in the wind, circling downward to take the pickings of the earth. Down they flew, where Matt now saw that the rhinoceros were dead, their horns torn from the bodies; the tusk-less elephant were dead, and the cooking fires of the villagers were the burning huts of the people. The rains had not fallen, the rivers were dry and, as the vultures circled lower in the wind, Matt had begun to scream.

# PART 6

# 1

On the 2 February 1990, President FW de Klerk made a speech in Parliament which stood South Africa on its head. Apartheid was dead, the ANC and the South African communist party were unbanned, and Nelson Mandela was to be let out of jail after twenty-seven years' incarceration.

The total onslaught had evaporated. The word with as many meanings as love, democracy, was mouthed by everyone, and the civil war in Natal took on a new intensity as the old forces of law and order were unable to understand which side they were fighting. The political military vacuum was to be paralysing.

The ANC camp in Angola exploded with joy at the news. They were going home. Amnesty had been declared. They had won their struggle, and Frikkie Swart in the wire cage of his prison watched them fire their guns in the air with the wry smile of cynicism. He was fifty-three years old, without an ounce of fat left on his body, a fully grey beard, and eyes that saw a distance far greater than his cage. Given a horse, a mauser rifle and an old felt hat, Frikkie would have looked like any Boer Bittereinder in 1902.

"Maybe they let you out, Boer," shouted a guard.

Frikkie turned away from him to disguise the half smile and the flash of excitement in his eyes. His people had enough arms stashed away to let the true Boers fight for their land for three generations. What was one little speech in a nation's history of three hundred and fifty years? They had fought the might of the British Empire, twenty thousand armed farmers against a million troops and, were it not for the concentration camps where the British herded women and children to die of disease, they would have chased the Brits into the sea. Africa had always been tough for the Boer. What had changed? The people, the volk, always stayed behind long after the politicians with their great new ideas were dead.

Frikkie did not believe that this was the end of all he stood for. Unlike his old enemy, Hector Fortescue-Smythe, Frikkie was sure his way of life would survive in one form or another, and that his faith would be vindicated. He already had some contingency plans in mind to prolong the present some distance into the future. And if not – well, he had prepared a comfortable refuge overseas.

LUKE MBEKI HEARD the news in London and it made him feel older than his fifty-seven years. They had told him he would be one of the first exiles to go home, and the enormity of the task ahead was evident for the first time. To change from a militant liberation movement to the government of the country and fulfil all the easily made promises was going to be more difficult than raising funds for the struggle. Luke made a silent prayer that they were good enough to govern a modern, sophisticated country that was immersed in a sea of Third World poverty.

Half an hour after speaking to the headmaster of Cranleigh School, the phone rang in Luke's flat.

"I have your son in my study, Mister Mbeki."

"Thank you … John. Have you heard? We're going home," he told his eldest son.

"And school?"

"You must meet your brothers. Go to school with them. You must become part of Africa."

"Where are we going to live, Dad?"

"Port St Johns. I said we were going home." Luke was excited.

"And Mother?"

"This time she will listen. We are not young, your mother and I. I will have a home. A place to offer. No more running away. She wants security, and now I can offer her all the security in the world. Chances are, John, I will be in the government. You will see. All our dreams we talked about are coming true. A free, democratic South Africa. All the sun and beauty, all the joy of belonging to a country. Pride. Future. Being able to do something that will really make a difference."

"When are we leaving?" John was somewhat apprehensive. He had never known South Africa. It made him feel insecure.

"Once de Klerk has signed my amnesty."

"Do you really think it will all happen?"

"Oh, yes, my son. It will all happen. For once in my life, I am going to find out what it feels like to be really happy."

"Will Sipho be there?"

"Of course. He's my son as much as you. Please thank the headmaster. I'm going to phone your mother right now."

PEACE GRAY WATCHED the incoming waves behind her with consummate care until she saw the one she was waiting for, and began to paddle with her hands. As the big wave swelled to carry up her surfboard, she caught its momentum and stretched up from her kneeling position to stand and ride the wave.

It was her thirteenth birthday and, so far as she was concerned, being a teenager made a lot of difference. Her body was tanned a rich copper and the curves that had been promising for months had taken shape. Her blonde hair was white from surfing and contrasted with the blue eyes inherited from her parents. Her skin was as smooth as silk, her face oval with high cheekbones and a strong nose. Peace was more striking than beautiful, but her best feature was her smile, the soft gentle smile of her father when he was relaxed and away from the troubles of the world.

When she came ashore, with the last of the sun burning the underbelly of the clouds a deep red, her brother Robert was waiting patiently on the beach. He was eight years old, and he and Sipho Mbeki shadowed Peace wherever she went,

"When will you teach me?" they both demanded at the same time.

"When Uncle Carel makes you a small board."

"He says we're too little"

"Then maybe you are."

"Can we carry your board?"

Matthew Gray, a much improved Matthew Gray, watched his young family walk across the beach to the path that would lead up to their home.

"They must have smelt the cooking," he said to his wife.

"She's frightened of sharks at night," said Lorna. "You think Luke coming back will change Sipho?"

"For us, you mean? Probably. We only had him to look after."

"I've brought him up from a baby."

"This is a community. We all belong to each other. Anyway, no one's going to separate those two boys, not even their fathers."

"Why should they ...? No, it's a change, Matt. Change always does funny things."

"Better get the food bowls out. Those kids are going to be hungry."

"You really are better?"

"Yes, I am," confirmed Matt, who was beginning to speak positively again. "Still the dreams, but I'm enjoying painting, and anyway those sods that did it to me are on their way out ... You know something, I think this paella needs a little more chilli."

"You think so? ... Maybe you're right. Isn't that a beautiful sunset? ... With all this change, I want you to promise me we'll never leave Second Beach again."

"Never, Lorna. I promise. We're going to grow old gracefully in paradise without any interference from other people. Give me a kiss. You look absolutely delicious back dropped by that sunset."

CHELSEA DE LA CRUZ looked around her small villa in Lisbon at all the small things she had bought to make a home, somewhere that was hers; a safe place, familiar, a place that left her content with her life after a rewarding day at her job.

When the men had been calling to take her out, there was a fullness to her life, but after she turned forty the flow of suitors came to a stop. In her mind she no longer felt attractive, could appreciate why men would no longer spend their money on a woman well past her prime. Her wide mouth was suddenly too wide, her big breasts were definitely sagging, and she no longer enjoyed the music with the same abandon. John's being away at boarding school had introduced her to the clutch of loneliness which made her reflect on the futility of her life.

What had she done? What had she ever achieved? A son out of wedlock and a job in the insurance industry that had once even seemed exciting. All she had to look forward to was a pension in nineteen years' time, and the four walls of her little villa with its pot plants and flowers and the peculiar sweet smell of Portugal, lush in its ancient history with more monuments to an ancient past than the last hundred years. And after her pension, how many years on her own?

And now he wanted her to go home; his home, not hers. Hers was long lost in African history, the country of her birth, Mozambique, torn to shreds by civil war and starvation. How could South Africa be any different to all the civil wars of Africa? The men plunged into their paths of glory. He was taking her son, and all the warnings of the more prudent woman were brushed aside.

Chelsea laughed out loud. He had promised her security and a home in a country with at least seventeen divergent factions, all armed. And all this they expected Mandela to weld into a homogeneous state! The best will in the world would not make a silk purse out of a sow's ear, an expression her mother, dead with her father in the Mozambique civil war, had quoted to make so many of her political points against Frelimo. But had Renamo, for whom her parents had gone back to Mozambique, been any different?

She had had her fill of African politics. For Chelsea, they were all greedy bloodsuckers with a terminal lust for power and a tendency to kill innocent people who got in their way. But she was lonely. Terribly lonely. They were all she had.

Lisbon or Luke? ... She wondered if he still played in a band, and giggled. And Matt and Port St Johns and Sipho Mbeki, whom she had refused to bring up. Luke said the colony was one big family, and if there was anything she wanted more in the world it was a family, somewhere to belong.

Chelsea waited a week before picking up the phone and calling Luke's flat in London. For the first time in many years, she was going to allow her heart to rule her head. A lonely slide into old age had become the most appalling thought in her life. She resigned her job and put her furniture into storage.

"Keep my pension contributions in the fund," she told them, with her last shred of sanity.

Whilst Chelsea was booking her flight back to Africa, Antonio van Perreira dos Santos Cassero, the man who had destroyed Teddie Botha's tank, was contemplating his year old coffee trees with satisfaction, the Angolan civil war the furthest thing from his mind.

Richard Williams, the old parish priest, looked at Hector Fortescue-Smythe with compassion. Hector had lost the thread of their game of chess some time ago and it was cold in the caravan parked at the bottom of the estate as far away from habitation as was possible.

Hector's only visitor for many months had been the village priest; the caretaker and his wife were forbidden to come anywhere near the caravan or to tell anyone the whereabouts of the millionaire recluse. The village bank manager held power of attorney to pay the household bills, and solicitors in London kept account of his considerable wealth. Smythe-Wilberforce Industries was run by professional managers and the family now had nothing to do with the running of the company.

The two men from the South African communist party, both white, had been watching the estate since ten o'clock in the morning, and had seen the vicar ride his bicycle down the rickety path and into the trees, where he had stayed longer than a winter's day suggested. The trees were leafless and the ground sodden under foot, only the occasional pigeon bursting out of the barren trees to fly below the low, slate-grey sky that had hung over Surrey for most of February.

The vicar opened the caravan door in answer to the loud banging. Two Spaniel dogs jumped down the steps and went off into the trees to relieve themselves.

"Mister Fortescue-Smythe?" The reverend gave them a queer look and pulled at the inside of his dog-collar with a finger.

"I don't allow visitors," bellowed Hector, "Call the prime minister. I told him quite plainly myself. No visitors." He was huddled in his old cavalry overcoat from his early days of national service, which contrasted with the slippers and his dishevelled head of hair. There was a faint smell of stale urine permeating the caravan.

"We're from the SACP. The party has been unbanned." The two men, one on the steps, were trying to look into the caravan. "We need your help. Money. You promised us money when the time came to take over South Africa."

"I don't have any money. Can't you see? Call the prime minister and please shut the door … My God, you let the dogs out! Where are the dogs? It's your move, vicar."

"It's yours, Hector."

"Oh, dear … Tell those fools to go away. Communism's dead. The dead dream. Gone with Perestroika. Gone with Gorbachev. Go away … Dogs, where are the dogs? Vicar, it's your move."

The vicar kindly took the men by the shoulders and eased them away from the caravan towards the tree and the brown, dead bracken.

"Gentlemen, your journey is wasted. He has withdrawn from the world. Maybe he is mad. Maybe not but, whichever way, he will not be rational under any circumstances. His London solicitors have applied to the court to administer his estate. Ask them for money if you will. Anyway, I wish you luck. Now, where are those dogs? … I wish he'd put a heater in his caravan and I wish he'd make the next move. Dogs! … where are those dogs?"

THE PORT ST JOHNS municipality tried to fill in the potholes down the main street and gave up, instead commissioning a large banner that they draped across from the Needles Hotel to a tree on the other side of the road. Lopsided but articulate, the banner proclaimed that the town was welcoming back the prodigal son, 'WELCOME HOME LUKE MBEKI'.

Farther into the three street town, old bunting hung from decaying buildings and ANC flags waved from some of the windows. No one was quite sure which day the great freedom fighter was returning, but they were not going to miss their moment of glory, reflected in the greatness of their prodigal son. It was Africa time. Comrade Mbeki was coming home, and nothing else mattered. The day of salvation was upon them, and all the poverty would be made to disappear.

The town waited a week and then ten days, the banner being put back in the tree three times, the last time smudged by muddy tyre marks when it had fallen down on a rainy night. The excitement of expectation was dampened by the weather and, when Luke stepped off the bus that had brought him from Umtata, no one knew who he was. The sign so early in the morning was on the ground and most of the bunting had blown off in the wind. The town looked its shabby old wonderful self, and Luke felt as excited as a young boy, picking up his small grip to start the long walk to Second Beach and his younger son and oldest friend, and the kraal in the forest where he was born on the same day as Matthew Gray.

Idly, he stepped over the mud-spattered banner and saw what it said. Ten brass bands could not have meant more; the tears came swiftly down his face and there was a small pain prickling behind his eyes. He was home. After twenty-nine years in exile, he was home.

By the time he reached the Cape Hermes Hotel to walk the short cut to Second Beach, the sun was shining. What had once been a grand hotel was empty of people, the road in front falling into the sea. It had been the same in Umtata, the capital of the Transkei, and the soil erosion on either side of the road down made him question more seriously their chances of turning the tides of poverty.

The population had exploded, with huts on every hill and goats chewing the grass down to below the roots, leaving the land barren. The images from his youth of lush grazing and fat sleek cattle were replaced by grinding poverty and dirt. The homeland had been independent for fourteen years, run by his own people, and the results were a disaster. The only new things he had seen in Umtata were the houses of the government ministers and the university, whose degrees were recognised by no one of importance in the world. The work to be done was prodigious.

He walked on, cutting across the tarred road, where he turned left and followed the coastline, his mind running ahead. They would have the magistrate marry them; Matt would give away the bride and their son would be the best man. With Matt's help, they would build a house in the kraal, and whenever he could be away from his work he would come back to his home and family to sit in the sun and drink beer, telling them the wonderful tales of all their success, watching them being happy and his sons growing, and no one would be lonely any more.

She had said she would come, and their son had said they would all have a home together and watch South Africa grow from the ashes of apartheid into a prosperous, free, social democracy that would give everyone housing, free health care, free schooling and jobs that would pay them salaries to let them live in dignity, free of the shanty towns and the shacks and the flooding when it rained. With the aid of his family, he was going to help South Africa throw off the last vestiges of colonial bondage and join the real world and the good life they took for granted in America and Europe, took as their right, as his people would take as their right. And only then would the struggle have been fulfilled.

MATT SAW his friend walk down the path through the milkwood trees and emerge onto the beach, a very tall, grey-haired black man, carrying a small grip in one hand and a long staff in the other. The big man hesitated, trying to get his bearings, and Matt grinned with pleasure. He stood up slowly from his seat outside the rondavel on the hill above the sea and walked to the edge, where he waved at the distant figure. There was no mistaking the height of Matthew Gray and Luke waved back and quickened his pace across the soft, white sand to the path that would take him to the hut that he had never seen.

"Better go to him, Chelsea," Matt called softly. "Luke's down on the beach," and he waved again.

Luke strode along the beach, his back as straight as an arrow, the long staff he had found on the side of the road touching the sand rhythmically. A woman ran out of the hut behind Matt and came tumbling down the path. In a moment they were running towards each other, and he had her in his arms.

All the pain was gone, as Matt watched from his height on the hill and Lorna came out, holding Sipho by one hand and Robert by the other. Out to sea, Peace waved from her surfboard, and Carel van Tonder came out onto the beach, followed by Raleen Urbach and Jonathan Holland, hand in hand, and Martin with the black beard. The word spread back to the kraal, and the people came running onto the beach, toy-toying and laughing and shouting, with Matt smiling down on all of them, forgetting the pain in his groin as he watched his beautiful daughter paddle in to shore to join the mayhem on the beach.

They made the fires on the beach that night after Carel came back in the boat with two, good sized copper steenbras. A pig was roasted with the fish; beer and wine were drunk, and the music played as the great night sky, free of pollution, showed them the three layers of heaven and the moon stayed hidden deep in the sea. Sipho met his father for the first time in his memory, and the boys went off to catch themselves a freshwater crab from the old, broken bridge over the lagoon. Chelsea knew she had done the right thing, and laughed as she had not been able to laugh in years.

"Luke, I'm so happy," she said.

"Not as happy as when I get you into the bushes."

"You wouldn't?"

"I would."

"Luke Mbeki, you're depraved"

"That's what makes it so much fun." Chelsea ran away from the light of the fire, and Luke chased her across the beach and into the darkness.

"Where's my dad gone?" asked Sipho, having decided the tall black man would do quite well as his second father.

"Questions like that you don't ask, young man," said Lorna, and Peace giggled from the other side of the fire.

A week later, John de la Cruz, or John Mbeki as he preferred to call himself, arrived at Second Beach to join his parents, and Luke and Chelsea's happiness was complete.

"We want you to join us, Matt," said Luke at the end of his second week, two days after the magistrate had married Luke and Chelsea in a simple ceremony on the beach, with everyone quiet and solemn and deeply impressed by the importance of what they were witnessing, a marriage that would have taken place years before were it not for the struggle.

"What do you mean, old friend?"

"The African National Congress. We need all the financial expertise we can garner."

"I'm a painter, Luke. Every time I have put my head above the parapet, someone has taken a shot, and the last one nearly killed me. I am more than content with my life as it is, and I have promised Lorna we will never again leave Second Beach."

"Will you support us?" pleaded Luke.

"Not if you are going to nationalise the mines, the banks and industry. Are not the communists in charge of the ANC? The Russian-style command economy has been a disaster in every country where it has been tried."

"We want a two-tier system. Leave most industry where it is and redistribute the country's wealth."

"If you want to win anything in this competitive world, you have to have only one strategy, and certainly not two that totally oppose each other. How are you going to redistribute industrial wealth and encourage it to grow, and create jobs at the same time? Let the men of the business conduct the nation's business, and you provide law and order and the legislation which promotes fair, competitive free trade with a social safety net only as wide as the country can afford. And that's my last word on politics, Luke Mbeki,"

"What are you going to do with your trust money?"

"An education trust. We learnt a lot with our little school."

"Who's going to run it?" Luke wanted to know.

"Sunny Tupper."

"When's it going to start?"

"When the country settles down with a freely-elected government. I have not been well. There were many times when my mind did not wish to return to my body. First I will paint, and then I will consider my other responsibilities."

"In the future, will you talk over my problems with me?"

"Whenever you come to Second Beach."

Matt's eyes strayed out to sea. "I wondered how soon it would take Peace to have your John on a surfboard ... He's a natural athlete. Look at that! He's surfing the wave kneeling on the board. She'll have him standing before he goes to school."

FRIKKIE SWART WAS RETURNED to South Africa on the same day that Luke Mbeki took up his post in the new ANC offices in Johannesburg, his son

John having been put into a secondary school in the black township of Soweto.

Frikkie was one of the numbers of political prisoners from all political spectrums to be released as negotiations between the de Klerk government and the ANC began its long, often acrimonious journey to find a solution to governing a country of tribes of peoples more diverse than all the tribes of Europe. The meeting of First and Third World, white and black, was taking place in South Africa as it was unable to do in the city centres of black America or the financial institutions of the world. South Africa, after years of sanctions and the work of the worldwide anti-apartheid movement, was the token gesture of a struggling new world order.

As the exiles and political prisoners returned to normal life, the financial wealth of South Africa bled through the torn cracks of exchange control. And, for every returned exile, a young, well-educated white South African slipped out of the country, taking his bloodline and genes back to the countries that had spawned them in the first place. Europe, America, Canada and Australia welcomed the new immigrants with their skills paid for by apartheid. And, being wise with their immigration policies, they only accepted the best.

Minister Kloss, late of the bureau of state security, was cleaning out his desk in his office of the Union Building in Pretoria when Frikkie Swart was announced.

"Which Mister Swart?" he said in Afrikaans.

"The one who was married to your daughter," said his secretary through the intercom.

"Have him wait." The minister had been whistling all morning as he put his retirement plans into operation. The new South Africa was not for him. They had done many things during the total onslaught that others might consider unethical, but if a man was a terrorist you must kill him first, by any means. No, he was going to Paraguay, and there were a lot of his friends farming there already. Why, they had even called a small village Johannesburg. He soon forgot the man outside who had killed his daughter.

"Mister Swart, Mister Kloss," spoke the intercom.

"Oh, well, better show him in. What does he want?"

Outside Frikkie Swart was allowing his mind to broaden with dreams of sweet revenge and, when the girl showed him into the minister's office, he was shocked to see the cardboard boxes and the signs of departure.

"You'll have to stand; chairs full. What do you want, Swart?" He had hoped the man would die in the ANC camp, but people like Swart had a habit of surviving.

"You leaving, minister?" said Frikkie sweetly, covering up his surprise.

"Not staying for the roof to fall on my head. What are you doing here? Should have enough sense to join your stolen money."

"Which is exactly what you are doing." He gave the minister a hooded, pained, don't-tell-me-I-don't-know-all-about-you look. "I have a plan. One that will turn this disaster into saving the volk for another hundred years.

"They are all coming into the open, every one of their sleepers, ANC, PAC, APLA, MK. All their structures. The perfect targets. Let them settle in for a while, and then we kill their leaders. We will use black men to do the killing. There were many bitter black men where I have just come from, men accused of working for us, tortured to confess. A few hit squads and we destabilise this country so the blacks will go on their knees for us to restore law and order. What I have in mind will set them at each other's throats and make life hell in the townships. And the first one we are going to take out is that bloody commie, Luke Mbeki. He's back, and the idiot doesn't even have a bodyguard."

It was hot in the Zambezi Valley, and Archie Fletcher-Wood was dying from a new strain of malaria. Aldo Calucci's Land Rover had broken down for lack of spare parts that were unobtainable in Zimbabwe. The safari camp on the banks of the Zambezi River was empty of paying customers, the new violence in South Africa chasing the foreign tourists out of the whole of Southern Africa. With a bottle of whisky, Lucky Kuchinski was sitting in a canvas chair next to his friend.

"I'm dying, Lucky," gasped Archie trying unsuccessfully to raise himself to a sitting position. His friend said nothing. "Remember the Congo? Getting lost? ... You leapt out of cars without opening doors ... Can you put on another blanket, Lucky? Africa got me in the end. I'm sixty-four. It was letting down Matt ...You think he understands? I was never like him. And Sunny. Took her for granted. You tell them how sorry I am ... maybe dying's a good thing. What have I got? Exile at the end of my life ... Let down my friends.

"Matt bailed us out. You tried to help and sent Swart to hell ... What did I do! Stayed in the house. Scared. A failure ... He came right into the Congo for us. He made me all my money and, when he needed me, I failed. You think he'd still be my friend, if I told him how sorry I am? Lucky, take off the blankets. The fever's coming. If I don't make it this time, thanks old buddy. Maybe two good friends were all I was meant to have. Maybe it was enough ... If only I hadn't let him down."

The big river flowed on, carrying the summer rains, and at dusk a small herd of buffalo came down to the river to drink. Lucky was drunk and lonely, not knowing what to do with the rest of his life. His best friend was dead and in the morning he would have to bury him.

# 2

When the Russian empire collapsed, it disintegrated in days making the swift decline of the British Empire look slow. One minute the world was faced with a menacing superpower, and within a week it was gone. The ripples of repercussion spread in all directions, catching the South African communist party and their ANC partners without financial or ideological support.

In England, in the caravan in the woods where the buds of spring had turned to summer leaves, Hector Fortescue-Smythe had lost all touch with reality.

"A new world, vicar. One government order. Gone. Anarchy will stay a thousand years. Your move, vicar. I told the prime minister to join the communists. He was a good man. A true socialist. Would have done. Your move, vicar. Helena was her name. A whore, vicar. To love a whore. They can have the stinking world, but for God's sake make a move, vicar!"

The two Spaniels looked up from the caravan floor where the mess was horrible. The vicar had not visited for a month.

CHARLES FARQUHAR, art expert and the manager of the Salvadori art gallery in London, twelfth earl of Lothianmore and one time member of the Second Beach colony at Port St Johns, was married in the small chapel of Lochlothian Castle on the same day that Ben Munroe, American journalist, landed in Johannesburg with his cameraman to cover the mayhem in South Africa's black townships.

The new countess of Lothianmore had paid the government the estate death duties, purchased four hundred hectares surrounding the castle and a ten thousand hectare grouse moor where she intended to entertain the finest in the land. She was rightly of the belief that within five years no one in the right circles would remember that her money came from her daddy out of pop music, that she had been born in a council house and her husband was ten years younger than his wife. It was a marriage of convenience, each giving the other what he or she wanted, and a marriage founded upon a promise more likely to last than the fickle torments of love. Charles, it appeared, was gradually losing his eccentric ways and unexpectedly beginning to fit almost into the mould of a Scottish country squire.

When Sophia van Hoek returned to Second Beach to come to terms with Charles Farquhar, her own marriage to her doctor having failed, she found she was too late. She was thirty-one. The only person happy that Charles was a long way off was Carel van Tonder and, when Sophia went back to the school to teach, Carel set about waiting once again. He had more to offer all of them than they realised, his stash of ANC weapons known only to himself and Jonathan Holland, weapons they would use to defend the colony in the rising tide of South African violence. "We're going to need them one day," he said to Jonathan.

"Not me, Carel. Raleen and I have been through one bush war. Not another civil war. We're leaving, going back to Zimbabwe where nobody is killing anybody. During the war I let go a young lad fighting against us in the Zambezi Valley. Jamba Sithole now has influence in Zimbabwe and Raleen and I have money up north. Jamba has got us back our residence permits."

"When are you going?" asked Carel.

"Tomorrow. I told Matt this morning. Raleen and I are going to buy a farm and settle down. Have some kids to replace her two the terrs killed. Matt said it was the best suggestion I had made for years. Said Mother would be happy. I'll be sad to leave you and the colony, Carel, but I can't take this violence. Leaves you in a state of suppressed tension. You'll be all right. You've got the guns. Look after them all. They may need you sooner than you think."

• • •

FRIKKIE SWART'S plan was to shoot up Luke's car when he went to work in the morning. Frikkie would use a mini-bus taxi and have it look like an extension of the taxi war that had exploded at taxi ranks and along the roads, taking black commuters to work and back.

His men had watched Luke Mbeki first take John to school every morning and then drive to the ANC offices in central Johannesburg. The man had established a routine and went about his daily life as if he was living in a normal society. The talks between the government, the ANC and the other political parties were going too well and the intention was to have the ANC walk out of the talks. Frikkie Swart was enjoying himself back in South Africa, and in eighteen months had established a network of agents across the country, financing his work from an assortment of parties opposed to a unitary state under black, communist-orientated rule.

BEN MUNROE, Matthew Gray's *bête noire* and one time protégé and lover of Gilly Bowles, was now recognised as America's expert on South Africa's transition to democracy having joined an American television station to beam into American homes the carnage in South Africa's townships and his prognosis was not good. Married for the third time to a journalist his own age, he enjoyed the hard work, occasional hard drinking with his new wife and good dinner in a downtown New York restaurant where television celebrities were left to enjoy their food. At fifty-two he was happier than at any other time in his life and had forgiven his mother and father for giving him a childhood that brought back few good memories.

Ben's new cameraman was twenty-nine years old, fearless, good-looking and determined to be right at the heart of news breaking anywhere in South Africa. He always took the pictures that made his network consider him one of the best television cameramen in the world. Clark Goss survived on excitement and adrenaline to make up for his dull upbringing in Kansas City, Missouri, and Ben Munroe was never far behind. Being at the scene very often from a tip-off, he was as aware as Ben that TV networks were used by politicians and terrorists, as the networks fed off the newsworthiness of the daily carnage spread across the world. If people wished to kill for political motives, it was Clark Goss's job to shoot the pictures and Ben's job to report the background into the camera at the end of the day.

A phone call warned them that Luke Mbeki was under threat, and Ben put the name to the face as they sped down the R29 to Alberton, Ben driving with Clark keeping his camera at the ready from the open passenger window. The commuter traffic was heavy for a Tuesday morning, as the previous week's boycotts had been called off and the black people of Soweto wished to make up for the lost hours of work, caused by the ANC calling for mass action to force the government to their point of view at the negotiating table.

The new year had come and gone with an increase in political violence. The low-key civil war in Natal had spilled over into the townships around Johannesburg, with the Zulu hostels warring with the ANC for political turf and the criminal gangs joining the battle on their own account. Generally, criminals were unlikely to be caught as the people were too scared to point fingers for fear of reprisal. Dead bodies lay in the streets in the mornings and the police could find no one to say how the carnage had occurred.

Both Ben and Clark wore bullet-proof vests whenever they entered the townships. Ben knew the streets of Soweto from experience, maps and aerial photographs, and he knew how to drive a car to the limit. Twice before he had arrived at the scene of action before anyone else and he was determined to warn Luke Mbeki before the assassination could take place. Twice he had interviewed the man and recognised him as an educated pragmatist who would be needed more than many of the other more militant politicians when it became the turn of the ANC to rule the country to turn from being the destroyer of the economy to the builder of a new, prosperous, democratic South Africa.

They reached the road leading to the school where John Mbeki was receiving an education that he would have laughed at had he not been drawn into the political mainstream of the school and their struggle for political liberation. His real education came after hours when they reached the small box home that he shared with his mother, half-brother and father.

John had just emerged from the car when he heard two cars speeding down the road to the school entrance in opposite directions: one a minibus, driven by a black with a black passenger, and the other by a white with his passenger pointing what looked like a camera out of the car's rear window. At first John thought the gun that came out of the black's window was to be used on the whites until he saw that the direction it was following pointed at himself and his father. He yelled at his father, "Dad, look out!" and threw himself flat on the pavement.

"You want to play this easy, Clark?" asked Ben, gripping the wheel band.

"Side-swipe him, and fast!" Clark kept his camera turning, having fallen over into the back seat, to film the oncoming mini-bus from the right-hand side, the assassin now half out of the high window with an AK47 rifle that began to fire.

The shots streaked towards the Mbeki car until Ben hit the driver's side a glancing blow, tipping the assassin out of the car with his gun, breaking his neck on the pavement ten metres from where John was covering his head with his hands. The car mounted the dirt pavement, hit the school wall and rebounded onto the road missing John's spread eagled legs and his father's car. The whole assassination attempt was shown to the world just ten minutes later when Ben had checked that Luke and his son were alive and the gunman dead. Chelsea saw the pictures on her television screen and screamed, not sure whether her husband and son were alive until Ben Munroe picked them up from the pavement, the camera switching from the disappearing minibus to film her family on the ground.

Luke had heard his son's warning in time to fall in the gutter next to his car, which took automatic fire down the left side, away from where he lay in the mud and filth. The garbage collectors had been on strike for a week, their mass action joining with the pupils and teachers to intimidate the government.

She waited all day until they came home and then she was hysterical, screaming at her husband and her son, neither of whom had thought Chelsea would see the assassination attempt on television. The telephone in the box house had been out of order for weeks, the white technicians who could repair the fault refusing to come into Soweto for fear of their lives. Chelsea's nightmare was back in living colour. Young Sipho listened to it all and wondered what was going on. He wanted to go home, to Second Beach and his mother Lorna.

Frikkie Swart shrugged. He had all the time in the world. To escape, Luke Mbeki had to be lucky every time. Frikkie only had to be lucky once.

"Keep his nerves tight, man. And the others. Not one of those top bastards will sleep well tonight." He was enjoying himself,

The next day, like clockwork, like puppets on a string, the ANC delegation walked out of the talks with the government.

"Maybe those Americans did us a favour after all," laughed Frikkie.

"Don't get more people looking at a soap opera than this. Those movies make it look good, man. People knew this one was for real; the guy falling out of the minibus was really dead."

"Think they can trace the dead man?"

"Not a chance. And if they do, they'll find he was a card-carrying member of the Inkatha Freedom Party. Relax, man; that dead kaffir was a Zulu. You got to think when you're stirring shit."

THE FREE AND fair elections for a democratic government in Angola had come and gone, and the loser, Jonas Savimbi of UNITA and the American surrogate when he had been fighting the Marxist MPLA had gone back into the bush to continue the civil war, causing the American administration to change sides once again and recognise the MPLA who had fought and won the election.

Antonio van Perreira dos Santos Cassero's coffee plantation was in its third year, with the farm self-sufficient in vegetables, fruit, eggs and meat. By the time the MPLA had swept through his plantation on their way to Huambo, Jonas Savimbi's capital one hundred and sixty kilometres to the northeast, there was not an animal left alive, nor a vegetable left in the ground.

He was forty-six years old. Cuba, without cheap Russian oil and high priced sugar sales, was one step short of collapse. Antonio had nowhere else to go. Laboriously, he set about restoring order from the army's chaos.

The South African defence force, which had fought alongside Jonas Savimbi in the days of the total onslaught of communism, the same war that had killed Teddie Botha and sent Security Lion Insurance and its associates into financial crisis, had left behind some of the most sophisticated artillery in the world, notably the new made-in-Pretoria-because-of-the-arms-embargo G6 howitzer that could take off a door knob at forty-seven kilometres. When the MPLA were routed by UNITA and turned back from Huambo, they went back the way they had come, and the MPLA brigade headquarters set up business in Antonio's farmhouse without bothering to ask permission, rudely forcing Antonio to leave his home. He caught a ride on an air force support vehicle giving his rank and squadron in the Cuban air force. The day he arrived in Luanda, the UNITA gunners were given the co-ordinates of the MPLA brigade headquarters. In five minutes there was nothing alive in the house.

In Luanda, along with other Cubans left behind to farm, Antonio boarded an aircraft for Havana. He had finally had enough of Africa and as the aircraft circled to gain height over Luanda, which was in MPLA hands and free of potential American Stinger air-to-ground missiles, he looked his last on the African continent.

"You know what," he said to no one in particular in Spanish "That continent will only come right when it's re-colonised and someone gives the people protection." The one thing he would not think about as the aircraft headed out to sea was his workers who had struggled with him for three years to build a farm that had been raped and pillaged in hours.

CHELSEA'S SHOCK turned to anger, and then to realism. It was how it was. She was married to him and, in retrospect, nothing was worse than the prospect of endless loneliness. The talks, he said, now on again, were going better than he had hoped, the ANC drawing pragmatically nearer the government, even though they were going to fight each other bitterly in the election.

The firebrands in the party, faced with the reality of imminent responsibility to govern, had been made to see that shouted words, slogans of anger and bitterness over the past were none of them able to fill empty stomachs and take the place of a leak-free roof over the heads of millions of homeless people. The realities of the world were becoming daily more apparent.

"The ANC are providing the family with bodyguards," Luke told Chelsea. "We can win the peace, and your soft and gentle presence at the end of each day is more vital to me than food. My precious Chelsea, we have come a long way. Back me now. Stay with me. There is more good in the world than bad, and this country deserves a better future than its past.

"We now have a date for the election, and then we will have given years of the parties with over five per cent of the vote governing the country together in coalition. We will lead that coalition. The consequences of not achieving our goal are too terrible to contemplate, so it will never happen. When John's school holidays come, we will go down to Port St Johns for some days of rest. Sipho misses Lorna and Matt. Then we are going to come back and win what I have been fighting for, for thirty-one long years.

BY MARCH OF 1993, Matt was able to walk without pain and his mind was clear enough to paint all day, paint without the shadows that had crossed his troubled mind. The world beyond his rondavel, his family and the colony and Second Beach was left to do that which it wished without his help or hindrance. Peace was returning to his soul and, when Luke and his family had visited, they talked of their boyhood together, of Sipho and Robert senior, of their mothers and the joys of a childhood spent in paradise. Death, wars and politics were not mentioned.

Every morning Matt went down to the sea and left his loin-cloth on the beach to swim in the warm salt water of the Indian Ocean, floating on his back between the troughs of gentler waves and watching seagulls in the sky.

He was sixty years old, and the years ahead gave pleasure to his mind. All the people who had wished him out of business, forced him out of business, had given him the greatest gift of all, peace in his mind, happiness within himself, and the time to pursue an art that gave his thoughts a way to show, with paint, what the world could be, a place of joy where man could live in harmony without greed. Each day the soft, white sand seeped through his toes as he walked the beach, tall and upright again, free of the pain his fellow-man had taken such pleasure in inflicting. He was a happy man once again.

VELI MOKOKA, schoolboy, was twenty-two years old and had yet to pass standard eight, a lower standard of education than that required from John Mbeki when he passed his common entrance examinations to Cranleigh School in England at the age of twelve.

Veli's chance of ever finding a job other than that which required thuggery was small. Since 1976, after the Soweto riots were launched to change the black education system, the black children had been incorporated into struggle and freedom was more important than education, the school term being more political than academic. School boycotts, teachers' strikes, arson and pillage were the order of the day, and the education system was reduced to fear and uselessness. Long-time students like Veli grew increasingly frustrated when they realised within themselves that their future could only follow the path of poverty without an education. The stronger the realisation, the more militant they became and the more likely to listen to the new slogan of the Pan-Africanist Congress and the militant youth leaders of the ANC, bent on their own agenda of destruction and lack of respect for their elders. "Kill a Boer, kill a farmer,' rang out from the mouths of children, and a Boer meant any person with a white skin.

The townships were on the brink of anarchy and the people slept with their clothes on, ready to run out of the shacks and box houses at the first sound of automatic rifle fire. Many could not sleep and many died in the arson and carnage perpetrated under the cover of darkness. Black political parties fought each other, rival black taxi associations fought each other for turf and criminals joined the fray. But everyone spoke of the third force that orchestrated the horror, setting brother against brother, tribe against tribe, yet no one could find the truth or alleviate the misery of millions of blacks trying to reach their workplaces through the taxi battles and armed rampages on the trains. They lived in fear with the inability, week after week, to get a good night's sleep.

The teachers' strike drew Ben Munroe and Clark Goss into Soweto to film and report the effect it was having on the black children's ability to obtain even a rudimentary education. For three days, the teachers and children marched in demonstrations against the white government, while others roamed the streets looking for trouble, mouthing the slogans, cheap and easy words fed to them by the firebrands who wished to take the country by force.

The white police captain warned Ben and Clark not to go into the township, which was enough to make Clark insist. There was something going on in the cauldron of the black, seething masses that needed his camera and, with the police no longer backed by emergency laws, the freedom of the press was paramount.

"I don't have enough men to give you an escort," said the policeman. "Better you stay out, man. It's bad in there. Too many big kids on the streets looking to express themselves. You take my word and stay out. They won't care that you're Americans, a TV crew. You're different in there. A target. Now excuse me; I have a lot of work."

Wearily the policeman went off to muster his forces in the face of the angry masses that took delight in killing policemen. The police captain had not slept for twenty-four hours and had been calling on the government to send in the army to restore order without any success, the political backlash in the talks being a greater problem for the government than the carnage in the streets.

The ANC executive decided to send in a high-powered delegation to calm the situation and to show that the party was the only authority to which the people would listen. Luke, an ex-freedom fighter and hero of the struggle, was given the task of leading the delegation. With his great height he was recognised by many of the people, though to many he was just another black politician with an axe to grind.

The quarrel between the ANC and PAC, the leading liberation movements, added to the tension, the teachers' strike being instigated by the PAC youth movement who were strong among the teachers and the older children. Veli Mokoka was a member of the PAC youth movement and all morning had been chanting, "Kill a Boer, kill a farmer." Leading his gang in the chanting and toyi-toying. He was high on dagga, which added to his fanaticism. The kids under him hero-worshipped the tall Veli and did everything he told them without question.

Ben and Clark drove carefully through the potholed streets, avoiding those roads with burning barricades, accepting the occasional rocking of their stationary car and the jeers of black faces staring hatred through the closed windows.

"Better get out of here, Clark," said Ben who was nervous.

"We're going to see something. This one's big, Ben. The world must see this. Think they'll ever get these guys under control? Just look at them."

"Don't know, Clark, baby. Want to get out. That 'Kill a Boer' bit makes me kind of tense."

"They won't hurt us, buddy boy. We're Americans. These guys like Americans."

"Think they'd bother to read my passport?"

"Accent, buddy boy. We speak American."

LUKE KNEW the temper in the townships better than anyone, the conflicting antagonisms coupled with poverty and fifty per cent unemployment rallying to a crisis that could destroy the negotiating process and propel South Africa into an unstoppable civil war. The United Nations peace officials were the first to give him the warning about Ben and Clark, and this was quickly confirmed by the bone weary police captain.

"Why didn't you arrest them?" said Luke to the captain. "Stop them? Anything!" Luke's voice was rising, which was not helped by the contemptuous look in the captain's eyes that told Luke the problem was his that the ANC had striven for years to make the townships ungovernable by reducing the people to poverty, through sanctions, strikes and mass action.

"With all due respect, Mister Mbeki, you want me to prevent an American news team from going where they want?" The unspoken sarcasm made Luke's temper rise again.

"Which way did they go?"

"Straight down that road in a white Mazda."

"What's the story for them?"

"School kids, maybe. The kids are getting ugly down at the secondary school."

"Can't you send men?" suggested Luke strongly.

"Mister Mbeki, the local ANC youth leader told me personally to get out of his township."

Luke turned to his delegation, which was travelling in three cars, all flying the ANC flag. "Who knows the secondary school here?" he asked.

"I wouldn't, sir," said the captain, over-emphasising the 'sir'. "That area's out of control."

Luke gave the man a contemptuous look and returned to the lead car, which he was driving himself.

After driving ten blocks, he saw clouds of black smoke rising from where the man beside him said the school was situated. Spasmodic gunfire came from the same direction and the streets were full of angry youths who were barely placated by finding black faces in the cars. Cars were wealth and privilege, and spoke of the oppressors. Using the car horn, Luke forced the small convoy deeper into the mass of seething, angry people.

"No one will hear you, even if you get out and speak," said his passenger. "Turn left at the next street and get out of here. This crowd has gone berserk."

"I can see a stopped car ahead. It's white. Could be the Americans' Mazda." Hooting hard, he pushed on into the crowd.

"Luke, the two behind have turned."

"It's Ben Munroe and Clark Goss," said Luke, ignoring the warning. "Those two saved my life."

As they watched, Clark was dragged out of the Mazda and willing hands in the screaming crowd thrust knives into his body. His camera fell to the ground as the youths, led by Veli Mokoka, dragged him away, kicking him in the face and body.

Thirty metres away, Luke scrambled out of his car and, using his great height to the maximum, advanced on the mob, shouting in Xhosa and using his strength to push a way through the youths. He could not see Clark Goss on the ground and, as he came to the centre of the struggle, Veli Mokoka turned to see the tall black man pushing towards him, obviously angry at what they were doing to the Boer. Through the thick power of the dagga, he realised the danger to himself and called his gang's attention to the shouting, gesticulating giant of a black man.

"Sell out!" yelled Veli Mokoka in Xhosa. "Kill him! Wants to save the Boer. Worst is the sell out! KILL HIM! KILL THE SELL OUT!"

The crowd turned from the dead American on the ground as Ben Munroe, speechless but with knee-jerk reaction, leant out of the car, picked up the fallen camera and turned it live on Luke, hoping the ANC executive would calm the crowd and prove to millions of viewers around the world that the ANC was in control of the townships. His mind was clear, objective, sick from the sight of Clark going down under the mob and desperate to film in the last few moments before the mob turned his way. The way out was blocked, the fire in the school was billowing black smoke and there was gunfire behind him as he concentrated, looking through the viewfinder, as Veli Mokoka turned his gang on Luke.

They pinned the giant's hands beside his body as an old car tyre was passed over the top of the crowd and rammed over Luke's head, the open side ready for the can of petrol that was passed quickly to Veli. No one listened to Luke's shouts. Then came the burst of flame as willing hands lit the petrol. All the time Ben rolled the camera, his mind set in horror and fear, knowing nothing else but to film and film, his voice croaked by burning flesh as Luke Mbeki died, necklaced by his own people.

# 3

The Wild Coast sun dipped below the horizon, leaving a sky ablaze with colour as rich as blood. Soon, from the opposite horizon, the moon would rise, to the right of the Gap. Between them lay the length of the Second Beach at Port St Johns, which was teeming with people.

The children were rushing to and fro in the near-darkness, splashing in the shallows, running hither and thither among adult legs, shouting for the joy of it. Many of the adults were scarcely less exuberant, some danced impromptu to their own music, others talked loudly and laughed in animated groups, while some supervised the cooking. A pig was roasting slowly, while a large catch of copper steenbras, brought in only an hour before, would likewise play a major part in the diet of the revellers. There was wine and beer for Africa, as they say.

In the centre of it all, relaxing near the fires was the tall figure of the man responsible for perhaps the greatest feast ever to be held on Second Beach. Matt, still walking with a slight stoop and with his hair long and white now after so much physical and mental suffering, perhaps perfectly fitted the image of a quiet, gracious elder statesman. He spoke less frequently now than perhaps at any time of his life, but his presence was no less evident, no less imposing.

It was two months since the holding of the South African elections, the elections that finally, after three hundred years, gave all the adults aged eighteen and over the vote and a say in the future of their country. These were the elections that enabled Nelson Mandela to tread the same path followed by so many of his counterparts in countries to the north of them, the direct route from prisoner to president.

These elections had been anticipated with considerable foreboding by the members of the colony. It was a fear of the unknown, and fear of the violence that seemed inevitable, before, during and after the elections. The colony had hitherto been in the domain of a corrupt, incompetent Transkei government, but one which had nevertheless maintained a state of peace and allowed the members of the colony to pursue their lives unmolested by politics. But the common fear, shared by peace-loving South Africans of all colours and political persuasions, was that the whole country would sink into a bloodbath as the likes of Frikkie Swart on the one hand and Veli Mokoka on the other fought their vicious war to ensure that, if they did lose, the victors would have nothing left over which to rule.

The colony had looked to Matt for leadership during the fear-filled weeks leading up to the elections. But it seemed to them that Matt, for once, was helpless. Whenever any of them had tried to elicit a response from him to queries, frantic or otherwise, about where the colony could flee or how it should defend itself against possible violence, Matt's reply would always be the same. He would simply stare past the questioner into the distance and say, "They're not here yet."

Perhaps that vicious interrogation in the square named after the late and unlamented John Vorster had finally robbed Matt of his ability to respond decisively to a crisis. Perhaps also the news of Luke Mbeki's tragic death had been the final blow to destroy all but the shell of the man who had once been one of South Africa's greatest business geniuses. Or perhaps (and nobody ever found out for certain) he did have some plan up his sleeve which he would have used had there been any genuine deterioration in the situation with regard to those dwelling on the Wild Coast.

Certainly Matt took a long time to recover from the shattering news of the death of his 'twin'; in fact, it was doubtful that he ever did. He seemed almost to retreat into the state in which he had been after his return to the colony from his experience with Frikkie Swart's thugs. His painting stopped, right in the middle of one of his best. He would sit by the shore for hours on end, with a thousand-metre stare, grunting in monosyllables but rarely even turning his head or moving his eyes to respond to any who tried to communicate with him.

He would occasionally mutter his friend's name with a deep, silent sigh, and it was clear his mind was back in the same location but almost sixty years before, recalling those wonderful carefree days of youth when the two of them played joyfully on the beach among the trees. The days before the grasping claws of all those vultures in the wind had reached out and destroyed their happiness. Matt himself had returned to his roots, but even here the outside world would not let him go altogether free. Now his hopes of persuading Luke to leave government to others and join him to share the final golden days of their lives together had been destroyed. Luke Mbeki would never come home. An occasional tear escaped Matt's eye and trickled down the side of his cheek. It was the only time Lorna had ever seen him cry.

The death of Archie had saddened Matt, but it bore no comparison to the grief he felt when Luke was killed. Archie had been a good mate, but with Luke there had been a unity of soul. Their lives had seemed bound together, right from the start; their friendship had survived every stress imposed on it by the world of racism and politics, and it had withstood the pressure. Matt had always cherished the belief that their lives would end as they had started; in the harmony of the paradise that was Second Beach, Port St Johns. But the blind hatred in the township of Soweto had put a horrendous end to all that.

But why had such hatred existed? Why had Soweto itself existed at all? The questions could be answered with one word: apartheid. Apartheid – the result of man's selfishness and greed. Matt could remember Lorna once quoting him a verse from her Old Testament: 'the heart of man is corrupt and desperately wicked'. It only strengthened Matt's conviction that humankind was on a headlong course of self-destruction and, whatever the result of the South African elections, nothing could stop it.

So for weeks Matt appeared to degenerate into a shrunken giant, in his eyes the gloom of despair. Were it not for the quiet, loving presence of his wife, it could even have been a death-wish. He responded not a whit when those who hoped to stimulate him told of the murder of Ben Munroe along with Luke in Soweto; Munroe, the man who had first driven Matthew Gray from the opulence of the First World and had inadvertently done him the greatest favour of his life by returning him to his roots in the Transkei.

Neither did he even show he had heard when they told of the fate of Frikkie Swart. Frikkie, with the arrogance of those who had manipulated politics with impunity for years, was a little too late in joining his overseas bank account. One evening, on his way home from work, he was shot by a hidden assassin. The bullet took him in the neck, irreparably damaging his spine. For the rest of his life, Frikkie Swart would be a quadriplegic. There were many who thought it ironic that this should be the fate of one who had contributed to the deaths or maiming of hundreds during his career, most notably Matthew Gray. But Matt responded to the news without pleasure, without vindictiveness, even without comment.

As the date for the elections drew nearer, the colony had turned to Matt for leadership, only to find he seemed unable or unwilling to give it any longer. Carel van Tonder kept very much to himself, awaiting the time to recover his cache of arms, more convinced than ever that he would need it now, with Matt apparently no longer capable of leadership. The suspense grew, as further reports came through of violence in the Johannesburg townships and in Natal, where Chief Buthelezi's Inkatha Freedom Party declared their intention of boycotting the elections. Civil war, no longer blacks against whites but now blacks against blacks, seemed inevitable. And in that case, there were few who could hope to escape being caught in the crossfire.

But it never happened. To the amazement and relief of South Africa and the world Buthelezi at the last minute decided to participate in the elections. The tension was by no means over, however, as it was unclear what he and his party would do when they inevitably failed to come out on top of the voting countrywide, although it was likely they would gain control of the province of Natal.

Yet there was, miraculously, no increase in violence in the townships either during or after the elections; Buthelezi, although still dissatisfied, did not respond with a call to arms; the right-wing Afrikaners did not rise to recapture their homeland by force; and the elections themselves passed off with remarkable good humour and even celebration by all sides.

Few of the colony went to vote. What difference would it make to their situation, their lives at Second Beach, who won the elections? If there was peace, which looked highly unlikely, they could live on just as happily, whether the president's name was Mandela or de Klerk or Buthelezi. If there was violence and civil war, as seemed unavoidable, no government would be strong enough to quell it.

Matt himself never considered voting. Vote for the National Party, even with an enlightened leader at the helm, after all the suffering they had brought to the peoples of South Africa? Matt could not forget that party's track record, and the evil little men like Frikkie Swart who had kept it in power for forty years at all costs. Or for the ANC, whose policy of disruption and confrontation had also hurt millions of people, and destroyed the life of the greatest friend he ever had? Or Inkatha, who had so nearly destroyed South Africa's only hope for peace? Matt didn't care who won. To him, they were all vultures, vultures in the wind, greedily seeking the pickings of the richest country in Africa.

Matt was probably as amazed as anybody else, probably more so, that the elections themselves and the aftermath passed off so peacefully, when all the indications were that mayhem would break loose, with Inkatha fighting the ANC and the diehard Boers fighting both, and the ordinary South African who wished for little more than to sit by his cooking fire and eat the labour of his hands caught in the middle. Typically, he didn't show it. Whenever anybody asked him his opinion, he would simply reply, "Wait and see." The euphoria of the colony at the prospect of being permitted to continue their lives of peace without restraint was not for him. He had suffered too much. For Matt, it was merely a respite.

And yet, in the end, Matt responded. For the first time since his arrival at Second Beach under the pseudonym of Mark, he actually invited visitors to the colony. He would not call it a feast of celebration, yet that in effect was what it was. Of course, he sought the approval of the other inhabitants of Second Beach and naturally received their unanimous approval.

And here they were, that glorious autumn evening on Second Beach in 1994, just weeks after the inauguration of President Mandela at the former capital of the Boers, Pretoria. All Matt's friends over the years who were still alive were invited.

Of course, it could never be the same without Luke. But Luke's family was here. Mrs Chelsea Mbeki, the widow of the lamented ANC Martyr, was present with Luke's two sons – and they intended to stay. Chelsea had had enough of politics, politics which had caused her years of estrangement from her husband and, after a brief but joyous reunion, an early widowhood. She thought of returning to Portugal, but found no joy at the thought. Her son, and Luke's son Sipho, were South African and this man who had been Luke's best friend had been right all along. She wanted nothing more now than to throw in her lot with him and live out her life away from the glamour, the politics, the greed, the self-interest that had caused so much destruction in her life. And to Matt, Chelsea and the boys were all he had left of his 'twin'. Their presence helped to assuage his pain, and gave him purpose as he made it his duty and his pleasure to look after them as his own kin in memory of Luke.

Aldo Calucci and Lucky Kuchinski were there, at the colony for the first time. It was unlikely they would stay, although they had no definite plans for the future. Aldo had had a little too much to drink and his English, which seemed to have improved not a whit over the past thirty years and more, was less intelligible than ever as a result. Lucky was quieter now than Matt had known him, and his once-black hair was almost entirely a snowy white. But one thing hadn't changed, Matt gave a wry smile as he watched Lucky chatting up an attractive female painter from the colony who was just young enough to be his granddaughter. She was humouring him marvellously.

Jonathan and Raleen Holland were present, and even Jonathan's mother, now a gracious elderly lady, had responded to the invitation to visit the place where her son had spent his lost years. She was thrilled with delight at the beauty of the place and, very wisely, did not ask too many questions about how her son had spent his time there.

There were even visitors from England. Sunny Tupper, now permitted back in the country with the new government, was there, having waited until after the elections before finally agreeing to take up Matt's offer of running their little school. The glamour of the big city still held its attractions for her, but even she realised it was clear that the feeling was unlikely to be mutual.

Even the earl of Lothianmore and his countess were there. Perhaps more than any other of his visitors, Matt had wanted Charles to come. Matt had always prided himself on his ability to judge character, but he had to admit that he had failed badly in this respect with Charles Farquhar. Yet, in the end, it was surely Charles who had saved his life during his incarceration in Pretoria. Charles had shown drive and initiative that Matt had never dreamed dwelt in the man. Now Matt had the chance to put the record straight, as far as he was concerned, and he gave his cousin and his wife a right royal welcome, fully prepared to apologise for his misjudgement of the past.

Charles, however, would have none of it. He was no longer as eccentric as in the past, having settled down to as normal a married life as could be hoped for in the circumstances. Now that he was a genuine earl with a genuine castle, his unusual airs and graces had diminished rather than increased, and he was affable without causing ridicule or offence. He seemed so genuinely pleased to be back at the colony and so delighted to meet all his old acquaintances again that they gradually warmed to him and accepted him as if he were one of their own.

Lorna sidled up to Matt and put her hand on his shoulder. "Peace, my giant, peace," she whispered, and she was not talking about their daughter now. "Are you happy?"

Briefly she regretted her question, as a shaft of pain flickered momentarily over Matt's face, and she knew he was thinking of Luke.

Then he looked down at her and smiled. "For now," he responded. "For now." And that was all he would permit himself. He had seen too much, suffered too much. He knew the avaricious nature of man too well to have faith in the future. Live for the present – that was all he could do. And this night he had all that he had valued most in the world.

Lorna smiled back and slipped away from him, away from the crowd for a moment. She still found it hard to believe that, despite the storm clouds that had enveloped the land, increasingly ominous as the years went by, they were able to live in peace now and even hope for the future, a future that perhaps would last to the end of their lives. Matt would never admit it, but even now he must be hoping the same.

Lorna looked up at the star-spangled heavens; the three layers of stars rising it seemed to eternity. "Thank you," she whispered. "Thank you for the miracle – and our hope." Hope. That was the key to their lives. Without hope, life was nothing.

A little gust of wind enveloped her for a moment. It was cold, a foretaste of the coming brief winter of the Wild Coast. Winter was coming – but, for South Africa, was there summer on the way?

She hugged herself tightly, and then gasped at the impertinence of her own thoughts. She had a sudden feeling that, after all those years, she was pregnant again. She was sure of it. Matt, in his sixties, would be a father once more! And this one, she felt, this one would be a daughter.

She would call her Hope, Peace and Hope. Matt, softly cynical when he was alone with her, might demur at first. But she would have her way with him, she was sure of that. "Thank you," she whispered again. There was hope for the future, hope for their lives together and hope for South Africa. The vultures need not win.

# EPILOGUE

Matthew Gray lived in his rondavel to the age of ninety-four, outliving Lorna by six weeks. After his death, the chest in which he had placed his writings was opened to find a two-thousand-page manuscript entitled:

---

The Tyranny of Democracy: the Decline and Fall of Western Civilisation

---

It was never published.

# DEAR READER

~

Reviews are the most powerful tools in our kitty when it comes to getting attention for Peter's books. This is where you can come in, as by providing an honest review you will help bring them to the attention of other readers.

If you enjoyed reading *Vultures in the Wind,* and have five minutes to spare, we would really appreciate a review (it can be as short as you like). Your help in spreading the word and keeping Peter's work alive is gratefully received.

Please post your review on the retailer site where you purchased this book.

Thank you so much.
Heather Stretch (Peter's daughter)

PS. We look forward to you joining Peter's growing band of avid readers.

~

# PRINCIPAL CHARACTERS

*Matthew Gray* — The central character; South African-born businessman
*Robert Gray* — Matt's father and former forester
*Isalin Gray* — Matt's mother; an artist
*David Todd* — Head and founder of Security Life Insurance Company
*Luke Mbeki* — Matt's 'twin', born on the same day at Port St Johns, Transkei
*Archie Fletcher-Wood* — Fast-living friend of Matt's
*Lucky Kuchinski* — A Pole; another of Matt's fast-living friends
*Sandy De Freitas* — Matt's first girlfriend
*Oliver Gore* — An inveterate snob, and workmate of Matt's in London
*Poppy (Sunny) Tupper* — From the East End of London; Matt's secretary
*Hector Fortescue-Smyth* — Descendant of a rich English inventor and manufacturer, and an active communist
*Frikkie Swart* — South African civil servant who rises through the ranks
*Helena Kloss*— Promiscuous daughter of a South African government minister
*Aldo Calucci* — An Italian; hunter and safari operator
*Mashinga* — Aldo Calucci's assistant
*Reverend Andrew Porterstone* — An atheistic church minister who is an active communist supporter

*Chelsea de la Cruz* — A beauty of mixed ancestry and wife of Luke Mbeki's wife
*Jonathan Holland* — Son of the founder of Threadneedle Insurance Company in England
*Ben Munroe* — An American; reporter for *Newsweek*
*Teddie Botha* — Grandson of David Todd and his successor in Security Holdings
*Lorna Gray* — Matt's wife, of Jewish parentage
*Martin; Melissa; Barbara (Baba); Carel van Tonder; Sophia van Hoek* — Member of the artists' colony at Port St Johns
*Bernard Strover* — Art fancier, employed by Security Life
*Desmond Donelly* — Former pop star who joins the anti-apartheid cause
*Antonio Van Perreira Dos Santos Cassero* — Cuban air force pilot and revolutionary, of mixed parentage
*Peace Gray* — Matt's daughter
*Raleen Urbach* — Widow of a farmer murdered in the Rhodesian war
*The Minstrel Boy (Wilhelm Marais)* — Member of the artists' colony at Port St Johns
*Gilly Bowles* — Journalist and girlfriend of Hector Fortescue-Smythe
*Anita Hylan* — Swedish anti-apartheid activist
*Charles Farquhar 12th Earl of Lothianmore* — Distant cousin of Matt's on his mother's side
*Tilda Blaze* — Johannesburg socialite who becomes Teddie Botha's wife
*Isidore Socrates Salvadori (Jack Kemp)* — Art Dealer
*Duncan Grenville Fox* — Art Dealer
*Sipho Mbeki and John de la Cruz* — Sons of Luke Mbeki

# GLOSSARY

~

*Baas* — Boss
*Bakkie* — Small to medium size truck
*Bittereinder* — Afrikaans term referred to the Boers of South Africa who fought in the Boer War
*Boma* — A safe enclosure (livestock enclosure, stockade or kind of fort)
*Braai* — Barbeque
*Chopper* — Helicopter
*Dagga* — Cannabis
*Dassies* — Rock hyrax (rock rabbit)
*Featherman* — A hawker or tradesman dealing in plumes or feathers
*Frelimo* — Mozambique Liberation Front
*Gook* — Terrorist
*Goy* — A non-Jewish person
*Impi* — Zulu word for any armed body of men
*Inkatha* — Inkatha Freedom Party (IFP) political party – Inkatha meaning "crown" in Zulu
*Jawling* — Having a party / free time
*Kaffir* — An insulting and contemptuous term for a black African
*Kopje* — Small hill
*Makori* — African Canoe
*Mealie meal* — Ground maize

*Muti* — Medicine
*Nats* — People who supported the National Party (Afrikaans)
*Oupa* — Afrikaans word for Grandfather
*Panga* — Machete
*Pap* — Traditional porridge / polenta made from mealie-meal (ground maize)
*Pot* — Cannabis
*Rand* — South African currency
*Renamo* — The Mozambican National Resistance
*Rondavel* — Hut / House
*Shabeens* — African drinking house (pub)
*Simbi* — A gong
*Stoep* — Veranda
*Veldskoens* — Bush shoes
*Very light* — White or coloured balls of fire projected from a special pistol
*Volk* — Afrikaans word for people

# ACRONYMS

~

*AAM* — Anti-Apartheid Movement
*ANC* — African National Congress
*BCom* — Bachelor of Commerce Degree offered in the Commonwealth nations
*D&C* — Dilatation And Curettage - gynaecological procedure
*PAC* — Pan Africanist Congress
*SACP* — South African Communist Party
*SWAPO* — South West Africa People's Organisation
*TUC* — Trades Union Congress
*UNITA* — National Union for the Total Independence of Angola
*WASP* — White Anglo-Saxon Protestant, a sometimes derogatory term used to describe American and English people of Protestant descent who control unequal social and financial power
*ZANLA* — Zimbabwe African National Liberation Army
*ZAPU* — Zimbabwe African People's Union
*ZIPRA* — Zimbabwe People's Revolutionary Army

Made in the USA
Monee, IL
15 August 2022

11695221R00267